A CHALICE *for a* KRAKEN

HIYODORI

Contents

1

WE SPENT ALL summer traveling. I attended an academic conference (under a false name) as Mori's guest; Wist mediated more skirmishes up north. We went to see my parents in the countryside. Here and there, I covertly broke mage-healer bonds. So far, I hadn't been caught.

My three-year-old passport was already thoroughly battered. I got a lot of weird looks and hard-edged questions at Osmanthian checkpoints. If not for Wist, I'd have been detained—and chucked back in prison—a dozen times over.

We traversed port gates in multiple countries. We boarded trains and airships and freighters. Occasionally we hitched a ride on the back of a tractor.

In late September, shortly after my thirty-seventh birthday, we dragged ourselves home to Wist's tower. This would mark the first time in months that we'd be able to stay over for more than a single hurried night.

Ginko—our only tenant, unless you count Wist's cat, fish, and other beasts—had worked diligently to keep our houseplants alive. They were doing a lot better than under Wist's care, to be honest.

The morning after our return, Ginko took us up to a large sunroom and pointed out numerous species that might be toxic to cats.

"Turtle won't touch them," Wist said.

"Why not?"

"Magic."

Most people would've left it at that. Wist was either the greatest or second greatest mage of all time, depending on who you asked.

Ginko didn't back down. "Cats are good at finding loopholes."

Wist turned to me as if this were somehow my fault.

"What?" I said. "I'm not a cat. I don't even get along with cats."

Turtle sat there blinking lovingly at the three of us. What a faker. She adored Wist and Ginko, but I'm pretty sure she saw me as competition. Just another one of Wist's pets.

Most elite mages would've ignored advice from a younger healer like Ginko. Wist didn't: she immediately started reexamining the magical protections around her plants.

She could take her time. I had some tests of my own to run.

The sunroom jutted far out from the side of the tower, which was held together primarily by Wist's power. Nothing separated us from the cloudless September sky except spotless sheets of glass.

I popped out my artificial right eye and tucked it in a pocket. (Don't fret: Wist had infused it with hundreds of cuttings. Her magic would compensate for unhygienic handling.)

An infinite Void resided in the depths of my hollowed-out socket. Even trapped inside me, it was still far from tame. I'd been its secret host for about a year now, though. If I was going to keep this thing in my skull for the rest of my life, the least I could do was put it to work.

Like Ginko, I was a healer of mages. I'd never possessed magic of my own. Besides, it would be dangerously arrogant to call the Void *mine*. It was a cosmic phenomenon that failed to fit any accepted theory of magic.

To be fair, the same description might also apply to Wist. Throughout written history, there had only been one other Kraken-class mage.

Ginko, ready to assist me, hauled over a clear jug packed with crispy brown insect shells. She'd spent much of the summer collecting cicada cast-offs for a citizen science project. Mori had helped her report her findings.

"You don't mind if some of these vanish?" I asked.

She unscrewed the lid. "Try not to eat all of them."

I tilted my head back. She took a cicada skin and dropped it in my empty right eye.

From her perspective, she may as well have dropped it in a bottomless pit. The Void caught at it like a carp snapping up crumbs.

I counted to ten.

I put two fingers inside my open socket, knuckle-deep, and swirled them around. Wist had attached dense tufts of magic to the bones at the entrance. It felt like pushing past rubbery flaps around a kitchen drain.

I never hit the back of my eye. There was simply nothing there.

Ginko was used to seeing this. She took it in stride—even though, by all appearances, I'd gone deep enough to dig a hole in my frontal lobe.

If I triggered them correctly, Wist's grafted cuttings could serve as a safety net, keeping the Void from instantly annihilating everything it swallowed.

Dried-up cicada legs tickled my fingertips. I seized the fragile shell. I pulled it out of my hollow eye, and out of the Void.

In the process, it got halfway crushed.

For a moment, Ginko looked mutinous. But she scooped out more cicada shells without being asked.

The Void gurgled in displeasure.

Wist and I called this maneuver Garbage Disposal for a reason. So far, I'd been more successful at retrieving hardy objects (like metal spoons) than delicate ones (like cut flowers).

It was much easier, at any rate, to let the Void consume at will. Extracting stored items felt like wrenching a chew toy away from an angry dog.

I'd done limited experiments on living creatures. Mostly flatworms and such, which could regrow after getting sliced up in two or more pieces. In my defense, I never sliced them on purpose.

I couldn't shake the feeling that the worms I withdrew from my eye weren't quite the same as before, even if they came out intact. The Void changed anything it touched. It had changed me, and not for the better. But I had no way to prove that.

There was no way to ethically test Garbage Disposal on human subjects, either. It worked well on vorpal beasts—they emerged largely unscathed. Perhaps because they were creatures composed more of arcane magic than flesh.

Ginko kept feeding the Void cicada shells. I got better at fishing them out without any visible damage.

I'd grappled with a mild headache all morning. Like having my skull held gently in the jaws of a creature that could easily crush it. I couldn't blame it on the Void: this felt more like weather-induced pangs, although we'd woken to an annoyingly clear day.

Wist, wearing a muscle shirt and a floor-length mesh skirt, still stooped intently over her plants. Some gave off a sharp herby scent when she moved them.

The invisible jaws of my headache clamped down harder. I passed Ginko another salvaged cicada shell.

It started with a dripping sound, strangely loud, like condensation plinking from the ribs of the ceiling.

But it was Wist's plants that were dribbling. Sweaty dew gleamed at the tips of heavy leaves. More drops welled up, and beaded together, and fused into shining strands of drool.

I mentally poked her.

Uh, Wist?

Did she know she was doing that?

Her plants retched, convulsing with effort. Vomit-like streams of water spat down against the floor.

"Ginko," I began, "you'd better—"

Turtle yowled and scampered out of the room. Ginko said something—too high and soft to make out—and ran after her.

They were both a lot smarter than me and Wist.

Wist wasn't stooping anymore. I recognized the look on her face. Her mind had fled to a different floor altogether, racing through the circuitry of magic beneath the skin of her tower. Below ground level, it stretched down into the earth like a well.

She took an unsteady step toward the glass wall. Her elbow hit one of her pots. It started to fall.

Something wrenched at the space between us as if straightening a wrinkled sheet.

That pot never hit the floor. It still rested squatly on the table beside her.

I kneaded my head, begging myself to keep it together. I tried to look where Wist was looking. Somewhere far outside the sunroom.

A single lofty cloud had appeared in the sky. A white ovoid shape. Or was it red, somehow? Or pink and pearlescent?

An elongated egg, I thought.

Or a cocoon. Smooth-surfaced rather than fuzzy. Every time I blinked, it drew closer.

My brain creaked. The Void vibrated with curiosity.

Brown cicada skins jostled in their jar, crackling with false life. The lid was still off. They leapt out in random directions, sizzling as they landed.

Hey, I said through my bond with Wist. *Hey!*

The looming egg spoke, and by then neither of us had room to form other thoughts.

It didn't speak in words. What came instead was a pressing sense of invitation. A siren lure. Something like:

COME TO ME.

COME.

It reverberated down our bond, music from a plucked string, singing on and on.

But anything I heard was incidental. The message was directed at Wist alone. It streamed along the outline of the tower to find her.

Blood trickled from her left nostril.

The egg in the sky had come near enough to darken the entire sunroom.

I stumbled over to Wist, slipping on the damp floor. All kinds of plants were still weeping. Directionless magic sloshed around my feet.

I shook her. I yelled. It felt like yelling at a standing corpse.

I grabbed the nearest ceramic pot—the one she'd mindlessly saved from falling—and dashed it at the floor. It bounced just before crashing, as if rescued by a hidden trampoline. Wist's magic acting on reflex. Again. But potted plants weren't made to bounce. Dirt went flying, and the whole thing came careening back down. This time it shattered.

Wist shuddered. Sunlight filled the room again. I gulped air. It burned, like inhaling water.

The egg outside was gone.

It had been large enough, physically, to knock out a significant chunk of the tower. It could've ground us both into a watery smear of human jam.

That wasn't the scary part. Our bond still quivered in the aftermath of that voice without words, a pressure as wide as the flawless sky.

"Wist." I caught at her. "Did you...?"

"I didn't do anything."

I looked pointedly out at empty air. Still no egg.

"I didn't do anything," she said again, with the same flat inflection. "It left on its own."

She used her knuckles to dab at her leaking nose. She pored over the blood smeared on the back of her hand. It didn't seem to tell her anything useful.

I picked up the dirty pieces of her broken pot. "You don't know what that thing was."

"No."

"We were supposed to relax at home," I said plaintively. "We were supposed to laze around and recuperate from all our travel."

Wist made a subaudible noise deep in her chest. More of a seismic tremor than a laugh.

2

LONG STORY SHORT: the egg in the sky was a Jacian machina. The supremely valuable type known as a chalice. A machine of war, deadly to its pilots, but powerful enough to deploy anyway. The pinnacle of Jacian magitech.

The good news was that hardly anyone saw it. Pretty much just me and Wist. So there was no mass panic, and no rumors in the press.

We both knew what chalices were. Giant magical machines with arms and legs—many arms, sometimes, and many legs. They could dice an airship like an onion. They could knock a skyscraper flat on its face. They could rain magma down on farmland.

No wonder we hadn't recognized that egg as a chalice. It had no limbs, no weapons, no mechanical visage. Trust me: it bore absolutely no resemblance to the fearsome sword-swinging titans shown in propaganda posters from previous centuries.

It hadn't harmed anyone, except for giving Wist a nosebleed. It hadn't done anything, in fact, except make a brief appearance near the tower. For all we knew, it would never show itself again.

But this chalice was a model hitherto unknown to Osmanthian intelligence. Worse, it had demonstrated an unprecedented ability to stealthily penetrate Osmanthian territory.

Most ensuing speculation took place exclusively at the highest levels of government. I could fill in the blanks, though. After Wist escaped from a torturous series of meetings, she told me I'd been spot on.

The more hawkish members of the Board of Magi interpreted this mysterious flyover as an assassination attempt. (Its target: Wist the Kraken.)

A few pointed out my own sordid history with Jacian conspirators, implying that *I* had somehow led the chalice to the tower. Or that it had shown up to collect me, an alleged sleeper agent. Nowadays, none of them had the guts to openly voice this within earshot of Wist. I would've admired them more if they did.

As soon as we got an inkling that the elliptical egg had come from Jace, I'd coached Wist on what to say. She couldn't mention standing there dumbstruck, blood leaking from her face. If they asked her why the machina left, she'd better keep mum. Let them think she had something to do with shooing it out of there.

For the sake of world peace, not to mention our own personal peace, people with power—both here and abroad—needed to believe that Wist could take anything they might throw at her. Anything.

So far, this had proven true. But she'd never faced Jacian war machines. The last open conflict between Jace and the continent had begun and ended before our time. Even then, they'd wielded chalices primarily as an intimidation tactic.

Things started getting twisty within a matter of days. Jace responded to back-channel negotiations with unusual alacrity. In a shocking turn of events, they actually apologized for the chalice sighting—albeit in diplomatic gobbledygook, not natural language. They blamed it on rogue elements.

And here's the kicker. They sought the Kraken's help with repossessing their rebel chalice.

Jace had been a hostile, closed-off nation for generations on end. They took enormous national pride in the fact that they'd never been conquered by the first Kraken's armies. This was all ancient history, but they acted like it had just happened yesterday.

They had never once requested any kind of aid from the current Kraken, or Osmanthus in general. They perceived Wisteria Shien as nothing less than an existential-level threat.

One might wonder why the Board of Magi would be so foolish as to send Wist on a covert diplomatic mission in the heart of enemy territory. Minus any meaningful backup. I sure wondered, all right.

The answer was simple.

Half the Board basically worshipped Wist. They considered her invincible. She was the mightiest mage in the world, yes; that much was indisputable. But her magic didn't make her infallible.

The other half of the Board couldn't stand her. They wanted nothing more than to get rid of her. She had far too much power for their liking. She wasn't merely an obedient soldier. If she disagreed with an order, she just wouldn't do it, and who could force her hand?

Her supporters sent her in because they thought she couldn't possibly fail. Her detractors sent her in because they thought she couldn't possibly win. They hoped to see her humbled. Or wounded. Or dead.

Anyway, that's how Wist the Kraken got sent to the archipelagic nation of Jace. Together with a young healer, a star duelist, an old friend, and an assortment of scheming diplomats. And—perhaps most surprisingly of all, considering my history—with me.

3

They sent us across the sea on a luxury superyacht. Shien Nerium's luxury superyacht. I know it sounds ridiculous.

Thankfully, Nerium wasn't there in person. He'd just lent his vessel for the voyage. What a patriot.

It was enormous, obviously, and treated with magic to induce an artificial sense of stability. Stay indoors, and it'd be easy to forget we'd ever left shore.

We cast off from a private harbor some distance north of Osmanthus Bay. Soon after, Wist spotted a beach laden with hundreds of napping sea lions. They were alive—I think—but suspiciously still, brown and torpid, packed together like the glistening aftermath of a mass die-off.

The wind turned. It swept their stench across the deck: an ungodly nose-burning mix of farm field manure and rotten fish. Someone behind us started gagging. Someone else laughed shrilly. We scrambled back inside.

For all the opulence of the interior, it had some questionable quirks. The toilets and showers were transparent—walled in one-way glass, so you could see out, but no one else could see in. Or so they said.

No one with authority had commanded me to stay out of sight. Still, it felt like a good idea to lie low. I holed up in Wist's stateroom.

Currently, there were three of us holed up together: me, Wist, and my duelist friend Fanren.

Fanren's magic—the skill known as Barrier—coruscated over the ceiling and furniture and carpeted floor and hand-painted wallpaper.

Wist was holding a gun. She held it as if it were about to come to life and bite her. She was the greatest mage of our time and all that, but she had no idea how to shoot a target. (Neither did I.)

Fanren waited another minute. Then he sighed and told her to hand it over.

For an icy moment, I thought she might shoot him right then and there. On the plus side, she'd probably miss.

I took my prosthetic out and put it on a marble-top side table.

"Can you hit that?" I asked Fanren.

"From this distance? How bad of a shot do you think I am?"

"It's pretty small. And you don't use firearms for magesports."

"I wasn't always a duelist," he said dryly.

He fired.

Silencing magic buffeted our ears.

My lidless eyeball, balanced on the table like a paperweight, gave us an accusatory look. The furniture appeared unmarked.

"The bullet evaporated," Fanren said. "Never touched my Barrier."

I retrieved my eye, reinserted it, and walked out in front of him—with my gaze on Wist, not the gun in his grip. Between the two, Wist was more dangerous.

Fanren aimed at my shoulder. Wist twitched.

"It jammed," he said, impressed.

"Was that my eye at work," I said to Wist, "or just you?"

"Your eye." But she sounded uncertain.

"Let's try one more time, then."

Fanren waved us out of the way while he tinkered with his gun. "Give me a second to fix this first."

Wist's hands were clenched. Beneath her skin, her magic branches were clenched even harder. But the next time I got back in position, she didn't intervene. She trusted the clippings she'd embedded in my prosthesis.

Silence slapped us all in the face again. Air puffed against my left eyeball—the living one—like a glaucoma test.

I felt nothing else. Once more, Fanren's bullet had disintegrated so thoroughly that it didn't leave a single speck of shrapnel.

"Had enough?" he asked.

"Sure," I said, more for Wist's sake than for mine.

"This doesn't mean you can dive in front of bullets," Wist warned.

"The protections seem plenty reliable enough to—"

"We haven't tested it with icearms."

"Whatever happens, you'd better keep your cool if someone shoots at me."

"Hm," Wist said neutrally.

Fanren shook out a cloth on the carpet, sat down cross-legged, and started doing something noisy with his gun. Cleaning it, or whatever. I dunno.

He looked much as he always did: black hair, stylish glasses, piercings galore. Facial piercings were apparently rarer in Jace than on the continent, so there'd been some debate about whether he ought to tone it down. In the end, though, our diplomatic superiors gave him permission to saunter into Jace fully beringed and bestudded.

The plan had come together with astonishing speed. Wist couldn't just drop anchor at a Jacian port and declare herself the Kraken (their most feared and hated enemy). Even within the upper echelons of Jacian government, few officials knew she was coming. Those who did know were, in all likelihood, just as divided as the Board of Magi.

She needed to go undercover. And we needed a pretext to get our people into Jace—which, of course, had no Osmanthian embassy. Or anything resembling normalized relations.

That was where Fanren came in. He wasn't just any old duelist. He was a celebrity with a remarkable backstory. An ex-con turned Continental Champion; a former underdog with tragic (and controversial) origins. Pure catnip for journalists.

Granted, there was no thriving ecosystem of magesports in Jace, where traditionalists frowned on any use of magic for entertainment. A frivolous waste, they'd say.

Your average Jacian had zero opportunities to learn about popular culture on the continent, anyway. But borders were a lot more porous for the wealthy elite. So Fanren had a handful of fans even in Jace— among the nouveau riche, at least.

While Wist and I struggled with our covert mission, and tried not to get killed, Fanren would be privately feted by top plutocrats. He wouldn't be alone, either. Shien Nerium must have been salivating over the prospect of doing business with Jace (a whole new market to exploit). He'd sent a trusted representative to schmooze on his behalf.

For now, Fanren kept fiddling with his gun. "You know this has got to be a trap," he remarked.

"Yeah," I said. "We've discussed it."

Wist made no comment. Her hair said it all for her, fretfully growing longer. It tumbled past her shoulders, then her hips, then her ankles: a dark veil like nighttime water, rippling with disquiet. Then it shrank back up to the nape of her neck. This was her last chance to go wild. She'd have to control herself to maintain her disguise.

At least her left hand was doing a good enough job of masquerading as ordinary human flesh.

Wist wouldn't normally use magic without good cause. She had every incentive to avoid it: one way or another, her power would always rebound on her. Popping pills didn't help much. The worst of her pain resided in her magic core and branches—not an organ anyone could treat with pharmaceutical means.

That's what I was for. After several years as her bondmate, I'd gotten better and better at keeping her branches from getting mangled.

She sometimes claimed she felt great. Her idea of *great* incorporated a much higher baseline level of malaise than most mages.

You'd think she wouldn't ever fidget pointlessly with her magic, considering the consequences. But the Kraken was still a person, and people pick at sores. People grind their teeth. Mage, healer, or subliminal— few of us treat ourselves with perfect loving care.

4

THIS WASN'T A pleasure cruise, and I didn't want to stand out. But that doesn't mean I never got a glimpse of open water.

Wist was preternaturally gifted at making herself seem unapproachable. At the same time, she cut a striking figure. If I kept my head down and walked in her shadow, watching eyes would skip past me, eager to follow the Kraken.

There were several sundecks. She took me up to the least populated one, which at other times might have been designated exclusively for Shien use.

Far below us, water smacked the hull. The sea looked cold and deep and depressingly empty. I'd heard talk of dolphin and shark sightings, but maybe we'd gotten too far from the coast. We drifted along as if traveling through the undecorated space between stars.

An Osmanthian airship would follow overhead until the yacht neared disputed waters. Camouflaged bombers would no doubt be arrayed on both sides. Submarines, too. If you wanted to start a war, this would be the perfect time and place to strike.

Weirdly enough, nothing happened.

Within a day, our Osmanthian escort faded away. (The official one did, anyhow. One way or another, I'm sure they kept tailing us.) Jacian vessels led us the rest of the way across the sea between the mainland and their islands. I'd been warned in no uncertain terms to avoid mentioning the name of said sea. They called it something different in Jace.

I didn't expect to be holding a lot of nuanced conversations. Technically, I was here in the guise of a low-ranking diplomat. Some sort of assistant attaché. Wist and I would split off from the rest of the group soon enough.

At top speed, we could've gotten to Jace in just half a day on the water. But the journey took over forty-eight hours: there had been a lot of stopping and starting and negotiating and reconsidering.

At last we all assembled in a grand, glittering dining room for one final meal aboard. (We'd previously made use of a glass-enclosed underwater eatery and a half-submerged bar area, too.)

There were a number of attendees I'd never met before in my life. Mostly diplomats, support staff, and intelligence officers with various fake and real titles.

One man hailed from the Gwindel family, which had taken an interest in this venture for the same reason as Shien Nerium. The Gwindels had an arms dealing branch, if I remembered correctly ... but that was none of my business.

On Wist's other side sat a tall black-haired woman who had basically been hired as a stunt double. She had a dueling background, so she'd fit right in with Fanren's entourage. Her job was to hang around him and look vaguely like Wisteria Shien. A helpful distraction.

Anyway, here's who I knew: myself, Wist, Fanren, Azalea Wren, and Shien Danver.

Poor Mori. His Jacian was already better than mine, but we hadn't been able to come up with an adequate excuse to drag him along. (It had been difficult enough to justify bringing me, a convicted traitor.)

Maybe we hadn't tried hard enough. We knew he'd be safer at home.

Parts of the yacht were always shifting and rotating, expanding and retracting. I'd thought this room had no view of outside, but now there were panoramic windows. They'd been doctored with magic to keep light from striking us too hard in the eye. Which meant we could all goggle fearlessly at the flaming sun as it sank.

Jace lay west of us, too. Just a few black hints of lumpy mountainous scenery on the gilded horizon.

Fanren happily chatted with security agents. Wist kept her thoughts to herself, and her impersonator followed suit.

"Soon we'll all be eating foreign cuisine," someone said to the table. "Hope you like it hot!"

He got a few polite titters. Then orchestral music came crashing out of a hidden melodium. The sound quality was unimpeachable, but the tempo seemed off.

People resumed speaking. I found it hard not to focus on the music. It sounded increasingly sharp and stretched-out. Wouldn't put it past Nerium to play this stuff as a form of psychological torture.

It wasn't just the grating melody that threw me off. All the plates had a purple wisteria pattern—which seemed indiscreet at best, if not outright mocking.

On my right, Wist applied herself diligently to the business of taking small methodical bites. She didn't much care for eating in front of others, and usually she'd shy away from meals of unknown provenance. Especially on a vessel owned by her brother.

As Wist cut and stabbed and chewed, her impersonator did the same. At first, every movement looked a beat too slow. Over time, they became so synchronized that I could no longer tell who was leading who.

The decoy only resembled Wist in a superficial sense. That made this distorted twinning worse, somehow, like looking through goggles with the wrong prescription.

Wist raised her glass, took a sip, and pressed her lips together when she finished. So did her double, not even a nanosecond behind, as if they were mimes who'd been perfecting this act for years.

For the first time since boarding, I began to feel a little seasick.

You can ask her to stop, I said.

Wist kept nibbling away without pleasure. *It's fine.*

Azalea (seated on my other side) said quietly, "If she didn't eat anything, perhaps the other one wouldn't, either."

At least Azalea was fun to catch up with. She'd been Wist's first friend at boarding school—yes, she beat me to it. Unsurprisingly, Wist had been terrible at staying in touch after graduation. But Azalea didn't seem to hold that against her.

All of us were less prickly than we'd been as students. Azalea came off as pleasantly tired now, with amiable lines around her eyes. She'd look increasingly impish with age. It wasn't hard to imagine her as a cackling grandma.

In our brief time on the yacht, she'd already laughed more than I'd ever seen her laugh at school. At this point, I suppose, she felt free from the pressure to prove herself. She was still a Class 1-1 mage, and she'd never taken a bondmate. But she no longer needed to care about snap judgments. Her credentials had been enough to secure her a seat here.

I passed her a silver transceiver pin under the table. It looked like a decorative brooch—specifically, like a clematis flower. (I could disparage Nerium's dinnerware, but sometimes Wist and I were just as obvious.)

I'd been given to understand that Azalea worked as a magical preservationist. She used archival and archaeological data to recreate lost old skills. The other half of her job involved recording and preserving contemporary skills, especially dying ones that only one or two mages still knew.

For the purposes of this expedition, she'd been assigned to shadow Fanren as he made the rounds of high society. Presumably she'd been recruited because of her aptitude for magical analysis. Somebody from some secret ministry was hoping that she'd be able to come back home and replicate bits of Jacian tech.

So I didn't need to explain why I'd pressed the clematis pin into her hand, or how to use it.

Magic perception isn't the same thing as physical sight, but a lot of people use their eyes as a crutch. Azalea didn't even look down. She just turned the transceiver about in her fingers, then slipped it in her pocket.

Our handlers would give us alternate ways to stay in contact. The problem was that Osmanthian allies were just as likely to undermine us as Jacian enemies. There might be two dozen other classified operations—all with contradictory motives—running beneath the surface of our ostensible mission.

The only people in this room I trusted were the ones I knew by name. And Danver was questionable, for a variety of reasons, so that left just Wist, Azalea, and Fanren.

"Watch over them," I said to Azalea, nodding at Fanren and Danver.

Wist turned to listen. So, awkwardly, did her impersonator.

"I won't mother them," Azalea said. She had a teenage son back home; she'd shown me pictures. "But I can try to keep an eye out."

"I can, too." I lifted my eyepatch and demonstrated. Spot-on comedic timing.

5

I'D HAD A testy talk with Manatree (my parole officer and/or case manager) before leaving for Jace. Much to her regret, she'd been considered important enough to get the full story about the chalice sighting.

"Jellyfish season is about to end," she said through her teeth. "I was planning on visiting the coast. With my family."

"Sounds lovely."

"Now I can't go anywhere. I canceled my trip."

"Oh. Well—"

"The booking was nonrefundable. What, pray tell, do you think I'll be doing instead?"

"Uh…"

"I'll be waiting around for your triumphant return."

"That makes me feel a lot better about all this," I said. "You've always been a pessimistic sort. If you think—"

She slashed her thumb across her neck. "My only role here is to serve as a handy scapegoat. Do you know how many times I've applied for a transfer? At this point I'd be pleased if they just let me retire. *But you've done such a good job with her*, they say. Hah! I've done nothing except take all the blame whenever you put a toe out of line. The rest of us don't have a Kraken waiting around to bail us out of prison."

Ah, Manatree. Always so comforting and maternal. I really was very fond of her. Sometimes I could fool myself into thinking the feeling was mutual.

She'd come to the tower so we could speak frankly. We'd nestled ourselves in cushioned seats on a protruding balcony. Turtle had made a big production of choosing to climb up in Manatree's lap, rather than mine.

Dull grey rain spattered down past a sheltering awing. Now that Manatree was no longer ranting, her tone turned dispassionate. "Warmongers will keep agitating for an attack on Jace."

"Thank god that none of this is public knowledge."

"Unless they get frustrated and leak it."

"They won't. The Board can't let the feelings of common rabble sway their battles. Sets a bad precedent."

"You're being set up," Manatree said.

"That's starting to feel like the usual course of affairs."

"Be serious, Magebreaker."

She liked to claim that I'd aged her, but she hadn't changed at all in the past four years.

"Which country is laying traps?" I asked. "Both, right? Heck, there might be third parties involved. Some of our neighbors would love for us to get bogged down in another protracted conflict. If we're lucky, maybe their acts of sabotage will cancel each other out. It could all add up to a big fat nothing."

Manatree stroked Turtle's back. "Don't count on that."

"We do have to go. The chalice is real."

"Its rebellion could be a lie. An alluring story."

"If it's true, we'd better catch their runaway chalice before it starts wreaking havoc. If it's false, that means they're in possession of a war machine capable of showing up anywhere on the continent—and they're already willing to use it. May as well stop it at the source."

"You'll be a target, too."

"For assassination, or recruitment?"

Rain bled from the awning. Manatree pinched the bridge of her nose. Turtle rumbled like a furry engine.

Needless to say, the answer was both. On the Osmanthian side, some would see this excursion as a chance to dispose of me. Wist might have a breakdown—she might even go berserk—but she'd be off in another country, and Jace would take the brunt of it.

Jacians, for their part, might target me in hopes of weakening the Kraken, or to spur internal conflict within the Osmanthian camp.

Alternatively, they might attempt to cultivate me as an asset.

"I'm not a wee lass of twenty," I said. "I think I can take it."

"You have a ravenous ego—"

"Says who?"

"—and you've never been to a nation where healers enjoy as much stature as they do in Jace." She eased Turtle off her knees. "Who might be tasked with taking you out if you show signs of defection?"

The Osmanthian team assigned to accompany us could be crawling with trained killers, but neither Wist nor I would let our guard down around strangers.

"Fanren," I said reluctantly. "He'll be busy, though."

I didn't think he'd go through with it. Not this time around. Our friendship aside, why would he put himself in a position to get slaughtered by Wist the Kraken? He'd seen what she could do.

"Please remember who will be made to suffer if you slip up. I don't just mean me and my entire lineage."

"No pressure," I said. My parents, Mori, Ginko: everyone I associated with was a potential point of leverage.

On a more optimistic note, many positive developments might hinge on our success in aiding Jace. The Board wouldn't ship the Kraken overseas without demanding concessions. More trade, more travel, gestures at disarmament, bilateral talks....

There was a time in my life when I would have been deeply invested in the political and economic particulars. Now I was more invested in trying not to care. If I got overly interested, that old inner howl would build up again: *Why can't you all just be reasonable?*

Historical grudges, painful symbolism, industrial interests, wealthy lobbies—there were too many competing currents. Any change in relations would be excruciatingly incremental. I could see it already.

As her parting shot, Manatree told me: "You can try to stay out of politics, but politics won't always stay out of you."

Would I have been any good as a diplomat? In some ways, yes, but I would've cut corners. When I was younger, progress had seemed to take far too much time. It was a moot point, regardless. The only Osmanthian healers allowed to have any kind of foreign service career were those bonded to mages on the same path.

Anyway, here we were on Nerium's offensively opulent yacht. Night had fallen, and we still needed clearance to disembark. We'd been waiting for hours.

Everyone looked ready to go. Even Fanren sported a new and enhanced pair of magical glasses (courtesy of his sponsors at Regalia Optics).

Azalea had a headful of springy brown finger coils. Not a hair out of place. She wore a comfortable blouse and slacks; an outfit that could be dressed up or down for nearly any occasion.

A curious piece of statement jewelry hung around her neck. The pendant resembled a stick-straight silver whistle. The gleam of polished metal helped hide the subtle magic tucked inside it. She'd entertained the table with droll tales of using it to call her kid home for dinner.

She'd already memorized the names of all our companions. When unfamiliar faces spoke, I looked to Azalea for hints.

Shien Danver was the one who'd surprised me the most. She'd visited Ginko a couple times over the summer. Usually when Wist and I were out of town.

Then she'd shown up on the yacht with a blond bob, styled like a CEO, carrying her own personalized Regalia Optics business card.

Some hanger-on introduced her as Shien Nerium's representative ... and his bondmate.

This was impossible. Not because of them being secret half-siblings. Officially speaking, they had no real blood ties; a believable story, considering the sheer size of the Shien clan, and how frequently it took in adoptees. Like my Wist.

I'd broken Danver's ties to her previous bondmate. I stood by my opinion at the time: she could never bond again. It just wouldn't work.

So her claim wouldn't hold up under scrutiny. Especially not if she or Nerium ever got examined by a bond-authenticating notary.

Listen closely, though, and it became apparent that Danver herself never said a word about being bonded to anyone. A black thread encircled her throat, but she neither acknowledged nor contradicted the flunkies who called her Nerium's healer.

The shadowy agencies that had arranged this expedition surely knew otherwise. But no one spoke up. Just like how no one brought up my legal history, which was far more of a open secret.

I could understand, to some extent, why Nerium would choose her. He was too risk-averse to visit Jace in person. Maybe he'd consider it later, but not at this volatile stage. He'd let others take the spotlight in moments of historical consequence.

Nevertheless, he wanted someone there to represent his interests. Someone who wouldn't easily fall under the sway of his rivals. Besides, his economic peers in Jace would be far more willing to engage with a healer—or a subliminal—than a mage.

And what was in it for Danver? Whatever the dangers, international travel did seem more glamorous than spending the rest of her life as a glorified maid at the Shien manor. However, I had a sinking feeling that she'd come for other reasons.

Nerium would be aware of her real motivation, even if she refused to acknowledge it. Maybe he thought he was doing his little sister a favor. The whole trip might implode in violence, sure, but she was an adult. That was her risk to take.

I was awfully curious about Nerium's business goals, too. Danver had avoided discussing specifics. Maybe she'd angle for permission to sell (and manufacture?) perception-enhancing glasses in Jace.

For an organization like Regalia Optics, though, consumer products were really just a fun little side venture. It would be easier to expand their market share on the continent. Nerium—and therefore Danver— were aiming to strike a different type of deal, I thought. Something trickier, and more ambitious.

But enough about good old Danny. As we stood around surrounded by luggage, waiting to deboard at a Jacian naval base, it became apparent that Wist had undergone a bigger makeover than anyone else. She now bore little resemblance to her double.

She wore opaque black sunglasses (despite the darkness outside the ship) and a cleverly tailored special ops uniform, with her chest bound down just about as far as it could go. She had Jacian-style mage gloves, too.

With her height and voice—not to mention the stony set of her face—most people would take her for an androgynous man.

Around anyone with less than a top-level security clearance, she was supposed to pretend to be a bodyguard (just as I'd been assigned to play a clueless clerk). Honestly, she looked pretty scary just standing there. Like a knuckle-cracking enforcer sent by some underground syndicate.

"What?" she said.

I'd been staring.

"She likes your costume," Azalea said wryly.

There would be plenty of time for discretion once we set foot on Jacian soil. I reached up to touch the sides of Wist's hair. It was almost as short as mine now—I could see both her ears at all times.

Wist kept thinking quizzical thoughts at me. I kept rubbing. Yes, I was plenty familiar with cropped hair, but there was nothing exciting about feeling up the back of my own head.

Few Jacians would recognize Wist on sight, with or without her disguise. All they might have seen of her were occasional caricatures in propaganda, if even that.

She hadn't dressed like this to fool the general public. We were more concerned about officials and agents who'd been trained to consider her their greatest foe. Many of whom might already be lurking on base.

"Wherever they take you two," Azalea said to me, several notches quieter than before, "try to bring back a souvenir."

"Like what? A box of cookies?"

"Anything you can carry. Any kind of physical artifact. Doesn't need to look special. Don't worry about assessing its value."

"You know, my primary goal here is to avoid getting arrested."

"What, you're not used to it?"

If anyone else made a joke like that, Wist would ... no, better not go down that road.

"Also," Azalea continued, unbothered, "keep your eye safe. Don't let anyone take it."

"Right. I've only got one left."

"I meant your artificial eye."

"This one?" I rapped it with my knuckles as if requesting permission to enter. "Go on, try stealing it. It's pretty well locked down."

6

I'D BEEN LOOKING forward to craning my neck around. A Jacian naval base would be a rare sight for Osmanthian eyes, to say the least.

We'd crossed the sea of many names, but the air out here pretty much smelled the same as it had at our port of departure.

We descended the stairs from the yacht to the dock. Various aides—now obliged to act as porters—held whispered conferences about the fate of our baggage.

My one working eye caught a miserly glimpse of blue-black sky—and lost it a second later. As soon as we set foot on solid ground, uniformed Jacians ushered us into a hastily fabricated tunnel.

Floor grates rattled with every step. The walls and ceiling looked about as sturdy as plywood.

Jarringly bright white lamps hung interspersed with sodium-yellow light strips. If the goal was to make it impossible to see anything through dark gaps in the paneling, they more than succeeded.

Wist could have picked up more intel by scanning our surroundings with magic. But she wouldn't risk it. Jacian tech might block or detect attempts at probing.

This I knew without being told: certain members of our delegation had been ordered to snoop everywhere they could. I hoped fervently that they would at least wait until Wist and I were far enough away to assert our innocence.

Our clanking parade of footsteps on the ill-fitted floor drowned out any interesting sounds from outside. Couldn't even hear the water.

The passage turned and snaked until I'd lost all sense of direction. Finally it deposited us in a building with flickering overhead lights and a sound-sucking carpet. Clearly we'd come through the back entrance: no echoing welcome hall, no banners emblazoned with military emblems. There was an aging scent of cooked fish, as if we'd passed near the kitchens.

Our escort dumped us in a conference room with so few identifying features that it looked like a joke. They left without a word of explanation about what might happen next.

There wasn't even a Jacian flag on the wall. Just a glass case holding a single taxidermied animal. It had been placed on a plinth that resembled a podium, like a professor about to give us a lecture.

No one breathed a word about this one lonely element of decor. The specimen looked like a small seal-brown otter standing on its hind legs, front paws clasped as if it were trying to beg a favor.

There's no magic in that, is there? I said to Wist.

It's just a stuffed animal.

An obvious hiding spot for analog recording devices. Or brutal explosives.

On that note...

Now that they've got us all in one place, think they'll try to gas us?

Her only reply: *Whatever you do, don't say that out loud.*

Would my prosthetic protect against poison gas?

What kind?

How many kinds are there? I have no idea. The usual sort.

In theory, you should be immune to toxic fumes, she said eventually. *Smoke, gas, or whatever else. But it's not guaranteed to—*

The door swung open. Three Jacians filed in: a rotund man with a wide smile, a taller twig-thin man with sunken cheeks, and a woman dressed like an assassin. Wist's gear had a similar aesthetic, albeit with bulkier body armor.

The assassin pushed a cart of drinks. Coffee, exotic fruit juice, infused water, all sorts of tea ... no spica, though.

Danver went as stiff as if she were bracing for a blow from a whip.

Ah, yes. The lady currently serving us drinks was the one-name Jacian artist known as Lear. When Wist and I first met her in Osmanthus last winter, she'd sworn she was neither a spy nor an assassin. Hah.

She'd gotten recalled to Jace in June, shortly after holding a highly successful solo exhibition. Danver must've been pretty torn up about that, although she had too much pride to confide in anyone. Except maybe Ginko.

Lear didn't smile. She betrayed no sign of recognition.

It took a while to get arranged around the table. Our countries had different customs regarding where the highest-ranked attendee of any given meeting was supposed to sit.

Thus ensued much hemming and hawing and fawning and fake deference. Eventually a satisfactory compromise was reached. Everyone bowed. In all honesty, kindergarteners would've worked it out faster.

The skinny fellow who'd come in with Lear turned out to be an interpreter. We had one, too: a matronly polyglot without a single drop of Jacian blood.

Osmanthians with a foreign parent or grandparent wouldn't have been permitted to join our delegation in the first place. Personally, I thought we should've brought over more bilinguals, but no one put me in charge of recruitment.

Our interpreter was also a certified toxicologist. As we started to sit down, she went around sprinkling grains of sand—or powdery spores?—in all our cups. Nothing seemed to happen after the spores dissolved, which was presumably the desired outcome.

The leader of the three Jacians observed this ritual with cheerful condescension. He was a military healer: short, confident, and paunchy, with a snake emblem on his breast. (Healers are called operators in Jace, by the way, but I'm not going to bother switching up my vocabulary in my own thoughts.)

He welcomed us with a few stilted words in Continental. Something like "Greetings and salutations!" After that initial volley, he switched back to Jacian, and our respective interpreters got to work.

Wist and I weren't supposed to look important. The Jacian healer addressed Fanren effusively (while ignoring every other mage in the room). Fanren smiled graciously: he was accustomed to getting showered with kudos in all sorts of languages.

Either the healer wasn't high-ranking enough to have been informed that our party included Wist the Kraken, or he was pretending not to know.

Our professional diplomats started talking in earnest. The discussion focused primarily on the itinerary for Fanren's group. No one inquired about—or offered an explanation for—the stuffed otter. I drained my cup of coffee.

Some minutes later, Lear wandered over to the drink cart as if assessing whether it needed replenishment. Wist and I discreetly got up and followed her out, mumbling something about going to help.

Danver almost ruined our exit by standing abruptly, white-faced. Azalea yanked sharply at her sleeve. Lear and Wist and I hastened away.

As soon as the door clicked shut, Lear abandoned her cart and started walking so fast that I had to run to catch up.

We turned several corners, then dove into a smaller room, also windowless. A taxidermied owl stared at us from the top of an otherwise barren shelf.

"'Auditor Lear of Special Branch,'" I said. That was how our interpreter had introduced her.

"It's a temporary assignment." Lear spoke fluent Continental. "I've been lent out to Special Branch."

"To protect visiting dignitaries?"

"Sure, why not."

I'd been wondering who might show up to meet us in Jace. I was just relieved they'd sent Lear. Better her than a total stranger, or any of the operatives I'd known in my twenties.

The lighting in here wasn't flattering. Not to us, and not to that pop-eyed owl. Lear still had the same purple-tinged hair and feline eyeliner, applied with an impressively steady hand, but she no longer wore any jewelry. Instead, she bristled with knives.

The two Jacian men had been trussed up in high-necked dress uniforms. Lear looked far more combat-oriented, but she wasn't clad in the stereotypical ultra-layered outfit of a Jacian battle mage.

Perhaps she'd been granted more privileges than other mages. She was neutered, as we'd learned late last year. Her magic core gave every appearance of being smooth and branchless. Most onlookers wouldn't be able to distinguish her from a regular subliminal.

On top of that, she still had a healer bondmate to watch her. (The bond had been established back before they neutered her. Very clever.)

"That smiley man in the room with the otter," I said. "Is he your...?"

"No," Lear said immediately. "Lord, no. Not him."

She'd asked me to break her bond if I ever came to Jace. Here I was—but whatever the case, I knew better than to bring it up unasked. Especially not smack in the middle of a military installation.

No one took a seat. Wist locked eyes with the stuffed owl, daring it to spy on us.

"We've still got your painting in our bedroom," I said to Lear. "Done anything new lately?"

She shrugged. "My art is much better received on the continent than at home."

So much for small talk. "Where are we headed?"

"An island."

"Yes, I'd gathered that much."

"Not one you've ever heard of, I think." Lear slipped on a distinctive pair of lacquer earpieces. They were bizarrely long and pointy. "We've got a train to catch," she said, with a ghost of her old smile. "I'll brief you on board."

7

WHAT WAS IT with me and peculiar little islands? I'd first met Wist at boarding school on a dinky barrier island off the Osmanthian coast. I'd spent my seven-year incarceration in an island prison. Now Lear was taking us to an island made of trash.

"A landfill?" I said. "Really?"

"Got decommissioned decades ago. But, yes, it was once the last landfill used by the capital."

"Sounds prestigious."

We'd boarded the military train without incident. We got on right there at the base, that very same night. Our luggage stayed behind with the other group—which meant, I suppose, that we wouldn't be gone long enough to need it.

As we settled in, Lear touched one of her earpieces and carried out a muffled conversation that mainly consisted of saying "Yes, sir," and "No, sir."

I nudged her after she wrapped it up. "So you're bonded to a man."

"A woman, actually. She just likes being called sir."

The Jacian version of the honorific had no gender connotation, come to think of it. I invariably saw it translated as *sir*, but why had I assumed that every single nuance would be the same?

Lear put a finger to the pointed tip of one ear cuff, as if testing whether it was sharp enough to cut. "You do realize that I could have been talking to anyone. Why would I need a transceiver to speak with my bondmate?"

Oops.

"There's no law forcing bondmates to speak mind-to-mind," I countered. "Some find it invasive. Or tiresome. Maybe you're using the earpiece for—for compliance reasons."

A pitiful argument, but Lear chuckled. "No, you're right. That was her."

The three of us had an entire compartment to ourselves. The floor squeaked like an abused animal, which effectively killed my urge to walk around.

I had a feeling that if I did go exploring, every linked car would be just as empty. Nothing but wasted seat space and the velvety reek of dust. Which made no sense. Surely they'd loaded the rest of the train with freight, if not passengers. But I couldn't shake that conviction of hollowness. We were stowaways clinging to the interior of a long lifeless tube.

Fortunately, Danver had made no attempt to stow away with us.

Wist slid into the window seat beside me. She'd taken off her sunglasses. Lear sat across from us.

All the windows were heavily tinted. Couldn't see a thing. The Jacian military seemed determined not to let us enjoy any local scenery.

"Wouldn't an airship be faster?" I said.

"There were arguments against giving you a peek at the inner workings of Jacian airships," said Lear.

"Ironic, considering that we're being sent after a mutineering chalice. Which by its very nature—"

"And that's how you know we're in dire straits."

The train started moving. It was so smooth and near-silent that we may as well have been going nowhere. Just sitting there like kids playing pretend. I half suspected Lear of rigging up an elaborate prank.

Something thumped the blacked-out window.

I swore and nearly somersaulted into the aisle. Wist caught my elbow.

Another soft thumping. I jumped again.

"What the hell," I said.

Lear looked up. "Relax," she said amiably. "We're not under attack. Trust your guide."

"What is it, then? Birds? Bats? Someone climbing around outside the train?"

She spread her hands. "Could be any of those. We're safe inside."

I sank lower in my seat, sulking.

After another ten minutes, the banging stopped. By then, the air in the car was starting to get a bit stuffy. Even Lear (who hated being cold) removed her jacket.

"Nasty bug bite," I said.

She looked puzzled. I pointed.

She rotated her bare forearm as if she'd never seen it before. The bug bite, not her arm. It was the same brown hue as the rest of the skin around it—but painfully puffy, with irregular edges.

"It doesn't itch," she said.

"Isn't that a good thing?"

She turned to Wist. "Kraken. I need to ask you a favor."

Kraken.

Something about this was as disorienting as being back on a boat again, miles from familiar land. Had Lear always called Wist by her title? She knew our names, but how much had she ever used them? In Osmanthus, would she have called me Asa, or Clematis, or Magebreaker? I couldn't remember.

We really didn't know her at all, did we?

Yet when Lear asked for help—arm upturned to expose her misshapen bug bite—Wist seemed to understand exactly what she needed.

The window was as unreflective as a sheet of rubber. Wist's eyes never left it. She had her chin on one hand, her body twisted away from us. Simply put, she couldn't see a thing.

She didn't need to see it.

Magic like a scalpel cut an incision down Lear's inner forearm, straight through the bug bite, all the way up to the crease of her elbow.

Lear made a winded noise. No blood crept out: Wist's magic must have forbidden it. There were hints of leakage at the edges, but it was a dampness as dilute as water.

Instead, white dots spilled out of the bisected bite. It went much deeper than it looked, like a buried cyst. Or a punctured egg sac. The dots were the same size as hard beads of fertilizer in packaged soil.

Then they uncurled. "Urgh," I said, trying not to heave. Pale worms scattered all over Lear's lap. I pulled my legs up onto my seat, trying to get as far away from her knees as possible.

The worms resembled living bits of thread, both ends waving about like competing heads—questing for warmth, or moisture, or skin. Once they started moving, they never stopped.

"Kraken," Lear said again, strained.

I almost took my eye out to experiment with the Void. I could vacuum up that smorgasbord of worms in an instant. But I couldn't guarantee that I wouldn't also steal a chunk of Lear's thigh. I needed more practice.

Wist still faced the impenetrable window. I dug out a tissue and dangled it in her peripheral vision.

"Here," I said.

Lear's throat gurgled dangerously.

The tissue tugged itself out of my fingers. Then—moving all on its own—it pounced on the skinny white worms and pinched them off with rapid efficiency. Some clung on till they snapped in half like rubber bands. It took minutes to scrape up all the leftovers: from Lear's wrist, and her pants, and the upholstered seat, and the floor.

The tissue wadded up its accumulated worms like sticky old gum. Hovering between us, it compressed itself to the size of a pearl. Then it winked out of existence with a puff of sulfurous smoke.

Lear exhaled. Cold sweat coated her brow. I wouldn't have blamed her for ripping all her clothes off and trying to burn them.

I leaned forward for a closer look at her slashed-open arm. It was surprising how much stuff you could see in there when loose blood wasn't gushing all over.

The membrane that had held the seeds of those worms had been woven from her own flesh. It was already dissolving into a gel of pink and yellow goo.

At Wist's direction, the lips of the wound clamped shut, leaving a puckered line like the edge of a poorly folded dumpling. She was rather slapdash when it came to physical healing.

Lear thanked her, still sounding faint. "Cleanly done," she said. "Almost painless."

How secure is this train? I asked.

Wist finally drew away from the window. She looked indifferent, as if she went around mutilating worm-ridden ladies on a daily basis.

"No one can eavesdrop," she said out loud.

I pointed at Lear and mouthed: "Except her bondmate."

Lear glanced at her watch. "She's a busy woman, and she goes to bed early. Speak freely."

In Osmanthus, she'd claimed that her bondmate was very hands-off. If that was still true, how could she prove it? And what would stop her from reporting our every action after the fact, anyway?

It almost didn't matter whether we did or said anything personally incriminating. If Lear's bosses wanted to cause trouble, they could just have her make things up.

I wiggled my fingers like worms. "So what was that all about?"

"The Parasite Guild," Lear said, still weary.

"Who?"

"Their emblem is a tick."

"Well, that's cute."

"They're hunters."

"Of people, I assume?"

She put her jacket back on, covering the ridge of sealed-up skin on her forearm. "The Guild is essentially a private military company. They take a lot of government contracts."

"Ah."

"I could've gotten those worms implanted at any point today. Or even earlier." She cursed softly in Jacian.

"What are the chances of them targeting the rest of our delegation?"

"The cultural ambassador, you mean?"

"Who—oh, Fanren? Yeah."

"If they find your friend, they're more likely to ask for his autograph."

"How worldly of them." I considered my next words. "You don't seem all that worried about Danver."

"Danny can hold her own."

"She's never left Osmanthus before. Or tagged along with a foreign envoy. She has barely a single season's worth of corporate experience."

"Nothing I can do about that, is there?"

"Have you been in touch since June?"

Lear leveled a wordless look at me. I could already feel us getting closer. Yes, this trip was going to be a real bonding experience for everyone involved.

Don't overdo it, Wist told me.

There were many, many islands in the Jacian archipelago. Some were larger than certain continental countries, and some were microscopic uninhabited rocks. The yacht had docked at an eastern port on one of the centermost islands.

Now this train was bearing us all the way across to the Natal Gulf on the opposite coast.

We still had hours left to go. I leaned against Wist and tried to doze off. This brought back memories of louder, shakier trains ... those older models had been easier to sleep in.

Once in a while, I squinted across and saw Lear rubbing her forearm.

What might have happened to her—to us—if Wist failed to purge those worms?

I opened one eye again. Wist was sound asleep. Her distant dreams thundered at the fringes of our bond like a mysterious noise filtering up from the bottom of the sea.

"Hey," I said to Lear, whispering. Every time I glanced at her, she'd been fully awake.

"Did you consent to that?" I tapped my own forearm, indicating the spot where I'd seen her bug bite. "Were you in on it?"

She looked deliberately at the blank window.

And yet, once the train got going, she'd found a reason to remove her jacket.

8

It was still dark out when the train deposited us at a naval shipyard. Yet another temporary passageway was waiting to shepherd us away from the station. For all we'd glimpsed of Jace so far, we might have never left the continent.

The walkway spat us out near a pedestrian underpass, which had clearly marked hours (it was supposed to be closed for the night). Lear stepped past the barrier—without getting electrocuted—so Wist and I followed after.

Space-distorting magic echoed through the garishly lit tunnel. I staggered; Wist didn't. My legs kept moving, but it was like the weeks after I'd first lost my eye. Nothing seemed to be in quite the right place. Not the ground, and not my own limbs.

We were only in there for a few minutes. By the time we waded out, though, I knew the shipyard would be far out of sight. The tunnel had sent us on a shortcut to some totally different part of the coast.

Wist brushed the back of my neck, and my nausea vanished.

Lear had a large bag with her. "What's in there?" I asked. "Weapons?"

"Supplies of all sorts. Just a precaution."

She'd produced stealth bracelets for the three of us: chunky resin cuffs with magic cuttings trapped in them like ancient organisms preserved in amber. They turned clear when in use. They were clear now, and cloaking magic clung to us like a veil of humidity. It would've been unbearable if we'd come to Jace at the height of summer.

We hadn't yet reached our final destination: the fabled garbage island. The underpass had connected us to a seaside park.

Hardy palm trees lined up like giant soldiers beneath the pre-dawn sky. There were dense forests preserved for hiking, and grassy narrow barrier islands a short distance away across tranquil water. And no other visitors in sight. A fairy wheel towered over a dark complex of barbecue facilities and overpriced restaurants, waiting for the start of its workday.

The coastal wind was constant and horrible: changing directions every half-second, drying my eye out, slamming grit in my face.

Snipers, Wist said absently.

Oh. As awful as it was, the wind did taste of Wist's magic. I didn't rubberneck—no way would I be able to spot a professional sniper—or ask further questions. If she was concentrating on keeping us from getting shot at, far be it from me to distract her.

I looked balefully at my stealth bracelet. The ones we wore were linked, so we could still perceive each other. It seemed entirely possible that they might also serve as deliberate magical beacons telling those hidden gunners where to shoot.

Even flawed cloaking was better than none, though.

The wind stuffed itself down my throat whenever I tried to speak; it made my nose run like a waterfall. I hacked out a disgusting series of coughs.

If Lear knew about the snipers, she was doing an admirable job of keeping her cool. Perhaps she'd received some assurance that they'd try their best not to hit her.

There was a lot going on in this sheltered part of the Natal Gulf. Hundreds and hundreds of years ago, even the ground we stood on used to be nothing but water. Intrepid engineers had filled in enormous swathes of land.

Now there were freight terminals stacked high with containers, civilian shipyards full of cranes, commercial piers, more nature parks, an aerodrome ... and, further out, dozens of artificial islands, some of which had begun to merge like amoeba. I could just about make out a few of them: distant blots like smears of charcoal at the edge of the sea.

On the train, Lear had delineated multiple ways to get where we needed to go. A hired boat, for instance (too slow). A magical bypass tunnel that ran beneath the bottom of the gulf (too predictable, and she thought the exit might've been walled off). Defunct portals once used for transferring massive quantities of garbage (promising, but dangerous).

In the park, she showed us an assortment of regional maps. Wist's mind was already far out over the water, coasting like a bird, triangulating our position.

In a pinch, Wist could have ported us all the way from the eastern base to this park; instead, we'd spent hours traveling. Wist could have cloaked us; instead, we'd used stealth bracelets. Anything to spare her unnecessary effort and unnecessary pain.

In some cases, though, the best solution was to rely on the Kraken.

Ready? I asked.

Mm-hm, Wist said.

She gave no warning. A giant fist around my torso squeezed and pulled me like dough.

When I blinked, left eye stinging, I saw double. As Wist ported us away, we left something behind. Husks of ourselves, like abandoned cicada shells: the figures of three women frozen in a moment of meditation. Gazing warily out at the gulf.

So they still have something to shoot at, Wist said. She enjoyed this sort of thing way more than she let on.

We rematerialized next to the wreck of a chalice. It might've shocked a yawp out of me if I'd been able to see. All I felt was its monumental shadow—the bulk of it lurked in my blind spot.

Wist didn't react, so neither did I.

Lear adjusted her bag on her shoulder. "That was abrupt."

"Are we on the right island?" I asked. Not that I doubted Wist's skills, but it never hurts to check.

"Looks like it."

My tear glands were still streaming from the abrasive wind in the park—a wind that had died down the moment we ported. I dabbed my face dry. My next thought: this place didn't smell at all like a landfill.

Things were looking up already.

The crashed chalice lay slumped against a low concrete seawall. Or maybe a breakwater. I wasn't sure of the difference. The wall seemed to have been built around the chalice, or altered to accommodate it, like a fence interrupted by a swelling tree trunk.

This machina looked smaller than the egg that had visited the tower, and much more ordinary, with a roughly humanoid structure. It was still large enough to trample any of the houses on the slope behind us.

Somehow, I hadn't thought there'd be houses.

Water lapped wanly against the discolored seawall and the rust-eaten chalice. Beetle-size crabs skittered about as if searching for hidden meat.

Lear peered at the wreck with avid interest. "Must be an old prototype. Cockpit looks empty."

"No skeleton?" I said.

"No skeleton. Someone came and dredged out the pilot."

Wist faced the sea, as still as a lighthouse. I kept an eye on the village at our back. It didn't look decrepit enough to be outright abandoned. Each residence was unaccountably narrow, shoved right up against its neighbor, with one-sided slanting roofs that jutted as steeply as the point of a knife.

"Seems like a regular small town," I said to Lear. "Not a research facility. Not anything sinister."

"No. Sorry, let me get my bearings."

I scanned the sky. Maybe the egg chalice would pop on over to say hello. But the only flying creatures in sight were a few dark cormorants.

I rolled my sleeves up—this stealth magic gave me the same prickly sensation as desperately needing a shower—then got cold and pulled them down again.

"Clem," Wist said.

What?

I trotted on over to her, right at the edge of the seawall.

"Try again," she said simply.

What? Why aren't you—

She couldn't hear me.

9

I GRABBED WILDLY for our bond, insofar as you could grab at anything that lacked a physical presence. Still there.

Delayed fear and relief crashed together and just about knocked me off my feet.

I sat dizzily on the seawall. The water looked docile. The concrete felt like nothing—neither cold or hot. Maybe the morning sun would warm it later. The light right now was too new and weak, an ineffectual gray wash.

Wist sank down beside me, legs dangling off the edge.

Lear observed us curiously. What else did she have to look at? She'd already done everything short of climbing up inside the machina and touring its weathered cockpit.

If I unclenched my mind, I could sense Wist trying to tell me something. Like words whispered underwater. As I strained to listen, she stopped and opened her mouth instead.

"There's a field around the island," she said. "Many, many layers…"

"Of what?"

"A power that distorts."

I lowered my voice. "Can you do anything about it?"

"Not easily."

"So we won't be able to speak in our minds. At all."

We were pressed together from thigh to shoulder, no air between us, and I still felt unanchored. As if it would be all too easy—even while seated—to slip and fall in the sea.

In the sea…

I flinched back. "Is that a body?"

Lear came closer, trying to spot it. "In the water? Looks like a deer."

"Do deer normally get that big?"

"Might be a young stock-elk."

"Right by the shore?"

"Maybe someone keeps a herd for research. Or food. The postal service might use them." Lear seemed bemused by my confusion. "Want me to climb down and check it out?"

"Don't bother," I said brusquely. "Might be diseased."

Gulls had started circling above the drowned stock-elk. Greedy birds: they'd devour carrion like a flock of vultures.

Wist and I got back on our feet. I consulted wordlessly with her—aggressive eye contact, a tilted head, a clutched wrist. I wormed a single finger inside her glove to feel the heat of her palm.

I hoped she was telling me to do whatever I thought best.

Better just have out with it. I tapped my skull at Lear. "I can't hear my own bondmate."

She didn't feign shock. She folded her arms protectively and said: "Not even you two, huh? That's a shame."

"You knew this would happen."

My anger crackled like something physically removed from my body, a warning snap of icy branches, a cold patch in the air behind me. But no—that was Wist, gloved hands light on my hips, as if the slightest hint of assent would be enough for her to shift me aside and show Lear the face beneath her mask of indifference.

Lear held her ground. She was looking determinedly at me, though, and not at Wist. She'd been under orders not to tell us. Or she'd kept it to herself just to see what would happen.

"One advance team reported an issue with comms," she said. "The details weren't clear." She slipped off her ear cuffs and tossed them in her bag. "These aren't working, either."

Wist took out a clematis transceiver. It lifted off her palm, wavering. Then, eager to please, it spun like a pinwheel. It spun until its pointed petals blurred into a seamless disc. It glowed white-hot. It started smoking.

"No good," Wist said tersely. The molten pin dropped back into her hand. I cringed—it should have branded her—but the metal had already gone dark, albeit rather more rubbery around the edges.

I caught Lear's eye. "Your bondmate won't be able to keep tabs on you."

"Not at all," she said cheerfully. "I'm glad. I had orders to shoot you."

She drew her hand out of her bag.

She held a pistol.

Wist didn't tense up. She wore her usual blank expression; she considered Lear about as much of a threat as the abandoned machina or the rotting stock-elk.

"Your bondmate wants us dead," I said.

"Not her. I'm on loan to Special Branch, remember? I have to follow their directives. My bondmate would never presume to tell me otherwise. Just between us, though, she would prefer if I didn't succeed."

"Great," I bit out. "I'm glad that's all cleared up."

Lear just laughed and rotated her gun, offering me the grip. The muzzle pointed sideways at the ocean. "If you think you might need it, go ahead and take it."

"How good are you with guns?" I inquired.

"I probably have more experience than either of you," she said diplomatically, "but perhaps you'll surprise me."

"Yeah, I strongly doubt that. Keep it."

She strapped on a holster.

"You must've been given a lot of conflicting orders," I said.

"Oh, it's been awful. My bondmate likes to play every possible side."

"Out here in the field, you're all we've got." This had a sarcastic ring to it, but it was—regrettably—true. "You can't screw this up."

"I'm much better at painting than covert ops."

"Don't sell yourself short," I told her.

A well-maintained road ran next to the seawall. No one traversed it, either on foot or in any sort of vehicle. The village on the other side of the street remained motionless. No boats on the water, either.

We'd landed on the natural end of the island: an unwieldy accumulation of hills. Once we got past the tallest ridge—not quite a mountain—the rest would be reclaimed terrain, flat and monotonous.

This island was known as Ashtereth. After retiring from service as a waste disposal site, it had been resurrected as a top-secret research base.

The research performed here had to do with chalice development. Experimental design and prototyping, for the most part (as opposed to mass production). Our Jacian hosts had alluded to the fact that our quarry wasn't any standard type of machina. It wasn't even supposed to function, really; it was a conceptual model. It had never been authorized for flight. After a quick joyride into foreign airspace, it had gone right back home to Ashtereth.

Wist was supposed to find and secure this hiding chalice. Then what? Would we mindlessly deliver it wherever Lear told us? We'd have frighteningly little incentive not to steal the damn thing for ourselves. A new wing to add to Wist's tower.

"How many advance teams were sent?" I asked. "What happened to them?"

"Three or four that I know of," said Lear. "We lost contact."

"They're still here, then. Dead or alive."

The timing felt off. Just a couple days had passed since Wist and I first sighted that experimental chalice. Even while the Jacian government dispatched commandos to Ashtereth, they'd already started making overtures to request aid from Osmanthus.

They hadn't waited to see what their own squads might accomplish. They'd leapt straight to the unthinkable: crawling to the Kraken for help.

"Why didn't your bosses just bomb the hell out of this place?" I said. "Barring that—why didn't they deploy more chalices? You've got others. Ones that haven't gone rogue."

"There are locals on the island. Civilians."

"Be truthful. Would that stop anyone from performing an emergency strike?"

Lear eyed the sky as if casing a ceiling for cameras. "They did attempt a strike," she said. "It ... backfired. The research director said he would only surrender to the Kraken."

"He's hunkered down here? But he can communicate off-island?"

"He could at one point."

Maybe this chalice-brandishing director was just pretending to rebel. Maybe he was secretly in cahoots with the highest levels of Jacian leadership, and this whole shebang was a diabolical scheme to snare the Kraken.

After all, he'd have no reason to involve a foreign mage in a run-of-the-mill attempt to overthrow the current regime.

Yet more so than myriad political considerations, more so than amorphous fears for the innocent populace of either nation, it was the chalice itself that had convinced me to follow Wist here.

COME.

That wasn't the kind of power you could safely run away from.

We were playing right into the hands of the rumored director. But there was no telling what might happen if we abandoned our mission. Would he stop at nothing to lure the Kraken?

Jacian or Osmanthian lives might hang in the balance. Both would hurt her. Oh, there were always groups trying to smear her name, but anyone who took a dispassionate look at her record could tell how much she'd bend over backward to avoid collateral damage.

"Lear," I said. "This director person. What's he called?"

"Datura Gray."

"And his chalice?"

"Reverence," she said in Jacian. "A virtue name."

I repeated the syllables back at her, and she explained what it meant.

All chalices had a call sign, like ships. This one was an old-fashioned choice. Classical Jacian literature and legends abounded in virtue names (typically for people, not machinery), but they'd long since fallen out of fashion.

"Anything else you'd like to tell us before we plunge into danger?" I asked.

"No need to plunge. We're already here. I'm surprised no one's started lobbing grenades yet."

"Still plenty of time for that later," I said sourly. "All they've got to do is lie in wait at the base. Where else would we be headed?"

"...Ah."

"What?"

"There is one thing you should know." She looked from me to Wist. "We ported to get here. But—no matter what—we shouldn't try to port out."

10

Something splashed in the water. I rubbed my good eye. Wist, hands in her pockets, had casually ported the bloated stock-elk from one side of the wrecked machina to the other. I was starting to think I could smell it.

Seagulls milled overhead, squawking as if they'd been robbed. The carcass appeared no worse off than before. (Then again, it was already dead.)

Wist looked inquiringly at Lear. It was easier to deduce emotion from those unchanging black sunglasses than from her actual face.

"Porting within the island works fine," Lear agreed.

"So does porting in from outside," I said.

"Right. One advance unit used disposable portals to get here. No problem. Since comms were down, they used another portal to send a scout back. She was supposed to report to Central, but she barely survived the trip. She's still not coherent."

Wist gave the stock-elk a sidelong glance, as if weighing the merits of hurling it off the island as a morbid experiment.

"Might be a long day," I murmured. "Save it for later."

We wouldn't recklessly port off Ashtereth, risks be damned. We wouldn't just take Lear's word for it, either.

But I left that part unsaid.

We left the seawall and started making our way over to the landfill side of the island. It wouldn't be that far of a walk—a good stretch for legs still stiff from hours on the train. Besides, going on foot would be more informative than teleporting sight unseen.

There were other reasons to minimize Wist's magic use. One, to keep her in tip-top shape for whatever might come later. Two, to avoid catching the notice of anyone scanning for unusual activity. Three, to keep her practical capabilities as mysterious as possible. Every skill she whipped out would inevitably get cataloged for mitigation analysis by hostile parties.

Our bracelets were supposed to conceal us from civilians. In the village, however, there was no one to hide from.

The houses were squished too close together to leave much individual yard space. Small bushes and flower boxes clustered out front. Old mud dauber nests grew from walls and eaves like brown warts.

Some windows were hidden by worn wooden shutters. Others were criss-crossed with packing tape to protect against breakage in storms. People did the same thing when typhoons hit Osmanthus City. It'd be a pain to peel off.

I would've felt better about all this if the settlement were obviously abandoned. The plants looked well-watered; the stoops had been swept. Fuzzy kiwifruit hung down from trellised vines, almost ready for harvest.

Half the streets were made of stone steps. One especially long staircase led up to a tree-shaded shrine with a circular gate. Wist's hand glided above the banister without touching it. She mumbled about containment fields as we paused for breath at the top.

"I see it now," she said. "If you port off the island, parts of the boundary will break off and stick in you like glass. It can shatter and repair itself over and over. It's designed to cause maximum injury to body and mind."

"Is this new tech?" I asked. Lear shrugged helplessly.

Tangled shrubbery rustled at the edge of the shrine.

Lear's hand jumped to her holster.

A black cat with one stark white leg stalked out of the greenery. It had a short, thick stump of a tail.

The cat glared at us, ears down, then ran to safety.

Across the way, Wist found an array of stainless steel bowls. A few still held clean water.

"Someone's been feeding the strays," I said.

Maybe the residents were right here where they belonged, tromping up and down the stairs, exchanging local gossip, paying homage at their shrine. If they too wore undetectable bracelets, they would be ghosts to us, just as we were ghosts to them. Two parallel worlds in the same geography.

We left the village and descended a series of eroding slopes. Woods grew around the dusty road, blocking our view of the sea. The terrain began to flatten.

Once upon a time, this stretch might have looked like an expanse of tilled dirt and grassy sports fields. But the landfill was long out of business: they had nothing left to bury, no reason not to let it go feral.

I stopped staring at the depths of the forest. I turned my head.

I was alone.

The Void roiled.

Sometimes I can't remember what it was like to see with two eyes.

Sometimes my enlarged blind spot presses at me like a living, tumorous thing.

I whipped around. On the inside, I was already calling for Wist. Instead of traveling down our bond, my cries echoed as if my mind—my self—were a sealed-off cave.

I'd forgotten about the blockade.

I'd never heard of magic that could garble the connection between bondmates. The potential applications were horrific. Worse, perhaps, than that anti-porting containment field. If I couldn't talk to Wist through our bond, I couldn't heal her from a distance, either.

I started forward. A shout died on my lips. Wist and Lear had been there all along, half-hidden by roadside trees.

"*You*," I said.

Their heads rose. Nothing had actually happened—I'd scared myself. I was jumping at shadows.

I modulated my voice. "Found something interesting?"

"Tracks." Lear indicated an area of trampled weeds.

"Like from a stock-elk? Or a boar?"

I surveyed the ground for prints, but there were no conveniently placed patches of mud, just layer upon layer of bent and flattened plants.

"A person," said Lear. "One or more. Someone heavy, or heavily geared up. They left the road here, see? And went over there"—she pointed—"and peed."

"You can tell all that from just this?" I said, impressed.

"I can't take much credit. The Kraken smelled it first."

I wandered closer, trying not to disturb any downy spiderwebs. Okay, yeah—it stank like an alley near a city bar.

If Lear was right, someone (perhaps someone in armor) had come through as recently as ... a few hours ago? A day ago? No one had ever taught me how to calculate the half-life of urine.

An interesting discovery, but it didn't alter our course. Sooner or later, we were bound to have company.

Once we got moving, I kept Wist on my left. Insects kept swooping at her: gnats, butterflies, wasps, you name it. As the tallest among us, she'd become an inadvertent decoy. Few of them bothered me or Lear.

Further down the road, we ran into a miniature city. Minarets and spires of lumpy sculpted dirt reared up in a glade where little else grew.

"Termites?" I said.

Wist took a step back.

"Ever seen tidal ants? They build castles on the shore." Lear gestured as if she were building one herself. "They've been accidentally awarded prizes in sand sculpture contests. It's a pretty common sort of local news story, down where I come from."

I had a feeling that she was pulling my leg.

While we (or at least I) admired the sights, Lear offered us water from her bag. She had an enchanted canteen that could desalinate and purify just about anything. Even liquid scooped straight from a sewer.

"Sounds expensive," I said.

"Well, none of the tools I carry are mine to keep."

Wist scrutinized the canteen, then pronounced: "This won't protect against brain-eating amoeba."

Lear was unfazed. "So don't snort it up your nose."

"There go my plans for breakfast," I muttered.

Once we finished passing her canteen back and forth, Lear pulled out a compact living scroll and showed us blueprints of the base.

"Might not be terribly helpful," she demurred. "The layout isn't necessarily static."

I elbowed Wist. "Sounds like your tower."

"My tower is taller."

"Guess you win, then. Congratulations."

Shortly afterward, we approached what should have been the location of the nearest entrance.

Wist did a quick scan. "Nothing."

"They moved it," Lear said grimly. "Or the blueprints were falsified. Lord. I would've liked to find the Ashtereth post office."

"What could we do at a post office?" I asked, dubious.

"With the current comms blockade, not much. I thought maybe—but no, it's not worth a detour."

I swatted a striped mosquito. Just a couple dozen steps into the woods, and I couldn't remember which way the ocean lay. The only audible birds were faraway gulls. The trees crawled with insects and vines and fuzzy, drippy fungal life. But it still felt dead quiet. The lack of sound made the air seem anemic.

Back to the road, then. The surface was coated with wind-rippled layers of powder-fine silt. Like unevenly applied makeup. Here and there, older pavement peeked through.

That dust should have been the perfect medium for taking footprints. Ours disappeared as we walked: behind us, Wist's magic swept them away like a broom.

"There are pylons out in the water," she said.

"Wind turbines?" Lear guessed.

"No. Those are on the other side of the island." Wist spoke as if she'd already seen it. She laid out her hypothesis. The pylons distorted all manner of technological and magical communication—and simultaneously magnified the anti-porting field.

"They're likely built for redundancy," Lear said. "You'd have to destroy half or more to take the whole system down."

She waved a bee away from her face. She was about to speak again when the bee came back for more.

It brought friends.

11

LEAR EXCLAIMED in Jacian. I ducked, swearing. The bees were sound-less—too many to dodge, too fast to see.

A sharp noise.

Everything stopped moving, bees and all. My ears throbbed woozily. Wist had brought her hands together in a single raw clap. I'd heard it a second too late.

The swarm hung motionless around us. While zipping to and fro, they really had looked like stinging bees. Once stilled, though, all they resembled were cheap office-supply thumbtacks: some translucent, some black.

"Anyone hurt?" Lear said after a moment. She sounded as if she were talking into a cup.

"Would we know if they'd stung us?" I asked.

"Yes." Wist left no room for doubt. "You would know."

The bee tacks fell to the ground all at once. Something drained out of them, leaving wet patches in the dust. The translucent ones turned clear. The darker ones turned the gray-white color of grubs.

"Your Guild again?" I said to Lear.

"It's not *my* Guild. Good guess, though. They do love their insect motifs."

"If someone was watching them attack us—"

"We're clear," Wist said, eyes on the thumb tacks. If she looked at a person like that, their heart might give out on the spot. "These operate autonomously. Their wielder isn't anywhere near us."

"Can you—?" I started.

"Easily."

"Save some to—"

"Done."

One downside of being unbeatable partners was knowing each other so well that a lot of our conversations came out completely garbled. Ordinarily, this rapid-fire half-speech would take place within the confines of our bond. Here, we had no choice but to conduct our unintelligible business out loud. Must have been annoying for Lear. To her credit, she didn't show it.

The tacks rolled over and, eerily synchronized, lurched into flight.

It was something about the way they vibrated: as soon as they got back in motion, they looked like organic bees again.

Half of them drifted off toward a stand of weathered pine trees, weaving drunkenly. The rest rose high above the road, then scattered like buckshot.

"You took control?" Lear said. "Just like that?"

Wist nodded. "Some of the tacks will hunt for whoever sent them. Some will scout out an entrance."

I sidled up to her and tidied her magic. "Can't we just look around for industrial buildings?"

"The facility is mostly underground," Lear said.

I wanted to question the wisdom of making this a subterranean base. Wouldn't reclaimed terrain be wetter (or less stable) than regular land? Also: the ground was infused with runoff from a mille-feuille of imported waste.

On the other hand, what did I know? Jace had been building artificial islands for thousands of years. We usually only heard about the ones they plopped in international waters.

We walked on. Further inland, we discovered a billboard draped with clinging vines. It pointed us at a roped-off plain where large signs introduced the history of the retired landfill.

There was a museum and visitor center, too: a wide, low-slung building that looked about as empty as the village. It was surprisingly nice, though. Clean and glassy. Who had paid for this, and who was it meant to impress? Visiting dignitaries? Machinists assigned to the secret base?

Lear located a colorful map board (the kind even a child could parse, with *YOU ARE HERE* marked in red). We compared it to her blueprints.

Most of Ashtereth's surface area was now a nature preserve, it seemed. Walking trails snaked all over: we could lose days to aimless wandering.

Wist had her eye on a white tower in the distance. It poked up like a chimney past wild meadows and woods.

"A lighthouse?" I asked.

"Too far inland."

Lear tapped the map. "It's a historical landmark. Part of an old incineration plant."

I went over to the plain marked off by yellow ropes. Inside were several square pits designed to show off a cross-section of the landfill, like an archaeological dig.

There were layers to it, yes, but I only saw various shades of gray-brown dirt. They hadn't just poured out the contents of a dumpster. Everything buried here had been thoroughly reduced—either burned to ash or mechanically pulverized to anonymous dust.

I'd thought it would be more like the detritus-filled cave that Wist and I had waded through in Manglesea. You know: ragged clothing and legless chairs and broken bottles. In the forest, there'd be creepy dolls with beetles crawling from their eyes.

Nope, nothing of the sort. Unless you were an experienced biologist or geologist, it would've looked like any other largely uninhabited island. A place mainly of interest to conservationists.

I'd been picturing a vast cemetery of entombed waste, its surface only lightly furred by grass the color of mold on old bread. Goes to show what I know. This place had already been something wholly different for decades. A locus for top-secret experiments. A womb for unconventional chalices.

I didn't look too closely at the text of the explanatory signs—my Jacian reading speed wasn't up to snuff—but I got the gist from skimming.

Aerial images showed how Ashtereth had grown over time. For complex regulatory reasons, the block with the tower was the oldest section of artificial land. They'd started there, then worked their way back towards the preexisting island with the hillside settlement, then expanded outward. The incineration plant had been some developer's pet project, an attempt to make Ashtereth an all-in-one destination for processing and interring municipal waste.

I didn't give much thought to garbage over the course of my day-to-day life. When Wist and I traveled abroad, different customs caught our attention—rules about recycling, the presence or absence of public bins, how severely they punished littering. That was about the extent of it.

Back at the academy, upper-level mage students used to transmute garbage with magic. Wist's tower took responsibility for its own sanitation, too. It sublimated all manner of waste, converting coffee grinds and tin cans into fuel for its ever-shifting structure. Yet there was only one Wist, and only one tower.

Nevertheless, waste management had been revolutionized in recent decades. All due to the increasing prevalence of vorpal holes. If a municipality happened to contain a stable hole in a safe location, they could expunge endless amounts of trash at no added cost. Like the Void in my eye, although the Void would've loathed the comparison.

People dumped junk without permission, too—which led to a lot of preventable accidents. If you had an unpatched hole floating at the end of your street, why not lug over your nasty old mattress and heave it in? No need to report it or wait for pick-up.

This generational shift toward using vorpal holes for waste disposal—both officially and unofficially—was more marked in Jace than anywhere else. After all, Wist the Kraken had never popped on over to seal the worst of their rifts.

12

Wist joined me by the landfill display.

"Anything from your bees?" I asked.

"Not yet."

A minute later, Lear asked the same thing. Wist started to give the same answer.

She froze.

"The bees?" I prompted.

She rubbed her left wrist. "A large group just disappeared."

We followed her hastily past the silent museum. It had a formal garden; flowers glistened as if glazed with sugar.

A short downhill jaunt brought us to a large pond. An elevated observatory overlooked it from the shore.

I jerked at the sight of devices on tripods—but they, too, were pointed at the water. Abandoned cameras?

"Wait," Lear hissed.

A tall stork-like bird picked its way among reeds. It had red-pink feet, a long rugged beak, the muscularity of an ostrich, and the posture of a man in costume on stilts. It walked through the water without a single ripple, poised to hunt.

"A trampler." Lear was still whispering. She motioned for us to slowly back up.

We skirted behind the observatory. I suggested sneaking upstairs to pry off a pair of window-mounted binoculars. Could be useful.

Lear shushed me, and we scurried away from the pond.

"Tramplers are nearly extinct in the wild," she said at last. "And very difficult to keep in captivity. Never seen one in a zoo. They kill large mammals for sport."

"Large mammals," I repeated. "Like us?"

"Those machina on the shore must have a mechanism to keep it contained." She shook her head, baffled.

"Might not be the only bird of its kind on Ashtereth. That dead stock-elk looked trampled, didn't it?"

She uttered a Jacian expletive I didn't recognize. "All the more reason to get down inside the base as fast as possible."

Wist took the lead again, putting us on a trail that wound through a chaotic grove of young trees. Branches clashed with spears of bamboo like bulls locking horns. Parasitic plants strangled every living thing in reach. Monkeys chattered back and forth above our heads, though we never saw any.

A dark hollow tried to swallow my foot. An animal den, perhaps. I didn't want to know what slept there.

Lear toyed with one of her knives. "You should have stopped Danny from coming," she said offhand. Like this whole excursion was my fault.

"To Jace? How?" I demanded. "She's a grown woman."

We were approaching the spot where Wist's bee scouts had vanished.

The path forked, then forked again, then trickled away into a mess of raging roots.

"Here," Wist said.

We'd reached a bald clearing. There was nothing within except a bank of identical outhouses. They looked incongruously urban, like accessories to a crowded concert.

Several on the left had been partly obliterated by a vorpal hole.

I only saw it for a second. I took another blind step forward and pressed my face to Wist's back.

The Void breathed darkly, expanding and contracting like a pair of bellows. I'd worked very hard to make it more tolerant of holes in reality. This one, however, had caught me by surprise.

I felt Wist's surprise, too, in the guilty tension of her spine. She thought I'd known. She'd thought she'd told me. I wasn't reading her mind: I heard her say it, stricken, not caring if Lear listened in. She put her arms behind her as though to hold me like a sling, apologizing in an uninterrupted tumble of murmured syllables. She loved me too much for anyone's good.

If not for the interference in our bond, she would have wordlessly shared a warning about the vorpal hole. I'd have been on guard long before it came into view. On this island—just this cursed little island—such thoughts no longer slipped so easily between us. I kept forgetting, too.

Lear didn't comment on the strangeness of me hiding like a child. She spoke to Wist: "That's what eradicated your scouts."

"They found an entrance to the lab. I pushed them to enter. When they tried to fly through—"

"A rift tore open?"

"Or someone transferred it from somewhere else," I said, muffled.

It was still an exceedingly rare ability ... but the techniques used for magically moving vorpal holes had been pioneered here in Jace.

This one could have been planted in just the right spot to block us. Or, yes, it could have spawned naturally.

I'd tried to study vorpal holes as a scholar would, as if familiarity might blunt the Void's hate. But no one can explain why reality might rip apart in any given place. No one pays attention to the thousands of fissures high in the sky—above the flight paths of airships—and at the lightless bottom of the sea.

Young kids might ask why they don't drain the ocean like a tub. Adults resort to pointing out that they don't siphon off all the air around us, either.

Of course, accurate vorpal detection was a life-or-death matter for naval and aerial vessels. Like Nerium's yacht. Yet just a couple generations ago, disruptive holes used to be rare enough that navigators relied on static maps (and good luck) to avoid them.

I had so little knowledge to cling to, but I clung to it like a raft. It was the only thing I could safely dwell on. I felt reduced to a lone speck floating atop the indefinable mass of the Void, rising and falling, lost amid ocean swells. If only I could convince myself that it would never come flooding out of me like water from a broken dam.

"I'll take a peek at the back," Lear said.

I couldn't stay useless forever.

I separated myself from Wist, though we were both reluctant to step apart. I followed Lear, head down. The hole was seared on my mind's eye like a splash of acid. Droplet-sized splatters pierced the air all around its perimeter.

The main opening wasn't a flat two-dimensional shape; it had a thickness to it, bulging inward. It had erased the front halves of multiple stalls in a row, and the stall on the end had lost almost its entire side wall, too. We returned to Wist and reported that even if we broke in through the back, there would be no room to stand.

She gestured at a damaged cubicle near the midpoint of the rift. "The entrance is in there."

"We could try hacking down the back wall anyway," Lear said. "Just to see in."

Wist dismissed this. "Too dangerous. I'll seal it."

"The hole? How much time will you—"

"Won't take long. If I seal it, we can go in the front."

Decision made, Wist sat down right there in the dust. Some semblance of the vorpal hole lay reflected in her sunglasses, even though it was a fissure of intolerable emptiness that shouldn't have cast any reflection at all.

My Void writhed. Her magic branches writhed, too.

She was currently doing the magical equivalent of picking an extremely complicated lock. Or defusing a bomb with touch alone. In any case, the crux of the matter was that she really, really needed to concentrate.

I stepped aside and said to Lear: "This would be the absolute worst possible time for someone to attack us."

She formed a chagrined smile. "I do realize that, yes."

We guarded the toilets in silence. For a bit. Until boredom overcame me. "They must have a way to stop hikers from using that one specific outhouse," I said.

"Can't imagine there being a lot of regular hikers around these parts."

"Spies might sneak in."

"Foreign nationals from the continent, for instance?"

"Exactly."

"If they put me in charge, I'd mark the stall out of order," Lear said. "Then I'd lock the door securely, with both magical and physical means. Boring, but effective."

That crucial door had been annihilated with a single poof of vorpal caprice.

Flies shaped like snowflakes traced wavering paths down from the foliage around the edge of the clearing. They looked dead tired.

I poked at my dormant clematis pin and wondered how the others were doing. Twenty years ago, Azalea would have been worried frantic by our immediate loss of contact. Nowadays, she could probably take it in stride.

Fanren wouldn't angst about circumstances beyond his control. As the main star of the delegation, he'd be too busy to think much about the rest of us, anyway.

Shien Danver, on the other hand, might secretly be out of her mind with some combination of fear for Lear and red-hot annoyance.

"I took leave to see my family," Lear said. "What's left of them, anyway. Before all this happened."

"You get vacation days?"

"Well, when you serve for a couple decades nonstop..."

"Generous of them."

"I can't complain," she said lightly.

I shooed a flake-fly away from my nose. "You spent all that time with Danver in Osmanthus. Why didn't you ever try to recruit her?"

"Who's to say I didn't?"

Danver might have joined this trip in part because Lear had already cultivated her as a Jacian asset ... or because Lear had continually refused to do so, to Danver's frustration, and now she was here to position herself as a more appealing prospect. While surrounded on all sides by Osmanthian counterintelligence. And pretending to be bonded to Shien Nerium.

"People with bondmates make for risky informants," Lear said.

"Even better. She'll never be able to bond again."

"My colleagues won't touch her, though. Not so long as she keeps playing Nerium's bondmate."

"And you?"

She grinned. "You don't want me to answer that."

"I've been rooting for you two," I told her. "But I gotta say, it doesn't feel like a winning bet."

She did something clicky with her gun. Sparks of magic showered down.

"Didn't mean that in, uh, an offensive way," I added weakly.

Lear took aim. At the woods, not at me.

A trampler bird stared back at us. It was fifty meters away—maybe more, maybe less; I'm bad at guessing distance—and it had a clear line of sight. All of a sudden, the trees and brush looked far too sparse for comfort.

13

I shook the clear cuff on my wrist. "It shouldn't be able to sense us."

Lear held her gun steady. "Stealth bracelets are optimized for concealment from humans."

It seemed like a bad idea to make any sudden big movements, which was the only reason I didn't just throw up my hands.

"Kraken," Lear said, "we're out of time."

Wist didn't hear her.

I didn't dare take my eye off the trampler. I nudged Wist with the back of my heel. A dull response stirred somewhere deep in our bond. It was like detecting a heartbeat in a buried coffin. Couldn't tell if I'd actually felt anything, or if it was all in my head.

I kicked her harder.

"Almost done?" I asked.

"Almost," Wist said.

"We're about to get mauled by a carnivorous bird with a beak as long as my arm, so if you can't finish in the next five or ten seconds, port us back to the seawall. Or levitate us high above the trees. Your choice."

The trampler shook its wings. They were much more robust than I'd imagined, nothing like the froofy fans of an ostrich. Surely not sufficient to bear a beast of its bulk aloft—it didn't have room to start flapping, regardless....

It tucked its wings in again, sleek as a diver, and started running.

It ran very fast.

My gut lurched. The ground shook with the force of each bounding step.

Lear immediately started shooting. One quiet *pop* after another—so suppressed that I experienced them only as a stabbing series of magical aches in my jaw.

I don't think she missed a single shot (not that I had much of an eye for this sort of thing), but the trampler didn't even stagger.

And it was huge, all right. Too big to fit in any of the cubicles behind us.

These thoughts spun out in the span of an instant, which was also how long it took the trampler to eat up most of the remaining distance.

Wist surged to her feet.

Lear was shouting.

The trampler had moon-yellow eyes—big, round, forward-facing, locked on us—and a beak like a greatsword hacked from pitted stone. It occurred to me, with the unhelpful clarity of burgeoning death, that I should've reached up to open the Void. Anything was better than getting decapitated or stomped on by a giant stork.

After all Wist's ministrations, the aperture of the vorpal hole had begun to shrink—slowly, like a lake in a drought. Its shape still burned at the back of my head.

Now, with the trampler thundering toward us, her magic seized the stubborn hole and *shoved* it away like a curtain on a rail. A different branch, crackling with a different skill, lassoed me and Lear and dragged us bodily through the gap.

Wist piled in after us, inhumanly fast, flinging herself past the missing doorway. A crumpled-up mass of vorpality hung off to one side like the world's most dangerous drapery.

A millisecond before the enraged trampler would've skewered all three of us, she *yanked* the hole back into place. It rebounded like a rubber band, stretching to seal the cubicle entrance. This time, it billowed outward. If it curved inward, it would have handily erased us from existence, sparing only an elbow or two. And perhaps the soles of our feet.

Squished up against Wist, I braced for impact. The trampler couldn't possibly have changed its trajectory. But there was no collision. No death throes. No squelching or spurting. Vorpal holes annihilate all matter instantly, silently, cleanly. Very eco-friendly.

Wist the Kraken was the only potential exception. She could, if pressed, use them for travel. Like an innocuous portal.

The trampler—lacking any comparable ability—was dead, leaving nothing but claw marks in dirt. It might have been taller than the upper edge of the rift ... but it had tilted steeply forward as it barreled towards us, neck outstretched.

We were alive and intact, crammed in there behind our vorpal veil. We had every reason to celebrate. I couldn't: I was on the verge of hyperventilating. My legs had gone as weak as wet paper.

The charging bird was gone. The hole that had extinguished it was still very close.

My Void bristled with rage.

Make no mistake, the Void didn't actually experience anything resembling thoughts or emotions. If I thought it seemed resentful, if I thought it seemed hungry, that was just the result of my pitiful mortal brain chopping the ineffable down into close-to-home concepts.

I mastered my breathing.

Earlier, Lear had peeped at each of the accessible outhouses on the opposite end of the row. She'd rated them according to their aroma, humidity, insect population, and supply of amenities. It was a close contest; they all seemed fairly hygienic.

The stall we now stood clustered in had no toilet bowl, or toilet paper. And no real stench except for whatever fearful sweat we'd brought with us.

In its original concave formation, the vorpal hole had eaten away much of the ceiling and sides. Sunlight seeped in from above. It illuminated nothing of interest except a square metal hatch.

The hatch would have offered plenty of standing room for one person. It hadn't been designed for three. All in all, this seemed akin to a fitting room with a privacy curtain of woven death.

"We should try to unlock that," I said, probing the hatch with my foot.

Wist's magic snapped against the floor.

We waited for something to happen. I began to crack a nervous joke.

The hatch tilted, then swung inward like the lid of a trash can. We went shooting down into darkness. Someone screamed. (I think it was me.)

14

THE HATCH IN the fake outhouse had ported us to an industrial-size tunnel. We were now much further away from that toilet-haunting vorpal abscess. The Void's agitation was already more bearable.

I would've complained about having to use an outhouse as our infiltration point, but clearly, it could have been worse.

There were no signs of life. On our right, multiple railway tracks ran off into the distance. On our left, the tunnel came to an abrupt dead end. It looked like the result of a cave-in.

Lear stopped to check her bag and do maintenance on her gun. Then she walked out onto the tracks and tilted her scroll this way and that. The blueprints glowed softly.

It was dim, but not dark. On both sides of the tunnel— every hundred or two hundred meters—backlit green signs pointed at emergency exits. Other lights studded the walls, too, but the space was too colossal for them to penetrate far.

"What is this," I asked Lear, "an old subway?"

"Definitely out of use," she said.

"So we won't get run over."

She closed her scroll. "When trash got ported in from other islands, these rails would carry it to the incineration plant, or wherever else it needed to go. Not sure if they did any pulverization along the way."

"It's not a bypass-style tunnel."

"No."

"Might take some walking," I concluded, "but we're probably a lot closer to the base now. Being underground and all."

Wist removed her sunglasses. "The hatch could connect to multiple locations. I picked the deepest one available."

"It'll be tricky for anyone else to use the same entrance," Lear said. "Stroke of genius, actually—the way you slapped that hole back across the door. What used to be a door, rather. You made it wrap around the missing side wall of the end stall, too."

"Just a fluke," Wist said impassively.

Most people wouldn't have been able to tell if she were joking, or being humble, or lying to downplay her talents. But Lear wasn't most people.

"Someone sent that bird after us," I said, switching subjects. "It didn't care at all when we first walked past it."

Lear began spinning a small knife. "Might not have been the same trampler from the pond."

"Either way—it started charging us with the vorpal hole in full view. Not very smart."

"Ah, well. Sometimes birds fly into windows."

Wist had gone quiet. She would usually have said a lot more. It's only around strangers that she comes off as the strong, silent type.

If we were alone, she'd have done a detailed postmortem of our confrontation with the trampler. Here's how it'd go: *I should've stopped tinkering with the vorpal hole sooner. Should've given that bird my full attention. There were innumerable other solutions. I could've thrown up a barrier.*

I might then cut in to suggest that even a trampler wouldn't survive running full speed at the equivalent of a titanium wall. An effective magical barrier would have granted it a much more painful death.

To which she'd say: *So I should have ported it away. Or frozen it in place. Or put it to sleep.*

We could go on like that for an half hour. But we wouldn't. Not here; not out loud.

What kind of magic would the Kraken reach for most readily under ambush? That might be a much shorter list than her full catalog of learned skills (which was too long to recite). And it was the last thing we'd want to tell a current or future enemy.

Maybe someone was listening in on us from the brain-like crenelations in the tunnel ceiling. Maybe not.

That wasn't our only worry. If Lear wasn't ready for me to break her bond yet, then she would have to find a way to keep living with her bondmate, her bosses, and every other source of pressure from the Bureau of Mage Management.

As far as Jacians went, she seemed to be trapped in the worst of all possible worlds. She lived with many of the same shackles as a branch-wielding mage, without even the meager benefit of being able to use magic of her own.

I couldn't particularly fault her if, in the end, she did report back to analysts about Wist's every word and gesture, every hint of fallibility. I was just glad that the comms blockade prevented her from ratting us out in real time.

She was vastly better at dealing with Wist than most of the officials we'd met on the yacht—our ostensible colleagues. She'd gotten close to other key members of the Shien clan despite the dual disadvantages of being a foreigner (a Jacian!) and, at least on the surface, a powerless artist.

In some situations, being effortlessly likable was more effective than any amount of magical bluster.

Lear twirled her knife again, then tucked it away with a droll remark about the lack of human guards along the rails. Lucky us.

After a few minutes of lively debate over her maps, we tried to leave through one of the nearest emergency exits.

The door, tucked in a recessed alcove, refused to budge. We took turns rattling the handle to no avail.

Lear and I admitted defeat. We stepped back. Wist stepped forward and ripped it open with magic. The ruined door hung dolefully on creaky hinges, curling like the pried-up lid of a tin can.

Wherever that exit used to lead, it was gone—nothing left on the other side but smooth cement.

The next door was the same. And the next.

"There's something alive up there," Wist said suddenly.

I glanced nervously at the ceiling.

"Higher," she clarified. "In a building."

"Something alive," Lear repeated. "You mean people?"

"No."

"A flock of tramplers?"

"No."

"What, then?"

"I ... can't tell."

We gaped at her. We must have looked like lost children.

I took a moment to collect myself. "Best not port up sight unseen, then."

We made our way down the middle of the tunnel. As we went, Wist used an echolocation-related skill to ping each emergency door, checking to see if any opened onto something other than a concrete slab.

Black millipedes slithered alongside the tracks, all traveling the same direction, as if trying to race us. I counted six before I started getting them mixed up. They were narrower than a shoe string, but implausibly long—two or three meters, or more. Their ends wove in and out of shadow.

They were wise enough to shy away from heavy footsteps. I made it my job to give warning stomps whenever they ventured near Wist.

The gravel between the railroad ties was composed of crunchy crystalline rocks that, gleaming with moisture, looked exactly like nuggets of ice.

Lear kept pressing her forehead. Maybe my stomping was starting to get to her.

"You okay?" I asked.

"Mm? Oh—sorry. It's my sinuses. Feels like allergies."

Between pings, Wist shook her head as if to clear her ears.

The air had acquired a mossy, absorbent quality. It soaked up every little sound except the clink of Wist testing those faraway doors—which was a magical noise, anyway; it didn't touch our eardrums.

Despite all their feet, the millipedes couldn't keep up. One by one, as if exhausted, they dropped out of our race. They rolled sideways, spasming, legs sweeping the air like panicked cilia.

The next time I peeked at Lear, there were tears streaking down her face.

I gripped Wist's arm, making her stop. No tears. But her eyes had gone all glossy.

"Cover your mouth and nose," I said furiously. "Both of you!"

They were slow to react. I forced Wist to look at me. "Can you make an air bubble? A filter? Like if we were in a fire—if you had to keep smoke out—"

She gazed at her fingertips as though they belonged to someone else. She kept pinging doors further and further down the corridor. She could use simple magic, but her thoughts were mired like bugs in a glue trap. I'd have noticed so much sooner if not for the muted state of our bond.

Lear doubled over, hands on her knees, breathing wetly.

I got on tiptoe and grabbed Wist's face hard enough to hurt. "Port *up*," I enunciated, all but feeding the words from my lips to hers.

This was the real issue with the protections on my prosthetic: Wist had no sense of urgency so long as I seemed fine.

"But"—her voice wasn't woozy at all, damn her—"the presence—"

"Maybe it's that chalice," I snapped. "Good! Just what we're looking for. Port now, and take all three of—"

She finally listened.

The chill of the tunnel fell away. I blinked, blinded by brightness.

We were in ... a classroom? A lecture hall? Nondescript gray-blue carpet. Whiteboards up front. Rows of table-desks sized to fit two or three students side by side.

It was a large room, and it was already packed. We'd dropped in at the very back.

Lear leaned on the wall, eyes closed. No one stared at us, so I guess those bracelets were good for something.

The people here were mostly on the older side—not special ops soldiers. They wore aprons and smocks and dingy coveralls. A few children lay flat on the carpet and traced abstract pictures with grubby fingers. A woman with a watering can approached the empty lectern and diligently went through the motions of watering it. (Nothing came out.)

Bored artists had sketched multiple iterations of the Jacian flag all across the whiteboard. None looked quite right, as if they'd been attempting to recreate it from memory. They kept adding weird bumps and extra handles to the goblet motif at the center. Sometimes they drew it half full, or dripping with condensation, or gouting red liquid like a fountain.

A tanned man in a sun hat walked down one of the aisles between desks, stepping over a languishing child. He stopped a few feet away from Wist.

My pulse skipped beats until I realized he was just staring into space. The space we happened to occupy, yes—but for him, it held no significance.

In his right hand he had a large white onion sheathed in papery skin. He brought it to his mouth like an apple. He took a huge, juicy bite.

Onion milk drooled down his chin.

By unspoken agreement, the three of us edged away along the wall.

The man in the sun hat stood there crunching his onion, as contented as a cow. That uncooked scent seemed to chase us all the way to the other side of the room.

"These people..." Lear said hoarsely. "They're the villagers."

None of them whipped around to listen, which emboldened me to talk, too. I pulled Wist's sleeve. "The lives you sensed up here—you were so sure they weren't human."

Wist turned a full circle.

"I was wrong," she said slowly. "I must have been wrong."

15

THERE WERE SEVERAL pallets of bottled water in a corner. Lear took some and refilled her canteen.

We were all raring to get the heck out of this room, let me tell you. Every time a stranger's gaze brushed dully past us, my back went as tight as a rope. No one was harming us, though, and we had no idea what lay outside. Might as well take a quick breather for Wist and Lear to recover.

Lear swallowed another shaky gulp of water. "The fumes in the tunnel—what were they?"

No one could say for sure. Scentless gases might have collected in the depths on their own. Or maybe it had been a deliberately timed attack: a devious mixture of airborne toxins and perception-dulling magic.

Wist's pain tolerance made her peculiarly vulnerable. She would always be the last to complain of dizziness, stinging eyes, a roiling stomach, an inexplicable tightness in her muscles and magic. She would be the last to notice herself struggling for breath, the last to topple over.

So I didn't entirely trust her when she claimed she was feeling better. At any rate, Lear still sat slumped with her back to the pale wall (which was a strange jaundiced color). I proposed that another couple minutes of rest might do the trick.

The onion man, now separated from us by many rows of desks, had fully demolished his prize. He sucked juice off his fingers with obscene intensity. He kept sucking until there couldn't possibly have been any lingering taste left. It began to look as if he were trying to strip a glove with his teeth, except that all he wore on his hand was reddened skin.

"Are the villagers...?" I didn't even know how to finish.

"Brainwashed?" Lear offered. "Enchanted? High?"

None appeared to be in immediate physical distress. With the possible exception of the onion man, although his hand wasn't bleeding. Yet. His gut might not react nicely to taking in an entire raw onion, but that would be a problem for later. I asked Lear if this sort of allium consumption was a common cultural practice in Jace.

She snorted. "I ought to say yes. Whenever you meet someone new, you're supposed to chomp an onion at them. It's the height of rudeness to skip it."

"Hope you didn't tell Danver that."

"I've only ever told her the truth." Lear paused. "In spirit, anyhow."

"Hah."

Wist kept looking about like a searchlight. A frisson of alarm went through me when she unhunched her shoulders, and stayed that way, as though to lord her height over the rest of us. She wasn't pleased about having been caught unawares in the tunnel.

"Why bring them here?" I said, meaning the villagers. "They're not doing anything."

Some moved their lips—not to speak, but as if exercising weakened muscles. There were no idle conversations, no laughter or sharp complaints. Most stayed at their desks.

The weirdest part was how they behaved as if they were sitting alone at home, unwatched. Every so often they picked their noses, or scratched themselves wherever they liked, but it wasn't just that. The unguarded limpness of their eyes and posture—it just wasn't how ordinary people would act in public.

"They're hostages," Wist said. She extended a gloved hand to help Lear to her feet.

"That would explain it," Lear agreed.

It was so frustrating that I couldn't talk to Wist mind-to-mind. I wanted to ask what she'd do if we needed to evacuate all these apparent civilians.

The old railway led nowhere, and she couldn't safely port them off Ashtereth. Not unless she found a way to destroy the containment field.

What else? She could conjure a boat (but could she protect it from artillery?). She could freeze an icy walking path across the gulf (some might go slip-sliding off the edge). She could fly them through the sky like birds (and get pursued by that mutinous chalice).

There were close to a hundred voiceless strangers in here, waiting for lessons from a teacher who had yet to show up.

We threaded a quiet path to the exit. The room was unlocked. No one else seemed remotely interested in leaving. We darted guiltily out and closed the door behind us.

The moment it clicked shut, it seemed impossible to believe that there were dozens of people in there, people with sun spots and ear hair and faded sweatshirts and thick brown socks worn together with sensible sandals. From outside, the room had the aura of an empty aquarium tank. No locals loitered in the hallway, either.

We'd already figured out that we were in a building connected to the old incineration plant. On the second or third floor, which was about as high as it went (not counting the tower).

Generous windows lined the hall, but there wasn't much to see except encroaching waves of forest. The tower stood on the other side of the complex.

We knew this because we found a display space with scaled-down models of the entire plant and its grounds. They seemed to represent different time periods. Each came complete with a white-painted tower and bushy fake trees, some faded to an unnatural blueish hue instead of green.

Lear knocked dust off a stack of full-color pamphlets. "Seems like they still do tours every so often."

"Let's book one," I said. "Sounds thrilling."

Wist was looking at a retro poster introducing garbage-themed cartoon characters. The designs were amateurish: bicycles and traffic cones and frying pans and candy wrappers all squished together into an awkward chimera with googly eyes slapped on top. (Look, I'm not saying that I could've done any better.)

"Actually," Lear said, "a self-guided tour might be just the place to start."

We gathered around a framed diagram of the plant interior. Arrows illustrated how trash would progress from one side to the other, fed into hoppers by metal claws.

"Looks like an arcade game," I said.

Lear's finger circled a series of pits below the garbage cranes. "These waste bunkers are huge. They go a lot deeper than you'd think. See the pictures back there? It's all concrete, and ripe for fortification. Air only flows in one direction—nothing can leak."

As an incinerator, the plant had been out of operation for decades.

But they hadn't let it lapse into disrepair. Ashtereth wasn't all that spacious to begin with: the research director must've found a productive new use for existing facilities.

Lear was right. Those abandoned waste bunkers might be just about large enough to store chalices.

16

Why hadn't anyone been posted to watch the hostages in the lecture room? Well, they didn't seem like they required much watching. Or perhaps they were being monitored in other ways. Perhaps we were being monitored, too.

We glimpsed a rooftop garden through shaded windows. The plants had gone all leggy. Indoors, a gallery showcased life-size wolves and horses that had been crafted (according to nearby plaques) by now-retired workers. They were made of great tangles of angry metal that had been dragged, unmelting, from the heart of the incinerator.

As soon as we turned a corner, I could no longer recall why I'd seen animals. The sculptures had been an abstract mass of wire hangers and mangled rods and black staples whirled into spiny balls. Where were the tails, the claws, the long panting faces?

Another corridor displayed a piece of an air filter, proudly claiming that the smokestack would only expelled purified vapor—as innocuous as steam from a kettle. I couldn't envision how it worked. No magic lingered on the sample, which resembled a pool noodle designed for a giant.

The hall ended in a squared-off area with cruddy old tape on the floor. A handrail ran in front of a ceiling-high window, which was coated in thick white paint, rendering it as unrevealing as the washed-out yellow walls.

We only knew it was a window because Lear said so. She riffled through her collection of pamphlets printed for nonexistent tourists. "This used to be a viewport down on the waste bunker. It's up near the ceiling, where the cranes hang. We'll have to survive a long fall."

"Wist can make us float," I said.

The paint had the matte opacity of correction fluid. Wist jerked her hand away just before touching it. "We can't break in through here. It'll drop us in an alternate slice of space."

"A what?" I prompted, more for Lear's benefit than my own.

"Parts of the incinerator have been preserved," Wist said. "Furnaces, burners, boilers, pulverizers. They're waiting in overlapping dimensional pockets. Someone took those working parts and slotted them neatly under the skin of the world."

"Like the Guild worms in my arm." Lear flipped a knife open and began scratching doggedly at the window. "Hidden hellfire, huh?"

"Let's not get burned to a crisp." I always gave the most helpful advice. "Wist, can you sniff out a safer route to—"

Lear exclaimed in triumph. She'd scored off a white chunk as fat as a wood chip. The glass beneath looked dark in contrast.

Unease built at the back of my throat. Before I could say anything, she leaned forward and put her eye to it.

Wist's magic clawed her away from the glass.

The flake on the floor flew up like a bullet. It slotted back in place, edges melting to blend with the rest of the paint. It looked a bit knobby, like a knot in wood. Otherwise, though, the hole was gone without a trace.

Lear took her hand away from her face and groped haplessly for the knife she'd dropped.

"Sorry," she wheezed. "Should've predicted that."

The white of her eye had turned as pink as corned beef. It glistened like a tongue.

She wasn't crying blood. Instead, it pricked its way up through the pores of her forehead and cheek. Watery stripes oozed down her jaw.

I held out a tissue. Several tissues. At this rate, I was going to run through my supply in less than a day.

"How's your sight?" I asked cautiously. One missing eye in our three-person squad was already more than enough.

"I'm not blind." She said it much more levelly than I would've managed.

More blood kept springing up. Her eyeliner smudged as if she'd slept in it. Eventually she just left a pink-soaked sheet stuck to her face like a moisturizing mask.

"I saw through the window," she added. "Just for a second. You could stash an entire city's worth of trash in that bunker."

"No machina?"

"It was over too fast to tell. Anyway, we're at the top of the shaft. Might not have a view all the way to the bottom." She curled her fingers around the handrail. "I get why they put this here. It's like looking down off the top of a skyscraper.

"But ... I don't know how much of it was real. There were bits of garbage floating around in the air like snow—paper, tinsel, shredded stockings."

We turned our backs on the whited-out window; we kept searching for another way in.

While building her ever-growing tower, Wist had inadvertently become the world's preeminent architect of impossible spaces.

This went largely unacknowledged. People tended to associate the Kraken with lightning and explosions and falling stars. Few associates received an invitation to the tower where multiple rooms and rooftops shared the same physical space, and doors and passageways could tunnel effortlessly between random floors.

Pacing through the incineration plant—even just the part of it designed for public tours—gave Wist a feel for its true metaphysical structure. I too became more attuned to the frameworks of magic in the building around us, but I couldn't extrapolate beyond the bewildered edges of my own perception.

"Not this elevator," Wist said. We kept going.

"What would happen if we took the stairs down?" Lear inquired.

"Can you swim?"

"Very well, actually."

"Can you swim in oil?"

"There's a first time for everything. Now, if it got hot enough to cook me—"

"Let's avoid the stairs," Wist said distractedly.

We passed a control room walled in glass. Instead of living scrolls or old-fashioned monitors, row upon row of static pictures hung on the wall. Graphs that would never be updated. Blurry snapshots of security footage. A livid orange-red image, like the inside of a forge—as if they'd had a porthole to observe the furnace at work.

Plump-limbed scarecrows sprawled in padded blue chairs, their backs to us. I couldn't tell if they had faces.

"This way."

Wist pressed the button for an elevator that looked identical to the one she'd rejected.

It was a lot roomier than the outhouse in the woods. Cold air gusted down from a ceiling vent.

The doors closed. The elevator cab remained still.

Wist reached for the metal panel of floor buttons and peeled it away as if prying off a fingernail. It flopped down and hung there, still attached by a bottom corner.

The buttons jutted out nakedly. There weren't many to choose from. Beneath them was a round socket with an icon of a pointing hand beside it.

"Uh," I said. "Maybe don't—"

She stuck her finger in. There was a soft, wet sound of suction. The elevator rocked like a train.

Wist took her finger out. Or tried to, anyway. A flexible braided hose—the spitting image of a pull-out faucet—emerged from the socket with her. The spout clamped around her forefinger like a biting snake. It kept stretching, spooling out to absurd lengths, even as she backed up all the way against the wall.

The elevator was still descending.

Lear took mincing steps to avoid the sprawling hose. "Need help with that?" she asked.

"No."

The carpet squelched like damp moss.

"It's flooding," I said, dancing from foot to foot, wishing I could scale the walls like a spider.

No liquid came from the hose on Wist's finger. It welled up from beneath the floor, as if we were being lowered into a bog. I let out a cry of grief for my socks.

"Stop moving," Wist said without sympathy.

Water lapped avidly against my ankles. It smelled stale and briny, like it had been trapped alone in the dark for a very long time.

"Is it … tasting us?"

No, never mind. I didn't want to know the answer.

Icy moisture wicked its way up my pants. Salt burned in places where I hadn't known I'd been cut. Greenish currents gummed at my heels and calves, testing the firmness of my flesh.

Lear stood without fidgeting, her expression distant, as if she were used to this sort of treatment.

The elevator clanked, swaying like a birdcage on a string. As it stilled, the inquisitive water receded, although I couldn't spot a drain.

"This is senseless," I complained. "As bad as wild magic. Who would rig security measures that get your feet wet on purpose?"

"Someone with a sense of humor," said Lear. She'd picked the bloody sheets of tissue off her face.

"How would you even justify the expense? Think of all the disparate cuttings you'd have to source from different mages."

"Someone with a very large budget, then. Or someone who knows they'll never get audited. Or"—an afterthought—"someone like the Kraken."

Indeed. I could imagine this taking place in some obscure corner of Wist's tower. In that case, it'd be emergent behavior stemming from the casual interaction of countless magical systems. All made from cuttings she'd birthed herself.

She didn't have to stint on complexity because the Kraken never had to buy, beg, or borrow specialized magic from other mages (or the corporations, clans, and government institutions that managed select skills as a form of intellectual property). If she really needed a new skill, she'd buckle down and invent it. She was limited only by practical time constraints and the excruciating knots in her branches.

Yes: her tower might easily develop something as impractical as self-flooding and self-draining elevators. Like a tree growing a crooked offshoot. Wist could foresee what might bud from the intersection of all the cuttings she'd planted—architectural, space-sculpting, protective, self-repairing. If it seemed silly or strange, but otherwise harmless, she'd shrug and let it be.

The elevator door rattled as if someone had bolted it shut. Wist yanked the biting hose off her finger—which was still all there, thankfully. Just swollen and purple.

The hose retracted into the wall. She attempted to bend her finger. It wouldn't go far.

"Wist..."

"It'll deflate," she said defensively.

The door parted with a ding. We stepped out on sodden shoes and then immediately halted, three abreast.

A body lay sprawled in the hallway.

The elevator dinged again, long and mocking. I dared a swift look back. And of course there was no elevator anymore: no door, no buttons, no evidence that we could ever leave.

17

No one moved. We contemplated the body.

Magic clung to it like dust. But then, magic clung to everything around here. Its source might be as benign as a tin of enchanted breath mints. Special agents can't always make time to brush their teeth in the field.

"That's a limbsuit." After further consideration, Lear amended her answer. "Half a limbsuit."

"You've got chalice suits and flight suits and now ... what?" (She'd used a Jacian word; I'd already forgotten how she pronounced it.)

"A limbsuit," Lear said. "For ground operations. Nothing to do with piloting."

"Hold still," Wist told us.

I stiffened, ready for fireworks. All that ensued was a sensation of desert heat: it blasted through my soggy shoes and socks and trousers.

"Come on," I said. "Of all the pedestrian ways to waste your magic—"

"Dry shoes are worth any sacrifice."

"She's right, you know," Lear added.

"Don't you gang up on me." I hip-checked Wist. "Thanks. We should probably go check that person's pulse."

"They're dead," she and Lear said in perfect harmony.

The hall had scuffed linoleum flooring and six enormous snake plants. You could bury a body in one of those pots.

At the far end was a single steel door, badly dented and scorched. It no longer fit well in its frame. Soot caked the surrounding wall and ceiling.

Wires sprayed like severed nerve endings from what might once have been a keypad. A sign high above the door remained inexplicably intact, flashing red characters like a display board for a train.

NOT YET

The words flickered on and off, synchronized and monotonous.

NOT YET

NOT YET

NOT YET

Wist asked me what the sign said (she didn't know much written Jacian). I told her. Before I could make any further suggestions, she spoke to Lear: "Check the body."

One unfortunate side effect of Wist's general affect was that requests tended to come out like commands. It didn't help that people expected the Kraken to be imperious.

But this time it was, in fact, an order.

"All right," Lear said stoutly. "Can't quibble."

"You can," I said, "and you should."

"No matter which side you're on, I'm clearly the most expendable member of our party."

She stepped toward the body, taking a blade out as if she were about to perform an autopsy. I started to follow her—no brilliant plan, just twitchy nerves—but Wist blocked me.

The Void itched with anticipation.

It would have been easier to hold my peace if I could sense Wist's intent as more than an ominous unreadable presence. Even with our bond at full strength, there were times when she felt as unknowable as—

As the chalice called Reverence. That blank-faced cocoon.

Lear began to kneel.

White strands erupted from a bloodless wound in the carcass.

But Lear wasn't there in the line of fire, not anymore. It was Wist. They'd switched places with magic as seamless as a card trick.

Those white straws gored Wist's chest like drill bits, spluttering dimly.

My eye sockets went hot. My head ached so badly that even my magic perception blanked out. It was like someone had dug sharp thumbs into the base of my skull and cracked it open to let out a burst of air that would otherwise have become a scream.

I was ready to use the Void, or to let it use me. I was ready to drown in the current. Here's the secret: if I truly wanted to surrender, not even the fake eye in my face could hold me back. It wasn't supposed to happen—but the Void could devour that eye if I let it. It could devour the booby-trapped body, the elevator hallway without any elevators, all of Ashtereth.

And why stop there?

NOT YET, said the red light on the wall.

Wist still hadn't made a sound. She convulsed violently. Her black-clad shoulders split like a beetle shell.

Then, as if molting, she climbed out of the seams of her own body. One ravaged torso slumped over the soldier's corpse, prostrated in a prayer for mercy. A second torso rose from the gap in her spine and stepped out to freedom one leg at time. It was like watching her peel off a pair of fleshy coveralls.

"I'm going to kill you," I breathed, swooning, bilious with relief.

Wist took another sticky step back. Her discarded flesh-suit wore the same clothes as her, although the cloven back gaped like a canyon, and the entire top half of the skull was missing. No eyes, not much in the way of ears, and no visible brain matter—just a hollow opening like a kitschy vase.

Hungry maggots of killing magic squirmed inside her double's gooey chest.

Wist coughed and, with reassuringly healthy vigor, spat out a fusillade of purple-red blood clots. They skated across the linoleum like tadpoles, glomming on to the bodily shell she'd left behind.

She'd emerged as sleek and wet as a seal, but now more and more ink-dark fluid ran down out of her hair and clothes and lifted off her skin like raindrops in reverse. She was stainless: even her swollen finger looked cured.

"What do you call this skill?" I said scathingly. "Meat Shield?

She coughed again, this time with less dramatic results. "Body Double."

"That old standby?"

Some double she'd created. She'd forgotten to give it gloves. The skin was a blotchy gradient of deep and light brown. An idiosyncratic mix of Lear and Wist herself—as if she hadn't quite made up her mind about who to kill in effigy.

"Those look like Guild worms," Lear said.

They still fed diligently on Wist's half-formed double. They were trying to kill and disintegrate something that had never really been alive to begin with.

The real Wist pressed a pained hand to the small of her back. Her double curled up around its ribcage full of burrowing worms and, slick as a pill bug, rolled away from the armored corpse. It left a smeared trail of something too thick to pass for fresh blood. But it didn't need to fool us; it only needed to fool a colony of mindless magic-driven parasites.

The skill known as Body Double was meant to produce a perfect physical replica. A lesser mage might fail to correctly deploy it—but it was difficult to mess up on purpose. Much more difficult than using a skill in accordance with its original goal. Wist had formed her double around her original body like a rubbery shield. She'd made it juicy enough to tempt those homicidal worms. And she'd done it all on the spur of the moment.

The ability to riff on existing skills—which were supposed to be a fixed quantity—was a high-level talent in and of itself.

Wist's double burst into flame. It burned without heat, without spreading, without any stench of roasted fat. In less than a minute, even its imitation bones had shrunk to ash. The skimpy gray powder left on the bland linoleum floor might have been produced by an incense stick.

She'd used the skill called Incinerator. How fitting.

Having been successfully dewormed, the dead soldier (or guard, or tactical officer) no longer posed much of a threat. I began picking apart a whorled wreath of knots in Wist's magic.

"Don't scare me like that," I said.

"You were scared?"

I smacked her on the butt. Her eyes widened minutely. Good. On Wist, that was a look of abject shock. I hummed, mollified, as I gardened her thrashing branches.

Lear had hunkered down to inspect the damaged limbsuit. It appeared to combine solid, shellacked plates with a scaly material that flexed like fabric.

In addition to chalices, demons, healer supremacy, insularity, and beating back the first Kraken, Jace was also renowned for magical camouflage and concealment. Even cracked all over—and with its full-face helmet hideously caved in—the limbsuit had obscured those lurking worms.

"A defender of the base, I think," said Lear. "But I wouldn't bet on it."

"Not a Guild hunter?"

"Even under government contract, the Parasite Guild wouldn't be allowed to use full-on limbsuits."

"It's like a chalice," Wist said out of nowhere. "Shrunken down."

"In the same way that a spark of light is a shrunken-down star," Lear replied. "Some of the technology—well, you're not completely off the mark."

She and Wist worked together to move the body into a more dignified position. The suit must have been far heavier than it looked.

As they finished, Lear said: "Our friend here was killed in combat."

"With who?" I'd prowled the hallway, but the snake plants hadn't yielded any additional clues.

"Guild assassins. Or one of the surviving advance teams. Or some other group of infiltrators targeting either Datura Gray, classified data, or the Kraken." She looked up. "At this stage, your guess is as good as mine."

"Whoever they are, the killers already got through that door."

"Perhaps we should thank them for blazing a path."

The lit-up board above the battered door now said: *OPEN*. As if we'd been queuing outside a shop.

The sign flashed.

WELCOME
WELCOME
WALK-INS WELCOME

NO APPOINTMENT NECESSARY
NO WAIT
NO SOLICITING
NO EXCUSES
NO VACANCY

It began to repeat itself.

"Reassuring," Lear said ruefully. "Shall we?"

18

We left the body in the limbsuit. Not to be callous, but its equipment seemed unsalvageable.

I caught at Wist on our way through the broken door. "Can you sense it here?"

She knew I was referring to Reverence. She didn't appear to know how to answer.

I changed questions. "Have we come any closer?"

"Distance is a matter of perspective," she said obscurely.

My inner ears rebalanced, taut with pressure, as I crossed the threshold. A bleating alarm had been set off somewhere far away, but not by our ingress. It was too faint for that, right on the border of unreality, like a beeping oven in a neighbor's house.

"You hear that?" I asked.

Neither of them had any idea what I meant.

We looked for blood, shrapnel, signs of combat. The walls were almost too clean: not a scratch on them. The ceiling, however, bore a greasy coating of brown-black gunk. More like decades-old nicotine than a blast from a bomb.

A startling quantity of plants hung overhead—strung up high enough that not even Wist was in any danger of needing to duck. Long strands dangled like hanks of loose hair.

Polished to a liquid gleam, the floor was as reflective as a puddle.

"Good thing we're not wearing skirts," I said. Lear let out a wan huff of a laugh.

I kept thinking I saw movement down there: mirrored glimpses of creatures like black hand-sized birds. When I looked up, the ceiling played dead—it held itself absolutely still, not even breathing, lacquered in filth.

I couldn't trust my magic perception, and I couldn't trust my eyesight, and my ears were starting to seem dubious, too. That distant alarm faded in and out, in and out, resurging just when I thought it might have finally stopped.

But the strangest thing about this space wasn't the greenery (better suited to an earthy restaurant than a secret base). Nor was it the spooky floor.

It was the lighting.

"Sunvine oil?" Lear muttered.

"This is true sunlight," Wist said.

The hall with the corpse had been lit like a low-rent office, brittle and white and artificial. Coming in here felt like stepping back out in the woods, with the morning sky and shifting leaves, warm and diffuse.

"Tubes," Lear concluded. "That's what's doing it." The way she described it, the bright ovals in the ceiling were bypass tunnels designed to shunt down sunlight.

We tried one door after another. Many were unlocked. We peeped in a locker room (empty), a laundry room (wheeled bins were piled high with towels and sheets), and a health clinic.

Bored-looking patients trooped from one station to the next. We stared, bemused, as nurses called them over to check their blood pressure, their weight, their hearing, their eyesight. They had more sophisticated tools, too, which fizzled menacingly behind the magical equivalent of blackout curtains.

We went unnoticed, thanks to our bracelets. A small erratic woman marched around with a paper urine cup thrust out in front of her, as if begging for change. Lear had to jump up on a chair to avoid a collision.

A smell like formaldehyde percolated throughout the waiting room. The nurses spoke to everyone, regardless of age or demeanor, as though they couldn't be trusted to listen: loud, hard, perky voices and oversimplified language.

"They're not acting like they're under siege," I said.

The people upstairs hadn't behaved much like terrified prisoners, either. Couldn't really judge by appearances.

When they released a man who had been under observation after getting blood drawn (five full tubes), we followed him out. Perhaps—if we were lucky—he might turn out to be a machinist.

He glanced impatiently at his watch. At the end of another sunlit hallway, he disappeared inside a laboratory complex. We piled in after him, just barely squeaking through before the double doors clanked shut.

Pipes, tubes, beakers, steel machinery ... we might as well have invaded a coffee roastery. I certainly couldn't tell the difference. I stopped to look over palletized stacks of—what was this, potting soil? Shredded bark? The bags were unlabeled.

Harsh scents warred around us: mulch, vinegar, cleaning chemicals. Wist discreetly attempted to breathe through her sleeve.

So far, we hadn't run into a single mage with branches. There were plenty of subliminal mages among the villagers and clinic patients, but they would never be at risk of using magic.

Statistically, it wasn't so unbelievable. Mages with true power were a tiny percentage of the population—and that percentage remained largely steady across international borders. (Despite ancient culling traditions in certain countries, and rumored attempts to birth more mages in others.)

But in Osmanthus, this sort of elite facility would be crawling with ambitious mages. The research director would be one, too, even if their role mostly revolved around bureaucratic wrangling, without any practical need for everyday magic.

At the back of the lab, an older woman stood fiercely in an open doorway. She held a stained wooden cooking spoon large enough to row a boat with. She made for a formidable sentry: none of us felt quite up to the task of squeezing past her.

They clearly weren't building or even designing chalices in this particular lab. We wound our way past freezers, complex distillers, and canisters of a mysterious substance (purplish, like blueberry powder). I was tempted to swipe a sample.

We took our leave.

At each subsequent juncture, Wist closed her eyes and picked which way to go next. Turn by turn, she steered us toward the waste bunkers linked to the former incineration plant. We were still banking on them having been converted to a chalice hangar.

We had yet to uncover evidence of anything more fiendish than small-batch drug manufacturing.

"We don't even know if what's-his-name is still in charge here," I said.

"Datura Gray?" said Lear.

"Yeah, him. Maybe someone overthrew him and sent out the chalice in his name. Maybe he did go rogue, but one of your assault teams seized control—"

"When?"

"Just before we arrived? I dunno."

"Whether it's him or an impersonator, someone risked everything to call the Kraken to Ashtereth. I think that's the part that matters."

"To slay her." I strode ahead. "Or to co-opt her. There can't be any other reason. But you'd have to be completely deluded to—"

I tripped.

Wist, businesslike, lifted me off my feet before I could fall on my face.

Someone had placed an iron snake in the middle of the hallway. That's not a metaphor. It was an imitation garden snake—matte black metal, devoid of magic. I'd taken it for a muddled shadow of something wriggly on the ceiling.

"There were a few scattered around the grounds of the visitor center, too," Lear said.

I was tempted to kick it. "Why, to scare off birds?"

"A trampler would probably see it as a challenge."

We had bigger problems up ahead.

A few meters past the floor snake, an emergency shutter sealed off the rest of the corridor.

Lear's hand hovered over the gun on her hip. "Did anyone ever give you a proper explanation of catastrophe ROE?"

"R O what?" I said.

"Rules of engagement," Wist put in.

"I can't speak to any complex legal nuances," Lear continued, "but basically, it's an excuse to attack on sight."

"Attack who?"

"Anyone who looks like an enemy."

"Maybe we ought to walk around waving the Jacian flag, then." I patted her bag; I'd taken over carrying it. "Got anything patriotic in here?"

Wist regarded the shutter, head tilted. It rumbled in warning, then slid up into the ceiling like a portcullis.

"Did you do that?" I asked.

She shook her head. Her magic lay fallow.

We encountered several more shutters. Each ground open in due time. I kept waiting for them to slam back down behind us, trapping us.

Something brownish darted along the floor, vanishing before I had a chance to point it out. A mouse? I would've expected better hygiene from a facility with high-security labs.

Sunlight still rained from above. The plants began to look grayer, though, to the point that I couldn't tell if they were even alive. Some had bloomed, but the flowers smelled intensely of mildew.

Past the gauntlet of shutters was an isolated door with a pristine label on the wall beside it. The position and styling of the text made the door feel like a contemporary art piece, not an actual entrance.

Rather than list the date of creation or the title of the work or the material it had been produced from, the label said:

Datura Gray

Director of Research

How helpful. It was all written out in Jacian characters, so I took a second to confirm my reading with Lear. Then I drew her and Wist a couple steps back.

"This is obviously a set-up," I whispered, "so let's talk strategy before we..."

Wist didn't hear a word I said.

She was glaring at the door, her face frozen behind those sunglasses.

Wait, I thought on reflex. *No, wait!*

It didn't reach her.

By the time I flung myself at her shoulders—shouting in my own head—she was no longer there, and neither was the door. It had fallen like a drawbridge.

Wist was already inside the room, too fast to see in motion. Lear, ever adaptable, had followed close on her heels. I bumbled in last, heaving Lear's bag.

As expected, it was a windowless office. The carpet pattern looked like a reproduction of chalk outlines from an old-school crime scene. Utilitarian filing cabinets lined the walls: cheap, ugly, and oppressively tall. Grow lights blasted four-tier shelves of desert plants with meaty leaves.

A child had come out from behind the desk. A young boy, maybe ten or eleven. He was as milk-pale as Shien Danver, with pin-straight white hair. Over his eyes he wore a heavy-duty black sleeping mask. He faced us without removing it.

To my utter amazement, Wist hunched over and vomited onto one of the cartoonish body-shaped outlines that squiggled across the dark carpet.

"Oh, dear," said the child, as if he could see everything through his mask. "Oh, goodness. Sorry about that." He had the voice of a boy. Not the voice of a devil.

Lear had drawn her gun.

Wist straightened up. She snatched a tissue from my pocket, wiped her face, and dropped it in her puddle.

Then she blurred.

A resounding crash. Before I could so much as open my mouth, Wist had flickered across the room—not quite dashing, not quite porting. A filing cabinet had toppled, although I hadn't seen her touch it.

She held the white-haired boy in the air by his throat. He didn't kick or struggle. He was so still; she might already have snapped his neck one-handed.

Lear had her pistol trained on them, her face set, and I couldn't even tell who she wanted to aim at.

19

19

"Wist?" I'd gone squeaky with panic. "I'm sure you're totally justified in strangling this child, but the optics really couldn't be worse!"

"It isn't a child," Wist said without turning her head.

I looked at him again. This time, I looked without eyesight.

Huh.

He wasn't a mage. He certainly wasn't a healer, or any kind of subliminal. In magical terms, this creature was about as human as the body double that Wist had used for deworming. It couldn't be killed with anything as straightforward as spinal damage.

With Wist's fingers warping his windpipe, the boy was difficult to hear. He did seem to be in good spirits, all things considered. He spoke pitch-perfect Continental.

"I'll tell you everything you might wish to know about who and what I am," he said. "If you would just set me down, please—"

Wist shook him like a dog with a chew toy. He gagged.

110

"If you put him down, will he rip us to shreds?" I asked. "Will the room blow up? Will the world end?"

If she said yes, I'd believe her.

Wist's arm was still rigid. A white streak shuddered through her short-cropped hair, a visible manifestation of disgust. As it subsided to black, she lowered the boy to the floor.

He dusted himself off like a little prince. He wore borrowed clothes: his sleeves and pants were rolled to fit.

Lear quietly holstered her gun.

"Introductions, then," said the child. "My name is Datura Gray."

"You're ten years old," I retorted.

"Fear not. We'll discuss that."

His face turned toward Lear. She got a disinterested *Hm*.

He glanced at Wist. Her sunglasses appeared about as impenetrable as his eye mask.

"Wisteria Shien, the second Kraken." He spoke portentously. But also as if coming in second (chronologically speaking) made her inferior.

"Hey," I said. "She's just as good as the first."

Now it was my turn to be scrutinized. "That's an interesting eye you've got," he said.

"None of your business, Director."

"Asa Clematis, yes?"

"You've done your research."

"Research is a rather salient part of my job." He had his hands clasped politely in front of him, his head held high. "You might have the makings of a scholar yourself," he told me.

"Yeah? What makes you say that?"

"I've read your prison writings. Some rather obvious gaps in knowledge, but for all that, you demonstrate a remarkable grasp of—"

I laughed him off. "There's no way, kid. You're bluffing."

"Why would I lie?" he said, wounded. "You put your theories out under various aliases, and some of it seems to have been heavily censored, and I won't claim it was easy to obtain copies from across the sea, but I collected all the papers I could get my hands on. I've got them filed right here in my office."

Lear contemplated the nearest cabinet. "Can't speak for anyone else," she said in Jacian, as if testing him, "but I would be pretty interested in getting a look at those."

"Absolutely not," I told her.

"You and the Kraken saw my private paintings."

"That's different."

Wist took off her sunglasses and folded them away out of sight.

"How'd you end up with native-level Continental?" I asked the boy claiming to be Datura Gray.

"He hasn't uttered a word of Continental," said Lear.

"What?"

"What?" she echoed. "Clearly he understands it quite well, but he's been speaking Jacian this entire time."

"Are you joking?" I demanded. "Is this some kind of subtle cultural humor that no one ever bothered to teach me?"

The boy smiled sweetly. "Don't bicker, girls. It isn't becoming."

On second thought, I should've let Wist break his neck.

We came to agree on a few pertinent points. Whatever he was, the boy spoke with all the authority and knowledge of the human research director who had previously laid claim to this office. Whenever he opened his mouth, Wist and I heard Continental; Lear heard Jacian.

"Come," he said. "Sit. Before the wolves arrive."

"Wolves?" I said, and then: "You've only got two extra chairs."

"I'll stand," Wist said flatly.

"Would anyone like a drink?" he inquired.

He held out a mug. It might once have been white, but the interior glaze was spiderwebbed with brown cracks. The liquid at the bottom wouldn't have been enough to feed an ant.

He sniffed the rim and set it aside. "Or maybe not."

Lear and I pulled cheap chairs up in front of him like we were here for a group interview. Two candidates gunning for the same job. Wist, deep in thought, twisted the ends of her gloves like a torturer.

The same old siren fluttered incessantly at the edge of my hearing. Maybe it was just a tiny sound trapped in the walls, like an evacuation bell for termites.

Datura Gray took his seat of honor on the other side of the desk with all the confidence of a pint-sized company president. "I was—am—an old man," he said. "Much older than any of you fine young ladies. I'm still old, and I'm still a man, but I'm also this."

He placed a proud hand on his chest. "The body before you was once a vorpal beast. A simple mimic, or a metaphorical parrot. Now it's me."

"Is it?" Wist said coolly.

He brightened. "That's an interesting philosophical question. My original body still exists. It's quite frail and wrung out—but alive, thanks to this fusion. Two bodies, one burden. And one shared mind? Well, that's what I think."

"You're deceiving yourself."

"Indeed. I might be the very paragon of a vorpal parrot. Just a mindless copy of a human personality, compulsively reacting the way he would react, saying the things he'd be most likely to say.

"A purely imitative monster might not have the right to call itself Datura Gray. But from your perspective, Kraken, is there really any meaningful difference?"

I cut in. "What's with the blindfold? Were you taking a nap?"

"Bad things happen when I look people in the eye," he said apologetically. "I don't have complete control over my more bestial instincts. Whatever you do, never unmask me. And never turn your back."

"You could've mentioned that earlier," I said.

"Oh, but there's just so much to cover. Sometimes I forget all the things that I know and others don't."

Wist looked at him with a particular kind of black-eyed blankness that stopped just short of loathing.

I leaned forward. The desk was marred all over with scorch marks and scratches and ring-shaped water stains.

"There was someone dead in a limbsuit," I said to the kid. "When we got off the elevator. One of yours?"

"My security forces were never provided with limbsuits."

Lear shifted in her seat as if she wished he'd shut his mouth.

"Couldn't you just make your own, then?" I asked.

"You have to understand that this isn't a dedicated production facility. Everything we build is bespoke. All sorts of one-off prototypes. Mass manufacturing is a problem for others to solve."

"So you're the equivalent of a high-end fashion house."

He wrinkled his nose, but not in reaction to my comment. "Such a smell it has."

"What, your cup?" I took an exploratory sniff. It was fetid, like old unwashed skin, but I wouldn't have noticed if I hadn't stuck my nose in.

Lear prodded her temples like a doctor searching for a sore spot. Wist, meanwhile, gazed with peculiar intensity at her own wrist, as if trying to tell time with an invisible watch.

More mismatched mugs—most equally grimy—hung on a rack by the back wall, near a utility sink crowded with fertilizer. At least that's what I assumed the bottle labels said: I could make out pictures of plants, but not text. A haze obfuscated my sight. Behind my prosthesis, the Void turned over with the languid surety of an sea-born creature swimming laps.

That lazy movement jogged something loose in my brain.

I hurtled myself across the desk, all but tackling the child version of Datura Gray.

"Gas!" I hollered. "They're using gas again!"

I had a sense of Wist's power emerging like a blade from a sheath, but all my attention was occupied with wrestling this boy around to face his mugs and his sink.

"Really, now!" he protested.

"Don't you dare turn your head," I hissed. "Face this wall until I say it's okay."

"You know I'm not actually a child who needs to be shielded from the sight of violence."

"You said you'll do something horrible if anyone shows you their back. They can't fight if they can't even afford to take a look at the doorway!"

"Be that as it may," he said pompously, squirming, "there's no need to take me out of commission. Why, I could be very helpful if you would just deign to point me in the right—"

His head exploded.

A delayed screech tore through my throat. It came as a message from another world, utterly disconnected from my watching self.

There wasn't any liquid to speak of. One moment I was listening irritably to that clear choir-boy voice, and the next moment, everything above his shoulders erupted in a brittle crystalline shower, flash-frozen and shattered. It dusted the air like spilled flour. I couldn't breathe for fear of inhaling him.

Someone fired ordinary bullets, too, but they all flew wide of me. The headless body jerked; I was now the only thing holding it up. My false eye had become a ball of bitter ice. The bone around it ached like teeth in winter cold.

Shards of freeze-dried flesh were strewn about our feet. My lungs flat-out refused to inhale until the cloud of aerosolized brain matter had drifted downward, too.

At last I gasped for air, reeling. I turned my neck, but I didn't let go of Datura Gray—I turned him with me.

Lear had taken cover behind a fallen cabinet. People in limbsuits floundered all over the floor, held down by a tremendous magical weight. A subversion of Zero Gravity, or a different skill altogether? They groped ineptly for unreachable weapons. They couldn't begin to get up.

The air around Wist shimmered like hot oil. She had both hands covering her eyes.

The chalk lines on the carpet came to life, pale ropes whirling up to tie down every last attacker. They went limp in their armor, as if the ropes had sedated or slain them.

The folding chairs had been dismembered. The desk was cracked down the middle; several vicious-looking blades stuck out of it.

All the grow lights had gone forebodingly dark. Miraculously, only a few small cacti had jumped off their shelves, and most pots remained unbroken.

"That was quick," said a voice beside me.

I thwapped Datura Gray on his newly sprouted head. He'd even grown back his sleeping mask, as if it were as much a part of him as his hair.

"Ouch!" he cried. "You can't hit children!"

"I'll hit you harder!" I said, fuming. "You're neither human nor a child. You don't count. Face the goddamn wall, would you? We're a little busy here!"

Elsewhere, Lear got up with leonine grace. She seemed mildly surprised to find herself uninjured. I barked at her to come babysit the kid. Then, abandoning them both, I rushed to Wist.

20

WIST HAD TAKEN her left glove off. She stared wonderingly at the blue bond thread on her wrist.

She smiled when she saw me, showing teeth.

"Clem," she said gently.

I went as still as the prisoners she'd lashed to the floor. If you don't think it's possible to be simultaneously paralyzed by overwhelming horror and overwhelming joy, that's just because you don't know what it's like to love the Kraken.

Even if I wanted to, I couldn't tremble. My body had made the executive decision that it would hide its visceral dread at all costs.

But of course she could see it in me anyway.

She cupped my face in her hands: one gloved, one bare. "What's frightened you? I'll take care of it. Tell me."

Her eyes were still black.

I sagged against the desk, boneless with relief.

She kept caressing me like she couldn't bear to let go. I basked in it for another moment, then said: "You're high off your rocker."

"I am?"

I reached behind her to unbraid her convoluted magic. "We got gassed. Remember?"

She must have done something to alleviate the physical symptoms. Lear, for one, seemed much less affected than last time.

Wist's hand crept up to pet my hair. "Clem," she said, frowning. "I can't hear you."

"You can't—ah. There's nothing wrong with our bond. It's this island," I explained. "All lines of communication get clogged. Thank god I came along, yeah?"

"Why wouldn't you come?"

"Don't you ever get tired of me nipping at your heels?"

She bent to nuzzle tenderly at my neck. I fiddled with her magic, making idle conversation like a dentist. It was easy enough to detect the moment, some minutes later, when comprehension caught up with her.

She drew back inch by inch, all but thrumming with dismay. That old iron control snapped right back into place. Well, her single-minded sweetness had been nice enough while it lasted, but I wouldn't want it all the time. Especially not in front of an audience.

Sometimes I can be a real saint. I didn't tease her—I kept my tone professional. Nothing to see here.

"I have to ask." I motioned at the figures on the carpet. "Are they alive?"

"Somewhat," she said, low and emotionless.

Lear called out a warning. We swung to face the other end of the office. She took Datura by the shoulders and rotated him away from the wall.

I pointed an accusatory finger at him. "You let them follow us to your lair," I said. "If you're going to use the Kraken to clean house, the least you can do is tell us what's coming."

He crinkled his smug little nose like a rabbit. "I did warn you. Anyway, that's one less group of infiltrators to fret about."

Lear edged away from him, keeping a eye on the floor to avoid tripping over wayward limbsuits. Wist and I backpedaled awkwardly, too. In this way, we gave ourselves a fuller view of the room without once turning our backs on Datura Gray.

We reconvened near the fallen door. He skipped over to join us. He was skinny beneath his clothes—the kind of child who would struggle to put on enough weight to grow.

"If they're alive," Lear said of our captives, "we'll need to decide what to do with them."

"Do you have a brig?" I asked Datura.

"This isn't a pirate ship, Magebreaker."

"Don't call me that."

"It's a term of respect."

Lear crouched by one of the tied-down limbsuits. "For starters, let's see what we're dealing with." She cast a glance at Wist. "May I?"

"Suit yourself."

"Wow," I said. "Was that a pun?"

"No."

Ah—nothing warmed me more than the familiar chill of Wist's voice.

These limbsuits encased each wielder like a translucent exoskeleton. Certain segments flickered in and out of greater opacity, as if glitched. Beneath it all, they appeared to wear dense wetsuit-type undergarments.

As Lear poked and prodded the nearest specimen, a strange conviction gripped me. It would be hollow, I thought. Headless. The Jacian military would give anything to develop unpiloted chalices, wouldn't they?

Why not start with empty armor?

"Why are they called limbsuits?" I asked.

"They do cover all your limbs," said Datura Gray.

"Do they eventually kill you? Like how your chalices kill pilots?"

"A mere limbsuit isn't an automatic death sentence, no. Although—"

With a quiet clack, and a hiss of release, Lear pried off the helmet. A pickled scent puffed out. The face beneath was the face of a stranger: cheeks slack, eyes unblinking, drool caked around the mouth. Breath came in and out with the steady regularity of a metronome.

"You locked them in their bodies," Datura said to Wist with delight. "All of them! Oh, I see—you've synced their respiration to your own. How very creative."

Wist stirred as if awakening from a dream. "I can put them under," she said. "I should—"

"They can survive a couple minutes of forced pacifism." Lear moved on to the next limbsuit. "Might ask you to let them talk, though."

"An interrogation!" Datura clapped, then visibly sobered. "Might not be very illuminating, actually."

"Worried about what they'll tell us?" I said.

"Not in the slightest. You just can't expect coherence. They've been trying to slaughter everyone in sight—sometimes including each other. It was all I could do to keep them running around the building in circles. These limbsuits don't react well to the presence of greater chalices."

"That kind of seems like a fatal design flaw."

"Ah, perhaps I misspoke. Conventional chalices would be fine. It's the type of machina we construct at Ashtereth that they seem to have a problem with."

"Still—"

He shrugged. "We're pushing magitech to its limits, testing the outermost borders of sheer possibility. You can't do that when you've got to maintain compatibility with every older framework. So it was quite sensible of Central not to equip my officers with limbsuits, yes? Although I assume the decision was made mainly out of budget considerations ... and I did always want to see what would happen. If only there were more time to take notes."

Lear had finished removing the last helmet, keeping her shoulders oriented toward Datura all the while.

Suddenly Wist strode forward. Together we looked down at the face of a villager from the third floor. The woman who had been waving around an empty watering can. Not a villager at all, then—an infiltrator who had been doing her best to blend in.

Datura favored each of us with a supremely satisfied smile. "Perfect," he said. "You drew them out, you tamed them, and you didn't even kill anyone. How pleasing it is to know that the Kraken respects the sanctity of human life. You should probably start taking them out of those suits, though."

"Right," said Lear. In Jacian: "Director, would you go look at the wall again? Way over there, please. This will take ages if we're all constantly shuffling sideways."

He complained—he certainly had the whine of a child down pat—but in the end, he trundled away to stand before the sink.

Lear showed Wist and me how to extract each immobile body from its limbsuit.

In the midst of instructing us, she said very softly: "If he turns on us, how will you destroy him?"

"That's easy," Datura Gray informed us from the other side of the room. He spoke as brightly as if he were explaining a favorite recipe. "Start with my original body. It's inside Reverence, in case you were wondering. There's a special connection between my two fleshly selves. If one dies, the other dies."

We all fell silent for a time, although he evidently had no objection to talk of murder.

"What do these actually do?" I said as Wist took a man by the armpits and dragged him away from his fragmented limbsuit.

"The suits?" Lear stretched her back. "They make you stronger and faster. They deflect a wide range of weapons. They repair injuries."

Datura chimed in again. "They don't feed on the wearer. It's the opposite—for every kill or casualty you produce, they get an enormous boost. A temporary boost, but still."

"That's a perverse incentive," I said.

"And that's why they aren't so widely used yet. Even in the military, it's a controversial topic. Can't slap equipment like this on peacekeeping troops. Which is not to say that it's never been tried…"

Datura Gray seemed eager to run his mouth about state secrets at every given opportunity. By this point, Lear must have given up on keeping him quiet. Probably considered it above her pay grade. For all that he was a traitor to Jace, he far outranked her, anyway.

We considered our array of nine paralyzed bodies.

"I think you just have to put them to sleep," I said to Wist.

"For how long?"

"A day. Maybe two. Or until someone comes to collect them."

If something drastic happened—like if a fire tore through the base—they'd be unable to flee to safety. But we could hardly take them with us when we trekked off to find Reverence.

"Can I turn around yet?" Datura asked.

He got our assent, then loped to his desk. Half of it bristled with swords, like an oversized knife block. He hopped up to sit on the other half.

"Always wanted to do this," he said, legs dangling. "I was never very good at comporting myself with the gravitas of age. I did try, though."

His head turned from side to side, running his blindfolded gaze over the team of nine that had tried to kill us.

"I can propose a different approach," he announced. "One more desirable than leaving them in my office to rot. On your way here, did you see any lab equipment? Like something from a brewery. You'll have to double back, but—"

Lear had abruptly started rummaging in her bag. She silenced him by holding up a palm-sized sachet of powder. Then another. And another.

My jaw dropped. "The hell? When did you—*I* was holding that bag for you!"

"I'm better at painting than at espionage," Lear said kindly, "but I didn't get sent abroad with zero training. You were thinking of trying to pocket some of this stuff yourself, weren't you?"

"Do you even know what it does?"

Datura answered for her. "That substance," he said importantly, "is as precious as anything you've ever touched. A single dose can open your mind to greater integration with compatible machina. We're still doing trials. But in the long run, it'll be essential for improving pilot performance."

"I thought chalice pilots all die after a single flight," I said.

"Wasteful, isn't it? That's always been my overriding objective: to extend the lives of pilots. A noble goal indeed. This"—he shook one of Lear's sachets—"is useful in a different way. It makes pilots more effective even if their first flight also ends up being their last. No redos. No chance to practice."

"I feel very edified," I said, "but we aren't about to make our prisoners board a death machine. Are we?"

He raised his pale chin and looked intently at me through his blindfold. "If you're volunteering their services—"

"No," Wist said.

"There are off-label effects, so to speak," he continued. "If you ingest it without actually climbing inside a chalice cockpit, it has mild psychoactive effects. Nothing nearly interesting enough to exploit for mass-market potential, I'm afraid."

"Doesn't sound very helpful," I groused.

"There's one more thing. Here on Ashtereth, it lets you hear Reverence."

"Your chalice talks?"

"In a way, yes. Once you start hearing Reverence, it's very hard not to listen. Reverence will guide them to a secure location."

They wouldn't suffer any nasty side effects, he said. Compared to sedation (magical or otherwise), the health risks were minimal. They would remain conscious and ambulatory, and utterly docile.

Wist and I washed and dried a bunch of dirty cups. The mummified debris from Datura's once-blasted cranium had become crumbled cakes of dust on the carpet, pink and dun and yellowy, like loose cosmetics. He must have ground it underfoot, restless, when we put him in time out.

After stashing him in a corner again, so we could move freely, Lear found a small precision scale and carefully weighed out each dose. The powder dissolved after a couple quick stirs. The tap water in the mugs turned murky purple.

I crept up behind Datura and said, out of earshot of the others, "If this is a trick—"

"You think it might be poison? A little murderous joke? No, no. But what could you do about it, anyway, if they all die as soon as you drug them?"

He seemed to be asking in the spirit of scientific inquiry. No fear whatsoever.

"Don't piss off the Kraken," I said tightly.

I went back to find Lear and Wist at an impasse.

"I'll dose them," Lear said after a drawn-out pause. "That's no trouble. You'll need to ease up on the paralysis, though. Enough for them to sit up and swallow without massively struggling. Asa—can you help me hold them?"

"I'll do whatever, but these folks are way above my weight class." Even petrified by Wist's magic and bereft of their limbsuits, they looked like they could eat me for breakfast.

An unpleasant idea bubbled up at the back of my head.

"Wist," I said, "just make them thirsty. Very, very, very thirsty. We'll do the rest."

Her face remained neutral. She carried out her role with silent, miserable expertise.

But this was better, wasn't it? Better than peremptorily executing them for the sake of convenience. Better than expending more of Wist's precious resources on keeping them continually knocked out (and vulnerable). Better than prying open their jaws to forcibly make them drink (a two or three-woman job). Better than using magic to convulse their throats against their will while their eyes—trapped, helpless—rolled about in a frenzied search for allies.

They were too blinded and deafened by thirst to think of anything else. They seized the mugs from me and Lear. They drank every last drop of their own accord, too fast to taste it.

Then, still stripped of their limbsuits like shelled crabs, all nine of them wordlessly filed out of Datura's office.

21

WIST SCRUBBED THE dregs from our borrowed cups. The ropes she'd used to bind our enemies melted back into the carpet, forming a new pattern, one more like a wide-holed net than a tracery of fallen bodies. The white lines were stained with purple dribbles from sloshing mugs.

I could no longer spot the patch where she'd vomited. The invaders in their limbsuits had trampled it all away.

"Now, hold on," said Datura Gray. "Before you start rushing around—you have questions. I have answers."

"Thought you'd be a harder nut to crack," I said.

He pouted. "I'm not trying to be difficult. I take full responsibility for inviting the Kraken to Ashtereth."

"What do you keep in these cabinets?" Lear had switched to Continental despite the fact that, to her ears, all his replies would sound like Jacian.

"Industrious, aren't you?" Datura said with approval. "Records, personal letters—you're welcome to take a look. I've already committed acts of insubordination severe enough to qualify as high treason. Consider me an open book. If they're wise, your superiors will assign someone to continue my research when I'm gone."

"Are you planning a suicide mission, then?"

"After obtaining such a remarkable new lease on life? Hardly. The world is much wider than most people seem to think. I've already seen a lifetime's worth of these islands."

After some consultation about magical locks, Lear prised open several cabinets. Wist peered over her shoulder as she rummaged around.

I backed Datura Gray into a shelf of plants, most in tiny pots—mere infants, fleshy cut leaves and stems just beginning to push out probing roots.

"You, absent the approval of any higher authority, made the conscious decision to send your chalice to Osmanthus," I said. "To the Kraken's tower. Then you sealed Ashtereth. You turned your little junkyard island into a fortress of rebellion. You basically blackmailed two entire countries to make us show up on your turf. Okay. Why?"

He spoke as distinctly as ever, addressing all three of us. "I have ambitions that far exceed the ostensible scope of my research. Ambitions that the organizations funding our work here would never understand or condone."

"Like what? Becoming king of Jace? Conquering the continent? You've already made yourself a semi-immortal monster, so—"

He laid a hand on his heart. "Ah, this—this was a gift. An unsought-for boon. Far beyond anything I might have dared to pray for. But I gladly received it." His tone turned reproachful. "Why does everyone always associate ambition with conquest? What a tedious line of thought."

"What exactly do you want the Kraken to do here?"

"Escort me to Reverence," he said. "That's the first step. Hunting

Reverence down is the next item on your to-do list, no? Our interests align."

He sure loved to hear himself talk, but his words weren't worth a whole lot.

Everything the creature calling itself Datura Gray told us, true or false, would be geared toward convincing Wist to fulfill whatever true purpose he had in mind for her.

At the same time, we couldn't afford to spend days questioning all the other lab workers, combing through their answers for inconsistencies. It was wholly possible that no one else had been privy to his plans. The rest of the island followed him out of blind faith, or because they were on psychedelics, or because they had been deprived of any alternative.

Ashtereth hadn't been locked down for long, at any rate. A particularly oblivious scientist, technician, or machinist might not even have noticed anything different. I had no idea how they normally lived here, or what they'd been told about their mission.

I pictured the mutilated end of his neck. If he could recover from that, he wouldn't require much protection. He acted as if he wanted an escort, but in reality, it was the opposite. What he really wanted—what he'd volunteered himself for—was to guide Wist to Reverence. And, annoyingly, we did need to go there anyway.

How long had he known we were on Ashtereth? Long enough to take our measure. He'd maneuvered us toward this office with a trail of open shutters. He'd placed himself in our path on purpose.

"Who was piloting your chalice when it flew by our tower?" I asked. "Some poor drugged-up sap?"

"Me," he said instantly. "Well—not *me*, precisely. My original body. It's still there, remember? Never left the cockpit."

"So why isn't your pilot body dead yet?" Lear called. "If it dies, you die. Right?"

He swiveled his head toward her voice. "I'm sorry," he said with renewed interest. "I'm afraid I didn't catch your name."

"This is Auditor Lear of Special Branch," I said in Jacian. I wanted to see if he would understand my intonation.

"Aural Lear? Oral Ear?"

Dammit.

"Auditor Lear," she corrected, too gracious to laugh. Papers rustled, and she murmured something inaudible to Wist.

"Young lady," Datura said to Lear, "what's the definition of a chalice?"

A cabinet door creaked. She cleared her throat; she played along. "A chalice is a magically enhanced superstructure that serves as an auxiliary body for the user."

"Textbook answer. Typical. And not inaccurate. But personally, I find it limiting. Can such a definition really cover everything from limbsuits to Reverence? Many traditional chalices are equipped with multiple sets of arms. Reverence doesn't even have one."

"It doesn't transform?" I didn't hide my disappointment. Part of me had been hoping that the cocoon would unfurl into some crazy shape. Like an armadillo.

"A chalice," he said sententiously, "is a magical construct that serves as a superior vessel for the user."

"That's what Lear just said."

"Only if you weren't listening closely. Classic chalices do act like a larger, more powerful extension of one's corporeal human body. Picture the sort of machina that can punch down tall buildings. But couldn't all that effort and power be channeled toward something other than warlike destruction?"

I grasped for an example.

"Like ... plowing fields?"

"Like predicting the future?" said Lear. "A chalice that could produce an infallible weather forecast would be incredibly useful. Even if it couldn't raze armies."

"Yes!" he cried. "That's more like it. We build these incredible machina, devices that no other nation has ever come close to reproducing in full. Sometimes even their designers and makers barely understand how they work. And yet we treat them like glorified battle tanks. How ridiculous!"

"Your problem," I said, "is that no one wants to die for the sake of a more accurate meteorological outlook."

Lear: "In fairness, I'm not sure that most pilots feel any better about dying in a dispute over the exact boundary of international waters."

"You see?" said Datura. "If we mitigate the fatality rate, so many other possibilities unfold before us. Every experiment we ever ran here—all of it starts from there. Small steps. Keeping pilots alive for a few extra hours, a few days, for multiple flights, and then...."

An old man's spiel delivered from the mouth of a child.

"Well, wait," I said. "Why'd you make your human self take the wheel? Or joystick, I guess. You said you were already decrepit."

"Not just decrepit. Deathly ill, until I gained a second body." He rested both hands atop his head. "But in this body, I'm too small to serve as a pilot."

"You've got to be kidding."

He chortled. "Reverence was developed for human use. It wouldn't respond well to some unprecedented human-vorpal hybrid."

"The most famous chalice of all time was piloted by a demon. Or something like that. Wasn't it?"

These days, Osmanthian scholars liked to argue that the legendary demon guardian of the Jacian islands was just another code word for secret technology. But I played it straight.

On the yacht, Azalea had mentioned that Jacian skeptics felt the same way about the second Kraken. They didn't believe in her ability to close vorpal holes. They accused her of merely veiling them, or shuffling them around like a cup trick. They thought she conspired with mainland governments to make herself look like a savior.

"I was just a grad student during our demon's previous emergence. Never met her." Datura spoke as if humoring an inquisitive child. "In any case, someone needed to pilot Reverence, and someone needed to stay behind. I had my work cut out for me."

"Doing what?"

"Prep for the communications blackout. Even so, this place was crawling with assassins mere hours after launch. I did my best to take care of them."

"For the most part," I said grudgingly. "Got any other machina sitting around in storage?"

"There's only ever been one fully operational chalice on Ashtereth. We've got plenty of partial builds tucked away in a hangar, if that's what you're asking. Torsos, legs, arms. And other isolated limbs."

"You had your own reasons for building Reverence," I said. "Something different from whatever you told your bosses to keep them happy. What's so special about it? What's it *for*?"

He walked from one end of the wall to the other, hands clasped behind his back. It made me twitchy, although there was no chance of him sneaking up behind us.

"You're human," he said, pivoting.

"I like to think so, yeah."

"I am no longer a creature of mere flesh, so I don't have to eat or drink. But you might as well pause to refuel while you can. I doubt you'll get another chance to rest."

"You're suggesting that we drop everything and have a picnic here in your office."

"Yes."

"With the Kraken's vomit ground into the carpet."

"I didn't put it there," he said, offended.

"You've avoided telling us anything pertinent about Reverence."

"Let's talk over lunch."

"As much as I hate to agree," Lear put in, "that's not such a bad idea. We might be here for hours more, and the Kraken's stomach is growling up a storm."

"Our cafeteria won't be open for business today," Datura said mournfully. "Blame force majeure. I'm sorry I can't feed you ... I wish I could be a better host."

Lear was already delving in her bag. "Don't berate yourself, Director. We came prepared."

22

DATURA GRAY, acting suspiciously cooperative, volunteered to go curl up in a tall utility closet that Wist had emptied of boxes.

I closed the door on him. "I didn't think this mission would involve shutting children in cabinets."

"You seem to be enjoying yourself," Lear said.

"It's a novel experience."

We could still hear him, and vice versa, although he had to shout to make sense.

Lear coached us on how to prepare packets of military rations. When I asked if we'd have to build a fire, she laughed and produced a chemical heating pad.

We companionably chewed mouthfuls of rice, fish, incredibly spicy stewed beans, even spicier pickled cabbage, and sheets of seasoned seaweed. Each set included extra packets of chili powder. Wist and I donated ours to Lear, who barely seemed to taste it.

Between one flaming bite and another, I brandished my bracelet and said, sotto voce: "Do these things ever work on anyone of strategic significance?"

"Ah, stealth bracelets," boomed Datura's cabinet. "A victim of their own success. During the experimental phase, they were much sleeker. Quite discreet. People kept forgetting they had them on. Someone walked out of a lab wearing one and got in a terrible accident with a skimmer. That's why they're required to be big and clunky."

I would've pushed him to hurry up and spill the beans about Reverence. But I didn't really want the dark truth (whatever it was) to get bellowed at us through a closet door.

"Why'd you cram so many plants down here?" I asked. "For synthesizing pharmaceuticals?"

He scoffed. "From my little shelves of cacti?"

"Out in the hallway—"

"Did that look like a proper farm to you? Come, now. Why should we be deprived of sunlight and greenery just because we labor underground?"

"So what's your drug made from?"

"Bark," he admitted.

"There you go."

"It's derived from a hardy coastal tree. We grow them on the other side of the island." He sighed gustily inside his metal compartment. "If I could do it all over again, I'd become a conservationist," he confided. "Now there's a noble career. Alas, we only get one life.

"We used to invite all kinds of ecologists to do research on Ashtereth. We worked below; they worked above. They attached nesting platforms to the old incinerator tower. Birds never took to it, though."

While we spoke, Wist began unobtrusively stripping off more gear. She'd already removed her gloves to eat. Her jacket joined the pile, followed by some sort of armored vest or battle harness. None of this revealed extra skin—just a high turtleneck. She rolled her shoulders.

"Wist," I said with false calm. "What's that on your back?"

She gave me an inquiring look.

Thumbtacks studded her spine like tiny knives buried hilt-deep, stapling her shirt to her skin. The fabric was too black to show blood spots.

Lear whistled softly, impressed.

I'd healed Wist multiple times since we came down through the outhouse. These creatures had snuck in beneath multiple layers of clothing, sure, and there were none on her lower back. But how could I not have noticed that she'd become a human pincushion? We were supposed to be bondmates.

"You co-opted them," I said to Wist. "You sent them out to spy for us. I thought they got eaten by—"

"What's this? You're talking about the Kraken's drone tacks?" An excited scrabbling came from inside Datura's cabinet, like we'd locked away a slobbering pet. "What's the big deal? You didn't know she had them? My goodness! You people are hopeless."

I gritted my teeth.

"I only lost one group of scouts to the hole in the forest," Wist said, unflappable. "I called back the rest."

"When?" I snapped. "We were together every step of the way!"

"Before we got to the clearing full of toilets. You were distracted—talking to Lear in Jacian. Making her correct your grammar."

The cabinet shook with laughter. At least one of us was having a good time here.

"Well, why're they stuck in you like a bunch of syringes?" I said.

"They need to feed."

"On ... your blood? Spinal fluid? They're fake bees. Feed them nectar!"

"Human victims work better." She made it sound self-evident.

Datura banged on the cabinet door. "Can I come out yet?"

Lear made him wait until she'd tidied up the packaging from our rations. The office still smelled powerfully of hot savory stew. It didn't harmonize all that well with the lingering reek of used limbsuits.

I pressed Wist for a clearer explanation of what she was doing with the tacks in her back. Yes, they hurt. How much? About as much as it would hurt to stick yourself full of regular thumbtacks. Yes, they sucked her blood—and accompanying fluids—but it wasn't blood that sustained them. It was the pain. The act of sacrifice, however minor.

While I interrogated Wist, Lear shuffled around stacks of paper and questioned Datura Gray about his files. She kept bringing up decades-old letters he'd received from someone up north.

Datura sounded bored. "Yes, yes, Doctor Bloodwood. May he rest in peace. Or was it Master Bloodwood? We really weren't that close."

"You were academic rivals."

"Back in the day, perhaps. And only by default—no one else took him seriously. It's a shame for a mage to be born with such a towering intellect. I vouched for him, but one man can only do so much."

He sat atop a shorter cabinet now, legs swinging. His blindfolded gaze kept wandering to Wist's pins. "Never saw anything like those drones in Osmanthus, did you?" he said gleefully.

This kid was an expert at getting my back up. "For heaven's sake. If you think we don't have surveillance magic—"

"*Surveillance* magic?" Now he was definitely mocking me. "That's entirely beside the point. Unlike you, my dear, your Kraken is a very quick learner. Has it even been a day since she first set foot on Jacian soil? No, no need to answer. What matters is that—working with an incredibly limited sample, and no guidance to speak of—she's already internalized the principles of sacrificial magic."

I sensed a lecture coming on. He bulldozed his way ahead before any of us had a chance to forestall it.

"In days past, sacrificial magic was prominent even on the continent. The Cressians perfected it—but now that entire tradition is lost. We islanders have our own stories of ancient civilizations. Nearly all Jacian magitech can be traced back, one way or another, to a cultural comprehension of the inherent potential of sacrifice."

"You slaughter cattle to send letters," I said.

"That's a marvelously childish way to sum up the complex magical workings of our postal service, but yes. Couldn't you have thought of a more relevant example?"

I'd just finished folding a piece of scrap paper into a crude airship. I sent it gliding across the room. "Chalices are powerful because they eat the lives of their pilots."

His smile disappeared. "I've always lamented that. I've studied ways to prolong each pilot's short career. Ways to extract maximum utility from each loss. I'm hardly the first to attempt this, but centuries of innovation have led to very little change.

"Years ago, I won platitudes for making a prototype that pilots could ride in again and again. Just a standalone cockpit—a simulation of a chalice. It fed on raw suffering, even without the finality of death."

Wist looked up. "You made a torture machine."

"I'll do anything to save a life," he said. "It didn't work with existing chalices. Truly, I never expected to live long enough to see a real technological revolution. But my studies might set the stage for it."

Lear listened with interest as he happily waxed eloquent. I left her to it.

"These tacks," I said, scooting closer to Wist. "How long do they have to keep feeding?"

"I've given them enough to last the rest of the day."

My hand hovered over her back. "Can I take them out?"

"If you wish."

Her shirt was pinned to her like paper to a corkboard. I pulled each tack out one at a time, working my way down from the top of her spine. It didn't take much force.

The tacks buzzed in my fingers, but they didn't take flight. I passed them to Wist—they were her responsibility—and she tucked them in a pouch like spare change.

Lear and Datura had become mired in a discussion about other infiltrators and enemies we might encounter on the way to Reverence.

"Is anyone on our side?" I said hopelessly.

It seemed clear, at least, that no one would come rushing to our rescue. If allied units landed on Ashtereth, they might end up like the crew in limbsuits: losing their minds, picking illogical fights.

Much political capital had been spent to get Wist across Jacian borders. Now we were more or less on our own. Whether they wanted to exploit or eliminate her, everyone thought that was the whole point of the Kraken—she didn't need or want backup.

I made Wist pull her shirt up so I could swab her with disinfectant from Lear's bag. The bee tacks had been very efficient. The red freckle-sized holes left by their stingers had clotted with unusual speed.

"Feeling sufficiently rested?" said Datura. "Come, children. I'll lead you to Reverence."

"Let's get one thing straight," I said. "No one is climbing inside that chalice. Not you. Not me. Not Auditor Lear. And definitely not the Kraken."

Datura arched his eyebrows.

"We'll secure your Reverence from outside the cockpit. End of story."

"You're certainly welcome to try," he said easily.

He didn't believe we could do it. Well, screw him. I kicked the nearest empty limbsuit. "Should we wear these, or bring one?" I asked the group. "For emergencies. They heal physical injuries, don't they?"

"They'll be far more effective if you feed them," Datura said.

"Like our bees?" I chewed my thumbnail. "Is killing enemy combatants the only way to boost a limbsuit?"

"Grievous bodily harm might work in a pinch."

"Got it." I looked around at Wist and Lear. "Let's put on suits and punch his head off. We'll take turns. Who wants to go first?"

"An ingenious proposal," said Datura, "and I would be delighted to cooperate—thanks for asking—"

"You're welcome," I interjected.

"—but you'll be wasting your time, I'm afraid. For the same reason that I couldn't make this body pilot Reverence. I'm not a suitable sacrifice."

"That's pretty much what I would say if I were trying not to get my head punched off."

"Decapitation does hurt, you know."

"When we first came in, you had concerns about optics," Lear reminded me.

"I should've trusted Wist's judgment. He's not a real child."

Wist flexed her fist.

"You have to wear a limbsuit first," I said.

She opened and closed her hand several more times, as though squeezing unruly thoughts into submission. "The communication blockade," she said to Datura. An abrupt change of subject. "You have a way to circumvent it."

He grinned. "Have you already guessed how it works?"

"Show us."

He leapt down from his perch and trotted over to the sink. A mass of exposed pipes and valves protruded beneath it. He got on his hands and knees to reach a squeaky wheel-shaped handle, which he twisted vigorously, grunting with effort.

A bare section of wall slid open. My head thumped; my brain shuddered in its casing. Behind that wall, like a mirror hidden in a closet, was a distorted vorpal hole.

23

Its edges were misshapen, like a blown-up diagram of melanoma.

"Come closer," said Datura Gray. "Much closer."

I didn't move an inch. "So you can attack us from behind? Or shove us in?"

"I'll be right here." He put his back up against the sliding wall panel next to the exposed vorpal hole, as if waiting for an adult to come measure his height.

Lear put a finger to her lips, then strode right up to him. I couldn't see her face. After a minute, she backtracked away from the hole and Datura Gray (meticulously maintaining the correct forward-facing line of sight).

"I spoke to my bondmate," she said. "Try it."

Wist held her hand out, wordless. I passed her a clematis pin. She blew at it as if to clean dust out of a delicate socket, and we approached the hole together.

"Asa?" said Azalea's voice. "Wist?"

Datura Gray smiled magnanimously, like a tycoon at an orphanage. I gave Azalea an extremely truncated recap of our time on Ashtereth.

"Might not be able to speak often," I said in conclusion. "If there's anything you need to tell us, say it now."

After a long pause, Azalea said: "Auditor Lear? The twins say hello."

"The who?" said Lear. "Oh, *those* twins?" She looked uncharacteristically befuddled.

"Don't you know them?"

"They might be fellow auditors..."

"They're mages," Azalea said. "Quite young. A man and a woman. They've been assigned to accompany Fanren. They'll warm up with him, compete in exhibition matches ... they're *very* friendly."

I snorted. "A honey trap? Someone didn't do enough research. He rarely goes for younger guys."

"Nothing to worry about, then?"

"No," I said decisively.

Fanren was as coldblooded as they come—he'd be good at playing along, but he didn't have a romantic bone in his body.

"That's a relief," Azalea said, her voice suppressed, "because we have much bigger concerns. Wist's double was killed."

I pictured the malformed body that Wist had peeled off like a wetsuit. But Azalea was talking about a real person: the Kraken impersonator who'd stayed back with their group.

"Killed..." My brain couldn't seem to get its act together. "How?"

"Not sure yet. We only found her about an hour ago."

And yet Azalea didn't sound remotely panicked.

A preservationist, was she? Did colleagues often get murdered in her line of work?

"Be careful out there," she said.

"Sounds like you might need to watch your back more than we do."

A dry chuckle. "Possibly. Listen—before you go, Shien Danver wants to have a word."

Danver's voice came through the transceiver next, and we had essentially the same conversation all over again. At last she came out with it. "Is Lear…?"

I elbowed Lear, who had appeared disinclined to respond.

"Yes, dear?" she said, rather unkindly.

A furious quiet ensued.

I took the silver pin from Wist—it was hot to the touch, like bread fresh from a toaster—and tossed it at Lear. She reluctantly caught it.

"You talk," I said. "Or don't."

Wist and I backed up all the way to the open door, giving Lear some vague illusion of privacy, although maybe we shouldn't have bothered. Datura was still pressed against the wall a foot away from her, grinning like a maniac.

Stifled murmurs reached us, but no distinct words.

I asked Wist how all this worked.

"Vorpal holes interrupt the continuity of the comms blockade," she said. "We should've looked more closely at the one in the woods."

"There was a giant bird trying to run us down."

"Not at first."

We'd kept our distance from that hole—right up until the moment we squeezed into an outhouse to save our own necks.

And all this time, neither of us had sensed the rift hidden in the walls of Datura's office. I found that particularly baffling, but Wist said the paneling around it blocked magic perception. Just like a fancy Jacian purse.

"They've got entire rooms lined with that stuff?" I grumbled. "It's going to get harder and harder to navigate."

While waiting for Lear to finish, we examined Datura's plant shelves. Water-plump leaves lay on sandy soil in mandala-shaped arrangements: an elaborate propagation project. A long green stem cutting had been curled like a mosquito coil and pinned down flat to fit its pot.

We tried speaking mind-to-mind, but we were too far from the hole. It didn't work unless I slipped a few fingers up inside Wist's sleeve, skin to skin, and I still had to form the words in my mouth.

I really don't want you going inside that chalice, I said. *Or any other.* All that talk of pilot death and torture was a powerful deterrent, to say the least.

I'm serious, I continued. *Don't pretend you can't hear me, damn you. Wist—promise me you'll never board a chalice.*

She still hesitated.

I sighed. *Look, I get it. Just promise to make an effort.*

I can make an effort, she said at last.

Lear let out a startled laugh. "Danny, you don't know who might be listening. Keep it to yourself."

Whatever Danver had to say in return sounded surprisingly lengthy. (She never wasted extra words on the likes of me.)

"It's not that," Lear shot back, strained. "I just—"

She cut herself off. The next time she spoke, her voice was much more controlled. "That's quite enough. Goodbye, Danny. Try not to get killed."

She hurled the pin over her shoulder. She didn't look to see where it landed. It didn't land, though. At the peak of its trajectory, it made a sharp, unnatural turn and went flying toward Wist. She plucked it from the air and put it back in my pocket. Residual heat seeped through my clothes, although it was already cooling.

Lear remained poised in front of the vorpal hole, shoulders stiff. If she bowed her head any further, she might lose the tip of her nose.

Datura Gray had the grace not to make any curious comments.

Lear's tension slowly leached away until she was back to her usual loose-limbed self. She raised her head, as if she'd come to a decision.

She turned on her heel.

24

THERE WAS NO time to shout. Lear had already realized her mistake—she swung back toward the towheaded boy by the wall.

He no longer looked like a boy at all.

Light shone out through his black sleeping mask, glaringly bright, almost mechanical. He'd hunched, lips spread for a rib-cracking cough. Something came shooting out of his mouth—the thick, supple neck of a water bird.

It must have been very sharp, that egret's beak. As Lear whirled to face him, it pierced her low in her gut and then ripped upward and out with a sound I never wanted to hear again in my life. Her legs started to fold beneath her, but his child-sized arms held her off the floor with ease.

My throat glugged like a clogged drain. I staggered forward—what did I expect to accomplish?—until Wist gripped my upper arm. I stopped, impotent as a kitten caught by its scruff.

Magic swiped Lear out of Datura's embrace.

Lear arced through the air, streaming blood. I dove to catch her. She weighed nothing until her heels touched the carpet, and then all her weight came back at once. I stifled a cry.

The boy-beast jumped up on the desk, haunches bent. The reddened head of an egret extended from his face like a chick worming its way out of an undersized egg. At the base of its long neck, his human mouth stretched to the point of splitting, teeth full of feathers, and his jaw looked irreparably broken.

"Down," said Wist—she who had no tells, who never needed to resort to the cues other mages relied on. The beast collapsed on the desk as if smacked flat by the palm of a giant. Wood cracked.

Wist knelt and took Lear from me. There was too much blood, too many other smells mixed nauseatingly with the aftermath of lunch, too many lumpy glimpsed organs I couldn't have identified even if you buried my face in an anatomy textbook. It all seemed horribly unfixable.

The oppressed heap of limbs and feathers atop the desk began to twitch.

Wist's magic—again operating like an unseen hand—picked the beast up by the ankles and dashed it against a metal cabinet. Then she threw it into a corner.

Her eyes were very still and very dark. She would need all the concentration she could muster to save Lear's life. But that egret's neck was already swaying up off the ground like a cobra. She'd have to hurl it into the vorpal hole to get some peace.

I grabbed Wist's shoulder for balance and clambered to my feet. The carpet squished just like it had in that flooding elevator. I had Lear's blood all over me. I wiped my fingers on the driest part of my shirt, then scooped out my prosthetic eye. I marched ahead on shaky ankles, holding the eye out on front of me like a talisman against evil.

"Hey, Director," I said. "Take a closer look. Which do you want to see first, the eye or the socket?"

I crouched in front of him, an auntie offering sweets. His human form looked considerably less shattered than it had even ten seconds ago. Except for his face, which at this point existed mainly to support the egret that rose from his oral cavity like a tree from a pot.

The egret was slick and wet all over, more scarlet than white, steaming with heat. It tilted its head, intrigued. Almost playful.

I used my free hand to stretch my right eyelid wide open in an exaggerated gesture of invitation. That razor-edged beak wove back and forth like the point of a knife, meandering closer, taking its time. The human body beneath it was clumsily posed on all fours, knees bent backwards.

I couldn't let my teeth chatter. *Come on*, I thought at the Void. *Come on!*

The tip of the beak dipped inside my empty socket, too close to focus on. In another second, I would throw up all over the pitiful remains of his human form.

I did throw up, albeit on bare carpet—look at me, just like Wist.

The Void and I had made our move, and the egret was gone. So was the boy it had grown from, and the nearest filing cabinet, and several boxes that might have been stuffed to the brim with important papers.

I stumbled to the sink, rinsed my mouth, and spat with a vengeance. I rinsed my prosthesis, too—fumbling, almost dropping it down the drain—and put it back in my face.

I was a little bit afraid to see Wist's reaction. I shouldn't have worried; she was still one hundred percent focused on keeping Lear from dying young.

"Clem," she said. "Bring a limbsuit."

I dragged one over. It was in pieces, so it took several trips. Even then, it was heavy enough to make me sweat. No matter what I did—even when I stopped to catch my breath—the Void slopped about like it was trying to make me lose my balance.

I helped Wist slot Lear into the limbsuit, helmet and all. It turned partly transparent, coming awake piece by piece, as we locked it in place around her. Her abdominal wound looked distorted, blurred first by the thickness of the armor and then, subsequently, by gobs of leaky fluid.

When we were done, I sat back on my heels. My arms felt like jelly.

Lear had no custom undergarment to help her meld with the limbsuit. Beneath it, she wore the same clothes as before—although we'd wasted a lot of time divesting her of her gun and myriad knives.

And even if we couldn't see it all that clearly, her torso was still slashed open, guts exposed. Unless this limbsuit could perform a veritable medical miracle, it would rapidly turn into a blood-stuffed sausage, ripe for necrosis.

"You think this'll be enough?" I said. "If it saves you from having to stitch her up, that's great, but she looks bad, Wist. Really bad."

Wist surveyed the empty patch of the room where there had once been stacks of records and a vorpal parrot with the mind of a man. She glanced at me, briefly, and my toes clenched inside my shoes.

She went over to the desk, which still had abandoned weapons sticking out of it. A real variety pack. She took hold of one that (to my uneducated eye) resembled a sword with an unusually long hilt.

"Under the right conditions, the limbsuit will repair her wounds faster than I can," Wist said, "and more sustainably."

She wrenched the sword out of the desk and walked back to Lear. She made Lear stand up, fully unconscious: the limbsuit supported her so she could be posed like a doll. Wist wrapped her gauntlet-covered fingers around the generous hilt.

Even after Wist let go, Lear held the sword stably on her own, unwavering. With that helmet on, she could've been anyone. An old corpse. A stranger. Someone I might gladly let die.

"No," I choked out, finally understanding. "You idiot! You absolute—"

My voice crumpled like paper. My head reeled. The Void rejoiced.

Before I could take a single step forward, Wist ported herself onto Lear's sword.

25

The silver blade jutted from Wist's back.

It had to be a trick. Another body double. She wouldn't just—

Like you said, murmured a voice in my head, *perverse incentives. Although I have to give limbsuits credit for being less bloodthirsty than a full-size chalice. Give your Kraken some credit, too—a body double wouldn't work, and she knows it. You can't cheat this kind of magic.*

It was the treble voice of a boy, pure and sweet, and it crawled about my brain like a centipede.

I applaud her, he said. *She made a perfectly logical choice. I suppose the Kraken must be much more efficient at patching her own wounds, yes? On an instinctual level, at least, keeping yourself alive requires quite a different type of magic than giving life support to others.*

If we were alone, I might have screamed to drown him out.

But I had better reasons to scream, didn't I?

Wist was impaled on an upward-slanting sword. She'd taken her body armor off during lunch, and she'd never put it back on. Dark blood splashed at her feet.

She flicker-ported off the blade. She was at my side again, magic blazing around her too ferociously to feel much of anything else. I was slow to notice her hand on my mouth, and even slower to notice why. I'd been howling like I wanted every enemy in the base to come find us.

"I'll recover," she said in my ear. "I'll survive."

My wrath peaked. I bit her palm. She released me, startled.

"That's not the *point!*" I roared.

I would've punched her if she hadn't just been stabbed. By her own doing.

She held her stomach. More blood seeped between her fingers and then beat a sheepish retreat, slinking back where it belonged. This repeated several times while magic welded her together from the inside out.

I felt her power all over my skin like a sunburn. I understood just enough to see that—although she'd patched herself in a matter of minutes—another person with the same injury would probably have died in the process. She could take shortcuts with herself that she wouldn't dare take with anyone else.

She had trusted me to do something about Datura Gray. I had trusted her to take care of Lear. Neither of us would agree with the other's methodology—but that, arguably, was business as usual.

I pointed at Lear's weapon. "Let me just say this. I reacted way better than you would have if I purposefully gutted myself on a pike."

"That's not a pike," Wist said.

She pried the wet blade away from Lear and slid it beneath the desk.

Despite the translucence striping much of Lear's suit, the front of her helmet stayed opaque. Our attackers had been the same, faces hidden until we stripped them.

In other ways, her suit began to look different. Stronger magic rippled through it like an electric current, innervated by her unwitting mauling of Wist the Kraken.

"Seems a bit conspicuous," I said.

The limbsuit moved her like a sleepwalker, sending her stumbling past the piled-up remnants of its brethren. Then—as if it had heard my complaint—it laid her on the much-abused carpet, face down, in an impressively convincing death pose.

That did make more sense. Observers might detect an unusual amount of magic at work. But that could theoretically represent normal standby activity for a sophisticated limbsuit. You'd need extra sharp perception to comprehend that the cuttings in there weren't just swaying like river grass, awaiting orders.

While Lear's limbsuit played dead, Wist limped to the wall. At this point, no doctor would see anything majorly wrong with her body, but the pain was still there. She'd prioritized rapid physical repair: she hadn't convinced her neurons that the problem was magically gone.

She put her head between her knees and breathed as if she didn't want to trouble anyone with the sound of her suffering.

I plucked at her branches (which were also in terrible shape). In her shoes, I'd have moaned and raged and milked it for all I was worth.

Very nice, Datura Gray said politely. *That was an impressive display of magic. Tell her I said so.*

My answer: *Shut. Up.*

Wist raised her head about half an inch, as if she'd heard a sound she didn't quite understand.

"Not you," I said reluctantly.

She gave me an unamused look. I crumbled.

"I didn't just devour the director with the Void," I said. "I used Garbage Disposal."

"He's alive, then."

"He's essentially a vorpal beast, right? At least in that body. So—"

"He's inside you."

"I thought we might want to keep him around ... you know, to pick his brain. No safer place to stash him."

I twirled a finger at my eye. I'll be honest: I hadn't expected him to talk back. He was—roughly speaking—being dangled over an infinite pit of nihilist doom, suspended by nothing more than an incredibly thin film of borrowed magic.

He'd acclimated to life in the Void with obnoxious speed. Then again, he was already used to sharing bodies. He also seemed to have a higher tolerance for physical (and metaphysical) peril than existentially anxious human beings. Maybe, in his current form, he wasn't capable of profound fear.

Why harbor an all-consuming Void in my head if I couldn't even use it to terrify my enemies? I mean, really. My Void was wasted on the likes of Datura Gray. I wanted to show it to someone who would appreciate its true horror.

You could let me out, he suggested. *I'll help you find a better pet to put in your eye.*

"We're not letting you out," I said aloud. "Absolutely not."

I couldn't blame Lear for turning her back on him—it had just been a matter of time until one of us slipped up.

"He talks to you," Wist stated.

"He's as talkative as ever."

"You can hear him. Without any special effort."

"Well, the Void is part of me, and he's trapped in the Void. So yeah. Whatever interference they've got going on here—it can't mess with what's already in my body."

Wist drew herself up. "You'll be able to hear him even when you can't hear your own bondmate. If we put our heads together near a vorpal hole, he'll be listening."

She stared at me—through me—with feral intensity. But she didn't reach for my prosthetic. She didn't tell me to get him out.

I put my arms around her. She hunched down smaller to fit. My heart pattered a guilty beat.

I could have just used the Void to erase him. Left alive, he might offer some guidance with regards to Reverence, but how much could we really trust anything he had to say to us?

On the surface of things, I'd captured him so Wist could attend to Lear. The truth of the matter was that I had other motivations, and she knew it. I'd already pushed Garbage Disposal as far as it could go with silverware and insect shells and nonverbal vorpal beasts. This could very well be the closest I'd ever get to performing a proper human experiment.

Not that this version of Datura Gray was truly human. Far from it. But he wasn't an ordinary beast, either. He was a hybrid with human memories, and links to an old man's body. I might never again encounter a being so singular in all my life.

I think I could talk out loud, he said, *if you take out your eye.*

Not on your life, I told him.

Would you prefer to constantly recite everything I have to say to the Kraken?

I grimaced. I would've preferred for him to shut his trap.

After much internal debate, I put my prosthesis in a soft pouch for safekeeping. Wist watched my every move without blinking.

"That's better!" chirped my empty socket.

"Oh, god," I said. "No, it's not."

Datura kept going, unruffled. "Be wary of the woman in the limbsuit."

"Who, Lear?"

"Was that her name? Yes."

"You almost killed her out of some stupid bestial instinct. Don't act like you were doing us a favor."

"She's Jacian—born and bred—and she's bonded, isn't she? A mage in spirit, if not in ability. With all the restrictions that entails. A rather fascinating case."

"We've been over this," I said. "She had orders to shoot us. We're not completely oblivious."

"Told you all about it, did she? An excellent way to make you think the crisis is already past."

"Why would I think that? We're stuck on your nightmare garbage island until we steal a chalice unlike any other, and I've got a creepy monster child talking out of a hole in my head."

"I'm just doing my part to help," he said blithely.

When he projected his voice from the Void, he sounded even higher and perkier than before. It wasn't so different from carrying on a conversation with a literal parrot.

Wist had mastered her breathing, and she was moving less stiffly. She knelt in front of me, and for a moment I thought she was going in for a kiss.

She put her mouth up against my right eye socket and said, quite casually, "I'll kill you, old man."

That actually got him to pipe down for a bit.

She wasn't in the best mood of her life, so I made sure not to say anything cheeky. I sorted out her magic, which kept cramping into tighter snarls (as if to spite me).

Lear still hadn't moved, but Wist seemed confident that the limbsuit would get her back in one piece. Eventually.

In the meantime, Wist gathered up all her own outerwear and extra gear. I helped her maneuver through confusingly cut armholes and a ridiculous array of straps. I also crawled around on my hands and knees until I found her gloves, which had gotten buried by a toppled stack of paper.

"So, Director," I said. "How'd you become a monster? Child sacrifice?"

"Most certainly not," said my missing eye.

"I mean, that might explain why you look like a kid. You kidnapped some poor innocent boy. You dosed him with your powder to make him compliant. You used the magical abilities of an advanced machina to fuse his body with a vorpal beast, and then you poured your soul in."

"You've got quite an imagination."

"Am I wrong?"

"Do you believe in vorpal beasts?" he asked suddenly.

"Uh, yes?"

"Do you believe in demons?"

Wist had crouched down to watch over Lear. But she definitely had her ears perked.

"Interesting question," I said. "I've never seen one."

"Would you believe in the existence of indefinable magical beings?"

The Void itself was no one's idea of a being. It was certainly unique, though, and maybe not that far off from what he meant.

I thought of Wist with long white hair. Without the fetters of morality or responsibility, she could become anything, couldn't she?

"Vorpal creatures have to come from somewhere," I said. "On the other side of a hundred thousand vorpal holes, maybe there are plenty of worlds filled with humans we wouldn't recognize as human, or human-shaped beasts, or great powers without any corporeal presence, or indescribable horrors.

"Anyway, what's that got to do with you regressing back to the form of a child?"

"First," Datura said, "I have to explain more about the drug—that violet powder. We call it Tuner."

"What's it named for?"

"A bit of an inside joke. One of my chemists gives everything she works with a nickname. A virtue name."

"Like *Reverence*?"

"No, much sillier. She alway picks from lists of real historical names ... but to modern ears, they sound like a joke. When we started testing all kinds of different recipes and concentrations, she called our most successful batch I-Turn-to-Please-the-Lord."

"I ... what?"

"Over time, it got abbreviated to Turner, and then corrupted to Tuner."

That cheeping voice tickled my empty eyelid. I held my palm up as if checking a corpse for breath—but no air puffed out of my socket. After all, he wasn't speaking with lungs.

Datura said: "We didn't invent the drug out of nowhere. Residents of remote islands have always used the same tree bark for rituals and recreation."

Were we about to get regaled with the entire history of his scientific career?

"During initial trials, subjects kept saying they felt a presence. Or heard a voice. A voice without words."

"Is that surprising? You called it a psychoactive."

"We'd fine-tuned the distilling process to eliminate overt hallucinogenic effects. So at first we saw it as a setback. Then we began to question ourselves, and our subjects. When one person heard that voice, everyone heard it. It was always all or nothing."

"Mass psychosis?" I said.

"Possibly. I was younger then, and more hasty. Desperate for success."

I could tell where this was going. "You started dosing yourself with Tuner."

"I did. Day after day. Over the course of years, it took a toll on my health. But I felt that otherworldly presence, too. A mind beyond language. Magic too vast to describe in terms of human cores and branches."

These sweeping statements would've been a lot eerier if he didn't sound like he'd swallowed helium.

"So you made contact with something like a vorpal beast, except way more powerful," I said. "Something distant and terrible."

"Something awe-inspiring," he corrected. "There was never any malice in it. Just pure curiosity."

He characterized the presence with various divine metaphors. He clearly believed what he was telling us—that he'd become acquainted with a transcendental deity or monstrosity. But he might just as easily have been describing a drug-induced hallucination.

"Kraken," he said. "You have a cat?"

I didn't like the fact that he knew this.

He compared the entity to a well-fed cat lying in a grassy yard. A benevolent predator.

Out of all the bunnies and rodents and tortoises and insects and salamanders and birds in the garden, some might see or smell it and instinctively shy away. But as long as it never attacked, they might eventually forget their fear. Others, blissfully unaware, would never even know it was there.

Perhaps it wasn't hungry, he said. Perhaps it just wanted to look. Perhaps it would content itself with gazing upon each small, vulnerable creature in turn.

26

I WISHED LEAR would show signs of life. I wished even more ardently that there were windows we could open to air out this blighted office. Ceiling vents hissed and rumbled, but whatever they were trying to do, they went about it too slowly for my liking.

With a brief glance, Wist and I agreed to continue humoring Datura Gray.

"We haven't reached the part where you become a kid yet," I said.

"First comes Reverence."

"Your chalice made you a child?"

"Close, but not quite," he said. "Reverence has no fists, no guns, no lasers, no bombs. It's more like the magical equivalent of a lighthouse. A far-reaching beacon in the dark. A communications tower, even."

The audacity of this man! It was almost enough to make me like him. "You designed an entire chalice—using taxpayer money—with the goal of getting in touch with your secret obsession."

"In the end, it saved my life," he said softly.

"When?"

This was the first word Wist had spoken in a good long while.

"Reverence has been largely complete for several years now. But I couldn't put it into long-term use—not until we found a way to stop churning through pilots. Meanwhile, my health declined. I got my affairs in order. I began to consider retirement. Then—"

"When?" Wist said again, more sharply.

"We did more activation tests on Reverence last summer. Bad timing, or so it seemed. The voice lay dormant. My body could barely tolerate Tuner. For my own survival, I knew I'd have to leave Ashtereth by winter, if not sooner.

"But in early fall—just about a year ago—the voice came back. I felt its presence more strongly than ever before. Even without a pilot inside Reverence, even without any open channels, it came down like an avalanche.

"I was too overwhelmed to even form prayerful thoughts. The presence sensed my illness, the slow death in me. It dragged a beast through the nearest vorpal hole. It squeezed the creature like clay and remade it in my image: a magic receptacle. All with nothing more than the touch of a powerful mind."

"You really looked like this as a kid?" I said.

"I did." He laughed dryly. "Minus the eye mask. Some of my most vivid sense memories are from when I was right around this age. Just snatches here and there, moments of no importance ... but they come back so easily, don't they?

"I used to run around with my schoolmates and play at being demons. I always took it much more seriously than the others. Once I bit a boy and made him bleed."

This alleged eldritch presence had reawakened—or gained new

fervor—a year ago, he'd said. Right around the time when we first encountered the Void.

I asked him for exact dates.

"Does it matter," he said, "if time is a substance that can be stirred with a muddler?"

Wist's shoulders tensed.

Okay. I was starting to see the shape of things. Datura Gray had insider information. He'd become metaphysical pen pals with an all-seeing creature that might have spied on us as far away as Manglesea.

That didn't mean he understood the significance of what he was saying, and it didn't mean he wasn't bluffing. If we got this windbag talking about the malleability of time, we'd be trapped on Ashtereth for weeks.

"You got your youth back," I said, "with just a couple inconvenient drawbacks. You've got a chalice designed for the particular purpose of communicating with arcane beings. You've been trying so hard to connect to your unreachable friend. But it's been going rather poorly, hasn't it?"

"I succeeded at piloting Reverence, at least in a mechanical sense," he said humbly. "In many other ways, I've fallen short."

"You want the Kraken to talk to your benefactor. You think she'll get much further."

His hum of agreement made my skull buzz.

Our interests wouldn't align for long. It'd all fall apart as soon as we reached his chalice. But first we had to actually find it.

On the floor, Lear was beginning to turn.

Wist reached out and flipped her on her back with ease, despite the substantial extra weight of her suit. She lifted off the full-face helmet.

Lear's hair was plastered flat with sickly sweat. Her smeared eyeliner had vanished, as if scoured bare, and her complexion had taken on a deep grayish cast. Wist supported her while I dug the canteen out of her bag and helped her drink. After several attempts at swallowing, her eyes fluttered shut.

An odor like sweet vinegar seeped up from the neck of the suit. A side effect of all the magic roiling down there, I hoped, and not a symptom of sudden rot. Wist was probably desperate to cover her nose, but she kept holding Lear without a word of complaint.

The front of the limbsuit had, obligingly, turned fully transparent. Lear's wound still gaped wide open, but much excess liquid had been cleared, and it no longer appeared to be actively leaking. Squishy lumps bulged together inside her abdominal cavity, swelling and receding, as if breathing. They were a pinkish hue like a litter of newborn animals, hairless and blind.

"Is that normal?" I said.

"She's improving," Wist said obliquely.

"Ready to depart?" Datura asked.

Wist slung Lear over her shoulder, limbsuit and all. Even with a touch of magical assistance, carrying her would require less effort than constant levitation.

Some of the files scattered around the floor might have been full of revealing secrets, but we'd run out of time to review them. Nothing interesting had leapt out at a glance; it was all in Jacian, which I would have to concentrate to read. The occasional graphs and number-filled tables looked even less comprehensible.

I seized Lear's bag and made for the exit.

Datura tutted. "My dear girl," he said, "this isn't the kind of place you can leave through a door."

27

JUST TO PROVE him wrong, I stomped out into the hallway and then back into his office. "Yeah?"

"To reunite with Reverence, we'll need to take another path," he said patiently. "The Kraken will understand."

I shot Wist a baleful look. "All right," I said. "Dazzle me."

Datura needed little encouragement. "The base here at Ashtereth is composed of multiple overlapping layers of reality. A familiar concept, no?"

"We already got a peek at the old waste bunkers," I said.

"A proper foreign spy could make their career with half a minute in our hangar ... but Reverence isn't stored there."

"What a letdown."

"The initial layer—we call it the surface. Doesn't matter whether you're above or below ground. Past that are the first, second, and third layers. Like basement levels in a building: B1, B2, B3. Reverence is accessible from the third layer. You're already on the first layer, by the way."

"Since when?"

"Since the elevator," said Wist.

He finally got to the point: "Designated objects span multiple layers. We use them to travel back and forth."

"Like a port gate?" I said.

"The nearest anchor is right over there in my desk."

Wist set Lear down and began opening drawers. Some popped out with ease. Others grated horribly, half-broken. She didn't give the contents more than a glance until she finished dragging at the deepest, lowest drawer.

She took out a colorful cardboard box.

Every inch had been meticulously laminated with parallel lines of patterned tape. The top of the box had a round aperture lined with triangle-cut flaps.

"I swear," I said, "if this is a prank—"

"It won't bite off your hand," Datura promised. "I use it all the time."

"I'll test it," Wist said before I could stop her.

She put her left arm in the box, and vanished as if the floor had swallowed her. A second later, she reappeared in the same spot.

I felt fretfully for our bond. What if it wasn't really her? I would know, wouldn't I?

"It's safe," she told me, "but we can only use it one at a time."

"My turn, then," I said bravely.

I pushed my wrist through the hole. The flaps were scratchy, like stiffened fabric. There was something soft at the bottom of the box. Heaps and heaps of it.

"Human hair," I said. "Really?"

"Cushioning material," Datura replied. "This is part of Ashtereth's legacy. Everyone likes to recycle. Would you have preferred piles of dog hair?"

"Yes, actually."

"Too bad. My other body is highly allergic."

I wasn't nearly as quick as Wist. I groped about in the nest of hair until my fingers closed on something hard.

I pulled it out to take a look.

It was a painted wooden egg. Larger than a chicken egg—large enough that my fist almost got stuck in the hole.

Datura's office collapsed like a poorly built set.

I stood alone in a hall of towering cement columns, comparable to the biggest train station I'd ever seen in my life. Except there were no guiding signs, no stairs, no commuters, and no visible infrastructure except those ponderous yellow-gray pillars—row after row, stretching as far as the eye could see.

"Put the egg back," said Datura, "so the Kraken can use it."

My gaze dropped. There was a box here, too. It looked the same as in his office, but it had been bolted to a stone plinth, like some precious artifact in an exhibition.

I released the egg through the flaps. It hit bottom with a muted thump. Long piebald strands of hair had caught between my fingers: brown, black, white.

By the time I shook them off, Wist had materialized beside me. She adjusted her grip on Lear, who looked completely out of it.

"No helmet?" I said.

"The limbsuit won't need it to stitch up her stomach."

Fair enough. Without her face covered, we'd be quicker to notice any changes in demeanor. And, I thought darkly, it would be harder for nefarious forces to secretly swap her for some other limbsuit-wearing stranger. Or a decoy stuffed with stones.

"You'll want to put on waders," Datura told us.

A vast range of sizes hung from wall hooks. They were all hip-high boots that hooked to a waist belt with garter straps, and they all had bright orange soles.

I understood nothing about Jacian shoe measurements. I started trying on random pairs.

"What is this place?" I asked.

"The second layer," he chirruped. "Patterned after a flood control channel back at Central."

"A sewer," I said.

"A special sewer, for special occasions."

"But this is a replica. What do you need it here for?"

"I do have some lingering sense of patriotism," he said piously. "I won't divulge classified information just for the sake of making small talk."

"Could've fooled me."

"Well, I never."

Wist deemed Lear's limbsuit sufficiently waterproof, so we didn't fit her with waders. We tied our original shoes to Lear's bag and set off into the old-growth forest of concrete columns.

Only a few thin puddles darkened the wide, flat floor. It was markedly colder than in Datura's office.

This space was not necessarily any lower in the earth than the health clinic or the Tuner distillery. In fact, it probably occupied the same physical footprint.

But it *felt* deeper. Like Wist's basement. These days, her tower stretched at least as far underground as it did into the sky above. Like a tree growing with perfect symmetry—half visible, half hidden.

The pillars turned out to be elongated, almost rectangular, in the way of concrete piers under a colossal viaduct. Old floodwater had dyed them; the rusty discoloration went up a good twenty feet. Even that marked only a quarter of the distance to the ceiling, which was implanted with piercing white lights.

I squinted. As severe as those lights seemed, they were too far away, and placed too far apart. Everything at ground level became dingy with shadow.

"That's—" I recoiled, bumping Wist. "That's a vorpal hole."

And not just any old hole. Its cancerous-looking edges precisely matched the size and shape of the one in Datura's wall.

But the duplicate hole and the box on the plinth were much farther apart than the entire length of Datura's office. The space of the second layer must have been stretched like elastic. It was the opposite of a time-saving tunnel.

"Director," I said. "Vorpal holes cut across every layer, don't they."

"Smart girl," he said loftily. It didn't sound like praise.

If we could just use this as a shortcut, we'd save ourselves a bunch of grief.

Wist had previously passed through vorpal holes, but only en route to other worlds: a desperate last resort. For anyone else, it would be suicidal to treat a vorpal hole like a bypass tunnel. Why attempt something so magically complex when you could rely on a regular porting skill instead?

Even so, she'd formed theories of how routine vorpal travel might work. She'd done object-based experiments, like me with cicada shells. But as long as other options existed, she wouldn't consider it worth the risk to dive inside a matter-destroying breach in reality.

Besides, the mere thought of it made the Void balk like an ill-tempered dog.

I kept walking. Datura's voice piped out of my head, rattling off trivia about vorpal holes. Stuff like what they used to be called in Old Jacian, and key differences between how insurance markets were regulated here and in Osmanthus.

Wist, still balancing Lear on her shoulder, had fallen back.

"Director," she said, her voice devoid of inflection. "Are these yours?"

She wasn't looking at the vorpal hole.

She moved swiftly toward a different pillar, sure-footed in her waders. I loped after her, anxious to see what she meant.

Datura Gray had yet to give an answer.

There was something stacked behind the pillar. A sloped snowdrift shape, taller than our heads.

The closer we came, the more it stank of fermenting laundry. And ripe household trash. Like the air that had collected, year after year, in Ashtereth's waste bunkers. Forgotten byproducts of daily life: wet tea leaves, skinned fruit, mummified tampons, moldy sponges, diapers....

That was the sum of the stench. But the pile wasn't made up of byproducts.

It was made up of bodies.

28

AT FIRST GLANCE, the bodies looked deflated: sausage casings with all their meat squeezed out for cooking. If not for Wist's reaction, I might have assumed they were fake.

The back of each corpse had tunnels bored in it. Like ragged holes for a homemade hand puppet.

They were still clothed, for the most part. The cement floor beneath them was dry, ringed with watercolor stains. No one bled.

"They were mine, once," Datura said, heavy with regret. "My people."

Their flesh had all the heft of a stack of jackets. Hands resembled flaccid gloves. Arms were boneless sleeves of skin. Necks twisted like scraps of an exploded balloon. Which meant we could see faces—many faces—despite the fact that every body lay prone.

Skulls had been reduced to less than half their usual width. A woman with curly hair and a hooked nose looked, in profile, like a bas-relief sculpture that had been chipped off a wall. A neighboring head, bent backwards and flattened, became a pallid upside-down mask. Others had been crushed at a careless diagonal, lips too distended to cover what remained of their teeth, tongue like a flap of dried fruit, eyelids sunken and puckered, as if there were nothing soft left beneath.

My most tangible emotion was a kind of clinical interest. Surely it came from outside me, not from within. Surely it had bled over from the Void, or from Datura Gray.

I stood before a stack of corpses that went higher than my head, and I didn't gag, and I didn't weep. They may as well have been a mountain of punctured tires.

In the moment, I was more distressed by my own lack of distress than by the actual carcasses. Maybe it would have been different if they were rotting, or less distorted, or fresh enough to drip.

Above all, I felt profoundly relieved that the vorpal hole was far on the other side of the hall.

None of this would seep through to Wist.

The flat eyes she turned on me, and the subtle rage in the set of her jaw—those were meant for Datura Gray. Because she couldn't see inside me. Because I'd twisted my face in all the right ways. Because when she took off her glove and touched my hand, it was cold with horror. She didn't have to know why.

Unsupported, Lear slid down off Wist's back. She landed in an invisible cradle of magic, scant inches above the ground.

Wist left her there, hanging suspended, and walked me into the pillar until I could go no further. That didn't stop Datura from trying. As my passenger in the Void, he had little choice in the matter, but he would've done anything to get more distance from her. My shoulder blades hit concrete. So, then, did the back of my head—which felt cumbersome, overbalanced, as if he'd bodily flung himself into the farthest cranny of my skull.

Wist's discarded gloves hovered back by Lear, orbiting the limbsuit like black guardian birds.

It wasn't me that she wanted to burn.

I snuck a glance at the bodies and blurted the first thing that came to mind: "They smell musty. Not putrefied."

"Preservation magic," Wist said shortly.

And so it was.

I'd detected the old slug trail of magic coating them, but I hadn't given it any conscious thought. Just like how I hadn't stopped to consider the state of their fingernails, or the lack thereof. There was too much to take in.

None died recently, Datura said in my head. *Most date to last fall.*

After he'd received his new body.

I didn't understand my vorpal self. Took several deaths to learn what set me off. I used to be very sociable, very well liked. And I was everyone's boss, at the end of the day. Half my job used to consist of flitting from meeting to meeting.

None of them knew the child was me, *of course. They thought I was a helper, maybe a relative. Some kind of prodigy. They were friendly—after all, I had the endorsement of the director himself. Everyone wanted to come meet this genius kid.*

It was easy to picture the outcome. He'd slaughtered the first person to face the wrong way. The others screamed and ran, or tried to attack him while he fed—either way, he got them all. And it kept happening. He didn't learn.

I was rapidly losing my ability to smell his victims. Maybe my nose had been ruined by prolonged abuse.

"You're scaring him," I said to Wist.

"Good."

"He'll confess to me, but not to you."

Her bare hand alighted beside me, fingers taut on the pillar. The untouched skin of my neck tingled with a kind of sick anticipation.

"Make him give his excuses out loud," she murmured, eyes on my collarbone.

I had no secret technique to force him to speak. But that high-pitched voice started spilling out anyway. Maybe he thought she would climb inside me and chase him down in the Void if he refused.

"I tried to overcome it." He sounded drained, and younger than ever. "I grew an eye mask from my own flesh. I armed my colleagues. I chained myself in place. I felt like a mythical oracle. I gave such simple instructions! *Never turn your back on me.* I couldn't explain that it would get them murdered, but I told them it was important. More important than anything."

"Did instinct make you preserve them, too?" Wist said coldly.

I could sense him picking and choosing which thoughts became audible speech. *The base has plentiful stores of preservation magic. Some all-purpose cuttings ... and some more specialized. You never know when you might need to make sure a biological specimen stays fresh.*

But—unusually for him—he'd embezzled that magic on impulse. No grand plan; no greater purpose.

"The truth is," he said pensively, "I'm not sure why I started preserving them. Maybe I thought I could fix it all later."

"Looks like a pile of trophies," I said.

"No! No—" He broke off as if Wist had reached in and strangled him. Her hand was a fist against the hard wall of the pillar, but she still hadn't touched me.

I've never been good at guessing the number of candies in a jar. I made no attempt to count the bodies.

Instead, I said: "You murdered dozens of your own workers. They've been festering for a year now."

"It wasn't on purpose." A child's protest.

"How has the base not fallen apart yet?"

"We've been operating on a skeleton crew ever since," he said sullenly.

"No one wondered where they all went?"

"My employees are very dedicated. Most of them rarely leave Ashtereth. Their relatives haven't raised many questions."

"Sad," I said. "And your surviving staff?"

"Reverence keeps them calm."

Reverence did everything for him, huh? A get-out-of-jail card in the form of a chalice. But even if he'd microdosed everyone with Tuner—Reverence would have to be up and running to soothe them.

Over the course of a full year, how many pilots had he fed it?

He spoke beseechingly to Wist, using my body as a conduit, as if they were alone in this vast gloomy space. Just the two of them and a mass grave.

"I haven't hurt anyone in months," he said. "I got smarter. I took more countermeasures. I ended nearly all activities on the second and third layers. This is my domain—no one goes here without my knowledge."

How conscientious, I thought at him.

Wist's palms settled with great delicacy on the sides of my head. I felt safe. Datura didn't.

"I suppose ... I should apologize," he said hesitantly.

"To everyone you killed?" she asked.

"To you."

Wist looked ready to lunge and bite. "Why?"

He replied: "Your bondmate was dead set against letting you board Reverence. But we're already here. Already inside."

It all snapped together at once. The baffling quantity of magic in the building. Intricate workings rivaled only by Wist's tower. Artificial layers of reality piled up like pancakes. The containment field that made it too dangerous to port off the island. The precision and totality of the communication-crushing blockade.

Wist grasped the truth of it faster than I did. She fisted her hands in my hair—a blind reflex. There wasn't a whole lot for her to grab, but she still got enough to pull me up on tiptoe, wincing, until I scraped at her wrists with blunt nails, and she saw what she'd done. She let go of me, and let out a violent breath.

"The most famous Jacian chalices are legendary for their size," said Datura. Had I just imagined him sounding shaken? "It's impressive, yes, to construct a machine that can stomp enemy soldiers like snails on a sidewalk. Scaling up leads to greater power—there's no doubt about that. Your brother would know."

Wist stared at me, uncomprehending.

"Your brother," he repeated. "Shien Nerium. He's been building giant magical observatories, hasn't he? Something called a SUPAS. They're like telescopes. The bigger the lens, the more you catch. What if you made it as big as a mountain? As big as a lake?

"Or what if you applied this principle to the magical scaffolding of a chalice? The shape you saw in the skies of Osmanthus—that was just the cockpit. A detachable unit."

"The entire base is your chalice," I burst out.

He shot me down. "Wrong. All of Ashtereth is part of Reverence. All the way out to the pylons in the water."

Someone would have to enter the cocoon component to serve as a pilot, to give the chalice directions. But everyone living and working here was already in its grasp. Fishermen, janitors, scientists. Everyone. No matter where they went on the island.

I had to stretch my neck to see the top of the hill of bodies. I tried to think calmly.

The rim of my eye—every place his voice touched—it itched like hell. I wanted to claw him out of my socket.

"You claimed it was an accident," I said unsteadily.

"I never meant to kill anyone."

"But these murders weren't wasted. They all died inside Reverence. They functioned as an unintentional sacrifice, didn't they? Does every death on Ashtereth feed your chalice? Every worm, every microscopic—"

My throat closed.

The more agitated I got, the greater his serenity. "Worms don't do a whole lot," he answered. "But it all goes to good use. Animal experimentation, unfortunate accidents—one way or another, it all leaches back into Reverence."

As a chalice designer, he'd obsessed over how to maximize the efficacy of each individual sacrifice. His work had paid off. His inadvertent massacre had allowed Reverence to remain operational for months. A constant whisper in the background, pacifying every resident who sipped of Tuner, keeping them devoted to the cause.

Wist had grabbed Datura Gray by the throat at first sight. If I were her, I'd be raring to do it again, except there was nothing left to grab. Would she make me retch him up out of the Void so she could toss him on this burial mound of hollow bodies?

Her shoulders bunched. Her expression remained unnervingly still. I was so used to feeling her through our bond that I'd forgotten what it was like not knowing—not knowing for *sure*—the trajectory of her thoughts.

Lear, on the verge of awakening, stirred weakly in her hammock of air. At last Wist took her eyes off me. The tips of my fingers trembled as if I hadn't eaten all day.

29

As Lear came to, Wist—out of some thwarted sense of decorum—donned gloves and bore her away from the mass of cadavers. Now she was back on her feet, already steadier than just a couple minutes before.

She had heard everything. "Even back in the office. When you thought I was dead to the world."

"So," I said, by way of confirmation, "you were listening when the director told us not to trust you."

"Yep."

"And when we talked about the drug," I said.

"I-Turn-to-Please-the-Lord."

"Wow."

"It felt like a dream," Lear admitted, "but the limbsuit kept me conscious. I know I didn't look it."

She wanted her weapons. I'd stuffed them willy-nilly in her bag, so we stopped for a bit while she (carefully) fished out her gun and blades—some sheathed, some folded, some jangling around without protection.

It was hard to assess the current condition of her wound. A confusion of light and shadow reflected off the glassy plating on her torso. I didn't know how wise it would be to let her walk on her own, but she insisted.

Before we moved on, I showed her the vorpal hole. "Need to do a wellness check?"

"With my bondmate? No, thank you. Once was quite enough."

We were already inside Reverence, technically speaking, but the egg shape was the key to the rest of the chalice. A kind of control room. Seize it, or neutralize it, and we'd have beheaded the metaphorical beast.

So we stayed on course, creeping along like microbes in the bloodstream of a giant. Datura Gray kept quiet. He had at least enough prudence to refrain from further provoking Wist.

Lear had adapted quite quickly to the fact that he was now being magically stored in my head. She put her blueprints up against my eye socket and made him take a look. Which was ridiculous. It shouldn't have worked. He wasn't hiding there in a literal sense, like a bluebird in a birdhouse.

He confirmed that her scroll only accounted for the surface layer of the island.

"Useless!" she exclaimed. "Well, that's no surprise."

Soon the carcasses were well behind us. I kept expecting to see more in the shadows.

Wist and I flanked Lear, ready to catch her if she stumbled. I waved a hand in the general direction of her wound (though it was covered by her suit) and asked if she planned on telling Danver.

"I think not," she said wryly. "A pretty pitiful showing, wasn't it?"

"There's nothing embarrassing about being mauled by a monster."

"I got careless." She spoke with a trace of her usual vim, but she still seemed wrung out. "I won't tell Danny because she'll love it. Hearing about me at my most pathetic—it'll make her day. It'll give her hope."

I mulled over the myriad virtues of keeping my mouth shut. Shien Danver wouldn't thank me for interfering.

My resolve lasted less than a minute.

"Yeah, she'd be thrilled to see you as a bumbling failure of a secret agent," I said. "Might get some real pleasure out of it. But that wouldn't be her first reaction, and you know it. If Danver were here, if she realized you were about to *die*—"

"Occupational hazard," Lear said thinly. "No point in scaring her."

Our arrhythmic, plodding footsteps made us all sound faintly injured. You'd think a space like this would echo, but it didn't. Sounds got sucked up by some invisible substance in the air—a suffocating layer of cotton stuffing.

This concrete channel didn't have much in common with Katashiro Caverns. And yet there it was: that same creeping dread. The pillars evoked images of a subterranean temple without an altar. Mineral stains congealed in corners like wax at the bottom of a used-up candle.

My thoughts rippled outward. The incinerator's chimney stack echoed the water towers all over Bittercress. For a different group of intruders, might Ashtereth have taken on a completely different shape?

Every time the end of the chamber came in sight, it jumped further away, taunting us. But we had to push onward to get to the third layer (and the cockpit).

"Is the whole second layer like this?" I asked. "Can't we go any faster?"

"It's not the quickest route," Datura said, "but this is the best way to avoid running into company."

The water blotches on the columns began to look fresher. The stagnant floor puddles spread wider, though they were still as thin as a layer of never-drying paint.

Even then, the scenery was repetitive enough to remind me of prison. Sometimes it had felt like living the same ritual day over and over. I'd stopped caring—as best I could—about anything outside my own skin.

I already knew what was left when you folded me down to my ugliest and least pretentious essence. It wasn't much to be proud of. It was me, though, and I didn't have enough shame to deny it.

Wist had said very little since we walked away from the mound of half-eaten corpses.

If not for the unidirectional containment field, she'd have ported them all off the island. The Jacian chain of command would ensure that they were collected, identified, sent home ... unless someone decided that the truth of the massacre was best left buried. We couldn't control that from here.

Accidentally or otherwise, Datura's murder spree had provided a year's worth of fuel for his chalice. It had to run out sometime, right? Was that why he'd shown his favorite toy in foreign airspace?

Immediately after his act of provocation, multiple assault teams had deployed to Ashtereth—a predictable response. A fresh supply of meat.

What about the combatants we'd drugged and sent off in a daze? We'd followed his exact instructions when mixing Tuner with water. Maybe he'd coached us into administering a fatal dose. They might already have become fodder for Reverence.

A standard battle chalice could chew through ill-fated pilots in a matter of hours, utilizing human lives like batteries. How much more of a sacrifice would you need to *create* that kind of magical mechanism? Was Reverence—which incorporated the entire landmass of Ashtereth—the biggest chalice ever made?

Internally, I peppered Datura with questions, but he didn't bite. Instead, he orated about how the theoretical framework of sacrifice might be applied in less violent ways.

For example: he'd witnessed a series of experiments in which mages had their branches permanently severed until only one remained. Such winnowing might strengthen the surviving branch—and thus prime it for imprinting with exceedingly powerful skills.

That sounded plenty violent to me. There wouldn't be any visible bloodshed, but it was still a form of castration.

You call it unthinkable, he said. *But no foreign government would turn down a chance to swipe data from our most vile human trials.*

Lear had undergone a similar procedure. She'd had every single branch excised, and she would never be able to use magic again, except by borrowing premade tools and cuttings. But she'd suffered from rare complicating factors. She'd been glad to get rid of it all, to become indistinguishable from a subliminal. Other mages would have no reason to seek amputation.

Our boots splish-splashed on and on through shallow water. Tarnished coins winked up at us from the wettest parts of the floor, as if this were a sewer for wishes. I began saying something sarcastic to the gremlin in my head.

Wist surged forward.

She seized me like a kidnapper; her hand sealed my mouth. I knew her touch, but it was hard not to splutter.

Lear, holding a throwing knife, skirted up beside us. Water lapped soundlessly at the soles of her limbsuit.

No one said a word about why we'd gone on high alert. I looked for more deflated bodies, spongy with moisture. Wist rotated me to face my blind spot. But there was nothing there to see.

30

It felt like staring at a print of a stereogram. What jumped out in my vision? Puddles and shadows. Nothing unusual.

Wist aimed me at the long gap between two pillars, rouged by past floods.

"Look at the reflections," Lear whispered. Her lips barely moved. None of us trusted our stealth bracelets to keep us unnoticed when it really mattered.

"Oh," Datura said, "that's just—"

Lear hissed at him to shut up. Wist clamped her hand over my eyehole. Datura whimpered like a muzzled dog.

Then I saw it.

A humanoid figure stood against the nearest pillar. At least eight feet tall, maybe more. It wasn't just the right color to blend with the concrete background: it perfectly matched every divot and seam, every irregularity.

It had very broad shoulders, but no head. Its camouflaged limbs were long and distorted, as if shaped from pulled clay. The feet looked oddly dainty.

It still hadn't shown any sign of movement.

"I'm telling you, it's harmless." Datura's voice buzzed in my orbital bones, muffled by Wist's palm.

She lowered her hand. "Explain."

"That's the dream, isn't it? An unmanned chalice. So far, the best we can do are remote-operated marionettes. We call them bipeds. The base technology isn't all that different from a limbsuit."

"There are more?" Lear said. "Where?"

"They aren't linked with anyone at the moment. Relax."

"Uh-huh." She didn't relax. Neither did Wist. Neither did I.

"Oh, please," he said, petulant. "I'm trying to help."

Wist: "You said that Reverence drives limbsuit wielders crazy."

Lear glanced at her borrowed suit with chagrin. "I should probably take this off, shouldn't I?"

"Go right ahead," Datura said, "if you don't care about your intestines flopping out. It helps that you're not wearing the complete outfit—no helmet—and you've got my approval. Reverence hasn't clocked you as a threat. You're safe enough as is ... and bipeds are fundamentally safer than any limbsuit. Ignore them."

We began seeing them everywhere. Lined up against the wall, hugging their knees. Frozen in the midst of a balletic stretch. The smallest was at least seven feet tall—the largest, more like fifteen. They never had heads, or more than two legs, but there were plenty with extra arms or tail-like appendages, thick and reptilian. A few lay in flat starfish poses in centimeter-deep water. One kept changing color like a dreaming octopus; its pebbled skin turned dappled shades of green.

We took care to stay away from them—and, most particularly, not to step on them.

As the novelty began to wear off, Lear spoke into the hush. She started off in Jacian, then switched midway through. "Director—you're well into your seventies, no?"

"Yes," he said, "but I have my wits about me, thank you very much."

"You didn't spend your entire adult life on Ashtereth."

"Of course not."

"And developing Tuner isn't what made your career. Even if you started working on it thirty years ago, you would've already been—"

"In my forties."

Lear had to be leading him somewhere with this. I just couldn't tell where.

"What was your focus?" she pressed. "Before pilot life support and pharmaceutical aids. Before Reverence. Your old rivalry with the scholar called Bloodwood—what was your shared interest?"

"Core extraction," he said.

We all stopped in our tracks. I couldn't read the look on Lear's face—a hint of disdain, maybe, or detached amusement.

It's not that I'd never heard rumors. But it seemed more respectful, frankly, not to believe them. Like how I wouldn't believe someone who came and told me that all Jacians were secretly cannibals.

"Permanent amputation of branches is one thing," I said, "but if you take out a mage's core—even assuming that's possible—wouldn't it kill them?"

"It does," he agreed, all innocence. "In the vast majority of cases. It's like playing roulette."

I didn't even know what to say.

"Core extraction is a time-honored practice with records dating back thousands of years. The problem with working in such a venerable field is that there's very little room for improvement."

"So much for the sanctity of life," Lear said dryly.

"That's another reason I changed career paths."

Lear flipped a knife in her hand and set off again, stepping over a scattering of brown-edged coins.

I tiptoed around a kneeling biped. The area which would have supported a neck (if it were human) had instead been hollowed out to form a water-filled bowl.

It gave the impression of going much deeper than it ought to. Like peering at my own empty eye in a mirror. The surface of the water puckered, stippled with undetectable seismic waves. Something about the reflected ceiling nagged at me....

I looked up.

There was someone tucked awkwardly in the nook where a pillar met the faraway ceiling. They stared down through a pair of protuberant goggles.

I hollered for Wist. But—being an irredeemable idiot—I did it in my head, where no one could hear me.

Almost no one.

Too slow, Datura said sadly.

Lear whipped up out of sight so fast that I almost thought she'd been ported. My false eye, safe in its pouch, let out an earsplitting whistle.

The water on the floor had turned to solid ice. I slipped and bumped hard into Wist. I clawed at her incoherently, ordering her to save Lear. My eye would protect me.

Gunshots sputtered high above us, as decorously muted as a spate of fake coughs.

A person-sized lump crashed down, cracking the ice like a broken window. I jumped back and nearly went windmilling down on my butt. The same thing happened all over again when another lump crash-landed seconds later. Wist gripped me so tight that falling was no longer an option.

Blood pooled beneath the lumps, suffusing a tracery of splintered ice. It was an oppressive blackish hue, as if completely deoxygenated.

Lear descended slowly from the ceiling, clinging spider-like to the end of a rope. Even after her feet touched down, she kept holding it for balance. She might have been a bell ringer in a grand tower, ready to commit her full weight to the task at hand.

Her limbsuit coursed with renewed energy. The gray undertones had left her face; the bruised-looking circles below her eyes were gone.

She patted me on the head, grinning savagely. "They tried to snatch you, too. But your protections held."

"Got a hell of a headache," I said numbly. At least my prosthesis had stopped shrieking.

"Still better off than these folks." She nudged one with her toe.

Then she caught Wist's eye. "Sorry," she said. "Jumped the gun, didn't I? You could've rescued me if I'd waited another second to shoot."

All Wist said was: "You're unhurt?"

"Quite unhurt. I think they were anticipating more of a hostage situation. Who's got time for that? Good or bad, this is the sort of thing that happens under catastrophe ROE."

Lear rotated her shoulders one at a time, wincing. The rope still dangled by her face. She batted it out of the way. It swung back like a pendulum, trying to thwack her.

I tested the tread of my boots on the icy ground. It was already melting into bloody slush. The sudden freeze had been Wist's doing, but not for any real purpose—the magical equivalent of a startled shout.

I pulled away from her and skimmed my fingers along her lower back, tinkering deftly with her tautest branches. Sometimes I felt like a harpist. No one could play her as well as I did.

Lear had stooped to check the bodies for signs of life, solemnly narrating her actions as she went.

I wasn't quite cynical enough to think that she'd let the ceiling lurkers nab her on purpose. But her step was much lighter now. She virtually sparkled with good health. Her limbsuit would be far more of an asset after two fresh kills.

"Director," I said. "Do these deaths count as a sacrifice for Reverence, too? Or did Lear's suit suck up all the good stuff?"

"Even a top-of-the-line limbsuit can't harness the full power of—"

"Yeah, okay. Gotcha."

Wist magically scanned the entire area—floor to ceiling, wall to wall, her eyes going distant. Datura had to talk her out of sending her bees out there, too. "Save them for later," he advised.

Neither of Lear's crumpled attackers had a limbsuit, or much obvious armor at all. They resembled acrobats in dark clothing, wiry and nimble, both wearing thick-lensed goggles, both thoroughly broken on the floor.

There was a distracting tang of blood in the air. Sucking my teeth just made it worse. I longed passionately for a toothbrush, or at least a bottle of mouthwash.

No one goes here without my knowledge, I quoted. *Your words, Director. So why didn't you warn us?*

Well, Datura said, *I might have noticed them more readily if I weren't trapped ... wherever you've put me.*

I hadn't told him anything specific about the Void, had I? Lear hadn't questioned it, either. One could write off all sorts of bizarre magical phenomena—rightly or wrongly—with reference to the Kraken.

Lear jabbed a thumb at the bodies. "They're from the Parasite Guild. Look at their tick marks."

"Are those hand-stitched?" I asked.

"Quaint, isn't it? They're real sticklers for tradition."

She uttered a few ritual words over the dead Guild members. A prayer, perhaps, or a curse. To my ears, she sounded much more ironic when she slipped into Jacian.

31

31

We didn't loot the Guild bodies. Lear was more comfortable with her own weapons, and Wist had already hijacked a full set of bee tacks.

As we forged on ahead, the water kept deepening—it crept up past our ankles—although the floor stayed flat. I looked over my shoulder to see if it were getting deeper behind us, too.

Datura's bipeds stood in a jagged ring around the fallen hunters and their still-dangling rope. They were just there, all of a sudden, somber as clerics in a historical painting. Hues of black and gray rippled across their skin, flowing contagiously from one to the next.

"You said they weren't linked to anyone!" I whispered furiously.

"They aren't!" Datura lowered his voice, too: it came out in a husky wheeze. "Not in the usual sense. They aren't set up with individual controllers—we don't have the manpower for..."

He trailed off, then said something about vestigial links to Reverence, and the pilot within. His human body.

But he swore he wasn't moving them around on purpose, and he couldn't explain what they were doing.

I glanced back several more times. The bipeds were all different heights. They had such skinny ankles. It was a wonder that they didn't topple over.

I never quite caught them in motion. Once, when I looked, the circle had shrunken. A biped hung from the central rope, as passive as a sloth on a vine. A few steps further, I whirled again. Many more had climbed partway up to join it, limps wrapping together in shapes like a sailor's knot. The lump of bipeds got bigger each time I averted my gaze, no matter how briefly.

Later, staggered pillars blocked my view. The rope must have broken eventually. Their fall must have shaken the floor like an earthquake. But we never heard a sound.

Without speaking aloud, I asked Datura why he'd so readily accepted his current predicament.

Not that I planned on explaining anything about the nature of the Void. That wasn't for him to know. But he was supposed to be a man of science, wasn't he? Where was his spirit of inquiry?

Ah, but you see, he replied, *the world is so full of inexplicable wonders. I can't go chasing every single one I meet. Especially not at my age.*

You know what's just as important as open-minded curiosity? Relentless focus. A commitment to your chosen pursuit. You have something of that in you, too. You've got potential, little one.

Call me that again, I said, *and I'll stick your egret head right up your—*

"Be careful of the current," he called.

Such a solicitous gentleman.

The water came up to my knees. It wasn't sludgy sewage, or floodwater choked with debris—it looked and smelled clean enough, at least.

My face felt naked without my prosthetic (although it was safe in my pocket). I had to struggle for breath, which was strange. I'd been making an effort to build up my stamina.

When Lear offered to take her bag back, I handed it over with a halfhearted apology. "You're injured. We should probably..."

She hoisted the bag high overhead and pumped it like a barbell. "Never felt better," she said gallantly. "My limbsuit's been boosted. Bet I could carry both of you."

"So could I," Wist said, deadpan.

"It's not a competition," I muttered.

"That's right," Datura said paternally. "No fighting, ladies."

"I'm going to drown you," I told him.

"So spirited!"

The space from wall to wall had grown as wide as a river. Lear didn't have to reach down far to fill her steel canteen.

Moving walkways shirred invitingly under the water. They seemed a hair too fast—I could see myself losing my footing, being dragged below. So I floundered along without assistance.

My gaze kept getting drawn inexorably to Wist. I knew the texture of her skin better than my own. She was all covered up again, but those needle-pricks had dotted her spine at intervals as regular as the marks on a ruler.

I resented the bee tacks for piercing her. Could I be jealous of a swarm of magical constructs without a single brain cell between them? Sure, why not?

I'd drawn more blood from her than they could ever imagine. So much blood that they'd bloat and burst if they drank it. One way or another, I'd stabbed her more times than anyone else alive. I'd stabbed her in the front, and I'd stabbed her in the back.

Hadn't I?

Shouldn't I?

Thoughts closed around me like a tightening snare. One wove inevitably into the next. I would hold her down, and she would trust me. I would rake her with my nails. I would open my face—my throat—the hollow of my eye—and let out my hunger.

I would love her no matter what shape she took. Hadn't I alway said so? I would love her even if she became a corpse like a set of empty clothes, soft and deboned.

I halted, panting. The current kept changing direction. It prodded my calves as pointedly as a flock of mischievous hands: little children swimming, never coming up for air.

Wist wouldn't sense any of this through the dulled conduit of our bond. She might feel my eye on her, drilling into a much-loved spot between her shoulder blades. But she wouldn't know that my throat throbbed, bloodthirsty, as though an egret lay coiled inside it. A neck as long and sinuous as a snake. A beak like a rapier.

Pangs of desire shot from my saliva glands to my gums to my jaw. My gag reflex hitched.

I made my feet keep sloshing ahead. I was used to this: I'd held the Void in me for a year now, and the Void lusted for things far more terrible than mere flesh. I was used to this. It was all the director's fault, anyway.

Don't sully my good name, said Datura Gray. *I haven't made you feel a thing.*

Not on purpose, perhaps. But his beast was bleeding through.

I could rid myself of these cravings in an instant. Borrowed magic— Wist's magic—held him like the winched-up claw of a construction crane. I could make it drop him. I could abandon him to the true finality of the Void.

If he died, so would his human self in the cockpit. Reverence would be left directionless. There'd be no great forces left to battle, except perhaps the mystical presence that had intervened to save a sickly old man.

Why? Jace and the continent were full of dying people, old and young alike. Why was Datura Gray the only one to get a taste of divine mercy? He didn't deserve it any more than I had.

For all his attempts to prolong the lives of pilots, he alone had obtained a second body and an artificially extended life. Some ineffable existence had blessed him from all the way across the cosmos. Just because he'd heard its voice? He'd thrown himself into serving it with the single-minded fealty of an ancient prophet.

Would the voice strike us down for killing him? Would it even notice? Had granting him a vorpal body been a whim, soon forgotten, like feeding sugar water to a weakened cicada?

None of us knew enough to judge what might happen. I clutched Datura Gray in the jaws of the Void. But his island-sized chalice—and his godlike ally—had the rest of us in just as much of a bind.

I've never treated human life lightly, he insisted. *I've always been consistent.*

I didn't bother bringing up his past participation in core extraction experiments. *You claim to be very passionate about pilot attrition.*

Because I am!

But, I said, *don't you see every life left on Ashtereth as just another log in a cord of firewood?*

I ignored his indignation. I waded faster. The burning in my thighs helped take my mind off the burn of longing in my gullet. I had to catch up with Wist. I had to stop lumbering along in her wake, slavering over the sight of her back.

32

I ASKED WIST to hold my hand.

Lear regarded us with unabashed fascination.

"It's been a tough day," I said stiffly.

Memories of bare skin consumed my brain. I saw myself scoring bloody lines in her with claws I'd never possessed. I saw myself bending, like a worshipper at an altar, to kiss exposed bone.

I clutched Wist's gloved fingers, and we trudged along together. The hand she held was a hand I couldn't use to impulsively hurt her.

If I complained of being tired, Wist would scoop me up in her arms—she'd do it gladly—but I had no hope of being able to return the favor.

Well, I'd sweep her off her feet one day, even if it meant I had to kick her ankles out from under her.

"I have a question for the Kraken," said Datura Gray.

"Have out with it," I told him.

"Very well, then." He projected his voice at Wist like a thrown ball. "Why her?"

A common question indeed. He asked it without guile or malice. Which was more than I could say for most people who eyed me with the Kraken and thought *Really? Her? But why?*

Not to brag, but I'm essentially immune to sidelong glares, gossip, and all manner of slander. Not everyone knew we were bondmates, or that our bond went beyond plain old business. I was happy for armchair analysts to conclude that my secretarial skills must be second to none.

Others concluded that—to have hooked my claws so deep in someone of such unparalleled power—I must be a master manipulator, a natural-born prodigy, right up there with any infamous cult leader.

I could see it. Cult leaders often turn out to be rather unimpressive in person. Shorter than you'd think. Not attractive in any physically conventional sense. I'm quite pleased with my own appearance, but I don't expect the entire populace to agree.

Unsurprisingly, real world-class charmers and beauties (of every gender) made plays at Wist all the time. Why wouldn't they? I hadn't publicly claimed her as mine; why paint a target on my back? And even if we'd been proudly married for fifty years, that wouldn't have stopped them.

It wasn't something I worried about. Her walls were as high as the sky.

"Did you hear me?" Datura said. "Why—"

"She's a picky eater," I said pithily, "and I'm a better cook than you'd think."

"If we boiled water in your eye, would it burn him?" Wist met my gaze in a way that—if she'd uttered any other combination of words—might have come off as very romantic.

"I don't think it'd be terribly comfortable for me, either."

"Pity."

To his credit, Datura Gray turned the same question on me next. Why her: why Wist? No one ever thought to ask *that*.

But it wasn't something either of us could explain in words without coming off as distressingly unbalanced, if not downright obsessed. Before I fell in love with her, I'd wanted to tear her open like an animal. That impulse had never really left me.

The water rose higher. A school of metallic streaks eddied past our knees. They looked too long and stiff to be minnows. More like knitting needles that had learned to swim.

Datura (with an affected air of chivalry) told us about a bathroom built midway up the wall. We had to climb a zig-zagging set of metal stairs to get there. A solitary jellyfish bobbed in the shadows beneath, trailing spaghetti-like tentacles.

Wist waited on the landing, which gave her the lofty vantage of a lifeguard. I went in first. There were four stalls, three sinks, and a one-armed biped with its shoulders cramped up against the ceiling. Its skin flawlessly replicated the yellow-beige tiles, the gray grout, the sink fixtures with spots of rust like old scabs.

It didn't look at me. (It didn't have eyes, but that's beside the point.) It appeared to have frozen in the act of squishing down toward the mirror, trying to glimpse the watery depression it had in place of a neck. If it bent any further, the liquid would pour out like puke.

The biped didn't budge—not after I emerged from my stall, and not while I washed my hands.

"Good luck with whatever you're doing," I said as I left.

Not long after we came down from the restroom, we finally made it to the other end of the reservoir.

I slapped the water's surface, hooting with joy, and tried to swim-run to the wall.

Wist intercepted me. She turned me around. The fabric of our waders rubbed together; that's how close she was standing.

She looked *through* me.

"What do you want from me?" she said to Datura Gray.

"I'll tell you after—"

"Tell me now." Her fingers tightened on my arm. I don't think she knew she was doing it.

Lear watched as silently as a headless biped.

"I wish to repay my debts," Datura said. "My dear Kraken—you can understand that, can't you?"

"Your debts to who? The people you gutted from behind?"

"To the voice that came from afar. To the being that heard my cries. It gave me more time, you see. No one ever gets that—not just because they want it. Not just because they ask, or pray, or bargain. I received an impossible and unmerited gift. I want to speak more with my savior."

Wist took hold of my chin and tilted my face up. I kept my lips sealed tight. I'd already argued enough with Datura in my head. Time for someone else to take a turn.

"Reverence should be capable of opening a window," he told her. "Or a door, if you will."

"You want to invite the entity in," Wist said. "As more than just an intangible voice."

"I could practice piloting all the rest of my days, and burn through every last resident of the island ... but I can't do this alone. I can commune with this presence, but I can't let it in. I'm just a scholar, and an aged one at that. You, on the other hand—"

"I've never boarded a chalice."

"Nevertheless. You're a far more suitable candidate than anyone I've ever met. I have every confidence in your capabilities, Wisteria Shien." He forestalled whatever she'd been about to say next. "Not simply because you're a modern-day Kraken. Although that certainly doesn't hurt."

"Why, then?" she said, unmoved.

"Because of your tower."

"What?" I blurted.

Wist's mouth opened around a single unformed syllable, then closed again.

"A chalice can be described as a magical superstructure. A chalice can become a second body—a more potent body. It harnesses power too great for any one human to wield unassisted. It acts as a cage for compiled magic that would otherwise be too wild to contain. It imposes order on chaos.

"A chalice," he continued, "can be a building. I proved that with Reverence. Isn't your tower already a type of vessel? An amplifier. An outlet. Your magic torments your inadequate human flesh. It always has, and always will. It's like a curse. Your tower helps contain it."

Cold water churned around our legs. My unprotected hips were damp from splashing.

The classic image of a chalice: a city-destroying machina, monstrously mobile and improbably limber, cleaving streets with a single stomp, turning battlefields into barren craters.

Lear was a just a blur beyond Wist's shoulder. My head spun as it had never spun before.

I coughed up the first flimsy argument that came to mind. "Her tower doesn't even have a cockpit."

"Does it need one?" He remained genial. "Its underpinnings are wholly original. Gather up all the machinists in Jace, and none of them could imitate the Kraken's work. That's why I had to see it in person to be sure."

He wasn't talking to me anymore. "Your tower, Kraken, could have been the greatest chalice ever made. But you built it up instinctively, didn't you? An act of compulsion, not conscious intent. Like a bird weaving an elaborate nest. It's a vessel, yes, but no one else can ever use it."

Once Wist started building her tower, she'd never stopped. She'd worked on it when we were together and when we were apart.

She had never been enamored with luxury or grandeur. She'd never wanted monuments. She was practically allergic to the Church of the Kraken. She would've been happy with me in a one-room apartment. And yet she kept coming back to her tower. Digging it deeper. Stacking it higher. It had more rooms than she would ever need in her life.

I mustered my thoughts and tried again. "Someone would have noticed. If any aspect of the tower's metaphysical composition is even remotely analogous to a Jacian chalice—if that's true, someone would've seen it years ago. Someone would've told us."

"Does the Kraken host many visitors?" Datura said archly.

"Academics have crawled all over that tower. I *live* there, and let me tell you, I take some pride in my magic perception. You're delusional."

"Ah, but you haven't invited over any Jacians, have you? Not that it would matter if you did. Few of my countrymen ever get to see a chalice close up. They wouldn't know what to look for."

"There's still a crucial difference," I said, rallying. "Her tower doesn't devour—"

"Think carefully, Asa Clematis. Has it never taken a sacrifice? Has it never slaughtered intruders?"

At these words, Wist let go of my face, my wrist, as if surrendering one weapon after another. I recalled the Extinguishers who'd come to kill her. But that was years ago. The roots of her tower had never needed to be watered with murder. Not in the same way as a Jacian war machine. Any structural similarities were at best a curiosity.

If her tower functioned as anything—and I'm not saying I believed it did—it was as a heatsink to offload excess power and excess misery. Or an enormous shock absorber. Perhaps, on some unseen level, it flexed like a quake-resistant skyscraper, easing the magical pangs that wracked her.

So we'd stumbled into a remarkable example of convergent magic. At least according to the voice in my head. So what? Even in Jace, Datura Gray was probably the only oddball who would look at a piece of architecture and declare it a chalice.

I grabbed her gloved hands, and I told her so. Why in the world would she help him open a window for a monster—out of some newfound sense of chalice-riding camaraderie?

"I expect you'll feel cooperative in the end," he said warmly.

33

A RECTANGULAR METAL box was bolted to the back wall of the reservoir. It had a rounded armhole instead of a letter slot.

Lear volunteered to test it first. She flicked in and out of sight. "All clear," she called before disappearing for good.

Wist went second. I was the last to grope around in the mailbox.

"You couldn't have reached this on your own," I said to Datura. I had to stand on my toes.

"Are you calling me short?"

"Shorter than me. You're a child. What'd you do, get a biped to lift you?"

"I have my ways."

The inside was wet. Grimacing, I fumbled until I found a bendy stick.

After some judicious twisting and tugging, it revealed itself to be the stem of a white chrysanthemum, waterlogged and partly crushed.

I was no longer up to my hips in a rising flood. I dripped on dry ground, and the mailbox was mounted to a painted post. I forced the chrysanthemum back through the rubber-lined hole. My skin prickled as if I'd been clutching an adder.

Wist and Lear were waiting nearby. Queasy with disorientation, I wheeled around to ask what they'd pulled from the box. Then I changed my mind. Wist's eyes had gone ever so slightly wider and blacker than usual. When Lear thrust the canteen at her, she took a very long drink. She wiped her mouth without saying a word.

The second layer had been rife with a listless mineral scent. I hadn't noticed till the change of scenery wiped it away. My lungs inflated as though they'd been starved of something essential.

It was so dark out. "Lear," I said, "What time is it?"

She glanced at her wrist. "Not night, that's for sure. It's not even one in the afternoon yet."

"Don't worry about the sky," Datura said. "It's just a backdrop."

Three moons, all identical, hung over the old incineration tower. Here on the third layer, the chimney stack was only about half its usual height. It flared out like an egg cup, forming a dramatic launch pad for the cocoon at the heart of Reverence.

It was really much too large for just a cockpit. The upper part looked stark white, though the bottom was shadowed—a muddier color. We'd been strolling around inside the skeleton of Datura's chalice all the while, but this was its core.

Or might it be better described as the fruiting body of a fungus? Wist's tower extended below ground, too. There was more to it than the simple, obvious structures that presented themselves for visual comprehension. Look agog at its height, stare until you strained your neck, and you'd still miss the roots that swarmed underfoot.

We sloughed off our drenched waders and tossed them down a chute near the mailbox. (The lid of the chute was engraved with a cartoonish pair of long boots.)

As we wriggled back into walking shoes, Wist dried us all with a blast of magic. It rocked me like an unexpected slap. That giant reptilian egg must have rattled her: a full minute later, my mouth still burned with the taste of her power.

You fear for her, said Datura.

I managed not to respond. But he knew I was listening.

You understand that her reliance on her tower is more than psychological. More than just a matter of habit. Now you see it as a vast vulnerability. Like her heart crammed in a box—the sole weakness of an evil sorceress. What if a more traditional chalice flew by her tower to blast it? What if airships rained down bombs?

Rest easy. The parts of it no one can see are much deeper and stronger than anyone thinks. They would have to destroy it on every layer—not just the surface—to hurt her. They would have to destroy it metaphysically as well as physically, and wherever she goes in the world, she'll know what they're doing. She'll fight for it no less fiercely than she would fight for her own corporeal life.

The tower isn't a place. It isn't an architectural wonder. It's an extension of her magical self. A mental prosthesis. In that sense, it's always with her. How many skills could she deploy at once, if she really tried? You don't know the maximum number. I daresay she doesn't, either. When her tower grows, so does she. I hate to reduce it to something as banal as the concept of parallel processing—but that's what makes her the ideal pilot for Reverence.

I set my teeth. It was as cold as winter out here, and there were plenty of reasons to shiver. I wanted to hold my ground, to argue hotly about how he'd gotten Wist and her tower all wrong. I couldn't; he already had me half convinced.

The trio of moons made the egg—and the half-tower that cupped it—cast an odd, underfed shadow. Other incinerator buildings crouched drearily in the background. No lights in any windows. On this layer, it might all just be set dressing.

We were situated at the upper rim of a stadium made of rock hewn into big white steps. And I do mean big—the sheer drop below each tier looked at least twice my height. The base of the tower was planted all the way at the bottom and center.

Four skimpy catwalks stretched out from the top step. If they were longer, they might have formed a bridge to the cockpit. But they sheared off in the middle of nowhere, jutting out like diving boards over a dried-up pool.

Lear found a set of human-sized stairs that cut a path downward. "Come on," she said, waving.

So far, no one had been wracked with a horrible headache, and no one had started bleeding copiously from their nose or mouth. But there was no need to tempt fate.

I stayed put. "There's plenty that can be done from this distance."

Wist was already on the move. She brushed past Lear.

I went rigid at the sight of her back, then forced my jaw to unlock. "Wist!" I yelled. "Wist, you—"

I careered straight into Lear's outstretched arm and hacked, winded. With the limbsuit reinforcing her, it was like hurling myself at a metal bar.

Wist kept descending. I lunged again, not caring if it sent me headlong down the stairs. Lear caught me just as easily the second time, and the third. She wore a practiced smile, her eyes in shadow.

I screamed at her to get out of the goddamn way. I screamed until I ran out of air.

As I heaved in the biggest breath of my life, my right eye socket spoke.

"Honestly, Auditor, I didn't expect you to be so helpful. Don't you dislike me? Don't you find me revolting? I can tell—I perceive much more than a human animal."

"It would be petty to hate a child," she said coolly.

Wist wasn't slowing or stopping. I'd reached the limit of what I could accomplish with fevered shrieks and kicks. I had as much of a chance of wrestling my way past Lear in her limbsuit as I did of splitting a boulder bare-handed.

"Wist," I said. Loud enough to be heard, but as steady as I could make it. Not desperate. *"Get on your knees."*

Her legs buckled. I saw it. She didn't kneel on the stairs, but she didn't keep walking, either.

Could I hijack her magic without touching her—and with our bond clogged by Reverence? Did I need to? That would be a last resort: trying to wear her like a limbsuit.

She was the Kraken, but sometimes she let me pull her strings.

I steeled myself. Deep down, I didn't think I could handle it. Not under these conditions. Not when all I had was my voice. I'd trained her to resist me, too. But I had to do something.

Lear's gauntlet-covered hand came down over my mouth.

"You had more Tuner," Datura said admiringly. "And your bottle is made of metal. The water inside could be any color, really. That's why you went to this layer ahead of the others. You must've poured the powder in lickety-split."

I made a pathetic attempt to bite Lear's thumb. My teeth rang like I'd hit a hidden funny bone in my face.

"I have a sedative injector," she told me, unaffected by my gnashing, "but I'd rather not use it just yet. I'm going to follow the Kraken into the cockpit. We'll go inside. After that—do whatever you like. How's that sound?"

All this time, Wist had faced the white cocoon as if she could hear it calling her.

Let me out, Datura said.

I made an inner noise of sheer fury.

I see what she wants, this auditor. Let me stop her.

You're on her side! I snarled. *You just thanked her!*

Wist's back was still squarely in view. To make matters worse, Lear had my arms pinned to my sides. I wasn't confident that I could eject Datura from the Void with thought alone.

I grunted into Lear's glove. I dragged my chin down in a small, reluctant nod. A realistic choice. What else could I do except cooperate?

She began to let go.

Don't go thinking that I had any great plan to tackle her, or barrel past her, or steal her gun. I know my strengths.

I raised my hand to my head, slowly, as if to massage a sore spot.

The Void churned with resentment. Datura Gray had been hanging there like a juicy lump of bait, perpetually just out of reach. Now I was about to pull him up out of its domain. What a tease. It had been a frustrating day for both of us, me and the Void.

Sometimes I fantasized about letting it run wild. It would spill from my hollowed-out eye like black oil. It would pool at my feet like a tar pit. Then it would eat, and eat, and eat.

I started to tell Datura that he'd better not even think of looking at Wist, or attacking her. And he'd better act quick.

Wist pivoted. She gazed up the stairs at us. I hastily shoved at my eyehole. Child-sized fingers had begun to feel their way out of there, grasping empty air like tentacles on a deep-water anemone.

In the lower reaches of my mind, Datura made a mewling sound of complaint. Too bad. I crammed his hand back into the shelter of the Void before Lear had a chance to notice anything strange.

Like me, she'd fixated on Wist.

Who was, abruptly, mere inches away. She'd ported right next to us.

The instant Lear registered Wist's presence, glue-like magic locked every joint of her limbsuit.

"You tried to drug me," Wist said.

Lear could turn her neck (though not far). Her expression had gone incongruously neutral. "I tried," she said, "and I'm fairly sure I succeeded."

I wondered if she'd been trained to resist interrogation. Wouldn't help much when facing a mage who—if she abandoned all morals—could crack your mind like a clamshell.

Wist opened her mouth. A thin stream of purple liquid leapt out, lashing the moonlit air like a whip-length tongue. Then it hurtled back inside her, chameleon-quick; she hadn't lost a drop. The only sign of it was a violet tinge on her lips. She looked so cold.

"I drank it," Wist said in a voice that, if I were Lear, would have made me wish I were dead. "I drank it all. Check your bottle. But I know when someone serves me doctored food, or doctored water. *I know.*"

I sat down heavily. My legs had decided to fold like a pretzel.

"You were playing along." A smile pulled at Lear's mouth again. Only for a second. There was no mirth in it, just twitchy incredulity. "Why bother? No offense, Kraken, but you never struck me as being much of an actress."

"I was planning on taking Tuner regardless."

"You were?"

Horrifically, I said this at the exact same time as Datura Gray.

"You tried to use me," Wist said to Lear. "You thought if I went on Tuner, the chalice itself would lure me over. We wouldn't waste time hashing out a plan of attack, or debating the necessity of breaking in, or going round and round in search of safer solutions. You thought I was your ticket to getting in the cockpit. You thought I wouldn't hear my own bondmate."

She paused. Her right hand touched my hair in apology. Just her fingertips.

She spoke to all three of us: me and Lear and Datura Gray in the Void.

"I have to go," she said. "But you'll stay."

34

34

"Real smart," I said to Lear. "What a plan! You must be proud." Boy, was I bitter.

Still magically paralyzed, she could only move her head and her face. She raised her eyebrows in a kind of substitute shrug. The same intangible glue that sealed her in place now married me to the frigid steps, too.

Wist had already gone out of reach—she'd ported right up to the sheer curved face of the egg. No time wasted.

She hovered there, a black speck dwarfed by that impossible white smoothness, and then I couldn't see her anymore. She must have shifted inside.

"Oh, she's good," murmured Datura Gray. "She's very, very good."

Not that I didn't agree, but it was extremely vexing to hear it from him.

God, it was cold. Wist would regret this if I got frostbite on my ass. No—with or without frostbite, I'd make her regret it.

Moments after she left, her magic began to unbind me. (It took much longer for Lear to finish thawing.)

Freed, I bounced upright. A heady mixture of jittery rage and abject fear propelled me down the steps. I didn't stop to box Lear's ears—although she would've deserved it. I was on a mission. If I'd seen a trampler just then, I'd have charged like a bull. Full tilt.

I didn't get far.

Pale headless figures rose ponderously from the coliseum of rock. They formed a moonlit circle around the uppermost tier, and around the lowest, too, like a ring of candles.

There would be no sneaking past them.

"She's in all of them," Datura said dreamily. "Every single one. They're hers to control. Tuner does help—it even enhanced the Kraken."

I glowered at Wist's army of bipeds. "She can't already be in the pilot seat."

"No..." For the first time, he grew uncertain. "My other self still sits there. But I would welcome her company. I would show her around the cockpit. I would ... I would be open to dialogue."

I stalked back up the stairs to Lear, huffing and puffing. She could now bend her finger joints about five degrees further.

In any other location, Wist and I would've talked this out in our heads. Reverence's interference (not to mention the monstrous little kid in the Void) made it impossible to hold any discussions in private.

She might pretend to go along with Datura, as she'd pretended to go along with Lear. She wouldn't mindlessly throw open a window to his idol.

But she wouldn't foist this whole mess off on the Jacian government, either. They very likely knew nothing of the distant being that had given Datura a new body. That inexplicable presence.

What manner of creature was it, and what world did it hail from?

Could it wriggle through a vorpal hole of sufficient size? Would Wist have to lay down the equivalent of magical caulk—on a global scale, mind you—to keep it out?

That's why she'd gone in the cockpit. That's why she'd gone alone. When she took a peek at Datura's savior, she didn't want it to peek back and see me, too.

A needless precaution. The creature had split an old man across two selves in a fit of caprice. Why couldn't it just look straight to her core and trace the indelible line of our bond?

I hadn't gone into hiding, and even if I did, it wouldn't matter. I was still on Ashtereth. The entire island had been integrated into the fabric of Reverence. And Reverence was, ultimately, a machine meant to facilitate communication with the ineffable. To amplify its voice. To swing open, like a secret back gate to all of reality, and let something inconceivable inside.

I was being a little uncharitable. Wist couldn't know what awaited her in the cockpit, or what Datura the elder might do when he saw her. It might have been too much of a challenge (even for her) to assess and deal with a world-spanning divinity, from deep in the bowels of an unfamiliar machina, while simultaneously protecting her comparatively useless bondmate.

I would've liked to bang on that egg till it shattered. I would've liked to yell righteously about how none of this was her responsibility. Let Jacians sort out Jacian matters.

All she had to do was put Reverence in the mechanical equivalent of a coma, rip Datura out of the pilot seat ... and report him as a serial killer, I suppose. That'd do the trick.

Then again, here I was with a Void seething where I used to have an eye. This wouldn't be our first encounter with a potential existential threat. No others would be better prepared to take care of it.

I couldn't get too pissed off at Wist's logic. But I could definitely vent my thwarted anger at Lear. "All your scheming was for nothing," I spat.

"It wasn't that much scheming," she said, self-deprecating. "I've never been in a position to plan far ahead."

"You got the Kraken in there," said Datura, "although it seems like she would have gone on her own. We—I appreciate your efforts, Auditor Lee."

"Lear."

"Was that it? Goodness, I'm becoming forgetful. I used to know the names and faces of every single employee on this base."

"Before or after you started eating them?" I sniped.

"That was an *accident*."

Lear had gingerly lowered herself to the steps. The ice-cold rock didn't seem to irk her. She stretched her legs out and bent her knees and ankles in slow succession. They still couldn't move very far.

Our faceless captors had joined hands. It made them look like oversized children about to play a big outdoor game. One circle above us, one circle below.

I was still very much in a mood to rag on Lear. "Why'd you start cultivating Shien Danver, then, huh? You think ahead all the time."

Her face briefly went blank. Then she laughed. "Danny turned out to be quite a good investment, didn't she? Oh, I figured she'd make something of herself one day. Just didn't think it would happen so fast. You couldn't have predicted that, either."

"I'm not in the business of making predictions."

"Star-crossed love is all fun and games as long as it stays in the realm of theory." Lear tested the range of movement in her joints, one by one, with grim determination. "In real life, it's just a question of who moves quicker to stab the other in the back. Timing is everything."

"Take turns," I said. "That's what we do."

"That might not be very good advice for mere mortals. Who else can expect to turn out like the Magebreaker and the Kraken? Imagine the chaos if there were more of you running around."

"It'd be great. We could finally go back on vacation."

I opened her bag and made her guide me to a soft cloth case at the very bottom. That, she said, was her sedation kit. She claimed it was standard procedure to bring one on missions with a mage, although she certainly hadn't told us upfront.

"But it'll work on anyone with a pulse," I said. "Not just mages."

Lear nodded and explained how to use the simplest tool in there. An autoinjector. I pocketed it, mentally daring her to complain.

"My suit might counteract it," she said mildly. "I can't guarantee that it'll work on the boy, either."

"Yeah, I thought not." I kept it anyway.

Lear's gambit had failed to get her into the cockpit. Now Wist had us surrounded by borrowed soldiers—for our own safety—and all we could do was gaze resentfully up at those triplicate moons.

Had the egg altered since she left us? The shadow on its underside might be turning redder, creeping higher. I couldn't recall if the squat tower that served as its dais had always been faceted. All angles, no curves.

I'd fretted about getting separated. I'd asked myself what I would do if one of us (more likely me) got taken prisoner. I just hadn't anticipated that Wist herself would hold me captive.

Our biped guards would never tire of their duties, or get distracted, or become sympathetic to our pleas.

"You didn't have much control over getting assigned to join us," I said to Lear.

"It was just a lucky break." She raised her arms over her head. She couldn't fully extend them, but her mobility had increased by leaps and bounds.

"And you basically did all this shit on a whim."

"I'm an opportunist," she said. "I saw an opportunity. I want him dead."

"I don't even know you," Datura said, offended.

I had been determined to keep Wist out of that cockpit. Wist, for her part, had silently come to the opposite conclusion: she needed to get better acquainted with the voice of Datura's friend. She wanted to know if it was a god or a devil.

Lear had assumed Wist would stick with my preferred approach of cautious surveillance and remote capture. She'd thought Wist needed an extra nudge to go in. And Datura the pilot, who had specifically requested the Kraken's presence, would open his control room more readily for Wist than for anyone else.

Lear hadn't sought access to the cockpit in order to commune with some cryptic entity, of course. There was one other thing she could accomplish there alone, and nowhere else. She could put two bullets in the back of Datura's human head. Or she could stick a knife in his throat. Maybe both.

If one dies, the other dies.

Why had the younger Datura—the vorpal parrot—even told us this? A taunt? A trick? Lear must have wondered, too. But in the end, she'd decided to try her luck.

35

"I USED TO BE a stunted mage," Lear said to the boy in my eye. "Sound familiar?"

He declined to answer.

"I was in constant pain until they chopped off my branches." She made a slicing motion with the side of her hand.

They could've done it much earlier, she continued. Her family needed to give permission. Then: she needed to come of age. Then: she needed to bond first, because otherwise, as a mage without branches, she would be forever deprived of the opportunity to become anyone's bondmate.

If I'd been born a layperson, bonding would never have been an option, she argued. Laypeople were much happier and freer. She knew this for a fact.

More importantly—with her branches amputated, she wouldn't need any of maintenance normally required by mages. She wouldn't ever be at risk of going berserk.

This surgery is so new, they told her. Who knows what might happen in a decade, two decades ... or even in your seventies? They had never seen any signs, ever, of a neutered mage resprouting. That didn't mean it was impossible. They had to take precautions.

Then I'll find someone to bond in my seventies, she said. If my magic regrows, so will my ability to bond. It'll all work out.

But no one listened.

She'd been a child when they removed her from her home in southern Jace. Still young, but old enough to practice diving for pearls. Old enough to know that her pain eased only when she swam.

People said it couldn't be true. The ocean had no measurable effect on magical aches. They took her away from the water, and away from her family. They said they would treat her. They said they would offer cures that could only be obtained in a place like Central.

Instead, all through her adolescence, they observed her. Asked questions. Took notes. Ran tests. They informed her, in tones of heartfelt sympathy, that her closest relatives hadn't given unanimous consent for surgery.

She wasn't alone. She stayed in a dorm full of child mages (though none of the others were stunted). They all became fast friends. They gossiped about their tutors, about the seemingly pointless exercises they kept getting asked to perform.

Her shared room was more luxurious than anything she'd ever seen back home. The food was fresh and plentiful; they even shipped tropical fruit up from the southernmost islands. Everyone received age-appropriate schooling—including exotic topics like music, and visual art, and foreign languages.

They're training us to be spies, some kids whispered.

They're training us to be pilots, said others. That's why they feed us so well, and teach us poetry, and coddle us. We're all going to die young.

But there was something thrilling about the notion of being chosen to pilot a chalice. Pilots were, after all, the ultimate patriots. If you were lucky, maybe you wouldn't get called up for years. Until then, you'd want for nothing.

One day, Lear looked around and realized she was the oldest child left. She was everyone's big sister; she taught them all the ropes. Newcomers kept trickling in, but one by one, her original classmates had quietly graduated.

"We weren't being raised to pilot chalices." She looked at me as if she could see through to the blindfolded boy on the other side. "Everyone who left, and never came back—their magic cores got taken out under the supervision of a researcher called Datura Gray. They all died."

"Not all of them," said Datura's childlike voice.

"Oh, I'm sorry," said Lear. "I was exaggerating. How uncouth. What happened to the sole survivor, then? Did he go on to live a full, healthy life?"

"Would you have preferred to make him a pilot? The survival rate for pilots is historically worse."

"It was just a job for you," she said evenly. "An unexciting phase of your otherwise illustrious career. By the time I got an inkling of what was happening, you already had one foot out the door."

"That's right." He sounded aggrieved. "I wasn't the first to dabble with core extraction, and I won't be the last. You've really got no reason to target me in particular."

She tossed a knife from side to side. Her fingers and wrists had regained full movement. "You're closest at hand, Director. A bonded woman like me—I'll take what I can get.

"Besides..." she went on, soft and hypnotic, "You're not my only target. That wouldn't be very logical, would it?" Her knife caught moonlight as she flipped it. "You never bothered to keep tabs on your predecessor, did you? Or your successor. I'd tell you to look them up, but I doubt you'll get a chance."

To the end, no one had nominated her for graduation. Had there been a heated debate about the pros and cons of extracting the core of a stunted mage? Or had other factions sought her for other experiments?

"If you want to kill him, go ahead," I said.

"No!" Datura cried. "I object! You can't just—"

"Tell your lawyer, kid."

He wailed like an infant.

I acted like I couldn't hear a thing. I rose, looking down at Lear. "I mean it. Just don't get in Wist's way."

She got up, too, and did a couple knee lifts. "Well, I already lost the element of surprise."

"What was the rest of your plan, anyway? Step one: follow Wist into the cockpit. Step two: murder your target. Step three: saunter off Ashtereth? Confess to your boss?"

"Oh, no. I'd ask you to break my bond and fake my death. One last favor."

I shot her a glare. "After all you did, you really think we'd still help?"

"You and the Kraken are both pretty soft, deep down." She wagged a finger. "And you, for one, can't resist a nice twisty love story. You want to keep an eye on me and Danny."

I protested almost as shrilly as Datura Gray had protested his own hypothetical assassination.

At the end of my rant, I said: "You know damn well that I can't break your bond. You've got to testify about what went down here."

She cracked her knuckles. "What should I say?"

"Might have to play it by ear. Speaking of ears...."

We divided up her pair of pointy ear cuffs. She kept one, and I wore the other. "In case comms come back," I said.

"Why don't you give me one of your pins?"

"You probably shouldn't get caught with foreign gadgets."

I reviewed our assets. Lear had a powered-up limbsuit, assorted weapons, and some degree of physical training. I had my intimate knowledge of Wist, crackerjack healing abilities, an annoying stowaway in my head, and the Void.

The lanky bipeds kept watching without eyes and listening without ears.

"Director," I said.

"What?" He'd become a sullen teen.

"Your bird thing. Can you do that even if no one shows you their back?"

He remained silent for a good thirty seconds.

"Answer the question, Director."

"I've never tried," he said with reluctant precision. "I'm not a thought-less savage."

"Of course not," I said soothingly. "You're just a little boy with a starving stork in your throat."

"No need to lay it on so thick."

"Seriously, though, why'd you call yourself a vorpal parrot?"

"..............."

"You could've been a lyrebird or a mockingbird, if we're thinking of mimicry. Or a vorpal heron. A vorpal shrike. A vorpal trampler. Any of those would feel more fitting."

My words fell on deaf ears. He'd been lost in thought.

A small voice emerged from deep in the Void. "...If you let me out, there's something else I can try."

"Will it clear a path to the cockpit?"

"As long as you move quick enough. You'll need my credentials to open the door."

"The Kraken didn't need them."

"She," he said haughtily, "is an invited guest."

I disliked his attitude, but there was nothing for it. I ordered Lear over to a safe spot at the side of the stairs.

I leaned forward as if I needed to retch.

For a dizzying instant, I was back at Wist's tower—skull creaking like a cracked bell, Reverence looming outside the sunroom. I stretched my right eyelid open and stuck one finger in until Datura seized it like a grasping infant.

It wasn't as bad as, say, giving birth through my face. I had a forefinger thrust in my socket, trying to make the Void vomit, and then Datura Gray was right there on the stairs, clutching my hand for dear life. Something from nothing. As slick as porting.

He was still splattered from his attack on Lear, as damp as the moment I'd tucked him in the Void like a pelican sticking prey in its pouch. Blood streaked his snowy hair, and the creases of his ears, and his cherubic cheeks, and his neck, and his once-white shirt.

At least his inner egret had retreated back to wherever he usually kept it.

"Stay behind me," he said to us. "And never, ever look at my eyes."

He turned away. I put a hand on his blood-spattered shoulder; so did Lear. When he rotated, we moved after him with shuffling steps.

He held his head high. Such a proud little monster.

He reached for his eye mask.

36

All he did was look.

The bipeds at the top of the coliseum fell like capsized statues. One tilted into the next, and suddenly half the circle had collapsed, avalanching down the slope in a brutal tumult of limbs.

The stairs thundered. The railing quaked—as did I. We'd be lucky not to get squashed.

Or maybe luck had nothing to do with it. The bipeds cannoned past us at gravity-defying angles. Even in freefall, heavy as boulders, they were frantic to avoid going near Datura Gray.

He whipped around. Lear and I scrambled to stay positioned at his shoulder. Other guardians came racing up the amphitheater to meet us, pasty arms swinging. They, too, went limp when he saw them. They bounced backwards, hitting sharp stone edges, unprotected. Their camouflage broke on impact. Shock waves of screaming color radiated across their skin, neon orange and yellow-green.

Datura lowered his eye mask. "Now," he said. "Hurry!"

Lear scooped him up with one arm and me with the other. I'd severely underestimated her limbsuit. She got us to the bottom in four soaring bounds, easily clearing the strewn bodies of all those giant tie-dye bipeds.

We hurtled into the base of the truncated chimney stack. Lear carried me and the boy and her bag like a traveler barging through the door of a train. The wall parted for us—or at least for Datura—then slid shut again.

Lear set us on our feet. I begged for a moment's rest, panting, as if I were the one who'd been sprinting.

"Take all the time you need," she said generously. Her limbsuit thrummed with the satisfaction of a job well done.

The smokestack wasn't just a hollow shell. Immense chimney tubes filled the interior, bracketed to the outer wall by thick struts. We stood lined up three in a row, me in the middle, and tried in vain to see all the way to the top.

For all my fears, it seemed unlikely that Datura's pal from another reality could force its way through to our world without significant help. If it could do that, it would've already moved in.

Heck, it might be the epitome of a compassionate god. Once we relented, everyone's lives might be paradise. You never know.

My treacherous brain suggested that maybe there was a different reason why Datura had felt compelled to lure the Kraken.

Oh, he'd given all kinds of pretty explanations about how only Wist could put Reverence to its true intended use. She'd proven her mettle with her tower. But what if his friend was just another starving beast? One with a more refined palate. One that wouldn't settle for anything less than an exquisitely singular and rarefied treat.

Maybe the cockpit was a serving platter meant to deliver the Kraken up to a predator of divine proportions.

Moreover: the entire island had been incorporated into Datura's chalice. Everyone on Ashtereth was a hostage.

If I were him, and if cajoling wouldn't cut it, I'd keep the locals alive only in exchange for total cooperation. He would prefer not to play that card; he still believed he had scruples. But that didn't mean he wouldn't try it.

One hurdle at a time, I thought.

Subtly—with all the discretion I'd ever possessed—I pushed a small pouch at the boy on my right. I kept pushing until he took it.

He gave me a fixed look from behind his blindfold. He was too smart to ask uncomfortable questions.

I arched my back, groaning ostentatiously, and blew out a loud breath. "Let's go on up, then. Not looking forward to all those steps."

"There's bypass magic on them," Datura said crisply. "We'll be there in a jiffy."

If bipeds banged at the secret door, we couldn't hear them. Couldn't detect any sound from above, either. We started up the stairs that spiraled around the tower walls. Our footsteps echoed like a cascade of falling rocks.

Our ascent was over after just ten vertigo-inducing steps. Each time I set foot on the next stair, I looked down (always a bad idea) and saw that I'd been vaulted a story higher. I gripped the banister like I was trying to throttle it.

The old flue pipes came to a premature end at the top of the corkscrew staircase, giving way to a platform mounted on metal connectors and braces. Cheap scaffolding wrapped all the way around the bottom of the great white egg.

We crossed the platform; the grating shook feverishly at every minor shift in weight. I clenched my jaw and made a good-faith effort not to hurl.

The smooth eggshell exterior of the colossal cockpit was completely uniform in every aspect, except for the fact that it had a door. Not a dilating door, or a retracting door, or a door jangling with fancy security. Just a boring old rectangle.

It was painted bright red, right down to the round twist-type knob. It could've been the front door of a city townhouse. But why make it garish red when the rest of the outer surface was—

Also red. Redder than arterial blood. A fair comparison, trust me: I considered myself something of an authority on spilt blood. We'd seen a lot today, and the crimson cockpit made it all seem like a dim faded memory. Why had I ever thought it was white?

Datura reached for the knob.

His hand jerked away as if he'd touched a burning stove.

Lear had put her gun to the back of his head.

He had nothing to fear except pain. He'd already been shot—and otherwise brutalized—multiple times in one day. His clothes were a mess, but beneath all the stains, he hadn't sustained a single lasting scratch. Hose him off, and he'd emerge with the clean skin of a child who had never been struck in his life.

The gun itself didn't mean much, anyway. Lear could deal out just as much damage with her limbsuit alone. She could twist his skull off like a bottle cap.

I'd slipped him my prosthesis, but truth be told, I didn't know how far it would go to protect him. Its halo of safety was really only supposed to apply to me. This was a whole different situation from Fanren taking idle potshots at my eye on a table.

Maybe Datura had guessed what it might do for him, and maybe he hadn't, but regardless, he hadn't found any time to pore over the contents of my pouch. He had his fist balled in a pocket, and his bravado had fled.

"Lear," I said. "Don't waste ammunition."

"Oh, I wouldn't consider it wasted."

"Save it for the real thing. We still have to get in the cockpit."

"You're real enough, aren't you?" she asked, grinding the gun harder into Datura's hair.

The door swung open, nearly bashing his nose. Wist loomed in the entrance like a wary homeowner.

"We meet again," Lear said brightly.

Wist looked unhurt. Physically speaking, that is. Magically—well, she'd hang in there.

A clacking sound issued from the unseen room at her back. She spared a brief, cool look for each of us: Lear, and the child being menaced by a magically augmented pistol—and me, lurking sheepishly behind them, empty-handed.

Last of all, her eyes traveled back to Lear's weapon. "Put that away," she said.

"Will you freeze me again if I don't?"

"You can't shoot," I said, urgent. "It'll go straight through. She's right there."

"Good point," Lear conceded. "Safety first."

As she spoke, she pointed the barrel down into the flesh where his neck met his shoulder.

She immediately pulled the trigger.

The magic-dampened blast socked me like a punch to the gut—more of a physical blow than an actual noise. Her gun hadn't jammed.

For a quarter of a second, time crawled as slowly as an ant. Datura sprang away with catlike speed.

That shot might have ricocheted off the floor. It might have hit any of us. But there was no sign of a bullet. A silvery substance reminiscent of vorpal mercury dripped from the muzzle in dense mucous strands, like Lear's gun had gotten gangrene. Her arms tensed as if she wanted to chuck it at the wall with all her might.

She didn't shout or throw things. After a cursory examination, she scraped the slime off on a grate and thrust her gun back in its holster.

"Had a feeling it wouldn't work, but I wanted to try," she said, unrepentant. "You don't plan on letting me in there, do you?"

This was directed at Wist. Datura, wholly unscathed, had taken shelter in the shadow of the open door.

Wist spoke low in her throat. She sounded sick, like she was holding back a cough. "I've taken control of every other person on the island—everyone not here at the nerve center. I sent them to the mouth of the bypass tunnel."

"The one that goes under the gulf?"

"The Ashtereth exit was blocked, but they're working to clear it. They'll be done soon enough."

"Wait," Lear said. "You mean all the villagers, lab workers, sanitation staff, Guild hunters, trespassers—"

"They're all there," Wist said levelly. "Everyone not already dead. That's why you have to leave."

Lear tapped her foot, making the grate shiver. She tugged at her earlobe. "You want me to lead an evacuation."

"Yes."

"Can't you send them away yourself?"

"Once they're off the island, they'll be outside my sphere of influence. They might grow confused in the middle of the tunnel, deep below the Natal Gulf. They might turn back."

Throughout this conversation, Lear—a self-proclaimed opportunist—had been casing the entrance for a way to break past Wist. That much was obvious.

With her supercharged limbsuit, perhaps she could have made it through the doorway. Even now, Wist was feeling her way around the metaphysical structure of Reverence, exploiting esoteric magic to simultaneously control hundreds of living bodies. It was a wonder that she'd been able to talk at all.

But the moment Lear charged in, that towheaded little boy by the door would glimpse her back. For all its speed and power, her suit wouldn't deter his vengeful inner bird. She'd suffer another set of mortal injuries before getting anywhere near her target. And Wist, too, might move to block her.

I cleared my throat and said: "If you've got any requests..."

She gave a short, bleak laugh. "No requests. Just a question. Tell me, Kraken, since you've looked behind the curtain—why him?"

Wist cocked her head.

"The entity. It gave him another chance at life. Why? Because he's a genius?"

"It wasn't a value judgment," said Wist. "On an individual level, it doesn't even know who he is."

Datura had gone inhumanly still. He stood very close to the threshold, his face tilted up to listen. I couldn't see his expression, and not just because of his mask.

"So it rescued him from the travails of old age without any real thought or premeditation," Lear said. "Like a cow swishing flies with its tail. Well, that's comforting."

People don't strike gold because they're deserving, I thought. They don't win wars because they're righteous.

Wist held her hand out as if offering a palmful of candy. Three tacks lay there, quiescent. One after another, they buzzed to life and started circling Lear's head.

"They'll guide you to the surface layer," Wist said. "There's an express elevator in the incineration plant."

I couldn't believe my ears. "We practically had to swim here! Why'd we take the long way?"

"The shorter route was littered with people," Datura snapped.

"Your employees, you mean."

"Saboteurs, too. If you wanted more fights—"

"All right," Lear said. "I'll go."

She gave her elongated earpiece a knowing tap. The three bee tacks alighted there like they'd discovered a spiky flower.

"If you open a portal to another dimension, our director will escape," she said. "Don't let him."

She retreated backwards down the stairs—gone from sight with a single step. Spectral echoes clanged far below.

For all his fuss beforehand, Datura didn't appear to be in much of a rush to enter the cockpit.

Wist still slouched in the door frame, blocking our path. If she were feeling ornery, she might port us right back to the biped-filled stadium.

"You could kick us out if you want," I acknowledged.

"You'll just take more drastic measures to be here."

"You had a job in mind for Lear. An important job, at that. What about me? Did you really expect me to sit around down there and wait?"

"Hope never dies," Wist said detachedly.

She stepped aside to let Datura in, taking care not to show him her back. The red door whooshed shut as soon as I followed him through.

37

It was considerably less cramped than my mental image of a cockpit. More like the bridge of a modest airship. Even so, this room occupied only a tiny fraction of that tremendous outer cocoon.

The illumination in the chute below had been colorless and unflattering. Here it shone with a warmth like the sun redirected through light tubes. The whole ceiling glowed, and the bright weight of it forced my gaze down. The white walls were shot through with an intricate relief of scarlet arteries. The pattern continued on the floor, thrusting up like branching roots.

"Cat got your tongue?" I said to Datura (the one who'd come in with us).

He shook his head, suddenly shy, and scampered over to the other side of the room. He stood up against the veiny wall like a sentinel. In these quarters, his blindfold made it impossible to tell which of us he was looking at.

Between us, an old man sat at an L-shaped desk. His chair was affixed to a set of sliding rails, like a captain's chair on a ship. Datura the younger had most definitely seen his back, but he'd gone past without attacking.

The chair swiveled. Its occupant wore a silk hair bonnet, loose checkered boxers, and not much else. His nose was topped off with a bulbous tip. He had light eyes, I think. A distinctly unmemorable hue. Patchy strands of silver hair grew (seemingly at random) from his chest.

First things first.

"Hey," I called to the boy. "You owe me."

"I could've taken any number of bullets," he said sulkily.

"The more you get hurt, the less you like it, and the more it hangs over you, and the more you avoid it. What saved you when you were about to get shot? Refresh my memory."

I looked straight at his eye mask until, lips pursing, he pulled my pouch out of his filthy clothes and threw it over. I jumped to retrieve it, two-handed. For once, my depth perception didn't betray me, although Wist would've caught it if I missed.

I shook my prosthesis out onto my palm, no worse for wear. I can't tell you how relieved I was to stick it back in my head. Just didn't feel right to leave the Void exposed for so long.

The old man said to the boy, in Jacian, "I ... you..." He frowned and tried once more. "*We* should have kept that. Quite an intriguing artifact."

"That's my eye," I said. "No thieving. Hello, Director."

"Hello, young lady." This, too, he said in Jacian. Oh.

I glanced from him to Wist. I'd thought she knew only a smattering of Jacian. Maybe (as was her wont) she'd been hiding how much she understood. Or maybe her newfound ability to tap into Reverence—a chalice created to enhance communication—made ordinary language barriers a bit less relevant.

"You already did your introductions?" I used simplified Jacian. My tongue felt clumsy, like it had forgotten how to form the right sounds.

"It was my great honor to meet the Kraken," said Datura the elder.

"Yeah, I'm sure she—"

"But that isn't her."

I reached out, and my fingers swiped through her as though I'd grabbed a cloud of smoke. Somewhere deep down, the Void laughed at me, rumbling like an underwater volcano.

Wist turned toward me, no longer shielding her back from Datura the younger. He didn't react. Then she was gone, collapsing with a near-silent *whump* into a meager pile of soot.

A lone bee tack vibrated apologetically in the empty space where she'd been standing.

The bare-chested old man spread his hands as if to say *See?*

"Where is she?"

I ought to get a medal for saying it quietly.

"On the fourth layer."

"The fou—oh, come on."

"It's the truth," he said. "Shall I send you there? I'm sorry that we don't have any proper chalice suits on hand. Mine's in the laundry. But Reverence was always meant to be user-friendly. No special clothing needed, really."

My brain had to work overtime to keep up with his dialogue. I'd been spoiled, I thought dismally, by Lear's Continental fluency.

I pointed at the little boy on the other side of the desk. "What about him?"

"I won't go," he said, sharp and high. "I won't go any further." He'd reverted to Jacian.

"This is your playground," I said. "What's the problem?"

"...I don't want it to look upon me."

"Be grateful—we must be grateful. It made us what we are." Datura the elder spoke like a chastening grandparent. Not at all like one man in two bodies.

I searched for a resemblance. Perhaps if they both smiled—but no, I couldn't see it. Too many years between them.

"Who's actually in control here?" I asked the man in the chair. "You? Your messiah? The Kraken?"

"As you can see, I'm still in the pilot seat," he said indulgently. He had his feet propped up on a built-in footrest. "Of course, I won't stop the Kraken from exploring. She doesn't need to rely on standard methods to interface with a chalice. And Reverence has fed very well over the past couple days. Very well indeed."

The only object on his desk was the most complex abacus I'd ever seen. Or numerous linked abaci: rows and rows of them, arrayed like an organ keyboard.

He ran his fingers over it lightly, lovingly, without actually moving any beads.

"You're in privileged company," he informed me. "Only one person has ever gone to the fourth layer and returned alive. You're looking at them right now."

"Oh, lovely," I said. "That's just great."

"Bring the Kraken back, if you can. Don't lose track of time." He flicked a single brown bead with his nail. "She'll be fine, I'm sure, but it would be a shame," he said meditatively—his voice had begun to fade—"if you lost your mind."

38

THE FOURTH LAYER felt like being shunted back through time. Morning light; the great outdoors; the cries of seagulls. Yet I couldn't see the ocean. Nor any modern buildings. No mechanical egg, whether floating or stationary. No tower in the distance.

Facts about my surroundings came to me with the certainty of dream logic, which required no justification. This was an imagined form of Ashtereth. I could walk this land for the rest of my life and never encounter other residents.

The sky was almost too blue, with a richness of color like an artist's replica. It added to the sense that this moment had already happened.

But that was an illusion.

I had to find Wist.

Forest-lined fields held a hodgepodge of slanted stones. From some angles, they were indigo; from others, pure black. Vorpal mercury trickled up through cracks in the ruins, unconcerned with gravity, glimmering silver and crimson. I couldn't spot a single other hint of red. No berries or cardinals, or early maple leaves.

The bee tack from the cockpit had followed me in. There were two of them, actually. They'd been so close together, practically overlapping, that I'd only seen one. Here, liberated, they spiraled in a giddy mating dance.

Someone coughed politely.

Again, a dreamlike lack of surprise. On my right—as if he'd been there all along—stood a middle-aged man in a lab coat. He had watery brown hair.

"Which one are you?" I asked.

"There's only one of me," he replied in Jacian. Suddenly I couldn't remember which language had come out of my own mouth. It could have been anything.

He was tan and outdoorsy, without the pallor of either his younger or older selves. He produced a lit cigarette from behind his back with a slight flourish, like a street magician, and started smoking.

I stared.

"One of the many reasons my health went downhill," he said pensively.

"You're still back in the pilot seat," I said.

"Yes."

"Is this your ... astral form?" I couldn't think of the right Jacian word for it.

"My spiritual form, you mean? Or my vorpal form?" he said curiously. "This is naught but a feeble projection of my will. A chalice can facilitate all kinds of astonishing feats if you don't force it to specialize in razing your enemies."

He gestured at the sky with his cigarette. "Well? What do you make of those?"

There had been nothing up there seconds ago.

Islands floated over our heads now: heavy dark shapes limned with greenery. They were too far away to discern many details. I saw the silhouette of a half-smashed water wheel. And that over there ... was that an upside-down ship? Multiple masts pointed at the ground—at us—like cannons.

"If I had an extra lifetime to play around with, I'd go back and become a conservationist," said Datura Gray. "Oh, did I already tell you? After that, if I got a third or fourth chance at life, I'd study the ancients.

"Even academics fall into the trap of acting like civilization started in the time of the Blessed Empire. Stuff and nonsense! What about the Cressians? What about these?" Another jab at the sky. "You look clueless, my child. That's no surprise. Continentalists care nothing for ancestral civilizations here in Jace.

"Ashtereth is the last remnant of a long tradition. Why, our ancestors did us one better—their landfills were huge floating barges made of trash. Long, long ago, when people marveled at our islands, which did they mean? The ones down here, or the ones up there?"

"Where's Wist?" I asked when he paused (for dramatic effect, if not for breath). "The Kraken, I mean. How do I find her?"

He didn't even blink. It was like he hadn't heard me at all.

Fine. I'd look for clues on my own.

I set off across the field of ruins. They cast long shadows: was it supposed to be morning here, or late afternoon? Small wildflowers coughed a haze of yellow pollen at my shoes. Taller plants grazed me with pinhead berries, hard and pale, like clustered moth eggs.

Datura followed, taking long drags on his cigarette, although somehow I never caught him moving his legs. My thumbtack companions came along, too, zipping jagged paths among clover.

My false eye bleated savagely. I sprang back, heart racing.

I'd almost put my foot down smack in the middle of a hidden bog.

The surface flashed as silver as vorpal mercury. I could've gotten dissolved to my bones, flesh sloughing off like loose clothes. No one else would look out for me: not Datura Gray, and not those bees.

On second glance, it was just water. Too deep, or too muddy, to see the bottom. Pudgy black finger-length shapes nosed about at the edge of the muck. Were leeches usually so obvious?

Daytime crickets rang out like sleigh bells. Other insects, less familiar, sawed away in a frenzy at my back. With each passing moment, their wheedling sounded closer and closer to that tenuous siren from the first layer, the maddening alarm that no one else had seemed to hear.

I'd been looking for something, but I couldn't remember what. In any event, it wasn't here.

I drew back from the water, patting my Jacian bag.

My hand stilled. This was the bag I'd used in Manglesea.

I'd left it at home on purpose. Osmanthian diplomats might call me unpatriotic for flaunting an accessory of Jacian make. There might've been questions about where I'd gotten it, and whether the bag itself had been compromised.

I held it out over the bog. Wist's bee tacks had been busy tormenting a dragonfly ten times their size, racing it across the water. When they saw what I was doing, they zoomed over and flew tight helixes around my arm.

Below, the submerged leeches stood on end like eager straws.

"Don't you want to see what's inside?" said Datura Gray.

The next thing I knew, I was on the move again, bag slung over my shoulder, feet eating up spongy ground. I couldn't recall deciding which way to walk, or why.

Strangling vines wound around spurs of rock that must originally have supported some greater structure. Now there was nothing left to hold up. In isolation, each standing stone had the quiet dignity of an intentional obelisk. The vines had lost the battle long ago, in any case. All were dead.

"Don't you want to see what's inside?" Datura said again, drifting beside me. His long lab coat never got dirty.

Important thoughts kept slipping away like a boat tipping over the edge of a waterfall. I clung tight to my last remaining fragment of incredulity. "How could you build a chalice like this?" I demanded. "How could you even imagine it?"

"I had hints," he said modestly. "Inspiration came at night and in daydreams, during long walks in nature, during baths. Perhaps it rose up from somewhere inside me. Or perhaps I had help."

The trash islands in the sky had changed position. Their shadows coasted across the land like ghostly boats.

My finger pointed up. "The first layer—you've got your office, your distilleries ... some oddities, but mostly practical stuff. The second layer—pretty weird, but maybe it works for field tests of your bipeds. I dunno. The third layer—okay, you want to keep the cockpit in a place that takes a little more effort to reach. Sure.

"But this—what's this for? If it's natural scenery you crave, your island is covered in it. What's the point of—"

He tsk-tsked at me like a disappointed mentor. "The Kraken works differently, no doubt, but for us, constructing new layers is more like baking than building a house."

"...Baking?" I said.

"Like developing a new recipe, except you really only get one shot. It's not as though I make drawings and tell my staff to put a tree here, and a rock there, and make sure the land lies just so. We might use references, yes, but there are always little surprises in the end."

That was an answer, all right. I had a feeling that my original question had been something quite different.

"Possession," he said.

"What?"

"Infiltration. Inhabitation. Occupation. Puppeteering. Your kind are called operators, yes? That'd be a good word to use for pilots, if only it weren't already taken."

One thing seemed certain: he wasn't here to help.

This man might be an echo. A construct parroting nonsense. Or the equivalent of a finger puppet. A doll getting waved around by a demiurge—a being hailing from some reality way past the outermost borders of human comprehension.

Or he might just be yet another avatar of Datura Gray.

Could the entity sense me? Could it make me its puppet, too? No strange voice had welled up in the back of my head. But if I were already being piloted like a miniature chalice, how would I stop it? And how would I know?

39

A SHORT DISTANCE away, the landscape shifted. The ruins lost height, sinking slowly into softened earth. A curved road of dead yellow grass ran between two endless rows of yew trees.

There was something menacingly mechanical about those trees. Corpulent mushrooms grew at their roots, purple-brown and white and dull maroon, as bulky as organs dissected from a cow.

My right eye twinged. Phantom pain? The prosthetic itself had no feeling. It better not—I'd been known to throw it like a rubber ball.

The sound of hard-driving rain filtered in from my blind spot. The type of rain that might dry up in just a few minutes. No matter how I turned my head, I couldn't see it. The sky was still that oversaturated blue.

Elsewhere, past the yew trees, water burbled even louder. A stream? I left the road and went to get a closer look.

"A birthing pool!" exclaimed Datura Gray. "How delightful."

"What's being birthed?" I said, followed by: "Eeeck."

Hundreds of mosquito larvae writhed in a shallow puddle. Minuscule brown threads; constant kinking motion. Forgive me—but if only they were longer, they'd have reminded me of Wist's branches curling in distress, inconsolable.

My bee tacks circled above the larvae like vultures.

Wist, I thought. The pangs in my false eye got worse.

I clutched my face. There was something useful I could do with that eye. Some sort of magic she'd lent me.

"Not *those* poor wretches." Datura stabbed the air with his cigarette, which had yet to grow any shorter. "Over there."

Larger shapes glided about a pool of silky mud. Lampreys? Eels?

One pulled itself up onto a shore of sodden rock and undulated, smearing mud every which way, like it was trying to write out a message.

It had the rings of an earthworm, but everything else seemed all wrong. An elephant trunk, perhaps. Not severed. Grown from scratch. Both ends opened and closed like soft toothless mouths. All it could do was flap and squelch.

Apropos of nothing, I knew what was causing that tug in my eye. It came to me with illogical certitude.

If I took it out, it would be as hard as ceramic. When I squeezed it into my socket, though, there were times when it seemed squishier. More accommodating. Fleshy enough to part with a scalpel.

Someone had sewn a seam across the surface of my prosthesis, as if stitching together a pair of rebellious lips. I felt it when the sutures shrank, pulling tighter, although I should have felt nothing.

How neglectful. A cut-and-dried case of medical malpractice. Look, someone had to get these out, and I wasn't about to ask Datura Gray.

The disembodied trunk kept contorting. Datura kept smoking, stinking up the air (which already reeked of standing water).

I took a rusty knife from my bag. Was it mine? No. Could I use it? Yes. It struck me as being the perfect tool for performing impromptu surgery on an artificial eye. In fact, I was fairly certain I'd done this all before.

"Mud forms flesh during the day, and sinks back down with the sun," said Datura. "Night holds other dangers. But night never comes here. The mud will rise again with no delay.

"I've bred marionettes of all shapes and sizes. I've spawned countless worms and amoebas. A homunculus that can regrow after you cut it in half—wouldn't that be the perfect sacrifice, or even the perfect pilot?

"No, it never quite worked. I'm still glad I made the effort. Sometimes it's the effort that matters. Formulating four separate layers of physical reality—that process, in and of itself, made us more receptive to...."

I stopped listening. I leaned over the mosquito puddle, trying to use it as a mirror. The larvae formed tight flat spirals, like microscopic ammonites, and stopped moving. The beached elephant trunk tied itself in a tortured ball, too.

The growing mist of cigarette smoke made my left eye sting and water.

I raised the knife to my right eye. I'd have to hunt to find those stitches. With the way things were going, it seemed liable to hurt. I had no anesthesia handy—the injector in my pocket would knock me out cold. And anyway, what would you use to anesthetize an artificial eye?

I dug the knife in.

My prosthesis wobbled. The rusty point slipped and just about stabbed me through the eyebrow. I'd sensed the pressure of it, but the sutures ached more. God, they pinched. I adjusted the angle of the blade and went in for another try. This was worse than piercing a grape with a fork.

The bee tacks veered over and launched a furious attack.

I yelped. I flailed. The old knife plummeted into the mud pool, never to be seen again. No matter how I beat at the tacks, it just made them angrier. It felt like getting swarmed by twenty bees, not two.

Datura didn't lift a finger to help. He gazed into the distance, sucking heartily on his cigarette.

Invisible stitches clenched at my tender fake eyeball. By the time those bees let up, I was absolutely convinced that I'd been pocked with hideous wounds from head to toe. I'd be dripping with blood. Scarred for life.

I ripped the useless bag off my shoulder, pitched it out of sight, and stomped back between the yew trees. The bee tacks followed, no longer assaulting me.

I frisked my face and neck and wrists and sides with growing disbelief. No visible pinpricks. Not even a spot of blood. They hadn't once broken skin.

My hands twitched around the remembered shape of that knife. The pulsing agony in my cornea smoothed out, all of a sudden, like a rope going slack.

Someone stood behind me. I whirled.

No one was there—not even Datura.

The empty road ran into a hollow filled with arched ruins. Not the same ruins as before. I couldn't return the way I'd come: the scenery kept remaking itself behind my back.

This whole island was a trap. This whole trip was a trap. Hadn't I always feared that? For every minute I frittered away here, wandering in circles, a day or a month or a year might pass on the surface.

Once more, something hooked the stitches in my prosthesis and pulled. Hard. I stumbled forward until it ceased.

I'd squeezed my left eye shut on reflex. My right eyelid stayed locked open, no longer responding.

The soft siren of hidden crickets kept keening away in the distance.

In occasional fuzzy-headed moments, I caught myself thinking of monocular vision as a natural part of aging. Like getting a sore neck from time to time. Something that might happen to anyone.

My prosthesis had never been designed to see much. It could distinguish between extremes of light and dark, and that was about it. With my left lid closed, I should've been essentially blind.

But I wasn't.

The sutures dragged at my fake cornea. The pressure increased until they snapped and came slithering painfully out, chopped-up strands thrashing like parasitic worms.

And, finally, I understood.

She had been there all along.

My good eye flew open. My voice caught in my throat. I immediately got seasick; I almost sat down in the dirt.

It was like the vertigo of borrowing someone else's glasses, only a thousand times worse. The scenery overlapped, blurring, misaligned.

I saw Wist with my right eye. I couldn't see her with my left.

40

I DIDN'T RUN to her. I fought to react with caution.

Keeping one eye open at a time, I glanced around. This Wist might be a hallucination, or a magical body double. Or Datura Gray in disguise.

Both eyes saw the same slanted yew tree at the end of the grassy road. Fungi spilled about its fissured base: an illustration of disembowelment. One pale specimen bore angry scorch marks from a fallen cigarette butt.

The cigarette hadn't shrunk at all while he puffed on it, but now it was barely the length of my fingernail.

When was the last time I'd sipped from Lear's canteen? Not after she'd drugged it ... for all I knew, though, maybe she'd added Tuner to our lunch packs, too.

I considered the apparition. Wist's hair had grown out in a sudden flood, long and white. When she turned her head, it gleamed black again, but only for the space of a breath.

Our bond lay as inert as an overfed snake. Yet for all my suspicion, I felt her there among the ruins, undeniable—*this* Wist, visible only with my prosthesis. I felt her like a heart palpitation in the string running between us, the sort of helpless wingbeat that makes you think: *Is this the big one? Am I about to keel over?*

I stepped closer, still hesitant. My inorganic right eye—alight with the pain of those ripped-out stitches—felt more alive and present than all the rest of me put together.

A cluster of flat-faced, almost featureless statues stared out from a squarish frame of rock. Their wide-set eyes were soulless indents. If I skirted around this installation, I'd be right there with Wist.

She moved sideways, briefly concealed by a jagged wall.

She wasn't alone, was she?

I stopped looking. I covered my face.

I peeped out through my left eye instead: remnants of a lost civilization, azure sky, black trees sprinkled like ink blots against pastoral green-gold turf. Long-legged flying insects, in no real hurry to go anywhere. And a fleet of sun-gilded rafts—conglomerations of hovering garbage.

"Wist," I said into emptiness. What a sour and demanding voice.

Her bee tacks swam a few woozy circles, then landed on my borrowed ear cuff.

I twisted off my stealth bracelet and threw it down in the grass. I switched to my right eye. I called her name again and again. She still couldn't hear me.

She was with a smaller woman. Short hair, mannish clothing, and a no-nonsense eyepatch. I only knew it wasn't me because I stood rooted here, watching.

I hadn't worn an eyepatch anywhere on Ashtereth. The woman with Wist had more muscle on her, like she wouldn't get bored shortly after starting any serious workout. We were otherwise identical.

My twin smiled up at Wist, arms around her waist. I felt a profound sympathy for anyone who had ever wanted to punch me in the face.

I lurched around the ruined wall, attempting to shout, to scare them apart. My voice came out weak and scratchy.

However much I lunged, they never seemed close enough to touch. They were a little further to the right, or to the left. Closer to the wall. No, closer to that crooked tree. I staggered to a halt, lungs heaving. A mere minute of this had rubbed my throat raw. Wist was still oblivious.

My twin looked over at me. Her smile turned thoughtful. She ran her hands up Wist's sides, possessive, shaping her like clay. Wist let her do it, eyes cast down with an expression that most would have seen as foreboding. On her, that was a look of languid indulgence. *Toy with me all you like*, it said. *Have your fun. I don't mind.*

Wist was real, and her companion was fake. This lodged itself in my body as settled fact. My copy was a high-fidelity reproduction, every bit as sophisticated as the artificial eye in my face. But couldn't we both be decoys, imitations of some other Clematis? Fear grew in me like a stomachache.

That smirking woman made a show of sniffing Wist's hair.

When she tired of taunting me, she reached for her eyepatch. She began to lift it like Datura the younger with his blindfold.

I knew only one way to fend her off. I tore the false eye right out of my socket and cupped it in my hand like a newborn animal, something feeble I couldn't care for, wet and exposed. The Void radiated scorn.

I couldn't think of how to prove that I wasn't the impostor, the human prosthesis. I sank down against the sheltering blue-black wall, head in my arms, as if doing a bomb drill.

I'd stood outside myself before. I'd watched myself with Wist. But this had to be different—she wouldn't tinker with time like that again. We hadn't even paid the price for what we'd done to secure the Void.

Thoughts began to leap out at me, faster and faster. They came to me in my own voice, but they weren't entirely mine.

No other mage could possibly twist time around like Wist had in Bittercress. All right, then. Look beyond the walls of our world. Look at where the seams might start to burst.

Maybe there were more worlds out there, beyond vorpal holes aplenty, than we could ever learn to imagine. And other types of power, terrible and implacable. They might not belong here, but that didn't mean we could stop them from coming.

Humanity, with all its collective knowledge, couldn't even prevent vorpal beasts from slipping through gaps in reality like an invasive species hitching a ride on a boat. There were just too many holes to plug.

What if Wist wasn't the only being out there capable of breaking the first Kraken's taboos? What if there were others—gods, angels, alien monsters—and what if they weren't remotely concerned about the repercussions?

Had Datura's patron cured his terminal illness, or had he already been dead? Had the creature brought him back? The boy in the eye mask—was that really a shared second body, or a whole new individual carved in Datura's image? Had we walked into a modern-day creation myth?

Panic constricted me, suffocated me, with the muscularity of a snake. Soon my bones would pop and crack like dry twigs. Soon my veins would burst.

If our enemy were a human mage, I could twist their branches till they stopped. I could force-feed them unspeakable pain, or hold their power like a pair of reins. I'd make them heel.

But this chalice around us was an edifice of magic without any single human author. Datura Gray had contributed exactly none of it: he wasn't a mage himself. More of a philosophical architect, or a conductor. He'd overseen the fusion of god knows how many cuttings from god knows how many providers.

Perhaps he'd also sealed a spare worker or two behind the walls of the cockpit, like servants getting buried alive to mourn an empress.

The eye in my hand stared bleakly up as if wondering why I'd removed it. It felt unyielding and glassy. Smooth all over. Impossible to pierce with stitches.

Wist and I were in this same place. I'd seen her by the broken wall. A membrane separated us—hair-thin, and yet insurmountable—as if we'd wandered onto different layers.

Were we being kept apart by the chalice itself, or by the will of the pilot? Or could his beloved entity have done this? My duplicate might be a shadow puppet dancing to its tune.

And that very thought might be something the creature had seeded in my head.

Both eye sockets, full and empty, felt like squeezed limes—no juice left. My prosthesis was grimy with sweat and tears and dust and pollen and fingerprints. I should've hesitated more before screwing it back in.

But Wist had slapped enough magic on it to keep me from getting a flesh-eating infection. It was too late to care, anyway. I'd hacked away at this same eye with a rusty knife.

Two sets of ankles came into view. Wist and my rival. I blinked grittily, with swollen lids. I didn't raise my gaze any higher. I didn't know the rules of this game, but it'd be a bad idea to look beneath that eyepatch.

I poked at my earpiece, nudging the bees into flight. They stayed close by my face. There had been a time when the slightest streak of motion near eye level would've made me startle, pulse racing, sweat seeping up through chilled skin. I'd gotten better about it, but not this good. I was just too deadened to flinch.

Would it help to make a sacrifice? I'd happily cut the heart out of my twin, but I'd never get close enough to try.

I clapped my hands around the slower of the two tacks. It didn't fight to escape. If I ground my palms together until the point drew blood, how much would come out—two drops? If it failed to do anything except energize my little friend, I'd have to start looking for sharp-edged stones or fallen branches.

Wist's feet moved. Two steps, then three. Close enough to walk through me. My right eye pinched shut before I saw it happen.

Only my left eye stayed open. I couldn't see my clone crouching down to look me in the face. I couldn't see where Wist had gone.

But I sensed her. Not her touch. Her magic, the whole sprawling tangle of it, close enough that she must've been pressed right up against my back. The Void leaned longingly toward her, trying to leak out through the base of my skull, looking for cracks to exploit. It wanted to smother her light and swallow down her searing core. The Void couldn't lie.

I opened my palm. A living bumblebee would have been crushed, but the tack lay there unharmed. I could've sworn that the short silver stud had punctured me as deep as it could go, but in truth, I'd barely scratched myself. What an embarrassment.

The tack lifted off and wafted over to place its pin against my earlobe. Its partner buzzed around the back of my head and gently touched my other ear in the same spot, where I'd never been pierced.

I reached back and, with sustained effort, made Wist's magic waver like a blown candle. That was when it dawned on me that her hands were on my shoulders. Her magic held each tack in place like a medical needle. She was there without body heat, without breath. She was there in the round throbbing bone of my right eye, in how the Void crashed against its shore in starving waves.

A trace of cold magic ran along the rims of my ears like fingers feeling a familiar shape in darkness. Hot blood beat its way up to the surface of my skin to greet her.

There are ways to communicate without an active mental link, and without coherent words. She knew me well enough to know what I'd want:

Do whatever it takes.

The tacks pushed through my earlobes with minimal resistance. It didn't feel like getting stabbed. Just a quick spike of pressure, and an answering pop of relief—of magical yielding—deep inside my head.

My knees were damp from well-watered earth and crushed clover. The smell of the ocean blew in, then gusted away. The wailing of foreign insects rose and fell.

I searched for my double's footprints, my double's pacing legs, but my prosthetic had gone dim. My sight was one-eyed again, and I'd never been gladder. I started to crawl forward. Wist reached from behind and pulled me back.

41

I DON'T QUITE recall slamming her down on her back, but I must have done something of the sort. If the ruins weren't sunk in silt, I might've cracked her head on a flagstone.

Wist listened tolerantly, that Queen-white hair fanned out beneath her, as I choked back a firehose of foul language.

She had no idea what I meant when I babbled about my evil twin.

"I couldn't see you," she said. "But I could smell you."

"What, do I stink?"

"Not to me."

I, for one, would gladly have buried my face in her sweaty cast-offs any day of the week. I was just too polite to mention this in mixed company.

I flopped forward onto her armored chest. "The fake me was wearing an eyepatch," I said.

"I never saw you with an eyepatch."

"Then what were you mooning over, huh? Don't tell me you were staring lovingly into empty space."

"I could hear you," she said. "Not your voice. Your footsteps. Like an animal crashing around in the woods."

"Oh, thanks."

"I knew it was you."

My other thoughts burst and scattered. Never mind all that rib-jabbing gear: for a few precious seconds, I lay flat and gave her all my weight.

"Is it listening?" I asked the side of her neck.

"We don't have to watch our words," she said, just as quietly. Which wasn't a no.

I reluctantly sat up and eased off her. The bee tacks were still stuck through my earlobes. No buzzing.

"These better not get infected," I said, pointing.

I'd never been interested in getting my ears pierced. A little too girly for my taste, I'd thought. Even though I appreciated earrings on others, regardless of gender—and I especially liked them on Wist.

Not much of a sacrifice, in other words. I didn't understand what about it had worked.

Wist ran her hand partway through her hair. It shook itself out without further assistance, curtaining the sides of her face. "The creature is fond of repetition," she said plainly.

Back in Bittercress, she'd temporarily turned her own earring holes into minuscule vorpal rifts. This time, she'd pierced my virgin ears with physical needles. More of a slanted rhyme than a reenactment.

"So—it wants a remix?" I guessed. "A fugue?"

"Reverberations across time," she replied. "It finds the echoes pleasing. It doesn't want anything in particular, except a wider window to slither through."

"Something different from a plain old vorpal hole?"

"It would have to be, if Lear is right about the director planning to use it for his own escape."

Of course he would. What else was left for him in Jace—in this whole world—other than a violent life as a two-bodied fugitive?

Each successive sentence came out of Wist with greater reluctance. "The thing that saved him doesn't experience pain, or hope, or any other shade of individual emotion. It communicates, but it doesn't speak."

"It's like the Void, then."

"The Void is more of an absence. This is a presence. It doesn't *feel*. It's too large for that. If it felt anything, it would feel caged."

Her lips were still purple from Tuner. I made her open her mouth and show me her tongue—also a deep blueberry hue.

"Any side effects?" I said, newly anxious.

"It helped," she said. "It helped a great deal."

I studied her for an extended moment, then—acting on instinct— pushed her hair back.

Smears of half-dried blood trailed from her ears to the edge of her turtleneck. The flow must have been sludge-like in its richness, much thicker than tear tracks.

Her gaze didn't waver. "It would have been worse without the drug. Remember how I reacted when Reverence first came by?"

I managed not to say anything overly biting. "Is the director right about your tower being a type of chalice?"

He'd phrased it as if she were an outsider artist, a clueless savant. Was she conscious of the purpose her tower served? Or had it always been more like ants constructing an anthill? Like scratching an itch?

She gave me a slightly injured look as these questions poured out. "Why ants? The director compared me to a bird with a nest."

"Fine, be a bird. Do you feel like a bird?"

"I don't know how birds feel."

"Oh, for—"

"You didn't summon me." Her fingers skirted my brow, then my right temple, lightly accusing. "After all that work to refine it...."

Her magic held my right eye—still in its socket—like a fist.

The most powerful function of my prosthesis was one I hardly ever relied on. I took pride in not needing it. But I could, under dire circumstances, force-port Wist from wherever she was in the world. She'd be with me in an instant.

I'd had occasion to use that function on Ashtereth, but I hadn't thought of it. Not once.

Wist's voice dropped. "You picked the best protections out of your eye."

I shrank. "I didn't..."

The rusty knife. Phantom sutures. Threads of power stitched through the cornea of my prosthesis.

Threads that, on reflection, were a whole lot like magic cuttings, weren't they?

Something had made them squirm and pull and pain me. I had no recollection of scratching them out myself; my inept bladework had ended in failure. But I could've done it. In this strange nonexistent place, I could've done it with my own desperate nails.

"I wasn't in my right mind," I confessed. Wist helped me up onto wobbly legs.

The sky islands had begun to aggregate, blocking the sun.

If my sneering mirror image had been a beast from the same genus as Datura the younger, Wist would have perceived her, too. A paranoid delusion, then, or a dream woven by Datura's friend.

"How dangerous does this presence seem?" I asked.

Her answer came at once. "No one else can be allowed to access Reverence."

"We can't take a whole island home with us. I mean, we *can*, but..." That would be an act of war. And where would we put it?

Wist felt my wrist, as if questioning why I'd discarded my stealth bracelet. I hadn't bothered to retrieve it.

I thought out loud. "The entire island is part of Reverence. We've got to make it unusable, and impossible to reconstruct. We can't just sink it ... we'll have to destroy the whole thing." In some ways, that might be the easy part. "But we can't wreak havoc with evacuees still halfway down the tunnel."

"They're starting to pass beyond the island's reach."

"Then it's almost over, isn't it?"

"There are a lot of people," Wist said. "There's only one of Lear. It's longer than most tunnels with the same type of magic, and the magic on this one is better suited for cargo. Some of them are bound to get sick."

Poor Lear. I cringed at the prospect of herding around vomiting villagers and scientists and children and staff. Well, whatever happened, she'd call for backup as soon as she got a sufficient distance away. Speaking with us would be a different matter: we were still swaddled in comms interference.

I asked Wist if she could open a vorpal hole.

"I'll borrow one."

The instant she said it (with a faint air of satisfaction), a hole gaped before us. Inside me, the Void stiffened. It was as though she'd pricked reality like the skin of a balloon.

I wondered if she'd altered its position elsewhere, too, or just here. The layers didn't have to physically align, after all.

That's the one from the outhouse, I said.

Yes. Just one syllable, and her voice filled me anew.

My throat bobbed. There was so much more I wanted to say. Some things could slip out more fluently when I didn't have to open my mouth or hear my own words. But we really had to get going.

I treated Lear's earpiece like an antenna, tilting my head in crazy directions until Wist reached out and awakened it with a single poke.

"Lear?" I said.

Her voice emerged with perfect fidelity. "We're still in the tunnel."

"How much longer?"

"Ten minutes—I hope. Just a guess. Don't hold me to it." She broke off and shouted in Jacian like a drill sergeant, ordering someone to keep moving.

"Listen," I said. "The chalice is unstable. I think it's gonna blow."

"Like a volcano?" she said distractedly.

"More like … a star collapsing." I floundered ahead despite my ignorance of astronomy. "A black hole. Nothing left to salvage."

"Oh. So I should dissuade anyone who meets me at the other end and thinks maybe it's time to send in the army."

"That's the idea."

"You'll be on your own if the island implodes."

"We'll live," I said recklessly. "Look—when you get debriefed, don't mention the kid. Keep things simple."

Incoherent yelling swelled in the background. Lear uttered a single piquant word.

"The evacuation—" I began.

"I'll let you know," she said hastily. "Later."

I called out again, but she was already gone.

42

Fresh blood oozed sluggishly from Wist's ears, despite her furtive attempts to hide it. The purplish tinge to her lips didn't appear to be just from Tuner, either. Her magic looked even worse: some branches had developed split ends.

I'd abandoned the notion of getting Datura Gray to open an escape hatch. He'd expect the Kraken to return from the final layer on her own. He'd consider it a test of her savvy.

I worked hurriedly to tease out the tangles in her magic. "How do we even get out of here?"

"A dialogue with the creature," Wist said. "A series of trials."

"No way in hell." The last thing she needed was further exposure to Datura's entity. "You can't port?"

"Within the same layer, yes. Across layers—there might be complications."

Well, that tracked. Datura had been very particular about using established channels. I used my last wad of tissue to soak up some of the blood from her ears. The flow was getting thicker, and—this was new—it gave off an incongruously floral scent. Sweet and poisonous.

"Only one other option," Wist said.

We both looked at the vorpal hole.

I spoke first. "We never actually tested if—"

"It's doable. It'll be simpler than traveling to another world altogether."

Her arm came around my neck. I wished she'd tighten it; I wished she would choke me. No need to face your fears when you've passed out from lack of oxygen. The one flaw marring this otherwise delightful strategy was that the Void wouldn't lose consciousness with me.

The Void had fed on her—deeply and thoroughly— before we left Osmanthus. We didn't want it acting up in Jace. But vorpal holes had always spooked it. Even now, after months of desensitization, apprehension glued it (and me) in place.

Those shrieking insects had begun to sound like raspy summer cicadas, as if time were leaking backwards.

Then again, there was no reason it couldn't be summer here, or a heatless facsimile.

"Originally," Wist said, "this was your idea."

"I talk big."

"And I listen."

Unlike some people—me foremost among them—Wist had never been one to overpromise and underdeliver. If she thought she could usher us through a vorpal hole in one piece, together, who was I to doubt her?

I clamped down on the Void (for all the good it would do) and closed my eyes. Wist shuffled me forward, gentle but firm. A soundless thrum went through our bond.

Don't do anything, I prayed to the Void. Just this once, don't lash out. She's already bleeding. She'll feed you for many more years if you don't ruin her now.

Usually I knew better than to negotiate with mindless forces of darkness. I had to occupy my brain somehow, though, or my body would've started a campaign of fruitless resistance. Wist already had enough weight to carry.

Nothingness engulfed us. There was no hunger in it. Just a total vacuum of sound, temperature, gravity, soil. There was nothing beneath our feet, and we failed to fall.

In the utter absence of other magic, Wist's core and branches deafened my perception. She blazed like an entire night's worth of fireworks set free all at once.

It ended after a measure of time too brief to define. The Void in me had frozen over like a glacier. My throat had closed too tight for gasping.

Once again, we stood on the uneven floor of the cockpit. The same vorpal hole had spawned behind us, just in front of the wall. No, I didn't look back. I could feel it there—in the pressure that bore down on my skull, in the way the Void cracked and thawed and shuddered. As for me, it was all I could do just to breathe shallowly and strain to see.

"Welcome back!" said Datura the elder, spinning in his chair. He seemed genuinely pleased. "Just look at you—how creative! Never thought I'd see humans step through a vorpal hole like beasts."

Wist slid me a questioning look.

"I don't..." Took me a second to figure out which language I ought to use with her. "Don't feel quite up to translating. Yet. Give me a moment..." I couldn't even be sure I'd heard him correctly. Maybe my mind was inventing fake Jacian to fill in the gaps.

He toyed noisily with his elaborate abacus, then said in accentless Continental: "How about this?"

Datura the younger had already demonstrated the same capability. Yet—somehow—it was much more impressive coming from a full-grown human adult. My mouth hung open.

He swelled with pride. "With a chalice that specializes in communication—"

"Right, okay," I said, recovering.

The boy against the opposite wall looked even whiter than before.

"Well," Datura the elder said chummily, "what did you think?"

He'd left his back wide open, but his younger self couldn't (or wouldn't) pounce at him. Guess that would be a form of suicide.

"This presence on the other side," Wist said. "It has no concept of debt. If you saved a worm, would you expect repayment?"

His eyes twinkled. "I'm a rather intelligent worm. I know what I was given. I'll pay my debts, or die trying. Which would be a better ending?"

He kept manipulating the abacus. He might have been sliding beads around at random, just enjoying the sound of it.

There were brown cigarette butts caught in the rails below his chair. Did he eat or drink in here, or bathe himself, or did the chalice do it all for him?

"That thing in your pocket," he said to me.

I pretended to be hard of hearing. "Hm? What?"

"Just a piece of advice." His tone remained avuncular. "This isn't a situation you can resolve by killing me, I'm afraid. Quite the opposite. The dominoes are already set to topple. Your Kraken is conversing with a mind that, I assure you, will keep her throughly preoccupied. Don't expect her to come riding to the rescue—not even from a mere three feet away."

He chuckled as if he'd told a real knee-slapper. I almost spun around to glare at Wist. She caught my shoulders, sparing me from getting gored by a long-necked bird.

It's been talking to you? I said. *All this time?*

She chose her words with care. *I wouldn't characterize it as talking, per se...*

"Thanks for the warning," I said to the man in the chair.

And to Wist: *The moment we hear from Lear, you need to close every single vorpal hole anywhere within range of the island. All the way up to the pylons, if not further. Check local airspace, too.*

I will.

Can you do it fast enough? I demanded. *Without killing yourself?*

I will, she said again.

I could still smell the sap-thick sweetness of her blood. Had Tuner made her reckless? Maybe—but I had to trust her. There was a time to undermine each other with intricate little schemes, and a time to just hold on and have faith.

Datura Gray spoke in a voice devoid of surprise. "I have a feeling," he said, "that you aren't planning to assist me with opening a window. Well, no matter. It was always worth a try. Bear witness, then, to the turning of history."

"Wait," I said. "You need Wi—you need the Kraken to do it for you! That's the entire reason you—"

"I would obviously have preferred to live," he said pleasantly, "but we can't always get what we want. While you frolicked on the fourth layer, I started the sequence. It's already in motion."

I didn't believe him. "Whatever you mean by a window—you're talking about a proper passage to another world. Like hacking open a vorpal hole, except a million times more complex.

"Regular mages can't even open regular vorpal holes. And you're not even a mage! You think you can sit here and operate your chalice like a magical forklift, and we won't lift a finger to stop you?"

"You won't. Think of how Reverence might object to interruptions.

Think of all the civilians. Evacuations take time. That being said ... another world?" His brow furrowed. "My child, you sound confused."

"I sound confused," I said. "*I* sound confused? You're senile, you old creep!"

Insults made no mark on him. "The voice that saved me never came from another world. I wouldn't have said that. Another world? Perish the thought. It's over on another continent."

"Another continent," I said huskily. "...Where?"

"Can't you guess?"

"Beyond the western seas?"

"But of course."

You knew, I said to Wist. *At the very least, you suspected.*

The bee tacks pierced through my ears shifted, just a smidge, as though twisting in guilt.

My stomach plummeted. *It's already here with us. Just an ocean away.*

Did it even matter what we did or didn't do with Reverence and Ashtereth and Datura Gray? Just the palest echo of that voice had made Wist hemorrhage from her face. She hadn't been safe even in the sanctum of her own tower.

No. We'd make it matter. We'd stick to our plan.

The beast was closer than I'd thought. All the same, something had kept it from crawling across those western seas. Datura had constructed an island-sized chalice in an effort to summon it, and he still hadn't succeeded. Eliminate Reverence, and his idol wouldn't show up on local shores. Not anytime soon.

How many minutes had passed since we last spoke to Lear? Not enough—the earpiece was still stubbornly silent.

Datura rotated his chair back around and beckoned to the boy. "Don't just stand there. You know what to do."

The boy shook his head.

"You're me," said the old man. "And I'm willing."

The boy's face pulled in several conflicting directions. At last it settled into a rictus of a smile. Pink pus-like tears seeped from the lower edge of his eye mask. Not quite water, and not quite blood.

"Yes," he said in soft soprano tones. "Yes."

I asked what the man was going to do with him.

"A final sacrifice. The eventual fate of all pilots."

"You said—*he* said he wouldn't be a suitable sacrifice."

Datura the elder chuckled. "Wishful thinking, or just a childish lie. No, I know—we must have been joking. It's been a long time coming, really." He patted his knees. "Would you prefer my lap," he asked the boy, "or the back of the chair? Your choice."

Datura the younger picked his way around the abacus-covered desk. He didn't look at me or Wist. His blindfolded face swiveled from the artery-laden floor to the captain-style chair.

He didn't sit on the old man's waiting lap. I wouldn't have, either.

"He's young," I said.

"You should know better than to judge by appearances."

"He isn't just you in a separate body." I had to stall for time; this was as good a chance as any. "Maybe he was at first—maybe you had equal parts of yourself poured out in each vessel—and maybe you used one body like your right hand and the other like your left. But your human self has been rotting away in this pilot seat for how long now? You left your boy outside to cope on his own. You made him do your dirty work. He's just a year old. He wants to live. You've grown apart."

"If you pity him so," said Datura the Elder, "then get your Kraken to help me open this window. That would spare him. Me. Us."

Did I pity him?

Datura the elder fussed with his extravagant abaci. Datura the younger stood facing us, right up against the back of the chair.

Veins sprouted from cushiony fake leather and shiny metal. They lashed him in place, jerking his arms back until he resembled a figurehead on the prow of a ship. They burrowed under his sleeves and his skin like a thicket of floss-thin IV drips. He let it happen—docile, head lolling.

More invasive roots latched onto the side of his neck. They twisted into a rope and probed both ears. They wrapped around his eye mask, binding it tighter. Then they wormed beneath the fabric. Fresh liquid licked its way down the yellow-pink pus-tracks on his cheeks. He made no sound.

Abacus beads clacked briskly away in the background.

I thought of the egret he kept tucked in his gullet. His boyish face had split open like a disposable mask. Would I have felt equally conflicted if he'd appeared in the guise of a naked biped, eight feet tall, with a color-changing epidermis?

I pictured the flattened husks of dead strangers stacked like dirty clothing on the second layer. Maybe he really hadn't meant to do it. But he'd known enough about this world to hide them.

"We won't die just yet." Datura the elder took a break from playing with his beads. "You can take a lot of damage," he added encouragingly to the boy strapped down behind him. "It's a very big window. It needs time to creak open."

"Done," Lear said in my ear.

It's over, I told Wist.

43

I THREW MYSELF at the man in the pilot seat. I was inanely glad that he only wore boxers—the less fabric in the way, the better. I aimed Lear's autoinjector at a pale flash of upper leg.

He saw me coming from the corner of his eye. He rolled his chair on its rails to escape.

I got the injector in him, but my fingers slipped off as the chair—and his thigh—went rattling out of reach like a runaway shopping cart.

Of course, the rails were of limited length. He could only slide so far.

He didn't instantly lose consciousness. No matter. I was burning with adrenaline and ready for a fight.

I would never dream of trying to take on a soldier—or, frankly, any physically able person over the age of fourteen. But a nearly eighty-year-old man, with sedentary habits, who had previously been ravaged by one or more incurable diseases ... for once in my life, there was no doubt that I could beat the crap out of this guy.

I dashed at him, and I tripped spectacularly on the vein-encrusted floor. Not only that: in tripping, I overshot him. I fell flat on my face—

Right in front of the living figurehead strapped to the opposite side of his seat.

I bounced up off the ground. But Datura the younger—head hanging, resigned, being eaten alive by shiny red tendrils of Reverence—had already gotten a blindfolded eyeful of my back.

I flung myself away, bruising my kidney on a far corner of the L-shaped desk. I went careening into the wall beyond as if he'd thrown me.

The egret had already erupted from his face.

I was still alive for two reasons.

One: he hadn't broken away from that torture machine of a chair. Even as the white bird neck extruded itself from his straining mouth, the rest of his body remained trussed up, as passive as a chicken prepared for roasting.

Two: Wist had flung a magical barrier between me and the egret. She had much more important things to do, but she'd saved my life (again).

Her body remained still. The rest of her was frantically attempting to cinch shut every vorpal hole anywhere on or near the island. Including those we hadn't seen in person, right down to pore-sized specks in the sky. And including the one she'd plopped here in the cockpit.

I would've looked to see if it had gotten any smaller, but the egret was ramming its head madly against the sheer prismatic sheet of magic about a foot away from my nose.

Its neck had extended much, much longer than when it went after Lear. As long and thick as a python. It could've tied itself in knots.

I was petrified, clinging to the vein-textured wall. Wist's barrier actually shook, buckling, when the egret struck it.

Another blow, and the long stabbing beak shattered. Black shrapnel wedged itself in Wist's magic, midair, like bullets in reinforced glass.

The egret screamed. I covered my ears.

Rather than beat its head to a pulp on the barricade, it pulled back. It swayed dizzily.

Then it sprang at Wist, neck unspooling. I waited for her to throw up another unbreakable blockade.

She didn't.

The egret slashed from side to side across her ribs, shredding all those elaborate layers of protective clothing. The broken edge of its beak flung her blood like a frenzied paintbrush.

I couldn't believe her. If she could shield me, she had no conceivable excuse—none!—for neglecting to shield herself.

The egret went in for another rabid swipe. It was louder than me wailing at her: it sang two notes at once, one deep and guttural, one shrill as a whistle.

Its movements slowed. Its shrieks petered out. Its head drooped— streaming red with Wist's blood, bright red right up to the rims of its eyes. It retreated, hanging low over the floor, neck hunching and bumping like an unwieldy garden hose instead of retracting smoothly back inside the boy.

Wist had a hand on the wet dark opening cut across her torso, holding it together. She didn't let out a single peep of discomfort. But that didn't mean she wasn't in pain.

The barrier walling me off had begun to melt away like mist.

Pink-white foam fizzed from the egret's mangled beak. The boy had split apart down to his shoulders, the bird swelling thickly out of him as if to discard him like a costume. But it hadn't been able to fully skin itself. The cracked-open halves of his jaw dangled around his chest and back, as bloodless as broken doll parts.

The vorpal hole in the cockpit had shrunk to half its original size.

Whatever the chalice was doing to Wist on the inside, it wasn't pretty.

Nor was the wound on her abdomen, carved cruelly with that splintered beak.

But she'd planned for this. She'd brewed that sweet curdled blood all on her own.

The egret was dazed and gurgling, but not quite dead. It wrapped the excess coils of its neck around the back of the chair, around its own mutilated human body. Like a living feather boa, mostly white, slow with confusion. It didn't seem understand where its human head had disappeared to.

Datura the elder had risen shakily from his chair. Those sedatives were taking way too long to kick in.

I edged closer. I kept a wary eye on the egret, but it just kept foaming at the mouth, keening wetly, cradling the remnants of the boy.

Datura Gray, still mobile, braced himself on the edge of his desk. He appeared utterly focused. He didn't glance my way. No flowery speeches, either. He pried at a fastened-down abacus. It broke free with a crack of wood. I stared: where was all this strength coming from?

He bashed the abacus against its brethren. Beads went flying. He pulled up another and snapped it over his knee—then, with zero warning, turned and flung it at me.

I ducked. It hit the wall. Brown beads scattered across the floor like an epidemic of marbles, pooling in the forks of protruding veins.

He slumped into his chair again, wheezing, white flecks all around the edge of his mouth. He waved a hand in my direction as if to tell a bartender that he was done for the night. Time for one final bill.

He scooted the chair forward, weakly, and pulled open a drawer. His hand emerged holding an open box of cigarettes—but he held it upside down, and they all came cascading down around his ankles. He eyed the heaps of unused cigarettes as if they had fallen somewhere impossibly distant.

I stole a glance at Wist. She leaned on the back wall, eyes closed, arms covering her bleeding stomach. The vorpal hole beside her was now just a wrinkled line in the air, a sutured wound.

Datura Gray reached up and tore the silken bonnet from his head. The hair beneath was wispy, though not completely gone. He crumpled the bonnet to his bare chest: extra padding for his heaving heart.

I grabbed a handful of abacus beads off the floor and shoved them in my pocket. I hurtled over to Wist just as the vorpal hole sewed shut without a trace, without a scar.

44

WE WERE IN a night sky with three matching moons. Wist's magic had borne us up as high as an airship.

It should've been a great locale for stargazing. The research base was mostly underground. The villagers would go to bed early. The wilderness and the surrounding sea would be as dark as anything.

But this was a pasted-on darkness, a backdrop for the third layer alone. With all the focus on those moons, no one had bothered to spackle the sky with the kind of stars we used to see from Guralta.

Viewed from above, the top of Reverence's control unit resembled yet another moon. A fallen one. A white circle about the size of a coin.

The air up here was breathtakingly clean. Especially after the carnage in the cockpit. The bee tacks in my ears must've been freezing, but I couldn't feel them. Wist held me close, promising not to bleed all over my back.

"Bleed wherever you want," I said. "Just stay conscious."

There was a tremor in my jaw. I couldn't blame it wholly on the cold.

I'd been worried, at first, that I wouldn't be able to see well enough to get anything done. But my physical vision didn't much matter.

I took one of Wist's hands and moved it to cover my left eye, like Datura the younger with his blindfold. My magic perception sensed the chalice built all through the island like fungal mycelium, a shining network denser than an urban nightscape. Our aerial perspective made it legible, like trick art viewed from a different angle.

The Void could sense the whole of it, too.

"Hold up," I said. Time for an infusion of last-minute panic. "What if this whole layer collapses while we're on it?"

"It will. It'll crumple and vanish—"

"But what about us?"

"We'll stay here as the layers drain away. I'll hold us steady."

There was a hitch of pain in her voice.

I still thought she should've just encased the bird-boy in a coffin of magical barriers and let him have at it. He might've fought his cage until there was nothing left but gore and feathers, at which point he'd regenerate and do it all over again, but by then it wouldn't matter. Any extra misery incurred along the way—well, it would all wash out in the end.

Wist thought differently. Despite being otherwise occupied, she'd contained him more humanely, with only a negligible percent of her full attention. She'd transmuted her own blood into a substance capable of subduing a vorpal hybrid.

It amazed me, still, that my moral lassitude had yet to completely corrupt her. But that didn't mean I had to endorse her methods. Martyring yourself as a last-ditch solution to every untenable situation: why, that's just another form of laziness.

I couldn't be too hard on her, though, and not just because she'd deliberately incurred mortal injuries for the second time in one day.

(Was it really just the second time? You know you're in trouble when you start to lose count.) She'd fended off the egret—and saved my skin—with minimal magical effort.

Meanwhile, she'd simultaneously sealed every last hole on or around the island. She'd had to do that because of me. Because of the Void. It had become remarkably tractable around vorpal holes, at least compared to before, but I can promise you that it would never willingly swallow one.

I tipped my head back and fished out my prosthetic. This took longer than it should have; my fingertips were numb.

"Don't drop it," Wist said.

"You hold it, then."

She lifted her hand off my face to take it. An icy wind ribboned weakly around our ankles.

Earlier today (although it felt like weeks ago) we'd viewed miniature models of the incineration plant. The physical terrain of the third layer—far below our feet that stood on air—didn't look so different.

But the dioramas had only included a few token trees around the edge of the grounds. Seeing the whole island put it into perspective. The grayish blocky roof of the plant, the village at the rocky end of the coast, the visitor center, the seawall: at night, all were hard to make out amid the froth of natural growth.

Datura Gray was the only living human left on Ashtereth—in all the buildings, and on all the trails.

Unless Lear had lied to us about completing the evacuation. No, she couldn't have: Wist would notice if people came spilling back through the undersea bypass. No matter which layer they hid on, she'd sense them. She'd stop me.

A sick exhilaration warmed me like a fever in my blood. All those unclaimed bodies. Records of the director's restricted research; untold volumes of data. Gulls and monkeys and tramplers and ant colonies. Life churned in soil that had once consisted only of ash and dredged silt and urban detritus crushed down like old seashells ground into speckles of gravel.

All of it would soon be gone.

This was by far the cleanest way to resolve everything in one fell swoop. The only obvious choice, really. But Wist hadn't wanted to put me in a position to do it.

She'd made the gash across her middle congeal just enough to avoid raining blood and guts on the land below. Sometimes I wished she'd hide in her tower like a hermit crab and send out a body double to do all her work. Preferably one made of titanium—or, better yet, untouchable vapor.

I would've said something about the false night sky being sort of romantic, but I didn't quite have the stomach for jokes.

When I twisted back, Wist bent her head for a good-luck kiss. I felt along her jawline, just above the edge of her turtleneck. It was still damp with blood from her ears, now a sticky gel like old jam.

I wasn't stalling, I promise. Hardly any time had passed since Wist ported us out of the cockpit. Each second—each heartbeat—crackled like thunder, portentous.

The hard part would be knowing when to stop. If she had to, Wist would cut me off. She'd do whatever it took.

For her sake, I summoned all the bravado I had to offer. I turned my magic perception back to the glittering island. I made sure my voice didn't shake.

"All right," I said, addressing the Void like a pet. "Ready to eat?"

45

I COULDN'T REMEMBER if I was in the Void, or if the Void was in me. I turned like a child getting tumbled by a wave, topsy-turvy in sandy water.

I settled, eventually, into the shape of my body. It felt meager and empty. The Void —despite its nature of nullity—was so much weightier.

And now it was extraordinarily well fed.

I felt as though I could reach for my throat and rip off my own worn-out skin, head to toe. I would emerge like the white egret slithering out of the boy who had called himself Datura Gray.

On Ashtereth there had been birds circling, and nesting boxes, and families of small mammals in burrows. There had been coastal ecosystems, and village houses full of weary memories, with thriving plants.

And all those abandoned corpses. It would have been too much work for Lear to drag them out, even if Wist made every able-bodied adult help her haul them to the tunnel. It would've taken too long.

Reverence had been inextricably intertwined with the island around it. The Void had uprooted them both. A clean kill—no polluting runoff, no industrial waste, no emissions. And no evidence except for the churning emptiness of the sea where there used to be land.

At a certain point, the fullness of the Void became harder to bear than its hunger.

When I came to, I was lying in bed. It felt cushier than a prison cot, so that already seemed promising.

I sensed a mage nearby. Just one branch.

I prodded Wist through our bond. All I got in response was an impression of deep preoccupation.

I sat up ponderously. Someone (I'm assuming Wist) had put my prosthetic eye back in. She'd cleaned it, too. My eyelid, though gunky, seemed way less inflamed.

Still: the Void exerted a demanding new gravity. I was more aware than ever that I had a bottomless pit in my head. My whole self seemed to teeter at its slippery edge.

Distended globes dangled from the ceiling. A thicket of pendant lights. Azalea sat—legs crossed, hands clasped—in a chair with fluted swirls of auburn wood. I couldn't tell what she'd been doing before I woke.

"Water-lights," she said, following my gaze. "Uncommon on the continent. How do you feel?"

"Alive," I croaked. "Wist—"

"Extremely busy, at the moment. She'll need healing soon enough. You were out for two days ... but you've been nibbling a bit, limping to the bathroom, sponging yourself. Remember?"

I didn't. "I'm in custody," I said. "Whose?"

She went to an end table and poured out earthy-smelling tea. The cups had tightly spiraled handles, like a snail shell. Cute, but inconvenient.

Once we'd both taken a few sips, and she'd ensconced herself in her chair again, she said: "As an honored member of our delegation, you're in Osmanthian care. We've come to the capital city."

"What is this, a state guesthouse?"

"The Grand Postal Hotel."

That explained why the table with the tea carafe looked like a modified post box, cast iron coated in heavy teal paint. The antique wooden bureau might once have been something similar; the drawers appeared to have mail slots.

Frames on the wall sheltered an extensive display of old Jacian stamps. They were arranged in neat, scientific rows like pinned insects.

Liquid sloshed unsteadily in the cup in my hands, never quite breaching the rim.

My mind kept excavating fleeting recollections of all the things I'd erased. Datura's little propagating succulents. Shredded bark lying around in sacks. Heartless bipeds left discarded like molted shells. Partially built chalices dumped in a bunker like sides of meat in a freezing locker.

There had never been any question of using Garbage Disposal to preserve our findings. I wouldn't ever pull the island back out of my eye. The Void had feasted, deeply and truly, unburdened by magical loopholes. Reverence was gone forever.

I ate that island. It was me, all me. You, the bed, the whole hotel and everyone in it—I could take it all right now. Don't believe me? Watch this. Look at my eye.

These thoughts weren't entirely new. But they seemed a hell of a lot more plausible now that I'd let the Void devour Ashtereth, bones and all.

Azalea pretended to scrutinize the gallery of artfully framed stamps. I pressed the rattling tea cup to my lips. I just held it there. I didn't take another drink until my esophagus stopped trying to gag on the truth. Eventually I scooted down to the other end of the bed and put my half-empty cup on the table.

"Nice accommodations," I said.

"You may have to spend a lot of time here."

"Am I a political prisoner?"

"It did take a bit of negotiation to decide where to park you. And the rest of the delegation, of course."

"That's the downside of not having an embassy."

Azalea eyed me over the top of her cup. She uttered a word in Jacian, slowly and clearly.

"What?" Without context, I had no idea what it meant.

She switched tracks. "Auditor Lear. Your companion. Hero of the hour. Do you know who her boss is?"

It had sounded, for an instant, as if she'd been about to say *bondmate*.

"No idea," I said. "Someone important?"

"The Postmistress."

I cast an inquisitive look around the room again. The water-lights shed a surreal blueish light, as if we'd been stashed in an aquarium.

"The Postmistress," said Azalea, "runs both the Jace Postal Service and a corresponding intelligence agency known primarily as the Service."

"Special Branch?"

"No, that's a different division."

"But Lear—"

"She was nominally on loan to them. Her permanent post is with the Service."

I couldn't even keep Osmanthian intelligence agencies straight. Jace seemed worse. Why would any country need more than one active spy bureau, anyway? Multiply them, and of course they'd work at cross-purposes.

Azalea pronounced that unfamiliar Jacian word again. Then, in Continental: "The Slaughterhouse. That's what political opponents call the Service."

Lear hadn't been entrusted with accompanying the Kraken solely because of her language skills, or our past acquaintance. She worked directly under someone with considerable influence.

That was probably a good thing. If Lear played along with the story I'd fed her during the evacuation, and if this Postmistress backed her up, her testimony might stave off any lingering doubts about what had happened at Ashtereth.

Someone had put me in soft button-up pajamas. I swung my legs off the bed and made a cursory effort to stand. My ankles immediately buckled under. The carpet was so foolishly plush—like fur skimmed off some fluffy northern animal—that I couldn't stop wondering how they cleaned it.

"I can't remember how we got off the island," I said feebly. When in doubt, fake amnesia. "It's all kind of a blur."

I don't think Azalea bought it, not for a second—neither my imploring gaze nor my claims of forgetfulness. But she answered obligingly enough.

Ashtereth had completely disappeared off the map, as if swallowed by a vorpal hole, except there was no island-sized breach left behind to explain its absence.

Publicly, its destruction had been characterized as a natural disaster. A sunken island; a localized quake. They'd even gotten seismologists and oceanographers to corroborate this. Which just goes to show that you can't trust scientific pronouncements from a dictatorship (Osmanthus, of course, was no better).

Personnel with security clearances heard an alternate explanation. Datura's last great chalice had been a creation of equal parts genius and hubris. It had spun out of control and eradicated its surroundings in a deadly implosion of wild magic.

It helped that the parade of evacuees had included units from rival agencies. Like our onetime attackers in Datura's office. They were too muddled to make much sense. But their reports supported the notion that something very strange (and decidedly unauthorized) had been going on at the Ashtereth research base.

"Make no mistake," Azalea said, "our Jacian counterparts aren't pleased. They lost an entire facility, and all corresponding records. And at least one completed chalice."

"Are they calling for Wist's head?"

"Only a vocal minority. And only behind closed doors."

That sounded like about the best we could hope for. Some would always claim that Wist had destroyed Ashtereth as a pre-planned act of sabotage. They'd describe Datura's death as a coldblooded assassination. They'd agitate for retaliation.

No one would suspect it of all being my doing.

How could they?

Even before this, open conflict had been little more than half a step away. Over the past couple centuries, Osmanthus had launched multiple unprovoked attacks (often in the name of liberating Jacian mages), and Jace, at other times, had been just as aggressive (often in the name of liberating Osmanthian healers).

Nationalist sentiment tended to be somewhat cyclical. People who had lived through the wars of forty-something years ago had a rather different view of foreign affairs than my generation, raised in peacetime. The latest crop of schoolchildren would see things differently still.

Our Osmanthian comrades weren't unreservedly thrilled with Wist's performance, either. Azalea had too much tact to state this outright, but I could read between the lines. Hardline patriots would've been disappointed with anything short of stealing Reverence and hauling the whole damn thing home as a glorious present for the Board.

On the flip side, much of the displeasure expressed by Jacian officials was a calculated act. A few were true radicals, but the rest knew that the more they fussed about the loss of Ashtereth, the more favors they could milk from the Kraken.

It was a singular chance to obtain Osmanthian aid in the guise of a fair trade. As a kind of compensation. This would, to some extent, let them overwrite the initial humiliation incurred by requesting Wist's presence. That whole unusual chain of events could be blamed squarely on Datura Gray.

The end result was that Wist seemed likely to be stuck in Jace for quite a while. She'd work overtime—doing the sorts of things only the Kraken could do—to appease our hosts. She'd already started closing dozens of decades-old vorpal holes.

And me? How was I faring after my days-long swoon?

The Void's ever-present hunger had almost gone silent. It was as though a cloudy bacterial film had peeled off my brain. I could see things with intuitive clarity.

Azalea, for instance. She'd grown into herself over the years—wider hips, softer padding, an aura of unimpeachable comfort. Her suit jacket (worn unbuttoned), her bow-tied blouse, those low-heeled shoes: she might have been waiting for a medical appointment, or a performance review, or a meeting with her child's teacher. That whistle-shaped pendant, tinted with magic, was her only visible eccentricity.

All of this was just as much a disguise as the chameleon skin of Datura's bipeds. If anything, she had sharpened with age. She just hid it better.

I wouldn't ask about her real job title. Frankly, I didn't want to know.

When we were students, she'd always been on Wist's side. She never wavered. Looking back, though, those years at Guralta Academy seemed incredibly brief compared to the rest of our lives. I'd spent a longer time in prison.

"You kept your promise," she said.

"Which promise?"

"To bring back a souvenir." She patted her leg. "You had something in your pocket. I assumed it was a gift."

I mimed holding a fistful of beads.

Azalea nodded. "Your clothes are being laundered."

I felt my upper earlobe. "What about my earpiece? The pointy one."

"What earpiece?" she said innocently. Guess she'd be keeping that, too. Sorry, Lear.

"I'm surprised you didn't confiscate these tacks," I muttered.

"Your earrings? Wist told us to leave them in. Watch it—don't poke them." She passed me a small spray bottle. "Saline solution. Use it once or twice a day. Wash your hands first!"

She brought me a pair of slippers and showed me the closet, the bath, and every other corner of the room.

She warned me not to take the tacks out for at least another six weeks. Unless I wanted the piercings to close. Some solicitous person (possibly Azalea herself) had capped off the pointy ends with little green chunks of floral foam.

Once I'd run out of postal-themed decor to remark on, I stopped by a wall hung with tapestries. The whole surface bowed when I poked it. Felt more like an accordion-style partition than anything meant to be permanent.

"What's back here?"

"The rest of the suite."

"I'm barred from seeing it?"

"Wist wanted you kept away from windows."

"What, did she think I'd jump out?"

Azalea answered in a tone of delicate neutrality. "We've already had our share of misfortune."

Wist's stunt double had stayed behind with Fanren's group—and she'd been murdered while we traipsed around Ashtereth. I'd completely forgotten.

"Did anyone else…?"

"Only one death," Azalea said. Then she reconsidered. "Well. Only one death in the delegation. An assassin came after Fanren."

"When?"

"While you slept."

"He killed them?"

"Ah, no. I did," she said modestly.

She lifted her silver whistle to her lips. It was a simple, slender rod, like a doll-sized flute.

"You talked about using that to call your son in to eat," I said.

"Dinner party stories don't often have much to do with factual truth."

"So how does it work?"

"Think of it as a blow dart." She let the whistle drop, reduced once more to a piece of jewelry.

Make the wrong kind of trouble, and I'd be next. We exchanged a short, humorless smile of perfect understanding.

46

I CLEANED MY EARS, brushed my teeth, and promptly crashed.

I was still shaky, but I couldn't work up an appetite. Even my natural nosiness had sunk deep beneath a shroud of satiation. The Void felt indolent, and so I slept the day away.

Without any windows, the room seemed to float somewhere outside the ordinary passage of time. Azalea had shown me a wall clock, but the numbering was strange. I couldn't figure out how to read it.

The ceiling pendants always emitted the same blue-tinged light. I kept thinking, as I padded back and forth from the bathroom, that I should've asked how to turn them off. But they certainly didn't keep me from sleeping.

At one point I stayed active long enough to soldier my way through a shower. The next time I woke up, pillow still damp, Fanren had taken over the bedside chair. Wist gave the same response as before when I pulled on our bond: a harried, wordless attempt at reassurance.

I'd be more reassured if I could see you, I told her.

Fanren wore a hand-knit sweater, black and red, with a pattern like an abstract broken flower. He indicated a glass of water on the end table. I drank obediently.

"Where'd you get that sweater?"

"From an admirer."

He'd been flipping though a book until I started stirring. "You can read Jacian?" I asked.

Upon closer inspection, he turned out to be holding the book upside down. I leaned over and fixed it for him.

"It's a collection of poetry," he said, "or so I've been told. I like looking at the characters."

"Even if you have no idea what they say?"

"Feels meditative, in a way."

I turned to a random page. "Uh..."

"What's the matter?"

"The person who lent you this," I said. "Was it someone with designs on your virtue?"

"Possibly. Why?"

"These are extremely ribald poems."

The next thing he wanted to know, naturally, was the exact content of each poem. I downed the rest of my water and, pleading ill health, went right back to sleep.

I wasn't conscious when Wist came in. But I felt her anyway. She seemed to melt through the door without the indignity of needing to open or close it.

The thumbtack posts in my ears moved minutely, stinging me awake. I lay there in a confused paralysis, mesmerized by the disorder of her magic. A thousand shining scrambled roads, and they all led to her center—

I remembered that I, too, had a body. I wasn't just a mote of awareness drifting along with the Void.

By the time I started to push myself up, she was already on me. She'd flickered from the door to the bed: the same half-magical movement she'd used when taking Datura Gray by the throat.

She seized me just as fast. For a jumbled moment, she held me up against the wall.

She'd instantly clocked the boy for a monster. No waffling, no wringing her hands. She just knew. If she ever made the same judgment of me, I wouldn't have much grounds to object.

The bed complained at the suddenness of our combined weight. I could breathe again—although I had always been able to breathe, even when she came at me in a flurry. I'd choked all on my own.

Thank goodness for low light. My embarrassment kept redoubling. She would've sensed the rush and ebb of panic in me even if she tried not to see it. Some emotions were too strong to keep from leaking.

It took effort to attune myself to the physical world: starting with the tipsy buzz in my piercings, and Wist feeling me all over as if expecting to find a secret broken rib or a knife sticking out of my belly.

On the other side of the bed, the temporary wall quailed. She'd whacked it with magic. Tapestries dropped to the carpet. The partitions separated and slotted away out of sight.

For the first time, I could see the rest of the suite.

She turned up the water-lights—again, using magic. Next, without so much as glancing over her shoulder, she lit a number of yellower lamps in the space that had previously been walled away.

Now she was just showing off.

"Reel it in," I ordered.

No.

"Wist," I said. "My love. My darling. My savory green pumpkin."

She winced at that last one. At least I had her attention. "Stop it," I said, serious again.

From the moment she slipped in here, she'd been throwing magic around for no reason. Given the current state of her branches, this was about as advisable as running a marathon on fractured legs.

I slithered off the bed. Wist tried to carry me; I swatted her away. The Void had drowned me in the spiritual equivalent of a food coma, but I wasn't actually injured. Just lethargic.

I told Wist this in the tone of a lawyer delivering a case-winning argument.

She responded by briskly stripping off my pajamas.

"Hey!" I cried, now clad only in briefs.

She pointed at my bare thighs. Then my sides and my shoulders.

I was covered in bruises, purple and black and seeping yellow.

Let it be noted that I'd showered and changed to new sleepwear. I hadn't just been wallowing in my own filth. But I hadn't noticed a thing, I swear.

"How did I..."

I trailed off. I'd fallen flat on my face in the cockpit. I'd flung myself all over the place, banging into walls and furniture. But any aches and pains had gotten scorched right out of me by the sight of what that egret did to Wist.

I yanked up her sweatshirt. A striking bluish streak cut across her abdomen, half an inch above her navel. It wasn't just the light that tinted it: I had similar scars myself. Used in a rush, restorative magic could leave permanent marks. If it happened every time, we'd both be blue from head to toe.

She'd magicked her hair back to black, but she'd left it long. Her braid encircled my wrist as I touched her, warning me not to fool too much with fragile skin.

Hunger and thirst took this as their moment to wage a joint ambush. I must've been giving Wist all kinds of desperate looks. She only faltered for a nanosecond before fetching my pajama top and threading my arms through it, as practiced as a nurse.

I rubbed my cheek disconsolately against her breast until she whisked me over to a table and began dispensing drinks and snacks.

The water was carbonated. The bagged popcorn was coated in fiery red powder. I mewled like a pet tricked into eating a pill. But all that burning did get me more securely grounded in my body.

Wist collected the tapestries that lay strewn across the carpet. She switched open the curtains over all the windows in the outer room. The glass had been treated to eradicate reflections. It was evening, the sun in evidence only as a narrow strip of sullen red.

I craned my neck to see if I could spot anything distinctly Jacian about the shape of the skyline, or fashion trends in the street below. When I loitered in this room, a prisoner in all but name, I had little sense of being in another country.

Once I'd had enough to eat, I went to floss popcorn from my teeth. I slipped the floral foam off my makeshift earrings, too. A nice gesture, but it wouldn't have stopped the needle-sharp ends from jabbing new holes in me if I tossed in my sleep.

I was beginning to suspect the bee tacks of subtly adjusting themselves to stave off careless pinpricks. I also suspected Wist of covertly feeding them to keep them active.

She came up behind me and examined my piercings one by one. I had to fight not to squirm at the tenderness of her fingers on the side of my neck. Seeing it all play out in the bathroom mirror made me as ticklish as if I'd never been touched. Sometimes it's awfully difficult to simply be still and be loved. Maybe I only feel that way because I'm a slippery sort of character, hm? Maybe you wouldn't relate.

"If you take them out now," Wist said, "it'll heal like nothing ever happened."

"You told Azalea not to steal them."

"It should be your choice to remove them. Not hers."

Even in the mirror, her eyes were as opaque as ever. She looked from my earlobe to the bruising around my clavicle, burgundy flecks and blotches spread out like a map of an unknown land.

I was sore, yes, the sorest I'd ever been. And yet I suffered far less than I should have. Wist's doing, no doubt.

"The tacks already served their purpose," she said. "You never wanted—"

I turned in her arms. "I never wanted a piercing from anyone else."

That, I thought, was why it had always felt vaguely unthinkable. If Wist wanted to pierce me, I'd thank her for the privilege.

"Go on," I teased. "Give me more. Riddle me with holes."

"Like Fanren?" she said tonelessly.

"...Ah, that might be a bit much."

47

Wɪsᴛ's ʙʀᴀɴᴄʜᴇs, too, had the look of a map—a nightmare subway. Civil engineers would be reduced to tears. I pored over her back for hours, unwinding threads of magic that had looped themselves into an endless interchange of curlicue turns.

Wist confirmed that Lear had said exactly what she needed to say about Ashtereth, and no more. She'd let Wist fill in the rest.

We both suspected that she'd squirreled away at least a couple papers from Datura's office. But it wouldn't be enough to reconstruct anything resembling a chalice like Reverence.

The same (I hoped) would prove true of the abacus beads I'd filched for Azalea.

Maybe Osmanthian analysts would make some interesting discoveries, or maybe not. Those beads alone wouldn't show them how to design Jacian-style machina from the ground up.

When I took a break from healing her, Wist hunched over my prosthetic and reapplied some of the magical protections that I'd ripped out like surgical stitches.

"I'm allowed near windows again?" I asked.

"Mm."

It was true night now, although we couldn't see a single slice of a single moon. We ate room service (carried to us by a young Osmanthian from the delegation—someone's harried assistant).

We left the curtains open, and we speculated about curiously shaped skyscrapers. One twisted like a drill bit. One appeared to be slowly melting. One was spangled in rainbow lights. One was riddled with deliberate hollows.

We spent a lot of time talking mind-to-mind about Datura Gray.

He'd sought Wist's help with creating a gate for his savior. But he hadn't made much of an effort to convince her. She'd refused, and he'd shrugged, and he'd initiated the process on his own. The Void had digested the island before his gate could swing open.

If we hadn't acted, Reverence would've gradually chewed both his bodies to bits. In exchange, a great portal would have been established over Ashtereth, a passage to a continent so distant that hardly anyone ever spoke of it.

He'd expended no small effort to lure Wist to Reverence. He'd put everything on the line—his career, his future, his legacy, his beloved landfill island, everyone who worked under him. Even after letting her invade his inner sanctum, there was much more he could've done to force her hand.

He never wanted you to open a window, I said. *He wanted you there to stop it.*

Wist's head had been bowed low over my naked prosthesis on the table. She looked up. *When we tried to stop him, he fought us.*

True. He tried to have it both ways.

He'd made a sincere effort to fulfill the wishes of the being that had granted his own greatest wish. It was important to him to live to the last as someone who paid his debts. But he hadn't necessarily hoped to succeed. He'd thought that only the Kraken might be able to block him.

He'd valued the gift of his own life so greatly that he would have risked anything to honor it. He would have handed Jace over to a nameless creature of untold power. Every other life lost along the way—every sacrifice that Reverence had absorbed ... those didn't matter quite so much, did they?

Knowingly or unknowingly, everything living on Ashtereth had been part of his project.

The appearance and nature of his second body hadn't just resulted from a whimsical roll of the dice. He'd looked like a harmless boy, and he'd acted like one, too, right up until you innocently did something to trigger his deepest instincts—instincts he hadn't even known he possessed.

That was a gift as well. A sweet outer shell, and a violently hungry beak, and the perfect excuse to reap a massive number of sacrifices for Reverence. It was no one's fault. He was just a boy. It was all an unfortunate accident.

And his involvement with core extraction? He'd have said in no uncertain terms that every loss was a tragedy, and no one would root for their own patients to die, and if the majority of them did perish anyway, well, that was just the nature of the beast. The experiments were too important to stop. They had gone on for generations. They would continue with or without him.

Datura Gray had never once killed anyone by choice. I, in turn, didn't feel terribly stirred by his death. Mass murder aside (there's a phrase I'd never thought I'd say), we'd known him less than a day.

As Wist labored to repair my eye, melancholy stole over the backs of my shoulders. If I had to wallow in guilt, it wouldn't be for Datura. It would be for the total loss of Reverence. Possibly the only chalice ever crafted for a purpose other than war and violence.

There had been a beauty to its intricacy. Like a great temple left standing for thousands of years. The sort of structure you might look at and wonder: what lost magic did they use to build that? It had functioned like a temple, too, being a space intended for sacred conference—for bringing seekers closer to some unutterable presence.

I would've condemned a military that bombed irreplaceable landmarks. I had to condemn myself, at least a little, for gleefully eating Reverence whole.

Wist, I noticed, had abandoned her bodyguard uniform. I was somewhat amazed that our compatriots had let her go out in a university hoodie. (A Jacian university, no less. She must have gotten it from Fanren's crew. They'd been swamped with free swag.)

Well ... she wasn't representing Osmanthus to the masses. Just to an extremely select group of those in the know. Heck, this getup could be its own kind of disguise. Few hired killers would expect the infamous Kraken to slink around like an overgrown student on an emergency grocery run.

I fit my false eye back in my face. We retired to a couch near a window, my legs in her lap, both too devoid of energy to do much more than clasp each other fitfully.

Wist lay back with heavy-lidded eyes, enjoying however much peace I saw fit to give her. I squeezed her knee, her bicep. I pushed her floppy sleeve up until it wouldn't go any further. I traced the subtle texture of veins along her inner elbow.

I laid my arm next to hers to compare our topography.

I blinked.

Brimming sourness touched a spot so far back in my mouth that I wouldn't have thought it had taste buds.

By the time Wist glanced away from the nighttime city and asked what was wrong, I'd pulled down my sleeve.

I tipped closer and dug my head at her, goat-like, until she slung both arms and legs around me and crushed me into a semblance of calmness.

I wriggled free, eventually, and took another look.

When I first measured my arm against hers, my veins had been black, radiantly black, standing out even where they shouldn't have, glistening through bruises of every color.

The Void stretched out luxuriously, from the beds of my fingernails to backs of my teeth. But now there was nothing to see but mottled skin.

When the Void ate Ashtereth ... what was I like? I asked. *How did I act?*

Wist touched me with the back of her hand, lightly, as if checking my temperature. "You were laughing." She said it without scorn. Without even a mote of concern.

I couldn't reply.

She continued. "You might laugh the same way if Jace launched an all-out attack on the continent."

"Wow," I managed. "You really know how to talk me up."

"It's a reflex. Like hiccuping. A body can't ingest disaster all at once. Your body protests with laughter. Others might cry. Others might vomit. Others might do nothing."

"Or," I said, skeptical, "maybe I was enjoying the hell out of myself. Maybe I loved it."

I chased her gaze. "You must've been able to tell, toward the end. When it chewed up enough of Ashtereth for the comms blockade to come down. Sooner or later, all that interference had to fail."

As I laughed, as the Void took its due, my thoughts must have blazed up against her soul like a brand.

She didn't tell me what I'd been thinking. Which, I figured, was an answer in itself.

She didn't look away, either. *It noticed*, she said. *The voice on the other side of the world. It noticed the Void drinking down Reverence, and erasing any possibility of Datura's window.*

So it saw us? I said, chilled. *It knows where we are?*

It's still far away. Still dormant.

I scoffed. *It mashed a human man together with a beast.*

Mostly dormant, she said, unswayed. *Any large-scale use of the Void might draw its attention. Draw its attention too often, and we'll shake it awake.*

There was only one correct response. But the Void had infected me: I wanted to cleverly argue my way around the necessity of not using it. I wanted to feed, again, on something bigger.

It was as if my long, long hours of sleep had caught up with me all at once. I itched for action. There were no obvious enemies and no righteous fights to be had in this room, though, unless Wist felt like indulging me.

My hands were cold and bloodless. I massaged them, punishingly, and said what I had to say. "Then we can't do that again. Ever. But what counts as large-scale use? Is anything smaller than an entire island still safe? I mean, where do we draw the line?"

She brushed a fallen eyelash off my cheek. "Keep the Void on a tight leash. The tighter, the better."

"It still has to be fed."

"Now?" And she pulled her hoodie over her head, right then and there, like she might as well get comfortable before letting it have a go at the tender roots of her magic.

"Not now! In general, you doofus."

She paused, stymied—the hair around her face all rumpled and wispy, arms still buried in her sleeves.

It was getting late. The buildings outside sparkled like stars reflected in a lake; the actual stars appeared quite sad in comparison. Not so different from Osmanthus City, then.

These past couple days, I'd rested enough for three grown adults. Wist, for her part, hadn't taken any meaningful breaks. I sighed and commanded her to come to bed. If anything dire happened, someone would wake us.

48

I SLEPT BECAUSE the weighted-down Void made it easy, and because there wasn't really much else to do. I didn't care to stroll in circles around my suite and reflect on all the subtleties of hospitality that made this different from an Osmanthian prison.

A box was still a box, and I was like an animal that needed to gnaw down growing teeth. Without anything of substance to bite at, my thoughts would twist inward, furrowing deeper and deeper into the muck of old resentments.

I became wearily familiar with all the features of the room. Those teat-like water-lights. The esoteric ink marks staining each set of framed stamps. The triangular doorknobs, which at first I had taken for a cultural quirk. Now that I thought about it, they might just be a weird design choice.

Wist stayed with me whenever she could, often arriving at odd hours. They'd put her on a semi-nocturnal shift. She knew all sorts of magic for going unnoticed in broad daylight, with or without a stealth bracelet. But Jacian authorities found it easier to gloss over prominent vorpal holes vanishing in the middle of the night.

My bruises got worse, then slowly began to recede. I took some pleasure in making Wist press them until I hissed through my teeth. I would've enjoyed prodding hers more, but she didn't have any left. I contented myself with running my thumb across the sensitive blue scar on her stomach.

"I think the Void made me a sadist," I announced to my audience of one.

"Clem," she said, without any change in expression, "you were always like this."

"Oh. Really?"

"More or less."

"But I was so sweet and innocent back in school. We both were."

She didn't quite laugh in my face, but her belly went taut beneath my palm. I grinned for both of us. I'd get her next time.

Later, too restless to lie still, she began doing one-armed push-ups on the floor beside the bed. (The furry carpet kept making her sneeze.) I put my feet on her back to give her more of a challenge. If I had better balance, I'd ride her like a surfboard.

Everyone agreed that it would be a bad idea to let me wander around town on my own. I had a history of political treachery. Minor acts of rebellion—like sneaking down to the hotel bar—would cause a major panic.

Not that Jacian guests would recognize me as anything other than an eccentric foreigner. That in itself was highly novel, even in a cosmopolitan-looking city like this. An Osmanthian accent would be particularly hard to explain.

I didn't want to give anyone an ulcer. Nor was I trying to ruin the career of whoever had been officially assigned responsibility for my antics. Some poor undersecretary, probably. Any missteps would rebound on Manatree, too.

So—believe it or not—I behaved myself. Wist's magic tangled rapidly enough to keep me from going crazy with boredom. I healed her in person and from afar.

Jacian military officials must have known almost nothing about Reverence's capabilities, I reasoned. Otherwise, they would've been far more enraged by its destruction. They'd had a mechanism capable of stifling all indirect contact between bonded mage-healer pairs, and they'd lost it without even realizing such interference was possible.

Only Wist and Azalea kept me updated on the fallout from Ashtereth.

Datura Gray had cultivated a reputation as an innovator largely on the strength of charisma and powerful backers—most of whom didn't know a thing about the technicalities of machina development. He'd made vague, sweeping promises, but offered few actual demonstrations. They'd most likely conclude, in retrospect, that he'd been blowing hot air for the sake of funding.

A parade of Osmanthian diplomats and security staff came by to keep me company. And (I assumed) to get me to babble more about Ashtereth. I talked their ears off, but not about anything of value.

I asked them to bring me Jacian magazines. They presented me with a selection on the following topics: native dog breeds, local travel, skimmer modification, home cooking, high fashion, fictional comics, beautiful people in skimpy swimwear, and financial advice for senior citizens.

My procurers seemed to think I just wanted to look at the pictures. Sometimes, inspired by Fanren, I let them see me flipping through pages in the wrong direction.

One day, Shien Danver came in and caught me faking illiteracy in front of yet another attaché. She snorted. "I thought you'd be bored out of your mind."

"Aw. Were you worried?"

"No," she said, and promptly left.

For my first authorized excursion—baby's first field trip!—I joined the rest of the delegation at a state-owned guesthouse. (Where none of us were actually staying. Perhaps the venue had been selected to show off what we'd been missing.)

I hung around with Wist, back in her bodyguard getup, and clapped politely for Fanren during a series of outdoor exhibition matches.

The mages who battled him seemed plenty competent, in a militaristic sort of way. To them, the rules of dueling must have felt totally arbitrary. Moves that made sense in the world of magesports might have little meaning in the context of actual combat.

Fanren, for his part, knew better than to crush them all in an instant. He deployed the same skill over and over, each time in a different way. He kept the action slow enough for inexperienced viewers to follow along. He let several opponents come surprisingly close to outscoring him.

On the far side of the field, Jacian healers and other observers watched from beneath the shelter of colorful sun shades. Each fabric sail bore the brush-stroke spiral that (or so I'd been told) stood for Central. The seat of government; the heart of all that mattered.

Lear was there, a flute of wine in her fingers, stationed near murmuring bureaucrats. Might one of them be her Postmistress? Danver—clad in a sleek belted jumpsuit and an exquisite mini hat—surveyed each Jacian face with unnerving ferocity.

Lear had no gloves, or mantle, or anything resembling what I understood to be a mage's formal uniform. How many guests knew that, despite her lack of branches, she was legally considered no different from the magic users who got sent out to perform like dancing bears? Being bonded would give her away in an instant ... but they couldn't easily perceive that. Even in the household of a prominent Osmanthian mage clan, she'd succeeded in passing for an anodyne subliminal. She might have tremendous value as a domestic spy, too.

Most of the mages who fought Fanren were stoic in moments of triumph, and just as stoic in defeat. They looked to management for permission before coming to speak with him between matches. But they loved him, I think. He made them look good, and he did it artfully enough to keep everyone satisfied, on both sides of the field.

After the show, there came a second round of refreshments. I would've loved to bound over and bludgeon unsuspecting victims with my awkward Jacian phrasing and spotty vocab. With ferocious effort, I restrained myself.

Azalea came by to inform me that the snails were delicious, and only lightly spiced. She waved an empty toothpick for emphasis.

"I prefer snails as pets," I said.

"Your loss, Asa." She ate another with gusto. "They're already dead."

She and Wist and I meandered over to a miniature garden. Even the very largest trees were rigorously trained runts, smaller than boy-sized Datura. Some grew from craggy boulders arranged like a cluster of mountains. Others stood on risers, pots disguised by a drapery of velveteen moss. Fishnet lichen trailed from branches like moth-eaten antimacassars.

Flat-faced, cattish dogs galumphed about the middle of the yard. They were a bright orangey brown and snuffled gutturally with every breath.

All of this—the decorative pets and the shrunken-down trees—felt like a testament to how much humans could alter their cosmetic surroundings without any reliance on magic.

Azalea said under her breath that the Jacian aversion to aesthetic magic use swung like a pendulum over time. Countercultural movements swelled and crashed and faded. If you had enough money and status, there were always ways to obtain a tacit exception. Those in power were expected to maintain a certain look, weren't they?

"Sounds like home," I said.

Danver and Lear had entered the garden ahead of us. They pored over opposite facets of the same mountainous boulder, as if they had nothing to say to one another, although I saw Danver's lips moving.

"Sometimes they look as though they're about to come to blows," Azalea murmured.

"Have they?"

"Not to my knowledge. They can do whatever they like, of course, as long as it's not in public."

"Is that the official stance of the Osmanthian government?"

Azalea widened her eyes in mock surprise. "Shien Danver is a private citizen."

Yep—Danver was definitely shaping up to be an intelligence asset for one side or another, or possibly both.

Later in the afternoon, we got roped into playing a couple games of vorpal bowling. Our hosts brought us to yet another sports field and, with great fanfare, unveiled the goal. A convenient rift in reality, perfectly placed. They must have shifted it there with secret magic.

The Void, still torpid, spasmed in revulsion.

Jacians had been the first to figure out how to move vorpal holes in physical space, but it was still a heavily restricted technique, even here. Wist (in typical fashion) had made it seem easy when she did it on Ashtereth. For other people, it would go disastrously wrong just as often as it went right.

The game they taught us involved using yo-yos to whack delicately stacked wooden pins at the hole. Wasteful, if you ask me. Once a pin vanished, it'd be lost forever.

But partial losses were to be avoided at all costs. Say a pin went flying and got sliced in two at the edge of the rift, one half falling in and the other half tumbling on the grass. An incomplete goal would make you lose all accumulated points. So everyone aimed for precision strikes instead of wild blows.

If they would just let me throw rocks, I might have acquitted myself fairly well, but my yo-yo handling left a lot to be desired. I joined Azalea on the sidelines.

Lear turned out to be capable of numerous fancy tricks (no surprise there). Fanren was a quick learner with deadly aim. Danver, who didn't appear to have ever touched a yo-yo in her life, had no chance of keeping up. Still, she refused to withdraw. Wist dropped out of the competition soon after I did, but she discovered a real knack for making her yo-yo spin on and on and on at the end of its string.

"Two weeks from now," said Azalea, "Ouro Fanren will have to head back across the sea. He'll take his entourage with him."

"Where's that leave the rest of us?" I asked.

"A new round of guests will arrive in exchange. They'll need another cover story. Trade negotiations, perhaps ... I'll tap out whenever my replacement shows up. Can't enjoy the life of a tourist forever. More's the shame."

Wist's yo-yo whirred discreetly at knee level, hovering like a hummingbird. If not for the sound, I might not have thought it was moving it all. She pulled it up after another few moments, then sent it down to sleep again.

I nodded at her. "There must be pressure to withdraw the Kraken."

"It goes in both directions," Azalea said. "Jace hasn't been this receptive to talks since before the war."

"Which war?"

"My point exactly." She paused while Wist's yo-yo zipped up and down again. "Business interests are thrilled."

"Isn't this whole thing supposed to be top secret?"

"If even a couple members from top mage clans know what's happening..."

There was a Gwindel with us. And Shien Danver, serving as a direct line to Nerium. And others, too, among the various functionaries and lobbyists who had wormed their way into what was supposed to have been a highly exclusive group.

"Some people want the Kraken to get back to solving problems on the continent," I said in summary, "but they've been outvoted by our corporate overlords."

"You could return ahead of her," Azalea said casually. "There's a place on the boat for you, if you want it."

The yo-yo whirled back up into Wist's hand.

"I think I'll stay," I said.

49

Stay—and do what? My presence was good for Wist's morale, but that may have been tempered by her worries about me getting abducted, assassinated, or extorted by foreign intelligence.

Back at the hotel, Azalea hinted that a number of Jacian parties were interested in my skills as a healer.

"I'd have expected them to look down on healers from the continent," I said. "They can't think much of Osmanthian education."

"You have ties to the Kraken. That's its own type of endorsement."

Or, just as likely, they wanted to talk to me because they knew about my trial, my sentence, and my nickname. Our countrymen would never consent.

"You're not listening," Azalea said a bit later. "Your souvenir has been well received."

"A scrap like that?" I asked, even as my brain begged me to shut up. Don't downplay it, you idiot.

"It's the biggest piece of a"—she used sign language, pretending to drink from a goblet—"we've ever acquired in modern times."

Allegedly, the Jacian Bureau of Mage Management had lined up some very unusual cases for me to look at. (It went without saying that the Osmanthian foreign service would put me through an arduous debriefing each time.)

"Permission will come down eventually," she said with confidence.

Whatever they had in store for me, it couldn't be all that strange, I decided. No mage could be more complicated to heal than Wist.

The more time I spent awake, the more intense my nights became. Maybe it was cabin fever, or my foreign-inflected diet, or something in the city water.

My prosthetic eye would give off clear signals if the Void became untamed. It would make me weep inky blood, or bloody ink. It would screech out for help. It would fight me when I tried to insert it.

I watched for these signs with the vigilance of a hypochondriac. What color was the morning crust around my tear ducts? Had my prosthesis kicked, soft as a heartbeat, against the tentative pads of my fingers? Was it keening like wind in a keyhole?

Or had that warning system been lost when I mauled my eye inside Reverence? Wist would have told me. No way would she have forgotten to tell me. And yet I still couldn't work up the courage to check.

Once I had a dream that she was gone. Not captured. Not dead. Just … somewhere else, unreachable. I woke up in a horrible mood.

I dreamed, repeatedly, of black veins tattooing me like streaks of infection. They were painfully full, as taut as worm-thin balloons, ready to pop out of my skin. A toxic sludge moved in them, slower than blood. Pins and needles followed, stippling my drowsing limbs.

A water-light burst overhead, and the Void rained out, drenching me, coating my nose and lips and every inner membrane in an oily unbreathable nothingness. When I came to with a start, the lights were intact, but I'd slobbered all over my blanket. I'd stuffed its fleece in my mouth like a gag.

On one such morning, a couple days before the end of Fanren's tour, Wist invited me out on a date. She sounded dubious when she said it, as if she were reading someone else's script.

It wouldn't be just us two, at any rate. We went down to the lobby and met up with Lear and Danver.

Lear took us—me, Wist, and Shien Danver—on a monorail ride to another part of the coast.

There were other passengers. They didn't stare, but none of us uttered a word except Lear, who occasionally tapped Danver on the shoulder and pointed out landmarks. She spoke in Jacian, spooling out trivia about the capital with the smooth patter of a practiced guide.

She was back in her guise as an artist. The purple undertones in her hair looked freshly dyed. She'd turned a brilliantly colored scarf into a headband, knotting it with the finesse of a sailor.

She was also carrying a paper takeout bag. "Gifts," she said when I eyed it.

We disembarked at a neglected station where no one else got on or off. Lear efficiently herded us over to the ticket gate for a ferry. A timetable indicated that it made only six trips per day. The line was short: just us four and an older man who looked like he spent a lot of time in the sun.

Cool seaside air tore at everyone's hair as we stepped up on board. The leathery man, who had gotten on the boat quicker than any of us, turned a corner and vanished. I, for one, never saw him again.

The ferry grudgingly shivered awake. We lined up on deck and watched the dock recede. Between the shrieks of gulls, chugging water, the absence of other visible passengers, and intermittent announcements from our unseen captain, it seemed impossible for anyone to overhear us.

"How long's the ride?" I asked in Continental.

"Forty more minutes," said Lear.

"Couldn't we have ported?"

"Isn't this the Kraken's day off?"

"Aren't there any port gates, though? Or tunnels?"

"This area isn't developed enough for a bypass." She rested her elbows on the railing. "Portals remember all who pass through them. We could've taken an airlift, but just imagine the red tape. Seems a bit too conspicuous, doesn't it? Where's the rush?"

"You think we won't be monitored just because we're going the slow way?"

Lear fired a lazy salute at Wist. "Your Kraken is already hard at work to cover our tracks."

Indeed she was. More out of habit than from any real understanding of where Lear was taking us.

"All we need," said Lear, "is a dash of distraction."

She turned and kissed Danver, holding the rail on either side of her.

It happened too fast to politely look away. I saw Danver respond with the thoughtless ease of habit. An instant later—after Lear backed off and stopped trapping her against the railing and addressed me and Wist again—she turned white.

"A double date away from the city, let's say, with two scandalous couples," Lear continued. "Love spanning castes and international borders. Juicy enough to make our destination seem less important, yeah?"

I spoke, weakly, since no one else was even trying. "I wouldn't quite put it like—"

"See those bumps?" She swept her arm at a couple lumpy islands on the horizon. Hunks of rock furred with evergreens. They rose from the water like half-drowned mountains.

"That's not where we're going," she said. "They're all uninhabited. Very picturesque, though. You might see whales."

She strolled off toward the covered part of the boat, whistling.

I shot a look at Danver—who immediately cut me off. "I know what she's like. I know her better than you do."

Cold as ice, that voice.

"Er, yes," I said. "I'm sure you're right."

Wist and I beat a strategic retreat.

At the Shien estate, Lear had played the role of an unusual guest, one whose mere inclusion would show the clan to be astonishingly open-minded. Her nationality would make her an inevitable target for suspicion. Her demeanor—and, most of all, her failings—would be taken to reflect on all other Jacians.

Success in this role, then, would require being broadly likable. She'd gotten along with everyone. She'd navigated familial tensions with grace.

She didn't have to be that person in Jace.

But maybe Danver had always seen past her ingratiating veneer. Maybe it had been the meaner, more opportunistic side of Lear that drew her: the hard core of practicality beneath her watchful eyes and easy laughter. Growing up as a Shien healer, Danver would have known that friendly smiles and sparkling conversation were by no means a sign of kindness.

I looked around; I took turns gripping Wist and the railing for balance.

Did we really come all the way out here just to see a ... penitentiary?

I didn't expect an answer. When we spoke without sound, Wist had alternately called it a prison, an asylum, and a hospital. She didn't know much, either. Only that it was located on another island, a short day trip away from the capital.

Lear had requested our presence through back channels. Officially, it was pure coincidence that we'd run into her and headed off together. A merry little band of misfits.

The sea frothed around the sides of the ferry, and wind frothed around our faces. A white bird hovered by the side of the boat, trying to keep pace with us. Or, more likely, hoping that someone would feed it.

I'd fretted that my thumbtack earrings were overly identifiable. In response, Wist had turned them invisible. That raised other potential issues. What if I forgot all about them, too, and stabbed myself? She'd assured me that the tacks would prevent it.

When a strong breeze touched my ears, they buzzed in a way only I could hear. A mechanical drone, low and soporific.

I'd worn Wist's local university sweatshirt, although it just about came down to my knees. I'd fastened on an eyepatch, too. Sometimes it felt better to place an extra layer of padding between the Void and the world around me.

A bit of fabric was, admittedly, a meaningless barrier. But with all this brisk fishy air blowing around, my exposed eye kept tearing up. I was glad I'd kept my prosthetic covered.

When we'd had enough of the deck, we ducked indoors. The ceiling bulged with bright orange life jackets.

Signs at the ticket counter had alleged that the ferry could welcome up to a hundred passengers. A hundred small children, maybe, if you really packed them in.

Lear had taken one of the cushier green seats up front, past the standing-room-only section and rows of unpadded blue benches. She propped her knee up to support a small sketchbook.

Wist and I wiggled into the seats behind her. The boat kept bumping as it puttered along—and, in spite of this, her pencil kept moving. Muddy light came in through the window beside her. The glass hadn't been cleaned in ages, it seemed: it was covered in yellow-brown scum like an abandoned fish tank.

"You lied," I said after a while.

"About what?"

"Those weren't sedatives."

Her hand paused.

I kept going. "Did you think I wouldn't do it if I knew it would kill him?"

"That stuff's not instantaneous," she said calmly. "I wasn't sure it would work, anyway. I thought his chalice might save him."

She hadn't known I could open up my gouged-out right eye and swallow the chalice. And its pilot. And the island it grew on—and through—like a mushroom colony on a log. Everything.

She still didn't know, and I still wouldn't tell her. Maybe she thought Wist had erased it all. Or that there was some element of truth in my tales of chalice implosion. She'd given me an autoinjector full of something fatal, and she'd coached me on how to use it. If she couldn't kill the original Datura Gray with her own two hands, she'd find another way to get it done.

"I did have a regular sedation kit, too." Lear resumed her sketching. "It's mandatory equipment."

"But that's not what you gave me." I leaned over her seat. She was drawing the back of someone's head. Hair in a short bob, ruffled by wind. A slim neck with a couple isolated freckles. I'd never looked close enough to see them.

"What'd you take from Datura's office?" I asked.

"You carried my bag more than I did," Lear said, amused.

"I didn't have time to comb through every single hidden pocket."

She drew more flying strands of hair. "I just grabbed a few sheets of his personal notes. Nothing revelatory."

"Like a diary?"

"He didn't put anything too incriminating in writing. If he did, he worded it broadly."

She rolled the pencil in her fingers. Wist, seated to my right, had her eyes closed and her arms crossed. I could feel her listening, for all that it looked like she'd dozed off. She'd move faster than a trapdoor spider if Lear did anything threatening.

"He thought very highly of himself," Lear said, dry as ash.

He'd criticized Jace for its insularity, she told us, and its continued enmity toward the continent.

That famous insularity had been more sensible during the time of the Blessed Empire. Jace had been the last free nation on this side of the world.

What about now? The Empire was long gone. What about the other side of the world, other continents, the enormous western ocean? The first Kraken had originally come from the west. Why was Jace always glaring east?

I saw the implication. Above all, Datura Gray had been an unrivaled genius at justifying his actions. If he failed to open a door, no harm done. If he succeeded, he'd force Jace to turn west, to perceive the possibilities that lay across the largest sea, to stop endlessly relitigating old vendettas.

It's a familiar story, he'd written. Nothing accelerates progress like the discovery of a shared enemy.

What went unwritten: he'd already enacted a proof of his theorem. If he hadn't gone rogue, it might have taken decades for Wist the Kraken to be allowed into Jace.

"At least he's not alive to take credit," I said.

Lear kept drawing with swift, vicious strokes.

50

THE ASYLUM AWAITED at the top of a steep hill (which locals called Asylum Mount). Raptors wheeled above, too distant to make out any markings. Danver irritably cleaned her glasses. The charms that kept them clear were less effective in salty air.

The view at our backs went down to the marina, surrounded by a tin-roofed village even smaller than the one on Ashtereth. The rest was all forest and ocean.

There was a large sign outside the asylum, one with such elegant old-fashioned lettering that I couldn't make out a single character. Oh well. I'd been so proud of myself for reading ads in the monorail.

The building was all concrete cubes and reflective glass, taller than it was wide, more like an ultramodern apartment than a correctional facility. Certain planes had been painted the color of a watered-down sky. At the right time of day, in the right weather, they would all but disappear.

We hadn't encountered any fences, locked gates, or magically delineated boundaries.

A cuckoo called out from a thicket of trees. It sounded exactly like a recording from a clock, but Lear said it was real.

I raised my eyebrows at a stretch of wall that looked like it might conceal a front door. She shook her head: we had to keep waiting outside.

"The structure extends far down into the hill," she said. "It's very clever—you'll see. Sunlight shunts in at all sorts of interesting angles, even in the parts without windows. A famous architect used to live here. That's her name on the sign."

"Isn't this kind of in the middle of nowhere?"

"Her firm designed or redesigned half the museums in the capital. She could've gone anywhere she liked, and lived like a queen. She retired here for her husband, I think. He had a sensitivity to magic."

Wist stopped studying the scenery.

She had veiled her magic from the moment we left our hotel room. But she'd ratcheted up her efforts as we climbed the hill. She almost came off as a one-branch mage now, her threads blurring into a single formidable rope.

"That's right," Lear said to her. "You already noticed, didn't you? This island is full of natural deposits of..." A perplexed look came over her face, as if she couldn't find quite the right word in Continental.

"...a material that blocks magic perception," she finished. "From an industrial perspective, it's pure junk, so it never got mined. Still, every bit helps."

"Magic sensitivity," I said. "Like having uncomfortably strong perception?"

"Not necessarily. It's more like an allergy."

A magic *allergy*? I'd never heard of such a thing.

But some people had fatal food allergies. Some people got itchy rashes for no particular reason. Some people were tormented by bright lights or loud noises or sharp smells. Why not magic?

"It's extremely rare," Lear said. "One way to cope is by moving somewhere rural—to a town without a post office, and little other magical infrastructure.

"But some can't even tolerate natural levels of wild magic. Some suffer extra because they're laypeople who just so happen to have a core. The nearest source of magic is always there inside them.

"The architect started a foundation to raise awareness. She donated this home to serve as a place of asylum for those who can't live anywhere else. There aren't many residents."

I said, by way of conclusion: "You brought us—you brought the *Kraken*—to meet someone with a crippling sensitivity to magic."

A cloud passed in front of the sun. I looked up; part of me expected to see an ancient floating landfill.

"The architect was a great supporter of core extraction experiments," Lear said dispassionately. "If laypeople could give up their cores, it would lessen the exposure of magic-sensitivity sufferers. It would bring them enormous relief."

"But there's no ethical way to cut out a core."

"No. Anyway, this place is a refuge of last resort. That's another reason we didn't come by porting. Flashy magic use ought to be reserved for emergencies."

A hunchbacked woman shuffled out of the building, arms laden with baggy neon vests. They looked like deflated life jackets. She made Wist and Lear put them on before she ushered us in. The fabric shielded the aura of their magic, like a lead apron for blocking radiation.

Even so, they weren't allowed to leave the first floor. Danver and I continued on without them. Lear gave us her takeout bag, which our guide inspected with a tool like a metal detector. A magic detector?

Most of the interior walls were made of exposed concrete, too, shafting together at peculiar angles. Whitish sunlight spilled down like a waterfall through unseen cracks.

The stone-faced woman led us downstairs. Her silence heightened my paranoia: why wouldn't she say anything? Had she immediately known we were foreigners?

She opened a door and motioned us through. She didn't follow. The room beyond was just a vestibule, coolly bare, with a two-seater table that might never have been used.

When she shut the door behind us, I listened for an imprisoning click.

A magic-blocking substrate had been hidden in these plain-looking walls. Something that made the whole building feel like walking around at the bottom of a Jacian bag. A black box for magic ... that wouldn't come cheap.

I asked Danver if Lear had told her anything about who we were here to see. She shot me a hateful look, then said that she probably knew less than I did.

There was only one other door. Also unlocked. I went over, footsteps echoing on the naked floor, and let us in.

51

The door led us into someone's living space. It didn't look much like my old prison cell. For one thing, it was decidedly less secure. If a patient walked out the front door, that lady in the lobby wouldn't go grab a weapon to chase them down.

The concrete surfaces and plain, dark furniture appeared austere at first glance. But it was a luxurious, award-winning kind of austerity. Stark sculptural objects stood guard on a shelf; they might have been architectural trophies.

There were no strange smells, and no detritus of a busy life. The only flaw I could spot were ashen crumbs sprinkled where the floor met the wall. A couple mummified dead bugs. Nothing egregious.

The man we'd come to visit was in a low, armless chair with his legs stretched out, head tilted back, communing with the ceiling.

"They're here," he said in Jacian.

Lear's voice came through an unseen speaker. "Talk freely," she said, also in Jacian. "Talk about whatever you like, or nothing at all. They brought presents."

I handed over her paper bag. The man placed it on a table shaped like a rounded-off triangle and reached in, with ceremonious gravity, to lift out a block of packaged sandwiches.

He seemed older than Lear, and older than me, with a narrow face and a prominent thin nose that looked prone to breaking. His stubble had grown in as a dappled mix of white and grey. His hair was greasy, or laden with sticky-wet product.

He had no core. A healer, then, or a subliminal healer.

He reverently unwrapped his sandwiches. They were rather plain, as far as Jacian food goes. White bread, fried pork cutlets, not even a hint of a vegetable.

We just sat there and watched, like observers of a religious ritual, while he consumed each half-sized sandwich down to the last crumb. He didn't get himself anything to drink. The only sounds in the room were the crackle of waxed paper and the smack of his lips.

Light from outside flowed down a slanted wall. Had the back of the hill been cut away to let buried parts of the building breathe? Or had strategic mineshafts been dug to ferry that light inside, like Datura's sun tubes?

A single undersized painting had been mounted on another wall, far behind our host. My eye kept interpreting it as a shadowed cavity instead of a picture. But it was nothing sinister. Just a pastoral scene of brown cows gnawing grass with hardly any color in it. More static than a still life.

I thought abruptly of the autoinjector I'd used on Datura Gray.

This man might be anyone—he might be another one of Lear's targets. It'd be just her style, wouldn't it, to hand us a deadly bagged lunch. She might not even need to use poison. Maybe he'd have a fatal reaction to bread secretly slathered in shrimp paste. Did his face seem swollen? Did his breathing sound different? Nothing so far, and yet...

As the man neared the end of his meal (without wheezing or hives), Danver and I offered greetings in Jacian. We introduced ourselves as friends of Lear.

His eyes widened. The funny part was that he started off understanding us perfectly—and yet, as he realized we weren't native speakers, it was like his brain staged a panicked rebellion and turned every subsequent sound into gibberish.

I gave him some time to let the fact of our existence sink in, then said (still in Jacian): "You have a sensitivity to magic."

I worded it a lot more clumsily than that, but you get the gist. So did he.

He swallowed the final bite of his final sandwich. "No." He had a soft, rusty voice. "Not like the others."

He dug inside the takeout bag again and produced a sealed wet wipe. He tore it open and cleaned his fingers. He was remarkably thorough.

He still had no core. But I'd begun to think I sensed something else there in his torso, beneath that shapeless beige sweater. A stain. A shadow. A memory of an absence.

It's hard to perceive a lack, or a wound without any physical evidence. Disconnected thoughts skittered through the back rooms where my mind overlapped with the Void. Sacrifices, metaphorical doorways, shattered windows. A crevasse looking out on another land, another world, another type of magic ... other places governed by alternate rules, or without any rules whatsoever.

What was I seeing, really? It might be illusory. My magic perception wasn't infallible, after all. Any sense could go awry from time to time—eyes desperately seeking out nonexistent patterns, ears ringing with made-up sounds.

The man smoothed his crumpled wet wipe and, after some consideration, tied it in a graceful knot.

"Only L sneaks me meat," he said. "I'm not really supposed to eat it."

"For health reasons?" I asked.

"Because of my history." He settled deeper in his chair, hands folded in his lap, and considered each of us. "You're both operators."

A reasonable guess. No one with a core would be allowed to descend to this floor.

"You aren't bonded to anyone," he said to Danver. "Not anymore. You were before."

Then, to me, before either of us had time to react: "You're bonded..." He leaned forward, slender nose twitching. "You're bonded to someone *very*—"

"Leave it," Lear said over the speaker. "Don't pursue that."

He scooted his chair a few inches back from the table, obedient, and averted his eyes. But the force of his attention remained as palpable as sticky fingertips. The gray walls—some in deep shadow, some white with sunlight—they all smeared together. I thought, lightheaded, that someone was bound to faint.

I stared at his knotted wet wipe until the room stopped blurring and I could hold longer breaths in my chest. Danver, beside me, had twin spots of angry red on her cheeks.

I tried to ask if he were a type of notary. A bond authenticator. I didn't know the right terms in Jacian. I had to explain myself with pantomime.

"No," he said, once he understood. "This sight is my gift."

He touched the part of his paunch where once there might have been the glow of a core. He kept speaking without prompting, as if he were used to telling the same things in the same order to all sorts of visiting strangers.

I remembered—unwillingly—my own early days in prison.

When they started trotting me out to hobble mages, they'd treated the whole project (and me) like a joke. Their security measures were the biggest joke of all.

Hobbling-related procedures evolved drastically over my seven years of incarceration, and even after I got released. In the beginning, there had been nothing to stop sentenced mages from seeing my face—or from talking the entire time, telling me they'd kill or rape me, begging me to let them out, begging me to help them die.

They'd be cuffed, or chained, or strapped to a chair. But a couple times, they briefly slipped free. I got punched in the eye, thrown to the floor, lashed with banned magic meant to induce the sensation of being burned alive. Guards would shamble over to intervene as if they'd just woken up.

The man here reminded me more of the calm, nonviolent type who liked to narrate what they'd done. How they'd earned a hobbling. They were delighted to tell me precisely who they had harmed, and why, as I came up to touch them.

I had strained so hard to divorce those nattering voices from the sweat-stained clothing right in front of my nose, the humid skin and flesh where magic grew like kelp in a filthy current.

This Jacian man described himself as a prisoner of sorts, as I had been, but he wasn't shackled to his room. Nothing—magical or physical—would prevent him from opening that unlocked door.

He had a name. Whenever we said it, his face contorted. So we stopped. We concentrated on listening. (From time to time, I had to make him explain unfamiliar words. I'll elide those parts—they're not worth repeating.)

He was five years younger than Lear, though he didn't look it. He was the only remaining survivor of the core extraction trials helmed by

Datura Gray. He knew vaguely of other tests, other researchers, but he had been ejected from the program after coming of age.

"In my twenties," he said, "I killed six people." He didn't fidget. "Two mages, and four branchless ... four laypeople with cores. Something came over me when I saw them. It came over me slowly, and then all at once. But it was gradual enough to stalk, and plan, and prepare."

Lear hadn't brought us here to assassinate him. Or if she had, the effort had failed. Not a single crumb of those sandwiches appeared to sit wrong in his stomach.

What Lear *had* done, however, was place me and Danver behind closed doors with a murderer. I was so intent on staying in tune with the flow of his speech that the actual meaning of what he'd said didn't penetrate until scalding fury welled up from some deep abyss in my gut, and I didn't get why.

Wist was seething. She wouldn't rush in (or bail me out) unless I asked. But she didn't like this. She didn't like it at all.

I couldn't tell if she'd gotten his story from my own understanding— had a tenderhearted subconscious part of me reacted viscerally enough to break all our dams and flood her with horror, as she now flooded me? She was listening, too, alongside Lear; maybe she'd made Lear explain it.

The man was thick around the middle. I wouldn't have noticed if not for the fact that he kept touching his belly. He caressed it artlessly, thoughtlessly, like he couldn't help it.

"I killed them," he said, "one at a time. I killed them, and I ... I tried to make myself careless. I tried to get caught. No one came to arrest me. No one noticed any change in me except L.

"I'll never be free, strictly speaking. But I never had a public trial, either. I'm safe as long as I don't see anyone with a core. I've stayed here for years now. No one ever had to chain me.

"Before all this, they took out my core, and I survived, which was celebrated. Unfortunately, all I obtained was a minor gift. Not a gift worth the trouble of extracting a core. But the things I did after they released me—that's an unprecedented new pattern. That's why I've been protected. As long as I stay alive, there's more data to be drawn."

He waited a minute, giving us time to digest. He recrossed his legs. He folded up his empty sandwich wrapper until the paper refused to bend any further.

The ticking of my heart seemed to come from somewhere outside me, like a clock hidden in the sleek walls of this room without any visible timepiece.

"That's not the only reason I'm still alive," he said. "I avoided sentencing. And yet ... it would be easy to kill myself, wouldn't it? Look around. Think of all the ways I could do it. I have enough freedom to pull it off. It would be the right and honorable course of action, if no one with authority will do it for me.

"It's devastating, the people I murdered. Objectively, it's devastating. I remember every moment. They were studying for class, or going shopping, or waiting to pick up their kids. None of them deserved to be hurt. But even though my teeth chewed gristle till it made me sick, even though my body ached from butchery, even though my hands set fires to hide the evidence, I can't feel like I was the one who did it. This thing in me won't let me want to die."

"This ... thing in you?" I said.

He rubbed his stomach again. "I once had a core. No branches. I was a layperson, not a mage. I would never have used my core for anything. Couldn't even feel it. I would've said it was good for nothing. I wasn't afraid of losing it. I was just afraid of dying.

"But when my core was removed, something else came in. You can't see it, detect it, or measure it in any way. You can't touch it or extract it. You can't smell the rot. But it's there. It has to be there, or nothing makes sense."

He leaned forward quickly enough to make Danver draw breath. With his index finger, he patted the wet glistening surface of his eye. No flinching, no blinking. His eye was flesh, but he touched it like I would. Like a prosthesis.

He said: "How else can anyone explain me? Long ago, all magic was wild. Long ago, people didn't know that tiny bacteria cause infections. Someday we'll become long-lost people from long ago, and the thing we're ignorant of, what we lack instruments to reveal—it's right here."

Tap. Tap. Tap. His finger came down harder now, pushing at his eyeball like a stuck button. On my left, Danver squirmed in her seat.

Suddenly he sagged back. He clasped his belly, gently, as though to reassure it. "Every time someone visits, I wonder if they've come to off me. It wouldn't be difficult. Wouldn't you come looking, if you'd lost your mother or father, your beloved friend, your twin, your child? Wouldn't you want to try?"

His voice lifted with hope. "You don't have anything else for me? No other food? No pill bottles, or medicinal parasites?"

"Nothing," I said. I upended the paper bag. Unused napkins fluttered out. "There's nothing."

The animation left his face. It was instant, like an extinguished light. Off-white napkins littered his lap and the table and the floor, but no one moved to collect them.

"I used to try all sorts of off-label medication," he said. "Anything I could get my hands on. Even regular cough syrup. There was always a chance it could help, I thought. It might transform me."

I knew, then, what Lear had put in his sandwich.

He didn't appear transformed. Or intoxicated, even. In the absence of a chalice like Reverence, the drug might have all the psychoactive impact of a glass of good wine. Lear must have been hoping for a miracle. Or perhaps she had no hope left whatsoever, but she gave it a shot all the same.

"Do you need to know how I did it?" he inquired politely. We'd been silent for too long.

"What?" I said. There was a throb in my temple. Maybe it came from me; maybe it came from Wist.

"The mechanics of it. I can explain. I'm good at explaining things—comes with experience." He made a sawing motion, as if miming his way through a meal at a carnivorous restaurant.

"No," Danver said in a low scraping voice. "Don't."

We talked of other things. Safe things. Childhood memories, perhaps. How Lear used to help him with math homework. I didn't retain a single word.

At the end he said apologetically that he'd studied Continental, too, but he'd never been good with languages. He tried a few sentences on us. Some of his greetings came out with textbook fluency. He'd misremembered other phrases in a way that completely inverted their meaning.

On some level, he understood what he had done. If he knew about the Void, maybe he'd have asked me to scoop his whole mind out, to leave him as empty as a scraped-out gourd. Or maybe he'd ask to have his existence utterly erased from this room, this house, this island, this world.

Should I have done it without being asked? Should I have concocted an excuse to be alone with him? I could've sent Danver out the door first. After all of Ashtereth, what was one more body, one more agonized life? That couldn't possibly count as a large-scale use of the Void.

52

The woman from the lobby waited outside the building for Wist and Lear to strip off their borrowed vests. She turned a gimlet eye on us before vanishing back inside.

I wondered if she knew why the prisoner was supposed to be on a vegetarian diet. Did she feel safe leaving his door unbolted? The other patients in residence—the ones with debilitating magic sensitivity, the ones who had been so quiet that I couldn't be sure they were real—did they have any idea who he was?

Danver blinked in the sunlight. She looked smaller, as if the gravity of that buried room had shrunken her.

Out here in the fresh, cool air of another island, Datura's entity seemed very distant and benign. A curious eye. A wordless whisper. A hint of indefinable danger.

Now it had lost its connection to this side of the world.

It had created the boy with the blindfold as a cursed offshoot of

Datura Gray, a skin suit filled with original sin. He, in turn, had murdered far more victims than the prisoner in the asylum. Perhaps it was unintentional. But he'd put himself in a position to attack his prey from behind.

Datura the elder, in contrast, had kept his hands clean. He wouldn't have gone in the operating room to amputate cores. He'd been a manager, not a frontline worker. His role would've been to sign off on proposals and allocate funds and counsel stakeholders and make high-level decisions.

Somehow, at the end of that, a cohort of children had died … except for Lear (who'd kept her core) and a man-made killer whose entire past and future had been consumed by the grand experiment.

"You want us to push for an end to core extraction," I said to Lear. "You could have just asked."

She waved at one of the blank asylum windows, although no one was there. "My boss's bosses want a whole lot more from your Kraken," she said. "There's plenty of room to bargain."

The Jacian government was starting to get a taste of just how much the Kraken could do. Sealing vorpal holes would let them reclaim abandoned farmland, impassable roads, desecrated cemeteries, lost towns....

An archipelago nation—even one composed of too many different islands to count—couldn't afford to be overly precious about usable space.

"Make it a human rights issue," Lear suggested.

Osmanthus didn't have the greatest record when it came to human rights, either. But magic core removal would strike the Board as being inexpressibly grotesque. Imagine them doing it to prisoners of war, they'd say. Imagine them doing it to us.

If we didn't shut it down, in fact, core extraction research might end up being the exact sort of thing that hawkish types would seize on as a pretext for invasion. Time to sally forth and rescue the downtrodden mages of Jace. Rouse your people with echoes of the same old cries. Let their fury flow out toward the sea with too many names.

History made the present feel like plagiarism. This, you see, was why I'd never cared to study it in any real depth.

We descended Asylum Mount. Lear noodled away at her sketchbook while we waited for the next ferry.

A whitish-silver dead fish bobbed in dark water below the dock. Wist and I kept a hopeful eye out for faraway whales.

"No one can prove that the loss of his core made him murderous." Lear sketched swift lines that, in a matter of minutes, turned into the shape of the dock, that bloated fish, a lonely figure in a dress.

"They can't prove that it's unrelated, either," I said.

"Yes. He'll be in limbo until the day he dies."

"Then what? They pull out all those cold cases and declare them solved?"

"Up north," she said, "the director's old rival pioneered another type of human research. At least one survivor came out of it with a massive settlement.

"Our islands aren't a monolith. Neither is the government. But the central lineage of core extraction—that continues to this day. If it's still ongoing, if it can't be written off as the work of a renegade, no one will ever admit any wrongdoing."

She started on a new page. "The experimenters weren't good to us for humanitarian reasons, you know. It had nothing to do with kindness or pity. There was a theory that pampering us might improve the survival rate. Datura Gray received a directive to test this theory, and that's what he did. He obeyed it to the letter.

"After his tenure ended, other schools of thought took over. They said people were stronger back in olden times, more understanding of the sacred value of sacrifice. Kids these days—too soft, too weak. Of course they'd die like flies. They tried to boost survival rates by toughening up their patients. Getting them used to adversity."

"...Fuck," I said.

"Indeed."

Once the ferry arrived, we filed on board. There were no other passengers on the way back.

I stood at the rail with Wist. Now that I knew what to look for, I could see the asylum at the top of the tallest hill, its painted parts blending eerily well with the sky.

I didn't know how to say this.

If you don't want to get involved...

"We'll stop it," Wist replied.

When the man spoke in that chicly furnished room, she had sensed, through our bond, every reaction I'd kept off my face.

We ducked beneath the roofed area of the boat and went to grab seats. We ended up taking one of the hard, flat benches at the very back—Lear and Danver had already gotten cozy up front.

I didn't gawk at them (okay, maybe just a little bit). Danver appeared to be asking about the wavy scar on Lear's forearm, the one left when Wist cut out those worms.

I'd been fine on our first ferry trip, but now my guts sloshed, unmoored. I hugged my stomach. I kept seeing the prisoner blissfully chewing his pork sandwiches, one hand raised to hide his mouth. He'd taken small, quick, grateful bites, battling himself to make them last.

53

It was time for Fanren and Azalea and Shien Danver (and most of their respective associates) to board Nerium's yacht. Wist and I would stay behind, but we'd come along to say goodbye.

Various Jacian military types in full dress uniform, Lear among them, observed benevolently from the wharf below.

I couldn't tell if we were at the same base where our vessel had first come in. It was daylight now, for one thing. Modular walls at the back of the dock—like something around a construction site—blocked prying eyes. They were marked with a repetitive cup-shaped motif borrowed from the Jacian flag.

We climbed the stairs to the yacht. Seen from above, those privacy barricades became a multilayered maze. Behind them rose an obscuring smog of magical concealment.

Fanren said he couldn't see past it, not even with his new Regalia glasses.

The only visible buildings appeared unusually far away: a shimmering white complex that might have held corporate offices.

I asked Azalea to please make sure that Manatree wasn't still waiting on standby for my repatriation. I felt bad for not asking sooner—our stay kept getting longer and longer.

I sought Danver out last. She gazed down at a small sketchbook, unsmiling. She held it as if she were afraid to drop it.

"What?" she said when she saw me. Her brows knitted together. "I didn't steal it."

"Uh, no one said you did."

A blue-bellied gull swooped past with a freakish ululating cry. A glob of white paste smacked the hardwood deck. Nice to see that even Shien Nerium's superyacht wasn't immune to a targeted bombing.

"Check up on the tower," I said. "You got souvenirs for Ginko? And treats for Turtle?"

"Why is that my job?" she complained, but she didn't deny it.

"Thanks. So—did you seal the deal?"

Danver glowered, then flushed. Wist poked me reproachfully. What?

"For your brother," I articulated. "For Regalia Optics. You know. The whole reason you came here. I obviously wasn't referring to fraternization with foreign—"

"You can't finalize that sort of thing in a single trip," she snapped.

"Oh, can't you?"

"We'll be collaborating with state-owned corporations. A joint venture. But it's practically illegal for them to have anything to do with foreign interests. It'll take years to carve out an exception. Getting permits will be a nightmare. The supply chain—"

"You've learned a lot," I said, "in a very short time."

"Are you calling me underqualified?"

"Hey, I'm the last person who ought to make insinuations about nepotism, or ... oh, never mind. You'll be coming back to Jace again, won't you? You think your brother's going to get that SUPAS built. Not just in Osmanthus. Here, too."

She tore her eyes away from her precious sketchbook. "Do you even remember what that stands for?"

"Er..."

Supermassive Passive Scanner, Wist told me.

"A Supermassive Passive Scanner," I said smugly.

Danver opened and shut her mouth twice in a row, like a goldfish. "...I never told you—either of you—my exact business here."

"You didn't, did you? So much for the Shien family spirit."

"Did Lear—"

"No," I said. "No one tells me anything. It was just a stab in the dark, honestly. I don't even know what you all do at Regalia other than make glasses. And humongous industrial lenses, I guess. Your brother mentioned working on a SUPAS in northern Osmanthus. Is it done yet?"

"It's not like baking a pie," Danver snapped.

I spread my hands. "He was already bragging about it last winter."

"It's not fully operational," she said, clipped, "but it will be. Soon. I brought over some initial data from the installation back home. That's part of what garnered interest in..."

She petered out. She must have regretted responding.

"Next time you visit," I said, guessing again, "you'll—hm, go location scouting, maybe? Or did you already do that? You've been busy."

She pursed her lips. Later on, she said a courteous farewell to Wist, but not to me.

We descended to the wharf, accompanied by a knot of remaining Osmanthians. Everyone engaged in several vigorous rounds of mutual bowing. Up on the deck of the yacht, Fanren leaned dangerously far over the railing to blow a kiss.

One of the Jacian soldiers waved and grinned, stopping only when a superior cleared their throat.

Let's not forget that Wist's impersonator had been assassinated just a day after our arrival. She'd been sent home in a steel case. Someone had come for Fanren, too. But in all this time, we hadn't been openly spat on, or heckled, or jailed, or poisoned en masse. We could have been subject to a far worse reception.

Lear finagled her way closer while our respective peers exchanged admiring comments about the yacht. I asked if she'd gotten a chance to paint Fanren. She'd expressed an interest, once, back in Osmanthus.

"No luck, sadly," she said. "His schedule was packed."

"You'll just have to do another residency in Osmanthus City."

"Ah, if only it were that easy."

Cheering erupted as the yacht started moving. Lear smiled and clapped right in time with everyone else.

"You sure you don't want me to...?" I put my fists together and pretended to break a stick.

"When you're trying to get things done, it helps to make a deal with the devil. I still need my devil."

"Your"—I stopped myself from saying Postmistress—"your devil helped send you to Ashtereth."

"Can't make that sort of decision on my own behalf." Her voice dropped. "I don't belong anywhere—not among mages, or operators, or laypeople. These days, my own hometown feels about as strange as Osmanthus."

Danver looked down from the departing yacht. Lear, imitating Fanren, blew a suave kiss. It could have been meant for anyone. It could have been snatched by a passing gull. Danver waited for a good long moment before spinning on her heel and stalking away out of sight.

"There are benefits to selling your soul," Lear said lightly.

Had refusal ever been an option? Had it been a sale between equal parties?

In Osmanthus, plenty of healers bonded with the first person to offer. Realistically, some had no other choice. Turn down a politically powerful mage, get yourself blacklisted—and then what? Could you scrape out any other kind of living? Who would train you, hire you, sponsor you, become your guarantor for housing?

The Jacian language was less finicky about distinguishing between subliminal healers and subliminal mages. They all got lumped together as laypeople. Jacians would never look at a subliminal with a core—a simple layperson—and call them any type of mage.

Lear had been neutered; she had no magic to wield in service of the state. She could've argued for recategorization. But by the time they severed her branches, she'd already been bonded. In the absence of every other qualification, her bond would be used to justify treating her as a mage (a broken and pitiful mage) for the rest of her life.

Back at Follyhope, she'd joked about asking me to free her. She couldn't possibly have expected me and Wist to show up on Jacian shores less than a year later.

"We'll be in the country a while longer," I said. "If you ever change your mind…"

"I can introduce you to others," she said, "who might want to take advantage of your services."

Wist stood there listening like a bird of prey.

I spoke into my fist. "I'd rather not cause another international incident."

"Better not get caught, then. Tread carefully, Agent BB."

Agent BB, Wist mused. *You liked that.*

Shush, I said.

The risks incurred by breaking bonds in Jace would be much higher than just about anywhere on the continent. I'd have to trust that Lear wouldn't betray us. Which, given her record, seemed dicey at best.

But my mind was already kindling with possibility. Wist's hand hovered at the back of my neck as if to protect a growing flame.

54

I couldn't remember what I'd dreamt of that night. I shot upright before daybreak, enveloped in dread, coughing dryly. Wist, still half asleep, put a cautionary hand on my flank.

The host of lights attached to the ceiling glowed dimly, pendulous sacs ready to hatch a swarm of gooey alien life.

The crystal pitcher on the end table reflected that blue glow. So did the glassy frames on the wall, and a mirror by the bureau.

A water wheel revolved in my mind, moved by a current I couldn't control.

A mirror, a looking-glass, a spyglass, a lens—

Regalia Optics built lenses.

Sometimes those lenses were unfathomably elaborate. Segmented, like an insect's eye. As large as an arena for dueling.

Would a SUPAS use mirrors in the same way as a telescope? Maybe not: the goal was to observe magic, not light.

A chalice is a magical construct that serves as a superior vessel for the user.

Supermassive Passive Scanners weren't meant to serve as a vessel for anyone. Nerium had said they would be placed in remote areas, far from human habitation. All the better to absorb ephemeral traces of natural magic. Like the faintest starlight, otherwise unobservable.

Reverence had been a kind of supermassive scanner, too. A cupped ear listening for the whisper of an unknown presence—a shadow so far removed that no other tool could detect it.

Then again, Reverence had been deliberately constructed as a chalice from the start.

I could buy the notion that Wist had subconsciously built one of her own, too, as she expanded on her tower. She'd developed a unique framework for a vessel-type construct.

But Nerium's SUPASes wouldn't be any sort of chalice, no matter how you stretched the definition. If it were that easy to throw together Jacian-caliber machina (for military purposes or otherwise), every country on the continent would've done so back in the days of the original Kraken.

A chalice is a magical construct...

Would a SUPAS even count as *magical?* I had no idea how they were supposed to work, really. Certain physical material would show a predictable reaction to the presence of magic. Might make more sense to use that than to puzzle out the recursive nature of magic scanning for itself.

Nerium had compared his scanners to a mountaintop telescope. They would be extraordinarily sensitive, to the point of having little historical precedent.

More sensitive than Reverence?

Datura's entity might notice them looking. It might channel all its curiosity into those finely tuned lenses. It might distort and disable them with the weight of its interest. Fundraising, grants, years of construction—all for nothing.

Or perhaps the entity would, all on its own, break free of the intangible barriers that kept it from coming to meet us. The simple creeping passage of time might eliminate any need for a magical door, an open window.

What if it perceived a completed SUPAS as an empty house?

That wasn't part of their conceptual design. SUPASes would have no pilot seat, no mechanism by which to meld with a human mind. But the same limitations wouldn't necessarily apply to greater beings.

Perhaps Datura's savior could make itself right at home in a stadium-size field of magically receptive lenses.

I hadn't said anything about this, either out loud or at the back of my head. I hadn't done much except take a shaky drink, spilling water down my chin. But by now Wist was wide awake, too, poised upright amid a tangle of covers.

I briefly entertained thoughts of becoming a full-fledged terrorist. The Void could consume each SUPAS— no matter how massive—in a single bite. But that very use of the Void might pique the entity's interest, too. There was no way to win.

I told Wist everything in a breathless rush. "It's all speculation," I said afterward, raking my hands through nightmare-sweaty hair. It hadn't gotten much longer, but I was increasingly tempted to make her help me shave it all off.

"If the voice on the other continent wants a vessel," she said, "why wouldn't it come after a regular Jacian chalice?"

"Too unambitious."

"What about my tower?"

"Already occupied."

"I don't think that much matters." She touched my wrist. I sank back into bed. "All that's changed is our own awareness," she said. "We've always been surrounded by hazards beyond our sight or understanding."

Point taken. The Void in my own head was the closest hazard of all. Then, of course, there were the temporal debts we'd incurred in Bittercress. But existential terror had a way of fading rapidly in the light of day. It retreated into the wings for weeks or months at a time, returning in a deluge just when I'd forgotten how to cope.

Despite all Datura's efforts, the presence on the other continent was still inexplicably caged in place.

When the right moment came, would it emerge like a moth from a cosmic cocoon?

That image would nestle itself in our most fearful recesses. It would haunt us on sleepless nights for years to come. Like living with the news that we were due for another thousand-year quake—but it might not happen at all, or it might be centuries late.

I did ask Wist to give me a buzz cut, in the end (albeit not that very instant). Autumn had been mild. By winter, hopefully, I'd grow enough hair to keep my scalp from freezing.

New faces came to join us not long after Azalea and the others left. Whatever happened with the future of core extraction—and other points of contention—I figured it would all hinge on Wist. Osmanthian agencies barely tolerated my presence. The last thing they wanted was my input.

I'd been allowed out of my room, yes, but only under Wist's supervision. She didn't often have time to escort me.

And yet, much to my surprise, the restrictions placed on me (by my own countrymen, mind you) gradually loosened.

Once the dust settled, Wist's account of Ashtereth came to be viewed in a generally positive light. Azalea must've put in a good word for me, too, or at least ensured that I got adequate credit for securing those beads. The last surviving fragment of a genuine chalice.

When other members of the delegation argued against letting me have unsupervised contact with any Jacian parties, no matter how carefully vetted, Wist put on a virtuoso performance.

In the interest of honesty, I'll say this: to me, it sounded totally fake. But no one else had ever heard her raise her voice, or seen her slam a table with the flat of her hand. She looked around the meeting room with eyes like black stone. I crossed my ankles and tried not to smirk.

The wall opposite us was tiled from ceiling to floor with decades-old greeting cards. I made a lackadaisical effort to count them while Wist preached about how I'd been to countries all over the continent and never caused any trouble. (This was at best an exaggeration, and would hinge largely on your personal definition of trouble.)

She pointed out, furthermore, that we hadn't been bonded during the series of events that led to my seven-year stint in prison.

Now I was permanently tethered to her—and therefore subject to mental monitoring no matter where I went. How inefficient, then, to insist that she accompany me every time I left the hotel. Physical proximity meant nothing to a mage like the Kraken.

I bit my lip. I strove to keep a straight face. If anything, I'd say it was the other way around. *She* was tethered to me. *I* gripped her leash, not that anyone knew it. I could control her through her magic, move her like an extension of my own body. I wouldn't, not unless she wanted it. But I could.

Wist wasn't done yet. "The only reason they caught her—the only reason she came to trial—was because I turned her in. You think I wouldn't do it again?"

In the trembling air of that room, no one seemed prepared to deny the Kraken.

Neither of us had any qualms about shamelessly weaponizing our history. Which said a lot, I suppose, about how far we'd come.

Sadly, sightseeing was never very high up on our agenda. I'd have loved to explore Jacian circuses and casinos, but Lear had mentioned that Central was too uptight for the good stuff. Its nightlife would pale in comparison with regional cities.

The sole touristy pursuit we made time for was a ride on a fairy wheel.

It was integrated into the top of a building: the tallest clock tower in Jace, a mammoth of glass and steel. Cantilevered balconies stabbed outward like thorns. Synchronized fairy wheels (four in total) rotated around the rim of each translucent clock face, offering a fantastical view of the tower's innards as well as of the city below.

Wist stopped to study the structure for a rather long time before we went in. It reminded me a bit too much of how she'd studied the magic woven through the walls of Datura's base.

We don't need a clock like that at home, I said. *No amusement park nonsense, either*. Imagine if she added a roller coaster or a bunch of drop rides to her tower.

Her eyes slid away. Guilt pricked my conscience. *I mean ... if you seriously want to recreate this, go wild.*

We'll see. She threaded her arm around my back, feigning disinterest. *Might be an inspiring exercise.*

55

THE GONDOLAS REVOLVING around the fairy wheel were each the size of a tram car. We paid to have one to ourselves.

The floor wasn't see-through, and it didn't dip like a rowboat when we stepped in, which I suppose was about all I could ask.

I don't love heights. (Flying with Wist doesn't count—there was an all-encompassing sense of security in her power that you couldn't get from any platform or railing or harness). But this felt more like riding an airship than leaning out over the edge of a cliff.

Go high enough, and the differences between cities start to vanish. Especially at a fuzzy time of day like this. The watery light of a slow-fading sunset painted all the rooftops dingy gray.

Wist sat up against the outward-facing window. I went next to her, gingerly, and uttered a silent prayer of thanks for the fact that the car didn't tilt.

"Listen here," I started. "No more being gouged, maimed, vivisected, stabbed—especially not at your own behest! And definitely no disembowelment."

"What brought this on?" Wist said, as if it had come out of nowhere.

"I haven't forgotten what happened at Ashtereth. It's bad enough that the Void wants to gnash up your magic. Spare your body from further mutilation, will you?"

"What if there's a good reason for it?"

"Nice joke," I said, although she'd been perfectly serious. "I'm supposed to abstain from eating all our biggest problems with the Void. If I can do that, you can avoid falling back on self-sacrifice."

Her fingertip found the sharp end of one of my invisible earrings. If I moved, even to sigh, she might draw blood. I kept my back straight, fists on my knees.

She lowered her hand and considered me as if I were a puzzle she still didn't know how to solve. Her mouth stayed in a straight line, but there was a very slight crinkling of amusement around her eyes.

If we were together, we'd never get homesick.

I was glad, truthfully, that we seemed set to stay abroad for months to come.

Remembered humiliation simmered up, hot and fresh, when I pictured us bedding down in her tower like nothing had changed. I would view it differently now that I knew it was more than just the eccentric magical equivalent of outsider art.

I should've questioned that tower more deeply. I should've wondered about it long, long ago. With all the pride I took in my perception, what else had I missed?

For Wist, extensive use of magic was a form of self-torture. Our bond—and my prodigious aptitude for healing her—had done a great deal to mitigate the worst of it. In the past, she'd been stricter in her avoidance of unnecessary magic.

Even then, she'd worked obsessively on her tower, which was full of frankly useless frills. She'd spatchcocked corporeal space to lay open all its possibilities. She'd stacked multiple chambers in the same location. But she rarely looked back. There were entire floors she never set foot on.

Datura Gray, with a single flyover, had deduced what that tower really did for her.

We Osmanthians didn't know the first thing about chalice theory. It had been too easy for me to explain it all away. After how she'd grown up, of course she'd crave a solitary stronghold of her own. A place where she controlled every molecule of running water, every speck of edible food. A place where no one else could lock her in or out.

And as she grew in fame as the Kraken, of course she'd want a refuge where she wouldn't have to use Disappearance all the time to avoid recognition.

The tower had been all that for her, and more. It had given her asylum. It had served as a structured outlet: a vessel for the painful chaos of her magic.

Knowing this ought to make me more fond of it. The tower had been there for her when I wasn't. It had saved her when I couldn't.

Maybe it was just an unfortunate feature of my personality that mortification came before gratitude.

I'd thought I understood Wist inside and out. Better than anyone else ever could. I'd made her magic my life's work. I'd locked horns with her as the Queen of the Void. We'd become bondmates twice over (or thrice over, if you want to get nitpicky).

There was still so much I'd failed to glimpse.

To hell with it.

"This would be a great place to propose," I said.

"Propose?" If she was surprised, she didn't show it. "You already did."

"Uh … remind me."

"You said we should get married if—"

"If?"

"If the Healers' Bill of Rights passes into law."

Ah. Yeah. I could see myself saying that. A promise very much along the lines of Lear telling me to break her bond … if I ever came to Jace.

Well, I wasn't about to go back on it. We were already tied for life anyway. But getting shown up by the likes of Datura Gray had ignited a old desperation. The Void was temporarily sated, but I'd gotten hungrier. More covetous, and more fearful. I wanted to lay claim to Wist in as many ways as I possibly could.

She nudged my fingers away from my face. I'd been biting my nails. Another bad habit creeping back.

We'd just reached the peak of our second revolution around the clock. I'd expected the fairy wheel to clank like a train, but it remained eerily soundless. A jukebox at one end of the gondola offered the option of paying extra for amorous music. No takers here, I'm afraid.

No flurry of kisses, either. That wouldn't be much to her taste, or mine, up in a panopticon like this. Maybe they couldn't make out our faces, but people were staring. In the street below, behind the pellucid clock face, on spiky jutting balconies all up and down the building.

I startled at the sight of human gargoyles. As twilight deepened, they became easier to mistake for lurking spies. They looked life-sized until the gondola shifted closer, and it became apparent that they were two or three times taller than Wist. A regiment of lithe feminine statues, leaning casually out from corners, highly realistic—except for their height, and their horns.

We'd been overseas for close to a month. It wouldn't be that burdensome for Wist to arrange a weekend trip back. Personally, though, I thought it'd be good for the mainland to remember how to cope without her.

Perhaps they could take some lessons from Jace, which had adamantly refused to lean on the Kraken throughout the entirety of her public career. They'd almost made it a full two decades before breaking their streak.

The following day, I had an appointment at … actually, I wasn't sure what to call it. A hospice, or clinic, that offered the magical equivalent of palliative care for mages who didn't respond well to regular healing.

Lear—together with a disgruntled Osmanthian security officer—came along to show me the way. I pumped her for information as we stepped down into a bypass tunnel. Must've been a busy one. The pavement was polka-dotted with blackened splats of ancient gum.

One patient, she said, was a stunted mage whose branches had been mangled during a botched amputation. Most others were natural outliers. (I thought of Fanren. Before we met, he'd been plagued by a congenital flaw in his magic.)

From the fairy wheel, the capital had looked uniformly barren. At street level, there were jacaranda trees everywhere, knitting into an airy canopy. I could've sworn I heard chittering monkeys, just like in the forests of Ashtereth.

Wist had left Central to tackle a string of vorpal holes littered throughout a critical mine. She still seemed closer, somehow, than either of my companions.

Pedestrians streamed around us in all directions, heading to or from work, or shopping, or other unavoidable tasks. None of them could see the way I carried the memory of Wist's teeth on my ear, every nerve standing on end. I sensed her in the tender spots between my fingers, too. Her ghostly hand stayed laced through mine even when she couldn't spare any thought to speak. She kept me from gnawing my thumbnail as my brain rebelled at the constant flow of foreign words, whirling half-syllables, hot oily scents, chipper jingles from storefronts.

Hobbling other mages was one thing, but healing them—I generally avoided that. I'd expected Wist to betray a smidgen of jealousy. But I should've known better. She would never begrudge anyone a chance to be spared the type of magical pain she'd dealt with ever since she was young enough to think she'd brought it all on herself.

We would worm our way deeper into this foreign nation that had little reason to trust anyone from the continent. Quietly, day by day, we would make ourselves indispensable.

Together, we would accomplish things that Datura Gray had never dreamed of. Maybe he and his chalice, now lost, could claim responsibility for bringing us to Jacian shores. But he couldn't control anything we did next.

We'd bargain for an end to core extraction. We'd keep all eyes turned east—toward the Kraken, toward the continent.

Let Jace and Osmanthus spend years quibbling and posturing over the minutiae of maritime regulations and International Vorpal Defense Council membership. Let them negotiate endlessly over how to set appropriate terms for public talks.

Beyond a much wider sea, on a different continent, an abyssal creature without a name would keep brooding and muttering, its voice unheard. It might be diminished without an audience. It might fester and wither and rot.

If we were lucky, it might forget us.

No way would we let Datura Gray get everything he'd ever wanted. It would be a long time—god willing—before anyone thought to look west.

A Note from the Author

First things first: a huge thanks to everyone who has been keeping up with the Clem & Wist series. Truly, I can't thank you enough for your reviews, ratings, and comments—and, above all, for doing me the honor of reading (and hopefully enjoying!) my work.

The funny thing about this story is that, seemingly out of nowhere, I became intensely interested in writing a more horror-influenced novel. I was maybe halfway through my initial draft when it occurred to me that quite a few of my previous books are, arguably, a lot more horrific ... even if I didn't necessarily have horror on my mind when I wrote them.

Chronologically speaking, *A Chalice for a Kraken* is followed by two standalone stories set in other regions of Jace: *The Forest at the Heart of Her Mage* and *The First and Last Demon*. I should also—for no particular reason—put in a quick plug for my latest standalone, *Masks Worn by Magical Wives*, which takes place somewhere very different.

For future new book alerts, join my newsletter or follow my Author Page on Amazon. (Newsletter subscribers will always be the first to know.)

Newsletter: **hiyodori-books.com**

Author Page: **amazon.com/author/hiyodori**

Hope to see you again next time!

– Hiyodori